CW01338413

FLOATING HOME

A Novel

By

LEONARD A. LAWSON

This book is dedicated to my two children, Kirsty and Robert.

I would like to express my grateful thanks to Janet Williams for reading my drafts and for her encouragement, support, and critical comment.

Copyright © Leonard A. Lawson 2014
All rights reserved.

Leonard A. Lawson has asserted his right
under the Copyright, Designs and Patents Act, 1988
to be identified as the author of this work.

No part of this publication may be reproduced, stored in a retrieval system, or transmitted in any form or by any means, electronic, mechanical, photocopying, recording or otherwise, without prior written permission of the author.

This book is a work of fiction. All characters in this publication are fictitious and any resemblance to places, real persons (living or dead), or any of the events described, is purely co-incidental and unintentional.

This book is published by the Author
and printed and distributed by www.lulu.com
ISBN: 978-1-291-97004-3
First Edition 2014

By the same Author:
Musings From My Mind (Published 2012)
A collection of reminiscences and short stories
(ISBN: 978-1-4716-7526-3)
Printed and distributed by www.lulu.com

Cover Picture: The Grand Union Canal at Gayton, Northamptonshire
(Photograph by the Author)

A Glossary of canal terms used in this book appears on page 384

PART ONE

CHAPTER 1

Alex throttled down the engine, and carefully steered the boat around the sharp corner of the canal, taking care to keep close to the towpath side. It wouldn't be the first time that he'd met another boat, coming towards him on a blind corner, going at a speed which would have made it difficult to avoid a collision. He tried to avoid such occurrences as much as possible, but sometimes it was unavoidable.

He was really proud of his boat. A canal narrowboat, with a steel shell, 58 feet long but just 6 feet 10 inches in width, it could accommodate two people comfortably, plus there was space for a couple of guests in the back cabin should he have visitors. Finished in a beautiful shade of royal blue, with a single coach line around the sides picked out in cream, he thought back for a moment to the events of the last couple of years.

18 months before, he and his wife Jennifer had sold their house to raise the money to pay for their new boat, and rented a small flat in the meantime, whilst the boat had been built and fitted out to their specific requirements for a life afloat. But then Jennifer had been taken ill and died suddenly. So, when the boat had been completed and handed over, Alex had given up the flat and moved onto the boat on his own, which he'd named *Jennifer Jo,* his wife's names. So at least his wife was with him still in both mind and spirit. For the last nine months Alex had been cruising the canal network, getting familiar with his boat, and gradually getting used to life without his wife and companion of the last 40 or so years.

They'd raised their two children, seen them both through university, and just as they'd been looking forward to their retirement years together, Jenny was gone from his life, and he'd been left on his own. They'd been married and lived together for almost forty years, and for the last twenty of those they had worked together as well, he as a Housemaster at a boy's boarding school, teaching maths and English, with Jenny as the House Matron.

It had taken him a long time to get used to being alone, but the camaraderie and friendship which he'd found amongst the boating fraternity had helped him a great deal to adjust to his new way of life. There was always someone willing to stop on the towpath and have a chat, and around the locks there were usually other boaters, or onlookers out for the afternoon, gongoozlers the boaters called them, to talk to. And when moored up for the evening, other boaters would come along for a chat whilst walking their dogs, and talk about the news on the cut, discuss various aspects of each other's boats, and so on. But the long evenings alone, with only the radio or television or a book for company, were the times where Alex was still finding life to be a little lonely at times.

As the boat rounded the corner, Alex throttled up again, and the boat gradually picked up speed, but then after a couple of minutes he slowed down to tick-over once more, as he saw in the distance the next lock coming up ahead. After a couple of minutes he carefully steered the boat towards the edge of the water, and deftly brought the boat to a halt some 30 yards or so from the lock, sufficiently far back to give him space to manoeuvre the boat into the lock when it was ready for him to take the boat in. Giving a cheerful wave to the helmsman of the boat which was just departing, having worked its way through the lock, Alex moored his boat against the towpath bollards with bow and stern ropes, and then walked forward to see what was going on there.

The lock was in a picturesque setting, well out into open country, away from the villages which frequented the canal further back. On one side of the canal, the towpath side, there was a low hedge, beyond which were fields planted with what Alex thought was wheat, the bright green leaves indicating the crop was growing strongly in the early summer sunshine which had prevailed for the last few days. On the other side, the offside of the canal, grazing meadows graced the side of the cut, but just past the lock they gave way to dense woodland. Just by the lock, the quiet country lane which had been running parallel to the canal on the other side of the grazing meadows for the last half-mile or so, suddenly took a turn and crossed the canal via one of the hump-backed bridges which adorned the waterway hereabouts. Alex had found that it was quite common for a lock to be built near to a road bridge – he surmised that it would have made it easier for the construction materials, such as bricks and timber, to be brought to the site of the lock by the horses and carts which were the only means of transporting goods and materials some two hundred years ago, when the canals were first built.

With a boat just having left the lock going in the direction he had just come from, Alex found that the lock was still set for him, but there were other boats approaching from both directions. Alex opened the bottom gate, and then went back to *Jennifer Jo* and carefully brought her into the lock, a procedure he'd now carried out many times before. In fact, he was getting quite expert at it now, although sometimes a strong side wind could make manoeuvring the boat difficult at low speeds when entering or leaving a lock. Climbing the lock ladder, he closed the lock's bottom gate and wound his windlass to raise the top paddles to fill the lock with water from the pound above. As the lock slowly filled, the other boats arrived and their crews made their way towards the lock, ready to chat to Alex and each other whilst they waited for their turn through the lock.

Alex knew from the design of the paintwork and livery of the waiting boats that all of them were hire boats, fresh out of the hire bases, as each boatyard had its own distinctive style for its craft. In fact there were two hire bases not far away, one about five miles away above the lock, and another some 4 miles distant below it, which he'd passed earlier that afternoon. On an early summer Saturday afternoon such as this, they would be spitting out new crews just starting on their holidays every 15 minutes or so, until all the available boats had been despatched.

As he waited for the lock to fill, a young girl, aged about 20-22, and dressed in dark blue shorts and a light blue top, came up and spoke to him. "Hello," she said, smiling sweetly. As he replied with a "Hi there," he noticed that the light blue top set off her fair hair perfectly.

"This is our first lock," she said. "We've only just picked up our boat this afternoon, about an hour ago. Would you be able to stop for a couple of minutes after you've finished with the lock, and show us what to do?"

"Yes, of course," replied Alex, "that's no problem." He had plenty of time to spare, and whilst he knew that the staff at the boatyard would have spent some time with their customers before they set off, familiarising them with their craft and telling them how to work the locks, he was also aware that there was no substitute for actually doing it firsthand. "Just starting your holiday?" he asked politely.

"That's right, she replied. "It's our honeymoon. We only got married this morning."

Alex looked back along the canal at the boat she had come from. Holding it against the bank was a young man, dressed also in dark blue shorts and a light blue top. Obviously a his-and-hers pair, to show that they were now an item. "Many congratulations," he said, smiling. "Is that your new husband along there?"

"Yes," the girl replied, blushing slightly. "I'm Anna, and he's Paul."

"Nice to meet you," Alex responded. "The lock's just about full now. If you open this gate, I'll take my boat out and moor it up over there, and then while your Paul is bringing your boat in, I'll pop back and show you the ropes. Locks are easy, really, once you get the hang of it."

"Thanks ever so much," Anna replied, with another smile. "See you in a minute, then."

Alex steered *Jennifer Jo* over to the offside, and moored her against the bank, beside a stretch of dense woodland. He knew that the woodland stretched along that side of the canal for another mile or so, and he didn't usually like mooring underneath trees, as they tended to drop twigs and leaves onto the boat, and the tall branches spoilt his TV reception. His boat was already quite dirty, it badly needed a wash-over to get it smart and clean again, and another polish was due. When he'd taken charge of the boat, the boatyard had advised him to polish the boat every three months or so to keep the paintwork in good condition, and Alex knew that another polishing session was well overdue. But he knew he wasn't going to be moored there underneath the trees for very long, and would be moving on again shortly, before mooring up for the night a little further along the canal. And tomorrow, if the weather was suitable, he'd take some time out to clean and polish *Jennifer Jo*, and spruce her up to 'as new' condition once again.

He walked back and helped Anna to close the lock's top gate, and then showed them both how to use their windlass to open the bottom paddles. Whilst they stood waiting for the lock to empty, they chatted idly together, and as they did so, Alex watched a tall man walking quickly along the towpath towards them, his dog trotting obediently by his side.

"Hello," the man said as he approached. Alex looked at him. Tall, thickset, with what seemed like a permanent scowl on his face, he was dressed in black trousers with black leather boots over them almost up to his knees, a black shirt with a black tie, and a black jacket, buttoned up tight, with some sort of insignia over the left breast, and wearing tight black leather gloves on his hands. The dog, a massive, vicious-looking Rottweiler, bared its teeth and snarled nastily as the man tugged on the lead holding it.

"Hello," Alex replied. How are you today?"

The man didn't respond to Alex's greeting, but spoke brusquely to him and Anna. "Have you seen a young boy around here? About 11 or 12 years old? Skinny? Scruffy? Dirty?"

"No," Alex replied, as Anna shook her head. "We haven't. Why?"

"He's escaped from Grant Hall. The children's home. About 5 miles away, over there." And the man waved his hand vaguely behind him. As he did so, Alex thought about the choice of words the man had just spoken. Not 'run away'. Not 'absconded'. But 'escaped'. It made Grant Hall seem more like a prison, rather than a children's home. But the man was speaking again. "Just he wait till we catch him, then I'll teach him a lesson he won't forget in a hurry." And there was a loud 'thwack' as the man angrily slapped the dog's lead against his other hand.

Alex didn't comment, just saying a quiet "no" once again, shaking his head as the man stamped his boot on the ground in frustration, and then abruptly turned around and walked briskly away, tugging at the dog's lead as he did so. Alex stood in silence as he watched the man walk the short distance down the towpath, up onto the hump-backed bridge which carried the country lane over the canal, and then disappeared off down the road. 'Oh dear,' thought Alex to himself, 'I don't fancy being in that poor kid's shoes when they find him.'

He turned and saw the lock was now empty. "Your boat's ready," Alex said to Anna, as he opened the bottom gate and would down the paddle. "You may go now. And enjoy your holiday, or should I say honeymoon."

"Thanks," Anna replied. "And thankyou for your help at the lock." Alex watched as she ran happily down the slope to where their boat was waiting and jumped aboard, giving him a cheery final wave as her new husband opened the throttle, and the boat picked up speed and went on its way. For a moment he felt a tinge of jealousy. Those two were just starting out on what would hopefully be a happy married life together, and Alex was now alone, left with just memories of his and Jenny's life together.

Alex stayed at the lock for another hour or so, helping the steady stream of hire boats as they negotiated the lock. Meeting people and talking to them was one of the things he found most enjoyable about life on the water.

By the time he'd at last cast off his mooring lines and set off again on *Jennifer Jo*, it was late afternoon. The sun had gone in during the afternoon, and dark clouds had started to gather. Alex knew from the morning's weather forecast that a deep depression was heading his way, bringing colder temperatures, strong winds, and heavy rain, and from the appearance of the sky it was almost upon him. But the forecasters had stated that the storm should blow itself out by early the next morning, and then the next few days after that were set to be warm and sunny.

He cruised along the canal for about an hour, as, all the while, the clouds grew ever darker and more menacing. The temperature was dropping and the wind growing in force and intensity, occasionally buffeting the boat as it passed a clearing in the trees. But eventually Alex saw, coming up ahead, a good spot to moor up for the night, sheltered by a line of tall willow trees on the offside. He once again brought *Jennifer Jo* in towards the bank, and jumped ashore. He quickly made the boat fast with bow and stern ropes, tied through chains threaded behind the Armco piling which lined the bank of the canal at this point, before stepping down into the inside of the boat, closing the rear doors, and sliding the rear hatch securely closed behind him.

He then set about making his supper, putting a pork chop under the grill in the galley whilst he quickly scraped a few potatoes and some carrots and put them on to simmer, after which he sat down with a mug of tea to write up his diary while his meal was cooking. He'd kept a diary of his travels ever since he'd first stepped aboard *Jennifer Jo*. Every evening, he noted down where he'd been that day, what locks he'd passed through, what other boats and people he'd met, amusing incidents he'd witnessed or been involved in, and where he moored up each night. And now, after a few months afloat, he'd already started to see people for the second, and even a third, time, people like himself who did not have a home base, but kept travelling throughout the year. Water Gypsies, they called themselves. Quite an appropriate description, Alex thought.

He also kept what he called a 'Git Book'. In this book he kept details of certain people whom he felt were worthy of the description 'Git', together with the names of their boats. These were boaters who did not keep to the (mainly unwritten) code of courtesy towards other users of the canal - for example, those who did not give way at narrow bridges even though they did not have the priority, and boaters who on occasion were downright rude, or who just did plain stupid things with their boats. Alex was well aware that, whilst canal boating was perhaps the safest form of boating there was, it was not without its dangers for the unwary. Silly or irresponsible behaviour only made the hazards even more dangerous. He preferred to keep well away from people such as those.

As he was writing up the diary, Alex heard the noise of the rain starting to come down outside. It was soon raining heavily, hammering fiercely upon the metal roof of the cabin. And the wind was getting ever stronger too, the gusts rocking the boat against the metal piling at the side of the canal. Alex was pleased he'd had side fenders fitted to the hull of the boat, their cylindrical rubber shape acting as a buffer between the boat and the piling. There was no doubt that the bad weather was set in for the night. Not a nice night to be outside, Alex thought to himself, as he decided that he'd light the fire in the saloon later, to make the interior of the boat warm and cosy.

By then Alex's supper was ready, so he sat at the dinette and enjoyed his meal, then cleared away his things and did the washing up, before sitting down again and enjoying an apple from the bowl on the worktop in the galley for dessert. Night had fallen whilst he'd been eating, and now it was starting to get cold inside the boat – the heat from his cooking had dissipated, and even though the boat was insulated, the cold temperature outside was starting to have an effect inside the boat. 'Time to light up the fire,' Alex thought, as he knelt down beside the small stove in the corner of the saloon and set to.

The stove was only small, measuring about 15" square by 15" deep and 15" high, and made of cast-iron, but it threw out a good deal of heat. Set on a quarry-tiled plinth, its small size meant that the metal casing got hot very quickly. There was an 8" diameter black-painted chimney pipe running from the stove up to the cabin roof, which also threw off even more heat from the rising smoke and fumes inside. Indeed, Alex had often gone outside and held his hand over the top of the chimney vent and felt the vapours coming out from the chimney. They were barely warm, indicating that all the heat from the coal had been given up, either directly into the casing of the stove, or from the chimney pipe itself.

Alex laid some sticks inside the stove and set them alight, and very soon the fire was burning nicely. The coal bucket beside the fire was nearly empty, but he added the few remaining coals into the fire, and then went to the front doors of the cabin which led out into the cratch, as he knew that he had another sack of coal in one of the lockers there.

He'd always wondered how the cratch had got its name. At the front of the boat, outside the cabin, there was a well-deck with lockers on each side, atop of which were some foam cushions, finished in a nice royal blue colour to match the livery of the boat. On a fine day boaters would sit there, enjoying the scenery as the boat cruised along. Like *Jennifer Jo*, many boats had a flexible plasticised canvas cover fitted over this well deck. It was called a cratch cover, a simple waterproof arrangement set over a simple wooden frame, and secured to the hull of the boat by flexible nylon loops. It was equivalent to a conservatory on a normal house, he supposed.

On Alex's boat, the front cratch board was fully glazed, with a glazed drop-down table fitted to it, so that, sitting in the saloon with the front doors open, one could see out of the front of the boat along the canal, and keep an eye on what was going on.

He dropped the two bolts securing the cabin doors which led into the cratch and pushed to open them, but to his surprise, the door only opened a few inches and then caught against some sort of obstruction. Alex pushed harder, as he knew there shouldn't be anything there to stop the doors being opened. As he pushed, he heard movement in front of the doors. There was something inside the cratch that moved! A dog, perhaps, or some sort of animal, was moving inside the cratch. Pushing again, he got the door open at last and was amazed at what he saw in the gloom.

For there, in the darkness, crouched in the corner of the welldeck, was a young boy, about 11 years old, with dishevelled hair and dirty clothes.

Alex looked at the boy for a moment as the rain torrented down on the cratch cover. "Right, get in here, will you," he told the boy who sat there. The boy just shook his head and stared at the floor in front of him, as Alex noticed that he was shivering in the cold. "Come on, in here, I said," Alex repeated. "It's a lot warmer inside." After a long pause, the boy nodded silently, and then stepped slowly down into the saloon. Alex went round behind him and closed and bolted the doors into the cratch, then turned and looked again at the boy in front of him in the light of the saloon.

The young boy stood there silently, still shivering slightly from the cold in the cratch. Although the flimsy cover kept out some of the wind, the cratch was otherwise unheated, and had very little protection from the weather outside. The bitterly cold temperature had obviously had an effect on the child, who had mousy-brown hair, and a face scattered with freckles. He was painfully thin, slightly under-nourished perhaps, and wearing only a flimsy tee-shirt, torn in a couple of places, the design on the front well-faded from being washed many times. His jeans were ragged, with a tear over the left knee, and the trainers on his feet had obviously seen better days.

"What are you doing in there?" Alex asked.

The boy didn't answer, saying nothing as he shuffled his feet on the floor a little bit, keeping his gaze fixed rigidly on the floor in front of him.

"What's your name?" said Alex. The boy mumbled something, almost inaudibly, but Alex couldn't make out what he'd said.

"Speak up," Alex told him, again asking him, "What's your name?"

The boy spoke more clearly this time, but still stared at the floor as he replied quietly, "Danny."

"Danny?" Alex repeated.

The boy nodded again. "Yea. It's really Daniel, but everyone calls me Danny. Always have done. Except my Mum. She's always called me Daniel. She says that's the name I was given, and that's the name she's going to use."

Alex nodded, looking at the boy carefully. "Are you the boy they're looking for?" he asked.

Once again, the boy nodded. "S'pose so," he mumbled.

"There was someone asking about you at the lock this afternoon, asking If we'd seen you," Alex told him.

"Yea, I see that," Danny replied. "You was with that girl off the other boat. She looked alright, she did, really nice." And the ghost of a grin flickered briefly across the boy's face.

"That's right," said Alex. "She's on her honeymoon. They only got married this morning."

"Cor," said the boy, "I bet the wind won't be the only thing rocking their boat tonight, then," as a sly grin spread across his face.

Alex frowned. He'd heard plenty of pubescent boys' smutty humour during his time as a teacher, and most of it had been much worse than that. But as soon as Danny saw the frown on Alex's face, the grin disappeared from his face. "Sorry, Mister," he said, sheepishly, "I shouldn't have said that."

Alex let it pass. "So where were you, then, when all this was going on?"

"In the woods near the lock. I was hiding up a tree, actually. Right by where you parked up your boat, after you done the lock."

"I see," said Alex. He paused for a moment, then added "that fellow looking for you seemed a bit cross."

Danny spoke again. "Yea. That was Hammond. He's the Head Warden."

"Warden?" queried Alex.

"Yea," the boy replied, adding "He's in charge up at Grant Hall. The children's home. He's a right evil bastard, that one. And the Rottie's even worse."

"Rottie?" Alex queried, a bit puzzled.

"Yea" said Danny. "Hammond's dog. The Rottweiler. He'll have your hand off and eat it soon as look at you. Hammond keeps him only half-fed, so as to make him even worse. It's the most horriblest dog I've ever seen. I was real lucky back there at the lock."

"How do you mean?" asked Alex, puzzled once again.

"Well," said Danny, "if Hammond'd brought Brutus across the lock, he'd have found me for sure. I wouldn't have stood a chance. But I was OK, he didn't."

"Brutus?" asked Alex. "Who's Brutus?"

"Yea," said Danny. "The Rottie. Hammond's dog. It's a real brute. It's well-named, the name suits it well. But after Hammond went off, it were easy to nip into your boat, when you were busy back down at the lock. Turns out I was right, I thought it were gonna rain tonight. I just wanted somewhere to kip outa the rain." And the boy dropped his head, staring at the floor once again, occasionally shuffling his feet on the floor, whilst still shivering occasionally from the cold which had permeated his frail body whilst he'd been hiding in the cratch.

'Well,' Alex thought to himself, 'what am I going to do now? What on earth am I going to do with this kid?' The spot where he'd moored was well out into open country, several miles from the nearest road bridge over the canal, and the evening was well advanced. To take the boy in and hand him over to the authorities would mean a long trek along the towpath in the pouring rain to find a bridge where a road crossed over the canal, and then another long walk along the road into the nearest village. And then Alex would have to hang around for ages, answering questions, and filling in forms. And then another long trek back again afterwards. The weather outside was absolutely foul, bitterly cold as well, and it was well set in for the night. After some consideration, he reluctantly concluded that there was nothing for it - he'd have to let the boy stay aboard the boat for the night.

"Right," he said at last. "The weather's pretty awful outside, and it's getting late. I've decided that I'll let you stay here on the boat overnight, then I'll take you and hand you in, in the morning."

Danny's reaction to this news surprised Alex. The boy started talking, very quickly, becoming more and more excited as he did so.

"No, NO, please don't. I'll be dead! You can't. You mustn't. No. Please don't hand me in. Just let me go. I'll go now, right now. I won't be a bother to you, no trouble. I promise! Just forget I've ever been here, ok? Forget all about me please, anything you like, but please don't hand me in. Please don't make me go back there, back to the Hall." And the boy's bottom lip started quivering. Alex could see that he was almost crying.

The boy looked nervously around behind him, at the cabin doors into the cratch, looking for a means of escape, but Alex had closed them and bolted them behind the boy a few moments earlier. Danny seemed painfully aware that if he tried to flee, then Alex would grab hold of him before he'd gone more than a few steps, and not even be able to open the doors. "Why, what's the matter?" asked Alex quietly, disturbed at how upset the boy had become.

Danny didn't answer, keeping his gaze firmly fixed on the floor in front of him. But, after a long moment, he put his hands onto the bottom of his tee shirt and slowly lifted it up to his chin. Alex was appalled at what the boy revealed. He was painfully thin, his ribs showing clearly through the tight skin of his chest. But it wasn't that which caught his attention the most. The boy's chest and abdomen were covered with a myriad of bruises, some still blue and quite fresh, others turning yellow and starting to fade. And there were lots of red weals across his body also, either from a whip or cane or lash of some sort. In some places, the boy's skin was broken, in various stages of healing. And some had become infected, red and raw from the bacteria which had become established in the wounds.

Slowly the boy turned around. His back was even worse, with more bruises and weals from a cane or similar.

Danny slowly lowered his tee shirt and turned back to face Alex once again. "Please don't send me back," he pleaded, a look of absolute despair on his face. "They'll half-kill me when they get me back." And he dropped his face again and stood silently there, staring at the floor once again, not moving, just the hint of a tear rolling slowly down his face.

Alex stared at the boy in astonishment. He couldn't get his head around what he'd just seen. In all his time as a schoolteacher and housemaster, the boys in his charge had been well treated, well cared for, and well looked after. This boy standing in front of him had been badly beaten, over a long period of time. What he'd just seen was abuse on a grand scale. He felt sick with rage that anyone could do such a thing to a young child.

"Danny, what have you done to deserve all this?" he asked. But the boy didn't answer, as he just shook his head and continuing to gaze solidly at the floor.

"Come on, you can tell me," said Alex. "Please. I need to know." But Danny didn't respond. Alex decided to leave it for the moment. Perhaps the boy would be more forthcoming later on.

"We'll sort it out in the morning, then," Alex told him. "Perhaps you'll feel able to tell me then, alright?" Danny shrugged silently, still staring fixedly at the floor.

"As I said, you can stay here overnight, at least," Alex told the boy. "OK? And then we'll see what happens. But if I let you stay here on the boat, you must promise me that you won't make off during the night. Is that understood?"

Danny lifted his head and gave Alex a faint smile. "Yea, OK then. I promise. Better than being out there. It's wet outside, innit? Thanks." The boy slowly looked around the boat, taking in the saloon and the galley. His gaze fell upon the bowl of apples sitting on the worktop in the galley. "Hey Mister, you couldn't spare me an apple could you? Please?"

Alex looked at the painfully thin boy standing in front of him. "Are you hungry, then?" he asked, but he realised that he already knew the answer to the question.

Danny didn't reply, just nodding once more.

"So, tell me, how long have you been on the run?" Alex asked him.

"Well, let me think............what's today?" Danny asked in response.

"Saturday," replied Alex.

"Oh........well, it were Wednesday when I got away, Wednesday morning." Danny thought for a moment. "So that's three-and-a-half days, innit?"

Alex nodded in agreement. "So, what have you done for food in all that time?" he asked the boy.

"Nothing, actually, Mister," Danny replied quietly, shaking his head. "There weren't nothing, nothing much at all. I didn't have no money, see? And I weren't gonna pinch stuff, was I? I'm not that sort of kid. I ain't had nothing much to eat since I got away. I did look in a few bins and such, so I got a few bits and pieces, but there weren't nothing much. Mind you, I didn't get that much at the Hall anyway. That's on account of they made me Black One."

"What's Black One?" asked Alex, curious to know more about what had been happening to the lad, and how he had been treated, or rather, mistreated. Was it punishment dished out by the authorities at Grant Hall?

Again, Danny didn't reply, studiously keeping his gaze firmly fixed upon the floor at his feet. Alex decided to let it pass for the moment.

"If you've had nothing since Wednesday morning, I think you need something better than an apple," Alex told him. "Would you like something decent to eat?"

"Yea, please, Mister," said Danny, looking up, with another faint smile fleeting across his face.

"I've finished cooking for tonight, and it's a bit late to start again," replied Alex. "But I could manage to do you cheese on toast, and I can open a can of beans. And a mug of tea. How would you fancy that?"

"Cor Mister, that would be great," said Danny, looking up, with another faint smile.

"OK," Alex nodded, "just give me five minutes and it'll be ready for you." He busied himself at the galley, then suddenly remembered what he'd gone into the cratch for, just a few minutes before. "But, while I'm getting it for you, can you please slip into the cratch, that's at the front there behind you, just outside the doors, and fish out a bag of coal for me? You'll find it in the locker under the seat, on the left-hand side. And you don't run, off, you understand?"

"OK, Mister, right away," said Danny, nodding, as he turned and unbolted, and then opened the saloon doors at the front of the boat and busied himself in the cratch finding the bag of coal.

Alex watched the boy out of the corner of his eye whilst he got the meal ready. He half expected him to lift the cratch cover and make off into the night, even though it was still raining hard, pouring down, the sound of the rain hammering on the cabin roof. But after a moment, Danny re-appeared, closing and bolting the saloon doors behind him. Without being asked, he carefully opened the bag and tipped its contents into the coal bucket, taking care not to allow the dust and small fragments of coal to spill onto the floor. When the bag was empty, Danny carefully folded it up and, walking forward, neatly dropped it into the pedal bin standing in the corner of the galley.

"Sit down here at the dinette," said Alex, "it's just about ready for you now."

"Cor, that looks good, thanks" said Danny, as he picked up his knife and fork and started eating.

Alex sat with a mug of tea and watched the boy as he ate. There was something about the way Danny was eating which disturbed him. It certainly wasn't the normal style which an 11 year old boy would adopt to eat his food. He knew from his many years as a school teacher that most boys of that age ate quickly, shovelling their food in as fast as they could. And if there was a chance of second helpings, if there was anything left after everyone had been served, then they put away their food even quicker.

But Danny was eating very slowly, taking small portions onto his fork each time, and then chewing the food very slowly and carefully, getting every last drop of taste out of each mouthful before swallowing it, and then repeating the same over and over again. And when he drank his tea, he cupped his hands round the mug, absorbing its warmth, holding it tightly to him, as if he was scared that Alex was going to take it away from him before it was empty.

Alex racked his brains for a few minutes while he tried to remember what it reminded him of. And then suddenly it came to him. He'd seen children eating like this, many years before.

After taking his degree, Alex had spent two years working as a volunteer with the Save The Children Fund. He'd spent most of that time in Africa, caring for the child victims of one of the many civil wars which ravaged that continent. He'd learnt then that children who'd been half starving ate very slowly, very carefully. Really savouring their food, since they were unsure as to when they'd get their next meal, or even if they'd ever get another one. They'd learnt to make the most of what they had to eat, whatever it was, wherever it was, and however it was that they came by it.

He remembered he'd spoken to one of the doctors about it. 'It's a natural instinctive reaction to being malnourished,' he'd been told. 'You see, starving children don't have sufficient digestive acids in their stomachs to properly digest whatever food they may have to eat. Which results in some of the food being passed out through the bowels before it can be fully digested. Chewing the food very thoroughly helps to break down the cell walls of the food, making the task of the digestive tract much easier. Also, prolonged chewing enables all of the flavour in the food to be extracted before swallowing. And finally, taking longer to eat whatever meagre rations they have makes the meal last longer, making it seem to be more there to eat than is actually there. I've seen it several times, in Somalia, Sudan, and elsewhere. It's a perfectly normal human reaction to there not being enough food to function properly over a long period of time.'

And now, Danny was sat in front of him, eating just as those children in Africa had done. That was what Danny's eating reminded him of. Alex looked at the boy's stick-thin arms, remembering the skin of his chest stretched tight over his ribs, his brief comment that he didn't get much food at the Hall anyway. The boy had been deliberately underfed, and for some time at that. No wonder he was so thin. And what was that Danny had said about being made Black One?

The more Alex sat and looked at Danny as he ate his cheese on toast with baked beans, the more and more concerned he became about the boy. There was something seriously wrong going on up at Grant Hall. But what? And why? And how was it being allowed to go on? And, if this was how Danny was being treated, then what about the other boys living there? But primarily Alex was worried about Danny. And he was even more worried that, with so many questions stirring around in his mind, he didn't know the answers to any of those questions.

But Danny had finished his meal. "Thanks, Mister," he said. "That was great. Really nice. You ain't a bad cook, are you?" Alex smiled. It didn't take a lot of skill to make cheese on toast, and open a can of beans and heat them up. But he was glad the boy appreciated it, and had now eaten his first meal for nearly four days. It certainly seemed as though he needed it.

"Where can I kip down, Mister?" Danny asked. "Down here on the floor, by the fire? Is that ok?"

"Oh, no," Alex replied, with a smile. "I can do much better for you than that. If you'd like to wait here a minute, I'll go and make up a bunk for you in the back cabin."

"OK, Mister, thanks," and for a moment another faint smile appeared on Danny's face.

Alex went through the boat to the back cabin, retrieved some spare bed linen from the locker beside the bunk, and quickly made up the bunk for the boy to sleep in. When he got back to the saloon, he found that Danny had been busy whilst he'd been away. He'd washed up and dried his tea things, and was just finishing putting the crockery back on the rack, and folding up the teacloth and placing it neatly over the oven rail.

"It's all ready for you," Alex smiled at Danny. "But before you turn in, there's something I should do for you."

"What's that ?" asked Danny anxiously, a scared look immediately flitting across his face.

"I've got some antiseptic cream in the first aid kit," Alex told him. "Some of your wounds are infected. The cream will help them to heal quicker. Would you like me to dress them for you?"

"OK, thanks Mister, that's really nice of you." Danny smiled again, a cheeky impish smile on his face. But Alex realised the boy was still very wary of him. He would need to gain his confidence if he was ever to find out about the boy's circumstances, and the treatment and abuse he'd been receiving,

Alex sat on the corner of the dinette and motioned Danny to stand in front of him. "OK, Danny, slip your tee shirt off," Alex told him, and the boy obediently did so. As he started spreading the cream on his wounds, Alex asked him "How did you get these, Danny? Was it at Grant Hall?" Danny nodded slowly, not speaking. It took a couple of minutes for Alex to spread the cream everywhere it was needed, but at last it was finished. "OK, all done," Alex told him. "That should help a bit."

Danny put his tee shirt on again, but then just stood there, hesitantly, not moving, as if there was something else he wanted to say. But eventually he asked, "can I go and kip now please?"

"Yes of course," said Alex. "Just go down the boat, you'll see your bunk all made up. And the bathroom is along there on the right. I've put out a flannel and towel for you."

"OK, then, Mister, thanks. G'night." And Danny went off to the bathroom, ready to turn in for the night, leaving Alex sat at the dinette, thinking about what Danny had just told him. A couple of minutes later, he heard Danny come out of the bathroom, but instead of making his way back to his berth, the boy came back to the saloon and just stood there, looking at the floor in front of him once again. What is it, Danny?" Alex asked.

"Do you have a mirror please, Mister?" the boy asked quietly.

"There's one on the bathroom wall, didn't you notice it?" Alex asked.

The boy nodded. "It's just that I need another one as well," he explained.

"I'm sorry, Danny," Alex replied. "I've only got one, that's the one on the wall in the bathroom. Why do you need another?"

Danny didn't reply for a moment, before saying hesitantly, "I've got some more cuts and stuff," he said at last, his gaze still firmly fixed on the floor in front of him.

"So, why do you need a mirror?" Alex asked, puzzled.

The boy was quiet again, his head down. "I can't get to them very easily,'" he mumbled eventually.

"So, where are they, then?" Alex was curious, and a little perturbed. "I'll dress them for you."

Danny just stood there, shaking his head.

"Where are they, Danny?" Alex repeated, and eventually after a long pause, Danny mumbled, "it hurts when I sit down. It's really bad. Much worse than up here, ever so much worse," as he raised his hand and tapped his chest.

Alex immediately realised what was wrong, and why the boy was so reluctant to admit to his other injuries. "You've been caned, or worse, on your bottom?" he enquired. Danny just nodded again.

"Then you must let me dress them for you," Alex told him, but Danny just shook his head yet again. "No," he said at last. "Not down there. It's private."

Alex thought for a moment. The boys' wounds on his chest and back were bad enough, and if his other injuries were worse, then it was essential that they were properly treated. Having been on the run for some days, it was almost certain that his wounds to his bottom had become seriously infected and were turning badly septic. And it was understandable that Danny was so shy and embarrassed with him, a total stranger. He would have to gain the boy's confidence, to persuade him to allow his wounds to receive the attention they needed.

"Danny, if they're as bad as you think they are, then it's essential that they're treated." Alex paused for a moment, gathering his thoughts. He needed to persuade the boy to allow him to attend to his injuries. "They've probably become badly infected," he went on. "You must let me see to them, straight away." But the boy just stood there silently, his gaze still firmly fixed on the floor in front of him, slowly shaking his head from side to side.

Alex racked his brains. He didn't want to let the wounds go untreated, and it was obvious that Danny was aware that treatment was needed, otherwise he'd have gone off to turn in for the night. But it presented a problem, as he seemed unable to attended to them himself, not being able to see the affected areas, and his terrible reluctance to remove his clothing in front of a complete stranger was perfectly understandable. "Why not, Danny?" he asked, but to no avail, as Danny quietly kept repeating, "no, private," again and again.

Then an idea crossed Alex's mind. He'd try a bit of gentle persuasion. "Danny," he asked, "if you were with a doctor, a doctor whom you'd never seen before, would you be as shy as this?"

Danny shook his head, saying nothing. "Why not?" Alex asked. After a long pause, Danny spoke quietly, "that's different. He's a doctor, ain't he? You're not."

"But, Danny," Alex responded, " I'm a fully qualified first aider, and I've attended to quite a few people who've needed attention at one time or another. The only difference is that a doctor has more medical training than I have. I share with all doctors the desire to do the best we can for anyone who needs attention."

Danny shook his head once again. "No, private," he insisted.

Undeterred, Alex decide to try another approach. "Danny," he began. "Have you ever seen people shaking hands?" he asked. Danny nodded.

"So, tell me, why do they do that?" Alex asked.

"It's when they say hello and goodbye," the boy replied quietly.

"Yes, Danny, that's right," Alex confirmed. "But people also shake hands when they've given their word to each other, when they've agreed something important between themselves. A business deal, or an agreement to lend or borrow money, or to buy something at an agreed price. Are you aware of that?"

Danny nodded again.

"Then let's make an agreement, here and now, between ourselves," Alex went on. "I'll give you my word that I'll give you my full respect and behave entirely properly towards you, just like any doctor would. And in turn, you must agree to let me attend to your wounds. And we'll shake hands on it, to confirm our best intentions towards each other. How does that seem to you?"

Danny looked up, a distrustful look in his eyes. "Are you sure, Mister?" he asked cautiously. "You ain't a perv, are you? Or a pedo? You're not gonna mess me about? Mess about with me?"

Alex shook his head, thinking about Danny's rather strange response as he did so. 'Why should he think that?' he wondered to himself. "No, Danny, I'm not, nothing like that, of course I'm not," he told the lad. "Why should I want to do that? You must trust me. I want to help you, if you'll allow me to."

Danny stood there for a while, undecided, his head down, but his eyes always moving, glancing furtively around the confines of the saloon, first at Alex, then at the doors into the cratch, still firmly bolted, then back to Alex again. It was apparent that Danny was aware his wounds needed attention, but the boy was so obviously scared stiff and really frightened.

Alex felt that he was losing this particular battle. "Danny," he said at last, "if your wounds are infected and are not treated, then you're going to get blood poisoning or worse, you'll become really ill, and you'll end up in hospital. And the hospital will be on the phone to Grant Hall within five minutes of your walking in through the door, because they'll have been told that there's a young boy out there somewhere who's on the run. Do you really want that to happen?"

Danny was quiet for a long time, shaking his head, staring at the floor all the while, occasionally shuffling his feet from side to side. Alex could only imagine the thoughts which must be racing through the young boy's mind. He was relieved when Danny eventually spoke again. "OK Mister, if you promise," he said, "but if you do mess me about, then I'm off. OK?"

"I understand, Danny," Alex replied. "Now let's shake on it." He extended his hand to the boy, who slowly held out his own. "Look at me, please," Alex asked him, as he took the boy's hand and shook it slowly, firmly, fixing Danny's eyes in his. "I promise that I'll behave properly towards you, and treat you with all the respect and dignity that any doctor would, Danny," he told him. "And in return you promise that you will allow me to address your wounds. Is that understood?"

Danny nodded again. "Do you agree, Danny?" Alex asked. "To mark the proper bargain between us, you must say that you do."

"I agree," Danny mumbled quietly. "That's fine," Alex replied. "Now, undo the top button of your jeans, lower your zip just a little way, then lean over the saloon table here. That will enable me to pull the back of your jeans and undies down over your cheeks and see to you, while preserving your modesty as much as we can. Is that alright?"

Danny nodded once more, as slowly and with obvious reluctance he moved forward to the table, and bent over it. But suddenly he stood up again. "You're sure?" he asked.

"Yes, Danny, I'm sure," Alex reassured the lad. "As I told you just now, you have to trust me." Saying nothing for a long while, Danny eventually nodded, then bent over again and loosened his button and zip as Alex had suggested. As Alex drew the boy's clothing down, he was appalled at what he saw. His buttocks were covered in welts and weals from repeated canings, some old, and some relatively new. The skin was broken in many places, and there were a number of wounds where infection was raging out of control. 'No wonder it's sore' thought Alex, 'it must be quite unpleasant.'

"Hang on a minute, Danny," he said, "this is quite bad. I've got some antiseptic lotion back there somewhere. The cream I used on your chest won't be strong enough to cope with this."

Seething with anger at seeing how this young child had been so badly treated, Alex went to the bathroom and searched for the bottle of Dettol which he knew was in one of the cupboards there. As he did so, he thought furiously about what he'd just seen. He decided that he had to have a photographic record of how bad the boys injuries were, so that no-one would ever be able to deny how Danny had been abused and mistreated. In a week or two those injuries would hopefully all heal up and be gone for ever, so it was important to get that record without delay. But with Danny being so frightened and suspicious of him, there was no way that he'd permit Alex to take pictures of his naked buttocks. He would have to take the pictures without first asking Danny, before he could refuse, as he almost certainly would.

Picking up the Dettol and a pack of cotton wool, he came out of the bathroom and closed the door, picking up his camera on his way back to the saloon. Without saying anything to Danny, he raised the camera and took a couple of pictures of the wounds on Danny's bottom. But as soon as he saw the flash of the camera reflecting round the saloon, the boy jumped up, grabbing his jeans up around his waist, and ran towards the doors leading to the cratch, where he crouched on the floor in the corner by the steps, like a scared rabbit caught in the headlights of an approaching car.

"Hey Mister," he shouted angrily, "you ARE a perv after all! You're just as bad as them others. You're a sodding pedo, that's what you are! What are you doing taking photos of my bum?"

Alex sighed. He'd worked hard to gain the tentative trust of this scared and frightened young boy, and now it seemed that trust had evaporated in an instant.

"No, I'm not, nothing like that at all," replied Alex. "But, what do you mean, 'them others'?" But Danny didn't reply. "Unlock the door and let me go, Mister," the boy whined. "Please."

Alex knew he was staring defeat in the face. He knew that he had one last chance to win the boy's confidence. "You can go if you really want to," Alex assured him. "But the weather outside is really foul. Please remember what I promised to you just now. You have to trust me. Let me tell you once again, you're quite safe here with me. It's much better that you stay here till the morning." He paused for a moment, then went on, "but now, I want to show you something, over here. Come on, come here for a moment," he added, as he beckoned Danny to come forward. Danny shook his head, but then as Alex stepped forward and took Danny's hand lightly in his own, he cautiously stood up and stepped towards him. Alex took him to the wall of the saloon, where there were a number of photographs in neat frames, secured to the wall.

"Here, have a look at these," he told the boy. "Here's me, with my family. This one, this is me with my wife Jenny, and our children, Robert and Christine."

"How come you're here on this boat on your own, then?" asked Danny, looking at Alex with a quizzical expression of his face, "if you're married with kids? Why aren't they here on the boat with you?"

"That's easy to answer," replied Alex. "This picture was taken several years ago now. Since then, sadly, my wife has died, that was about 15 months ago. And my children, well, they're grown up now and living their own lives. My son Robert is in America, in California, doing post-graduate research on crop improvements, hoping to improve the yields of crops, breeding drought-resistant strains of wheat and so on. And my daughter Christine's in New Zealand, she's teaching there."

"And this picture here, that's my House at the school where I was a teacher and House Master for more than twenty years. And my wife Jennifer was the House Matron. The school was run by the government for the sons of people who worked in the Diplomatic Service. Usually their diplomats were given postings to embassies abroad where they could take their families with them. But other postings were to countries which were less stable politically, and it wasn't deemed suitable for the families to go abroad with the diplomatic staff. In such cases, their sons came to our school. I like to think that we gave them a good environment in which to live and learn. Many old pupils used to come back and see us, sometimes for years after they'd left and gone on to university."

Danny looked at the picture. It showed Alex dressed in a smart suit, with his academic gown over it, and his wife Jennifer in her Matron's uniform. Surrounding them were about 40 boys aged much the same as Danny was. All the boys looked happy, and were smiling and laughing. Danny looked at Alex, the unanswered question still in his expression, mistrust still spread all over his face.

"No, Danny, you're quite ok with me," Alex told him. "Trust me. All these boys did. And their parents. Believe me. Let me tell you one more time." He spoke the next few words slowly and carefully, to give them greater emphasis. "You are quite safe with me."

"Are you sure, Mister?" Danny asked. "How do I know I can trust you? Why did you take those photos of my bum?"

"There's a very good reason for that," Alex told him. "Would you like me to explain that to you right now?"

Danny nodded once again. "Then sit down here, at the dinette, and I'll tell you," Alex went on. "But be assured, please, I'm not a pervert who's interested in young boys. Nor am I a paedophile of any sort. No way."

Nervously, the boy sat tenderly down on the dinette, facing Alex across the table.

"Now look here, Danny," Alex started. "You've got some severe injuries on your bottom, which are badly infected, and also some nasty wounds on your chest and back as well, which are starting to go the same way. I'm really angry about what I've just seen. I don't yet know how or why you've been treated like this, but what's been done to you is completely unacceptable. It's very very wrong. Whoever did this to you must be called to account. But that can't be done without evidence. Your injuries are evidence of the abuse you've suffered, the sort of evidence that will be needed to secure a conviction in a court of law. But in a few weeks time, hopefully they will all be healed up and gone, gone for ever. The evidence will have disappeared. These photos will preserve that evidence, for as long as is needed, until justice can be done. And justice must be done. I suppose this has all been done to you while you've been at Grant Hall?"

Danny nodded, saying nothing.

"Even though you're not at Grant Hall now," Alex continued, "I imagine other boys are still there, being ill treated and abused like you have been. And that will go on, they will continue to be abused, and others after them, until such time as a stop is put to it, and all this is put right. That is why I took those photographs. They will help to bring what is happening a Grant Hall to an end. Without them, it might never be possible, and the abuse will continue."

Alex paused for a while to let Danny consider what he'd just said, then quietly asked, "are you alright with that now, Danny?"

For a long while Danny didn't respond, obviously thinking about what Alex had told him, but eventually he nodded silently, not saying a word. Alex waited patiently, and after a while Danny stood up, saying, "I s'pose so, Mister. You'd better carry on," as he loosened his clothing and bent down over the end of the dinette once more.

"This may sting a little bit, Danny," Alex told the boy, as he dripped some Dettol onto a small pad of cotton-wool. Alex felt a little bit guilty as he spoke. He knew that he wasn't telling the whole truth. He knew that the Dettol wouldn't just sting. It would be really really painful. But it had to be done if the infections were to be given any chance of clearing up and healing. As he applied the Dettol to the wounds, Alex fully expected Danny to cry out, but the only reaction he observed was a slight clenching of the boy's buttocks as he dressed the wounds. It took quite a while, but eventually Alex had finished. 'That's a brave boy I've got here' he thought, as he capped the bottle of Dettol and told Danny to get up. "OK Danny, all finished," he said.

"Thanks, Mister," Danny replied as he stood up and fastened his jeans once more.

"You'll need it all done again tomorrow. Bottom, chest, back," Alex told him. "And for a few days after that. But with luck it will all heal up alright."

"OK, then," Danny replied, adding "can I go and kip now please?"

"No, not yet, Danny," replied Alex. "I need to take some more photographs, of the injuries to your back, and your chest too. We really need to have a complete picture of your wounds. Is that alright?"

Without saying a word, Danny lifted his teeshirt while Alex took the photos he needed. "That's fine, thank you, Danny," he said eventually. "You can go and turn in now."

"OK, then, Mister, thanks," Danny replied, as he turned and slowly made his way to his berth at the back of the boat.

Alex sat thinking about Danny for a while before turning in himself. He seemed to be a well brought up child, but how and why he'd ended up at Grant Hall, Alex as yet had no idea. The little he'd heard from Danny about it didn't sound good, and the injuries the boy had sustained were clearly unacceptable.   How was it that the Social Services and child protection people had not taken action about the abuse which seemed to be going on? Was there some sort of connivance and cover-up taking place? And what was that about being Black One? Alex realised that he had to get Danny to talk to him, so that he could find out a lot more about what was going on. But first, he had to work to gain the boy's complete trust, as Alex knew without that, he wouldn't stand a chance of getting to the root cause of it all.

He put on his coat and went out of the front doors into the cratch, then, lifting the cover, he stepped off the boat and onto the towpath into the rain to check the mooring ropes, as he always did every night before turning in. They had been known to pull loose during the night, causing the boat to knock noisily against the metal piling at the side of the water. But they were sound. Alex went onto the stern deck, and locked the rear access hatch from the outside with the padlock he kept handy for the purpose. Alex had learn that it was not wise to leave your boat unlocked during the night, as thieves were known to frequent the towpath on occasion, preying on unsuspecting boaters. Also, that night in particular, he had an additional reason to keep his boat locked and secure. He didn't want Danny to disappear during the night. He seemed quite capable of making off again, perhaps in the early morning after the storm had blown itself out, whilst Alex was still asleep.

Back on the boat, Alex locked the front doors and made up the fire, which would keep in for most of the night, and then he made his own way to bed. Unusually, he didn't slip off to sleep straight away. He kept thinking about Danny, about what the boy had told him, and about the injuries the boy had shown him. He was very disturbed about the treatment which had been handed out to the boy, and he felt determined to find out what was going on. Whatever it was, it was wrong, wrong, wrong, and had to be stopped. But how that could be done, Alex as yet had no idea, no idea at all.

CHAPTER 2

The next morning, Alex woke at his usual time of 7.30 after a restless night's sleep. He'd not slept well, as he'd been unable to get Danny out of his mind. He was worried about the boy. Why was he on the run? And, from what? He hurriedly dressed, made his way to the galley and brewed himself a quick cup of coffee. Then, donning a coat, he went out through the front doors of the saloon and, lifting up the cratch cover, climbed out onto the towpath and walked round to the back of the boat. Stepping onto the rear deck, he undid the padlock which he'd used to secure the rear hatch and doors the previous night.

He went down into the boat and made his way through the back cabin into the engine room, passing Danny on the way. The boy was still fast asleep, curled up into as near a foetal position as the narrow confines of the bunk would permit. The boy's innocent face belied the grief which he must have endured over the past few months. Alex noticed that, even though they were quite dirty and appeared to be well past their best, the boy's clothes had been neatly folded and carefully placed on the locker at the foot of the bunk, with his trainers equally neatly placed side by side on the floor beside the bunk. It reinforced Alex's view that Danny had had a good upbringing, and made him more determined than ever to get to the bottom of this sorry affair.

He checked the oil and water levels in the engine, a routine he carried out every morning before setting off. Passing through the back cabin again, where Danny was still fast asleep, he moved out onto the rear deck and started the engine. Then he went back onto the towpath and untied the mooring ropes, and gave the back of the boat a gentle push out into midstream. Engaging a slow reverse with the engine, he backed *Jennifer Jo* away from the edge of the canal, and then, putting the tiller hard over, Alex engaged forward gear and set off along the canal.

He was adopting the routine that he'd become accustomed to after a few months afloat. He'd learnt it from other live-aboard boaters along the cut. The idea was to get under way early in the morning and cruise along the canal for about an hour. This allowed the water in the domestic hot water tank, known as a calorifier, to be heated up using the waste heat from the engine. *Jennifer Jo* also had a gas-fired boiler, which could be used to heat both the hot water and radiators throughout the boat, but it was much more economical to use the engine to heat the domestic hot water system whilst cruising along, as much as possible. After an hour or so, the water would be hot enough for him to moor up, take a shower, make a leisurely breakfast, then decide what to do for the rest of the day.

Alex had very quickly learnt that a life afloat did not consist of nothing else but cruising along the canal. Food and provisions had to be obtained at regular intervals, as there was only a finite amount of storage space aboard, there being a limit to the amount of cupboards etc which could be provided in the confined spaces of a narrowboat, even one as long as *Jennifer Jo*. Often this meant a long trek to a nearby village, as there were few shops right adjacent to the canal. Alex had obtained, specially for instances such as these, a folding bicycle which he kept in a locker in the stern of the boat. It had a carrier frame on the back, and with this it was relatively easy to cycle along the towpath to a nearby bridge, and then make his way along the road to the shops. But even this had its limitations, the bike couldn't carry that much. Best of all were those places where there was a supermarket close to the canal, as he had found at places such as Leighton Buzzard and Rugby. There, all the boaters would moor up and stock up on everything that they could carry, often making several journeys to replenish their boats with supplies of food, cleaning equipment, toilet rolls, and all myriad of household items which were always needed.

Alex cruised for about an hour and a quarter before he found a suitable place to moor up. It was a pleasant spot, with a low hedge on the towpath side and an occasional tree bending slightly in the dying wind, with pasture beyond. Across the cut was a large meadow, with a flock of sheep busily tugging at the grass for their morning feed. In the distance beyond the meadow, in a slight cutting, ran a railway line, on which there appeared to be a regular service, as every so often the peace of the morning was broken by the hiss of a fast electric train going on its way.

The sky was now starting to clear from the previous night's storm, with the sun beginning to peep through the gaps in the clouds. Alex knew that they would soon clear away completely, and there was now the prospect of good, warm, weather for the rest of the week. The spot where he'd chosen to moor was ideal for what he had in mind for the next day or so.

After mooring up, Alex made his way through the boat to the galley, finding on his way through the back cabin that Danny was still sound asleep. 'No wonder,' Alex thought to himself, 'he's been on the run for several days, and probably not slept properly at all during that time.' Picking up Danny's clothes, he took them through to the galley, where he opened a cupboard to reveal a small washing machine. He put Danny's clothes into the machine and set it to work while he cooked himself some breakfast.

Just as Alex was finishing his breakfast, there was a loud 'ping' from the washing machine, indicating that it's cycle had finished and Danny's clothes were done. Alex removed them from the machine and made his way to the engine room, where he hung the clothes on a line strung across between the bulkheads for exactly that purpose. Even thought the engine was stopped, its residual heat would keep the room warm for some time and quickly get the clothes dry, much quicker than they would if he was to hang them outside in the dying breeze. He then returned to the galley to clear away and wash up his dishes.

He was just finishing the washing up when a tousle-headed youngster appeared in the doorway to the galley, holding a blanket around his waist.

"Hey Mister," Danny called out accusingly. "Are you sure you're not a perv? Or a pedo?"

"No, of course I'm not. I told you that before," Alex replied. "We went through all that last night. Why, what's the matter?" But Danny eyed him suspiciously, still perhaps not entirely sure of Alex's intentions.

"Well, where's me clothes, then?" demanded the boy.

"Oh, that's no problem," replied Alex. "I put them in the wash for you. They're done, and hanging up to dry in the engine room. If you'd looked a little bit harder as you came through, you'd have seen them hanging in there. The heat from the engine will have them dry in about half an hour's time. Slip back into bed, and I'll bring you some breakfast. Would cornflakes, then sausage, bacon and eggs be alright? With some toast and marmalade to follow? And a mug of tea?"

Danny nodded, and disappeared off back to his bunk in the back cabin. Alex set to, getting some breakfast for the boy. When it was ready, he set it all on a tray, and took it through to the back cabin, putting the tray down on top of the locker by the boy's head.

"Cor, Mister, that looks good," said Danny, smiling broadly. "I ain't had a breakfast like this for ages, ever since............". His voice tailed off as the smile disappeared from his face, to be replaced with a wistful look, causing Alex to wonder yet again about the boy's background and history.

"Eat up, and enjoy," replied Alex. "Take your time."

"Thanks, Mister," Danny replied, "thanks ever so."

Leaving Danny to get to grips with his breakfast, Alex carried on up to the back of the boat, where he opened one of the rear lockers, from which he took out a blue plastic bucket and some cloths, followed by a can of polish. He was going to use the morning to give the boat its much-needed wash and spruce-up after the previous night's rain, it was even dirtier than ever, and desperately needed a clean. He filled the bucket with clean water in the bathroom, and then went out onto the towpath, and then, starting at the bow of the boat near the cratch, commenced to wash down the side of the boat, thoroughly cleaning all the accumulated muck and grime away, taking special care at the gunwales, where dirt had penetrated into the joints between the welded steel sections which made up the boat's hull.

He took his time to wash the cabin side down properly, as he knew that it was essential to carry out a good wash before applying the polish, otherwise the paintwork might become scratched and allow corrosion to set in. He slowly and gradually worked backwards towards the stern of the boat. He'd been working for about 20 minutes, and just about reached the second saloon window, when he heard the sound of the fresh water pump inside the boat purring gently. Glancing along the hull at the heavily-frosted bathroom window, Alex saw a soft opaque white shape moving around in the bathroom, and realised that Danny was taking a shower.

A few minutes later, the sliding hatch at the rear of the boat opened, and Danny appeared on the rear deck. He stood there for a couple of minutes, taking in his surroundings, looking around at the rural scenery of this stretch of the canal, and watching what Alex was doing. Then he walked forward, took up the can of polish and a polishing cloth, and without a word to Alex, silently started to polish the area Alex had just washed.

The pair carried on cleaning the boat all morning, never speaking, Alex busy washing the cabin side, with Danny following on behind, applying the polish, and then buffing it off till the paintwork shone as new. A narrowboat the size of *Jennifer Jo* had a lot of cabin wall to clean, and it was well past mid-day before Alex had finished washing the side of the boat. Looking back, Alex saw that Danny still had a bit more polishing to do before he too would be finished.

Alex made his way back into the galley, passing first through the back cabin en route, where he noticed that Danny had made up his bunk, with the pillow neatly placed at the top of the bed, indicating that the boy was planning to stay for another night. He quickly made some sandwiches for lunch, placing them on a tray with two glasses of squash and a couple of apples from the fruit bowl. Then, taking the tray up on deck, he went over and sat on the grass beside the towpath, where he sat down in the warm sunshine, took a sandwich, and watched as Danny finished his polishing. When he'd done, the boy came and sat down beside Alex, reaching out for a sandwich.

"Uh, uh," called out Alex. Danny quickly took his hand back, a disappointed look on his face. "Oh, sorry," he said.

"No, it's OK, Danny," Alex told him. "They're for you as well."

"OK, thanks," the boy replied, and he stretched out his hand again.

" Uh, uh." Alex called out once more.

Danny looked at him again. "Yes?" he asked.

"Haven't you forgotten something?" asked Alex, finding it difficult to conceal a slight grin upon his face.

The boy thought for a moment. "Can I have a sandwich, Mister?" he asked.

Alex smiled at him, as he said "try again."

Danny thought for a moment, a slight furrow on his brow. "May I have a sandwich, PLEASE, Mister?"

Alex laughed. "Of course you can, Danny," he told the boy, "but you've forgotten something, one of the most important things that you should do, when on a boat afloat."

"What's that, Mister?" asked Danny, slightly perplexed at the riddle Alex had set him.

"Well," said Alex, "the golden rule is, before eating, always but ALWAYS wash your hands. The water in the canal is filthy and full of nasty bugs. It's not fresh running water like in a river. The only current that there is, is caused by water being flushed through a lock when someone moves their boat through it. But water-borne bugs aren't the only hazard, there's other things to be aware of as well. Lots of people bring their dogs for a walk along the towpath, and they do their business everywhere, and whilst some owners clear up after their dogs, not all of them do so. You could easily get a nasty illness from any number of causes. Always wash your hands before eating, OK?"

Danny nodded, as Alex continued "someone like yourself, with open wounds and cuts, are even more at risk from bacteria in the water. Get a nasty bug into your bloodstream through a cut or sore, and you could end up very seriously ill in hospital. So you should be extra careful until all your wounds have healed. And if you ever have the misfortune to fall into the water, be sure to get into the boat and have a shower and a good wash as soon as you possibly can, even if the water hasn't been heated yet and it's only a cold shower. And, of course, change your clothes and get them washed straight away."

"Yea, OK then, Mister," Danny responded, as he disappeared into the boat and made his way to the bathroom, emerging a few moments later with clean hands, and a big smile on his face.

"Can I have a sandwich now please, Mister?" he asked, as he sat down on the grass beside Alex. "Of course you can," said Alex, smiling back at him. "I bet you're hungry now. There's ham or cheese, whichever you like. Help yourself, and enjoy your lunch. You've earned it. Well done, and thankyou for helping me."

They sat in the sunshine for a while after their lunch was finished, as Danny slipped off his tee-shirt, laid back on the grass, and basked in the warm sunshine. Alex looked at him as he lay there, seeing again the boy's wounds, set against his ribs sticking out under his skin, and wondering just how he'd become so thin and skinny. Leaving him there for the moment, Alex got up and took the lunch tray into the gallery and cleared up their lunch things. He then fished out some plastic carrier bags from the cupboard under the sink, and, going outside again, he said to Danny "Come on, we're going for a walk."

The boy immediately jumped up off the grass, pulling on his tee shirt, a wild look of fear and mistrust on his face. "W......w.........where to...............what for................why ?" he asked, nervously looking up and down the towpath, seeming as if he was going to run off at any moment.

"No, it's OK," said Alex. "Come here. Look at me, will you?" Danny stepped forward and raised his head, as Alex fixed him directly in the eyes. Placing his hand on the boy's shoulder, he gave it a gentle squeeze, at the same time saying "you must believe me, Danny, when I tell you there is no secret agenda. You have to trust me."

"Are you sure?" said Danny, the nervous look still on his face. "I've been pissed about before."

"Yes, Danny, I'm sure," said Alex. "I can't help you if you won't trust me."

"Well, OK, then," replied Danny, a little reluctantly it seemed. "Where are we going, anyway?"

"Just along the towpath for a while," said Alex. "Here, take some of these bags. We'll need them."

"What for?" asked Danny, curiously.

"You'll see," Alex told him. "Come on, let's go." They walked along the towpath together, then suddenly Alex stopped. "Here we are," he said, as he stooped down and picked up a small twig laying on the grass, blown off from the tree above by the previous night's storm, and dropped it into one of the carrier bags he was holding. "Just what we need," he said.

"What for?" asked Danny.

"Well," replied Alex. "I'm always in need of sticks and twigs to light the fire with. You can buy packs of kindling at the boatyards and chandleries along the cut, but why pay for what you can pick up for nothing while you're out for a walk? There's always plenty of bits and pieces lying around after a storm like we had last night. Look, there's another piece. Pop it into your bag, will you please?"

"OK, Mister," Danny said. "And here's another piece as well. Is that OK?"

"Yes, that's fine," Alex told him, "get that too."

They walked along the towpath together, and after about ten minutes they'd filled their carrier bags, so they turned round and made their way back to *Jennifer Jo*. "Right, Danny," Alex told him, "I'll slip into the galley and make a drink, while you can put the twigs in the engine room to dry. You'll see that there's two large plastic boxes near the front of the engine, they've got some sticks in them already. Take the one nearest the engine into the saloon and empty it into the wood box by the stove, then put the second box nearest the engine, and then put the new twigs into the first box. Got that?"

"OK Mister," Danny replied, and he set to as Alex put the kettle on and made two mugs of steaming tea.

"Let's sit outside for our teas," Alex told Danny, and they went outside and sat on the grass in the afternoon sunshine.

They sat in silence for a while, drinking their tea, and then Alex turned to Danny and asked him, "Danny, will you please tell me something about yourself?"

"OK, Mister," replied Danny. "But, what do you want to know?"

"Well, Danny, I need to know how you ended up in Grant Hall, why you've been so badly treated, and why you're on the run," Alex told the boy.

Danny nodded, but remained quiet for a while. Eventually, he turned to Alex with a pained expression on his face. "Mister," he said, "I dunno where to start really."

"Well," said Alex, "why not start by telling me what your full name is, and when's your birthday. Tell me about your family. Tell me where you lived, and where you went to school. Things like that."

"OK, Mister," Danny replied. "Me birthday's on May 18th. It was me birthday about 3 weeks ago so I'm twelve now. But I never got no cards or presents or nothing. Fat chance when you're at Grant Hall."

Danny paused for a while, in reflection, then spoke again. "Me name's Daniel Marshall. Daniel Harrison Marshall. But like I said before, everyone calls me Danny."

"Harrison's quite an unusual name to have," Alex commented.

"Yea," said Danny. "It were me Mum's maiden name, before she got married, see? And I think she had a crush on Harrison Ford , you know, that actor? She were always fond of him, she always watched his films when they were on the TV."

Danny fell silent again. "Tell me about your mother and father," Alex prompted him. "Do you have any brothers or sisters?"

"No, I ain't got no brother or sisters," Danny replied. "but I nearly did. Me Mum, when I were about six year old, well she got pregnant again. But one day, I come home from school, and there she were, lying on the kitchen floor, blood all down her legs, blood everywhere. She were bleeding from............." Danny paused briefly, a little embarrassed perhaps, struggling to find the words, but then he continued "well.... you know where. She got me to phone for the ambulance, cos Dad was at work, see, and Mum couldn't get up to get to the phone, and they come and took her away to hospital, she lost the baby. She didn't have no more kids after that. I don't think she was able to after that happened to her. I think there were something gone wrong with her insides. So I never had no brothers or sisters after that, no one else to play with, without going out to me mate's houses or whatever, or one of me mates came round, but they did that quite a lot."

"Where did you live?" asked Alex, gently prompting the boy once again.

"We was in Anchor Street," Danny replied. "It weren't nothing special to look at from the outside, it were in a row, what you call a terrace, I think, but it were really nice inside. When I was about seven or eight, me Dad made an extra room up in the loft, that was my playroom. I could have my trains out all the time and my Lego models and all my other toys and stuff, it were great. Loads of the other kids round about used to come in to play, specially after school, cos the school, it were Heath Road Primary, it were only just around the corner."

Danny fell quiet again. Alex prompted him once more. "So, Danny, Tell me about your Father?" he asked.

Danny thought for a while, then started talking again. "Me Dad, he were great. He used to play with me loads, and he made me the playroom, like what I just told you. But about a year after mum lost the baby, when I were about eight, he moved out. I'll always remember the day he left, I'll never forget it, I'd just come home from school that afternoon, and he took me on one side and he told me that he loved me such a lot, and he loved Mum as well, but he couldn't live there with us any more. I'll never forget seeing him walk out of the door, he took the key outa his pocket and unlocked the door, and he gave the key to my Mum and blew her a kiss and he gave me a big hug and then he went out the door and he were gone. I never seen him since. But I wish he were still about, cos then I'd probably never have ended up at Grant Hall."

"Yes, Danny," Alex asked. Tell me about how that happened."

Danny was quiet for a while, not talking, just looking around him and playing with a long stalk of grass which he'd picked, putting it in his mouth and sucking it. Alex didn't push him. He realised that they were getting to the difficult bit, and that Danny would tell him some more once he'd collected his thoughts.

Eventually Danny started speaking again. "It were when I was ten, nearly eleven, I remember that cos I'd just started at the new school, up Cowthorn Lane, it was quite a long way to go, it were on the other side of town. I think we was right at the limit of the catchment area, but all the kids round our way went there. Mum had bought me a new bike to get there with, all the kids from round our way went there on their bikes, we all went together and came home together. It were alright as long as you remembered to lock your bike up when you got there, or some other kid would pinch it. Anyways, just after I started there, Mum got took ill again, she went to the doctor several times, and then she got so she couldn't get out much, she stayed in bed nearly all the time, and then the doctor came in a couple of times, and then eventually she got put into the hospital again."

"No-one seemed to be bothered about me, cos I was at school when she was taken into hospital, when I got home from school that afternoon, I just let myself in with my key as usual and there was this note what she'd left me, saying she'd gone into hospital and would be home in a day or two. So I just carried on living there on my own and going to school and that, and every Saturday and Sunday, I'd go round to the hospital to see Mum. She were very poorly, but I dunno what exactly was wrong with her. A couple of times, they wouldn't even let me in to see her, cos she was in the insulation ward, they wouldn't let anyone in there."

Alex interrupted him. "You mean the isolation ward, don't you?" he asked.

"Yea, that's right," said Danny, "that's what I said, the insulation ward. Anyway, I knew where mum kept some spare money for emergencies, so I used that to buy food and stuff. But after about six weeks I ran out of money, it were all gone, and then one day I came home from school and there was this bloke on the step knocking at the door. He said we owed some money for something or other what Mum had bought, I forget what now, but I just said Mum's away but she'll be back tomorrow, so come back then, so off he went. The next time he came I just didn't answer the door, and he never came again after that, or if he did it was while I was at school or visiting Mum in the hospital."

"But one day, I'd just got home from school and there was this bloke there just getting out of his van, he said the electric bill hadn't been paid, and he made me let him come in, and he cut off the electrics at the meter, so after that I only had cold food, but it were only for few days anyway, cos then these two Social Workers came and took me away. I think it were Mr. Chambers down the road what told them about me, I'm sure it were him that tipped them off about me, cos everyone else were OK with me being there on my own, all the neighbours and such, they were keeping an eye on me like, and making sure I was OK, but old Chambers, he were always a nosey parker, sticking his nose into other peoples' business."

Danny paused again, and was quiet for several minutes. "What happened to you then, Danny?" Alex asked. "Is that when you went to Grant Hall?"

"Oh, no, said Danny, "that were later. They sent me to live with this Mrs Bradley. She lived near the new school, so I was able to walk from there to school. She were really nice, at weekends she'd drive me up to the hospital in her car and sit in the cafe there and have a cup of tea and a cake, while I went up to the ward to see Mum. It were a nice house she lived in, like, her husband had died a few years ago, and her kids had grown up and left home and got places of their own, but they came round to see her sometimes while I was there. They was ever so nice, they'd bring sweets or some chocolate for me and Freddie. This Mrs. Bradley, see, she fostered kids for the council. That's how come Freddie was there."

Danny paused again. Alex didn't push him. He was pleased he'd been able to get Danny talking at last. Maybe being able to talk to someone about his background was doing the kid a bit of good. But after a while, Alex asked him, "Tell me about Freddie, then. Who was he?"

"Well, when I first arrived, Mrs Bradley sat down with me and we had a cup of tea and she told me about her place, and she said I could have my own bedroom if I wanted, but she'd got Freddie staying with her as well as me, he'd been with her about four or five weeks by then, he'd just turned nine years old, and he'd been badly dramatised cos he'd had a really bad experience." Danny paused.

"Don't you mean traumatised?" asked Alex, taking advantage of the gap in Danny's story.

"Well, yea," Danny said. "That's right, you should listen more, that's what I said, he were badly dramatised."

Alex smiled, but let it pass. "Go on, then," he said, "tell me more about Freddie."

"Well, it seems that he was at home with his Mum one Saturday afternoon, and then his Father had come home from the pub in a drunken rage and his wife hadn't got the tea ready for him or something like that, so he picked up a kitchen knife and stabbed her and killed her right in front of the kid. And since then Freddie had retreated into his shell and wouldn't speak or talk to anyone. I saw him sitting in the next room, that first day I was there, and he were just sat on the seat with his hands around his knees, he were just sitting there and rocking backwards and forwards on the edge of his seat, you could tell straight away that he weren't quite right in the head."

"I went in to say hello to him, and he just looked at me and didn't even speak or say hello or anything, he just sat there rocking backwards and forwards on his chair, all the time he was doing that, nothing else, not playing with his toys or anything. Like what I just said, Mrs Bradley told me that I could have my own room if I wanted, but she thought it might help Freddie having someone else in with him, so I said I'd share with Freddie, cos it were obvious he weren't right, and I thought Mrs. Bradley might be right, if I was sharing with him, then at least it might help him to come out of his shell a bit."

"So that's what I did. The very first night I got woke up in the middle of the night by this funny sound, I didn't know what it was at first, but then I realised it were Freddie, he were sitting up in bed and he weren't crying or anything but he were making this funny noise, like he was just snivelling a bit. It weren't very loud so I don't suppose Mrs Bradley had ever heard it, her bedroom was down the corridor a little bit and up a couple of stairs, and anyway the bedroom door was shut. So I got out and sat on his bed and give him a hug and a cuddle and stroked his head a little bit and whispered to him that he was OK now cos I was here for him, and after a while he stopped and I settled him down in his bed and he went off to sleep again."

"Well, that carried on for several nights, and then one night I woke up in the middle of the night and there was Freddie getting upset as usual, and after I'd calmed him down a bit, he wouldn't let go of me, so I picked him up and took him back to my bed and we got in my bed together so I could keep on cuddling him. And then, when he'd dropped off back to sleep, I got out of my bed where me and Freddie were, and I went and slept in Freddie's bed, cos it don't seem right for two kids to be in the same bed together all night, do it? And anyway, there weren't much room for both of us together in the same bed, cos they were only bunk beds and they were a bit narrow and not as wide as a normal bed, like what I was used to. And it were like that for ages, every night for ages."

"Anyway, Freddie, he still weren't speaking or anything, but the next thing I remember with him was when I was out in the garden doing some watering of the plants with the hose for Mrs Bradley. You see she'd got a vegetable patch up the back of the garden which I got to look after for her, and there hadn't been much rain lately so I was there with the hose, and Freddie, well, he was there just sitting watching me and rocking backwards and forwards like he always did."

"But then I got in a muddle with the hose and I tripped over it, cos it got all wound up round my legs, and I fell over on the grass and the hose was pouring water out all over me. Then I heard this funny noise, and I looked up and it were Freddie, he were sitting there laughing at me on the grass with all the hose wrapped around my legs and me getting wet through. It were really funny I suppose, but I just sat there and laughed as well, cos Freddie had actually laughed, he'd never done that before. I was really pleased about that and so was Mrs. Bradley, when I told her about it afterwards."

"So after that, I used to mess about when I knew he was around, and try to get him to laugh and after that first time he did that more and more. I'd sit down with him and just talk to him, and I kept asking him what his name was, but he never replied or said anything back. I tried for a few minutes every day, and then one day, it were a Saturday I remember it well, we was out in the garden, me and Freddie, and I asked him what his name was, and Freddie just said very quietly 'Freddie,' and when I heard that I knew that he'd turned the corner, and was gonna get better. I was so pleased with him, and so was Mrs Bradley, cos he'd had therapists and everyone to come round to see him and they'd never got anywhere with him at all."

"Anyway, by the time I'd been with Mrs. Bradley about three or four months, Freddie, well he was back to normal and he was talking like any other 9 year old, and I used to play with him, and we'd kick a ball about together, and he was, like, alright again, you wouldn't know there'd ever been anything wrong with him at all. And then eventually his adoption papers came through and he moved away, and when he went, he went out of the front door and then turned and gave me the biggest hug I've ever had, that was really nice. He were a lovely kid, he really was. I hope he's gonna get on alright with his new people, he deserve better than what he's had so far."

"Mrs Bradley, she was really pleased with what I'd done for Freddie. She baked me a special cake as a reward, it had cream and jam inside and icing on the top, it were lovely. I was able to eat it all to myself, cos Mrs Bradley, she was diabetic, you see, and weren't allowed to eat any stuff like that."

Danny went quiet again, pausing as if in reflection about little Freddie, the youngster who'd had such a bad time, and whom he'd helped to get better. "I hope he's OK now," he added wistfully. "I'd love to see him again, to see he's alright and getting on OK. See if he remembers me."

Alex thought about what he'd just heard. He thought about Danny helping Freddie to overcome his traumas, or dramas, as Danny had called them. But, thought Alex, perhaps dramas wasn't very far off the mark after all. It showed that Danny had a very thoughtful nature. It seemed as though he had a very thoughtful, caring, young boy sitting with him on the grass beside the canal in the afternoon sunshine.

After a while, Danny started talking again. "I were with Mrs Bradley about 7 months altogether. Then I was told that I'd gotta move on to somewhere else, cos Mrs Bradley, she was moving away, cos her sister's husband had died and she and her sister were going to move down to Brighton or Bournemouth or somewhere like that and share a house together. It were really nice living with Mrs. Bradley, she looked after me and Freddie really well. And like what I said just now, she used to take me to see my Mum in the hospital every week. She were nice like that. I think she'd helped loads of kids like me. It was a real shame she moved away. I wish I were still with her, I really do. Perhaps if she hadn't moved away, then I wouldn't have ended up at Grant Hall."

Danny paused again, thinking perhaps of what might have been. "So, that's when you went to Grant Hall?" Alex asked. "When you left Mrs. Bradley?"

"No," Danny said, "I got sent to Harding Court after that. It were a long way away from where we lived, and it were miles from the hospital as well. That were a strange place, it were. It were run, see, by this religious group, they were always stuffing religion down your throat. There was prayers every morning and evening, and prayers before and after every meal as well. They never stopped. That weren't the worst thing about Harding Court, though. You see, they had this very strict routine and there weren't no one allowed to do anything different. There was school for five days a week of course, and on Saturdays it was games out on the playing field down the road, football mostly and rugby sometimes, and on Sundays you had to go to church three times a day. It were awful, cos I don't do religion or anything, and they never let anyone do anything different from their normal routine, so I never got the chance to go and see my Mum, who was still in hospital all that while. They never ever let me go and see my Mum although I asked loads of times. She weren't getting any better and I never knew what exactly was wrong with her."

"Anyway after a few weeks there, I bunked off one Sunday instead of going to church, and I went to see my Mum in the hospital, I got there and back OK cos I borrowed a bike off one of the other kids, mine was still at home cos I hadn't been able to take it with me to Mrs. Bradley's. But when I got back, there were hell to pay cos I'd bunked off, and they were really cross, and they said that if I did it again then I'd have to leave and go and be looked after somewhere else. But I didn't believe them, I didn't think they'd throw me out, cos if they did, then they'd lose the opportunity to convert me if I weren't there, wouldn't they?"

"So the next Sunday I bunked off again to go to the hospital, and it was after that when they told the Social Workers that I was disobedient and didn't respect authority, and I'd got a bad attitude and behavioural problems, and so that's how they sent me to Grant Hall. If I'd known what it was gonna be like at Grant Hall I'd never have bunked off, having them at Harding Court stuffing religion down your throat all the time was loads better than what happened to me at Grant Hall."

Danny paused again, and Alex didn't press him to continue. He knew that the boy would carry on when he was ready and had collected his thoughts together. He just sat there beside him, and thought back to the previous day, to the short encounter he'd had back at the lock with the Warden from Grant Hall. Hammond, Danny had called him. He'd thought then that Hammond was a nasty piece of work, and what Danny told him next confirmed that view, many times over.

"When the social workers took us there, there was two of us took there that day from Harding Court, me and another kid, Jamie Roberts his name was, I thought it were gonna be such a nice place, cos there was a really blue sky and the sun was shining and the birds were singing, it really was a nice day. It was a couple of miles outside the town, you go through a small village and then turn off the road through this really posh gate by the church and then there's this long road, dead straight it is, through some sort of parkland. I remember there were sheep in there eating the grass, and then about half a mile down this road you turn off and you can see the big house, that's Grant Hall, right in front of you, but its surrounded by a big tall red brick wall about 8 feet high. So you go through another gate in this tall wall and there you are."

"It were only after Hammond and the others had signed all the papers and what have you, and the social workers had left, that I first got some idea of what things were gonna be like. As soon as they'd gone, the Wardens, they closed the big door and bolted it top and bottom, and two of them came along with their keys and they each locked the door, cos you see the door had two separate locks and each Warden had only one key, so there was always two Wardens needed to unlock the door. But us kids were never allowed to use the front door, it was only for visitors and people like that, we had to use the door round the back by the kitchen, and that had two locks as well, it were kept locked nearly all of the time."

"After the social workers had left and the big door had been locked and bolted, they showed me round, and I noticed that all the windows had bars on the inside, even the upstairs windows, you can't really see the bars from the outside cos they're in line with the little wooden bits between the small panes of glass in the windows, and when they took me up to the dormitory there was bars on all the windows there as well. There's some nice big windows in the dorm, but you could see they'd been fixed shut with these big screws, there weren't no chance of getting them undone, and anyway even if you could get through the bars, none of the kids fancied crawling around on the window sill. It were a really long way to fall down, and there weren't no drainpipe or anything to climb down, and it was too far to jump without getting hurt, the ground directly underneath the windows was concrete, not soft grass or flowerbeds or anything like that."

"I was in a dorm with about nine or ten other kids, they was all about my age, although the dorm had twelve beds in it altogether, there were some that weren't being used. There's kids at Grant Hall what are older and younger than me, but they try to keep all the kids what are much the same age all in the same dorm, but in our dorm I was the oldest. The dorms are upstairs, on the first floor, and there ain't no heating up there, so when it's cold outside it's really cold in there sometimes, and they only ever let you have one blanket on your bed. When it's hot outside its stifling in the dorm, cos like I said the windows have been screwed shut, and you can't open them to get any fresh air in."

"The floor above the dorms is the Wardens quarters, and they've got heating up there, but we're not ever allowed to go up there, but I did once when they wanted some furniture moved. You normally have to stay indoors all the time, except when they allow you to go out. Like I said, there's only one other door to get outside apart from the main door, and that's round the back near the kitchens and they kept that locked and bolted all the time as well."

"At night they closed the gates in the wall round the Hall, and Brutus, that's the Rottie, Hammond let him run loose in the grounds inside the wall, so if you ever managed to get out of the Hall, then the Rottie would get you and have your leg off for its supper. And there's automatic lights out there as well, if anything moves out there at night, then the lights come on. Brutus used to set them off sometimes. It were more like a prison than a children's home."

"The next surprise after I got there was at suppertime, cos there weren't much to eat at all, just some sort of meat stew on your plate, and a slice of bread and glass of water. Nothing else. It were always the same, they hardly ever served up anything different. And there weren't much stew anyway, cos I soon found out that it was like that on purpose, they deliberately kept you short of food, so that they could keep control of you, they reckoned that if you were hungry all the time then you'd behave better."

Alex thought back to the previous night, to the manner in which Danny had been eating the supper he'd made for him, and had later slipped off his tee shirt off to show him his wounds, and Alex had seen just how skinny the boy was. He was now starting to realise just why Danny was so thin. But Danny was talking again.

"They always keep you short of food. For breakfast there's porridge. Nothing else. The same every day. And you don't get much of that, anyway. They only have small bowls, so it seems more, but there ain't much there really. Lunchtimes all you got was a sandwich, just one slice, halved, with something inside, weekdays it were jam and on Saturdays it was cheese and on Sundays you got a real treat you got a bit of ham in your sandwich. But you always got an apple at lunchtime as well, so I suppose that filled you up a bit, although sometime they weren't really worth eating, cos quite often they'd got loads of bruises and were going brown inside."

"The real shock was after supper that first night. Cos that's when they dished out the punishments. They called some poor kid's name out and he had to come and stand out the front and they read out what he'd done wrong, and then he'd get whatever punishment they decided on. Hammond wrote it all down in this big red book he had. But the only punishment they ever did was either caning or the lash. Running in the corridors usually got two lashes. Talking at mealtimes was two lashes as well. Leaving food on your plate was two strokes of the cane, but there were fat chance of that there were so little to eat, the only reason anyone left anything was cos it wasn't worth eating, like when the apples were all bad inside, or the meat in the stew was all gristle and fat."

"Being cheeky or answering back to a Warden got four strokes. If you got caught talking in the dorm after lights out, that were two lashes for everyone in the dorm, not just the ones who were doing the talking. And Black One, he got everything. Whatever anyone done wrong, and got the cane or the lash, Black One got the same, even if he'd got nothing to do with what was wrong. So if three kids got two lashes each, then he'd get six lashes. It weren't fair. They reckoned that if the kids knew that someone who was innocent was getting punished as well as them, then they would behave better. But no one did anything wrong on purpose. I mean, Jimmy Watson was on kitchen duty the other day and he tripped and dropped some plates, and he got four lashes for that, cos there were four plates got broken. And then Black One got four as well. It weren't no fun being Black One, I can tell you. There was a Black Two sometimes as well, he got half of what Black One got."

Alex took advantage of a break in Danny's account of his time at Grant Hall to ask him a question. "Danny," he asked, "you told me last night that they'd made you Black One. Why was that? What did you do to deserve that?"

Danny was quiet for a moment. "Nothing, really," he said. "But you see, they want total control, absolute domination of all the kids what are there. They try to break you, break your spirit, make you subservient to them. Everyone tries to keep out of trouble, just like I did. But you see, I upset them. They didn't like that."

"How did you upset them, Danny?" Alex asked quietly.

"Well, everyone knew what was going on was wrong," Danny replied. "But whenever I could, I used to just stare at the Wardens. I didn't ever say anything, but whenever they were punishing one of the kids or telling them off or sorting them out, I'd just stand there and stare at them. Most of the other kids would just look at the floor, but I didn't. I just used to stare, stare at their faces, because I knew what they were doing wasn't right. They didn't like that, It un-nerved them, especially Hammond, he hated it. And whenever I got the cane or the lash, I never cried. Some of the other kids did, especially the younger ones. But I never did. They didn't like that either. Because I never cried, they tried harder and harder to make me cry. But I never did. So they made me Black One, so I got all the punishments what every other kid got, to try and break me. And when you're Black One, they put you on half rations, you only get half what the other kids get, and that ain't much anyway. So I never got much to eat at all. But I never gave in. I never cried or anything like that. And I kept on staring at them whenever I could. They hated me because of that."

Alex realised now how Danny had received all the weals and marks on his body. "But, Danny," he asked, "that doesn't explain all the bruises. How did you get them? And why? Did you get them at Grant Hall?"

"Yea," Danny replied, pausing again, then adding a little later, "that were the ball game."

"Oh, so you were allowed out to play games, then?" asked Alex. "Was it football? Or rugby, perhaps, how you got those bruises?"

Danny thought for a moment, chewing the end of a blade of grass as he did so. "No, Mister, we weren't allowed to play any games like that at all. We got to exercise three times week, though. That was on Tuesday, Thursday, and Saturday afternoons. They made sure the gates in the wall were closed and locked, then they made us run round the Hall in the grounds inside the wall. We had to do that all afternoon, without a break or anything. We were always tired out after that. The last one to finish each circuit round the Hall got put in the book for a stroke of the lash that night. That was supposed to make you run harder, but there was always someone who was going to be last, I mean, there had to be, didn't there?"

And when we were out running, well, Hammond, he was always there with Brutus. There weren't no chance of getting away, even supposing you could climb the wall, it were really high, and there weren't no trees near the wall or anything what you could use to climb up and jump over the wall. You could see where there used to be trees, but they'd been cut down, there were only the stumps left sticking out of the ground."

"But once, we rebelled a bit, cos it was really cold and raining, it were pissing down all afternoon, and we were only in our tee-shirts and shorts. Instead of running round the Hall, we all just got together and walked round instead, we were already soaked through anyway. The Wardens were furious, especially Hammond, he was beside himself with rage. Everyone got two strokes of the cane that night. Every one. It was lucky I weren't Black One then, or I'd have been flayed half to death. There weren't no Black One when we did that, cos the kid who was Black One had left the previous week. I think he'd turned sixteen and been turfed out, they only keep you there at Grant Hall till you're sixteen, after that they let you go and you've got to fend for yourself, but even that must be better than being there. It were me what were made Black One the following week. Hammond had sussed out that it were my idea that we should all walk round, instead of running. That's another reason I was made Black One, as well as the staring. Like I just said, they didn't like that."

"So, Danny, tell me about the ball game then," Alex asked.

"That weren't no fun either," said Danny. "You see, we'd go up to bed at night, and then it was lights out, and we'd try to get off to sleep. And then, a bit later on, we'd hear footsteps on the stairs and coming down the landing, and we'd all lay there, hoping that they'd go past our dorm to someone else's. Sometimes they did go past and sometimes they didn't. Sometimes the door to the dorm would open and one of the kids would get called out to go downstairs. Sometimes it were the ball game and sometimes it were something else. That were even worse."

"The ball game was what they did with you when the Wardens had been drinking and getting drunk. You see, there's this big fancy staircase down from the first floor, down into the main entrance hall, it's all white stone, its marble I think. Anyway, they'd make you take your jarmies off so you were naked, except you were allowed to wear a pair of briefs, and they'd tie your hands behind your back and then they'd put this cuff round one of your ankles. Then they got this big ball out, it were huge."

Danny held up his hands to give Alex some idea of how large it was. Alex reckoned it was about three feet across. But Danny went on, "It had three compartments inside, and they'd fill one of them with water so it was really unstable, and there was this rope attached to it, they tied the end of the rope to the cuff round your ankle. Then they stood you at the top of the stairs and pushed the ball over the edge so it started to roll down the stairs. It was always really unpredictable as to where it would go because the water wasn't in the centre of the ball or anything like that. It always went slowly at first, but then it gradually got faster and faster, all the way down the staircase, and it would eventually go right to the bottom, but as soon as the rope between your leg and the ball got tight, you had to try to stay upright, and go down the stairs with the ball. But in the end, the ball always got the better of you and pulled you over, and then you got dragged all the way down to the bottom of the stairs, feet first, you see the ball it were really heavy and you couldn't do anything about it, the ball always got the better of you in the end, and you got bounced about and bruised as the ball dragged you down."

"And the Wardens, they used to laugh when you fell over, and also, they used to have bets on how long you'd last before you got pulled over, how many steps you'd got down on your feet before you got dragged over, they bet huge amounts on it. Hammond was one of the worst, and when he lost a bet he got really cross. They used to get me to do the ball game a lot, cos I got to be quite good at it, at staying upright the longest. I could last almost half way down sometimes. But when the ball pulled you over, as it always did in the end, you got dragged all the way down the stairs to the bottom by the ball, and that really hurt, and that's how I got all those bruises. Sometimes Hammond got really furious when he'd lost a lot of money betting on me, he lost £50 one night I think. Once, he was so cross he got his cigarette and burnt me with it, he was so cross." Danny paused again, thinking no doubt about the horrors of the ball game.

"Danny, tell me, you said you boys used to get called out of the dormitory some nights for something else, as well as the ball game. Can you tell me what that was all about?" Alex asked. He had his suspicions, and his heart sank as they were confirmed by what Danny told him next.

"Well," Danny said. "Sometimes we'd be up in the dorm and we'd see these big posh fancy cars turn up outside, one of the Wardens used to go and open the gates and let them in, you see our dorm was at the front of the Hall, we could see them arriving, and if it was dark, then the automatic lights would come on, so we could still see what was happening. It was usually every Tuesday night, every week without fail, I suppose they told their wives they were at the Masons or something. No-one in the dorm looked forward to Tuesday nights, but it weren't just Tuesdays, sometimes it was some other nights as well. There was always men in them cars, posh men in really smart clothes and fancy suits.

And then a little later you'd hear the footsteps in the corridor and it might be the door to our dorm what would be opened by one of the Wardens, and one of the kids would get called out to go downstairs. Sometimes it were me, but it could be anyone, it just depended on who they fancied that night. They took you down into a room and left you alone with one of these men what had just arrived, he got you to take of your jarmies so you were naked, and then he did things to you, or got you to do things to him. They always wore these posh clothes and suits and stuff, but once they'd taken their clothes off they were all the same underneath, the same as anyone else. Dirty bastards. They used to hand over some money before they left, I saw one guy once giving Hammond a load of money, I reckon it was easily £100, it could have been more, though."

"One night, a kid from our dorm got called out, it were Micky Rhodes, he came back a bit later and he'd been hurt, cos his jarmie bottoms were red at the back, he were bleeding from his bum. After that, some of always made sure we stayed awake till whoever had got called out came back, so we could be sure he was alright. But one day, Jamie Roberts, he got called out and he never came back. It was awful."

"What do you mean, he never came back," asked Alex.

"Well," said Danny. "We waited and waited for Jamie to come back, but he never did. We waited for ages, but in the end, the two of us who were waiting, we just fell asleep, we were really tired cos it was a Tuesday, see, we'd been running round the Hall all afternoon. In the morning, his bed had been stripped, and his blanket and sheets and pillow had all been folded up and stacked at the end of the bed like the other beds what weren't being used, and all his stuff had gone out of his locker beside his bed. We never knew what happened to him, but Peter Bullen, the next morning he asked Hammond where Jamie was, and he got four strokes of the cane that night for being important and not minding his own business."

"You mean impertinent, don't you?" asked Alex, trying to suppress a sly grin, for he knew what the answer would be.

"Yea, that's right, he were being important," said Danny. "Like what I said, important." He turned to Alex. "You really should listen a little better, Mister."

Alex nodded. "Yes, OK then, Danny," he said, smiling to himself. "I will in future. Do you know who these men were?" he went on. "Who came to Grant Hall at night?"

"No," replied Danny. "No idea. But they must have been important people, cos they all had these huge cars, they looked very expensive, nothing normal like the Ford Fiesta my dad had, or anything like that."

"You can't remember their registration numbers or anything?" Alex asked.

"No," Danny replied. "I suppose we could have seen them, cos like I said, there's automatic lights what come on when anything moves outside at night, but we never thought of doing anything like that. Anyway, what would we have done with them? Told Hammond? I don't think so. Fat chance, you'd only get the cane again, or the lash, I mean he were in on it, weren't he?"

"OK, then, never mind," said Alex. "Tell me, was there anything else done to you boys there? Anything else going on?"

"Well," said Danny, after a pause. "There was rumours about something called the Dark Room. Nobody really knew what it was, and nobody had ever been there, but the rumour was that it was something really awful what Hammond had dreamt up, and he used it when he wanted to punish someone really severely. It was supposed to be the worst punishment of all. But like I said, no-one had ever had that done to them, not any of the kids, not all the while I was there anyway."

"OK," said Alex. "But, Danny, weren't there ever any inspections or anything? By the local authority, the council's childrens' department, or social services, or whatever?"

"Oh yes," replied Danny, "the inspectors, they came round every few months. But of course, Hammond knew in advance when they would be coming. For the whole of the day before, were we all put on cleaning duty, so the whole place was spick and span and really clean and tidy. And the evening before the inspection, Hammond would give us a lecture, saying that we weren't to speak to the inspectors without being spoken to first, and not to volunteer any information or anything, and not to mention anything about getting the cane or the lash, or anything like that, because if we did, then whoever it was would be caned every day for the whole of the following week. So of course no-one ever said anything, anything at all."

"On the day of the inspection, he'd make sure we all had a shower before breakfast, and there'd be haircuts the day before if anyone needed one. One of the Wardens did the hairs, you always had to sweep up your own hair off the floor afterwards and put it in the bin. And there was always clean clothes to wear that day, too. The inspectors, they didn't ever suspect anything. He always gave them a nice lunch, too, in the dining hall, not the stew we got served up every day, and they always seemed to go away happy. Hammond really pulled the wool over their eyes, he did."

Alex nodded. He could well understand the climate of fear which must have pervaded the life of the boys who had to live at Grant Hall. For about ten minutes, he and Danny sat quietly together side by side on the grass in the afternoon sunshine, not speaking, Danny reflecting on the treatment he'd received at Grant Hall, whilst Alex contrasted the un-paralleled brutality of Grant Hall with the kindness and support that he and his fellow teachers, and his wife Jennifer as Matron, had shown to all the boys in his care at his school where he'd taught and been a Housemaster for a good part of his life.

Eventually, Alex turned to the boy and asked him, "Danny, you said it was like a prison at Grant Hall. Tell me how you managed to get away. Was it when you were out of the Hall, at school?"

"No, we were never allowed out of the grounds of the Hall, except when we were on gardening duty down the kitchen garden," said Danny, "and even then they watched you like a hawk. Fat chance of going out to school. No, they had a couple of teachers who came in every day during term time. Actually they were quite nice, really. I don't think they had a clue about what was really going on. And in the evening, we had to sit in the schoolroom and do homework like any other school, and anyway that gave us something to do, cos there weren't no television or anything like that for us."

"I'd sussed out quite early on that there weren't no chance of getting away from that place undetected. It was too well guarded, and Hammond was always around with Brutus. I hadn't been there long before I realised that the only way out of Grant Hall would be to walk out of the front door, with the gate in the wall open in front of you. But eventually I was able to do just that, cos I got lucky. I got the toothache."

"It's not usually lucky to get toothache," said Alex. "Most people would consider it to be really unlucky."

"Well, no, it were lucky for me, anyway," Danny replied. "I'd bitten on a piece of bone or something, when we were having the stew at suppertime a couple of days before, and I'd broken a bit off one of my teeth. It really hurt. So I reported sick, and they just gave me a couple of aspirins and told me to go away, they always did that to shut you up whenever you report sick, and it was only when you'd been back several times that they ever called the doctor or anything. You never went out to go to the doctors, they always called someone in to see you."

"But it was really really bad, so I went back the next morning and they gave me some aspirins again. But it still hurt really bad so when I reported sick again the next morning, they realised that I weren't putting it on and they phoned the dentist, and got me an appointment for a couple of days later. They never took you out to the doctors they always called him to come in and see you, but with the dentist it's different cos he's got to have all his kit and stuff all handy to sort your teeth out."

"Anyway, the next morning, they were deciding who was going to take me to the dentist's, and one of the Wardens, Mr. Wilkins it was, he said that by chance he'd got an appointment at the same dentist that morning, so he'd take me in. Mr Wilkins was really nice, he didn't live in at the Hall like the other Wardens, he lived in the village and came in every day, he came in on his bike unless it was raining, then he'd come in his car, he'd got a little blue Ford Fiesta like my dad used to have. He's another one what didn't know what really went on there, he was only there during daytimes, nine to five or something like that."

"Anyway we got to the dentist, and I was lucky cos I got called in first. That really was lucky, because If Mr Wilkins had gone in first, then I wouldn't have tried to get away, cos my tooth was hurting so much, it really needed fixing. The dentist poked me around a bit, and then he gave me a couple of injections and built my tooth up and then he put a filling in somewhere else what he said needed doing, and then I came out and Mr Wilkins got called in.

When he went in, he asked some other guy who was sitting in the waiting room if he'd keep an eye on me, and this bloke said yes, OK. But as soon as Mr. Wilkins had gone in and the door was closed, I told this guy I needed to go to the toilet, they were in the lobby by the front door, you see. So he said OK, don't be long, and he just carried on reading his newspaper. So after I'd had a pee, I didn't go back to the waiting room, I just nipped off out of the front door and ran. I'm really sorry about Mr. Wilkins, cos he was really nice and he's probably going to lose his job for letting me go, but I didn't want to stay at Grant Hall any longer."

"So what did you do once you'd got away?" asked Alex.

"Well, I ran and ran and ran as fast as I could for as long as I could. I was used to running, I suppose all that running round the Hall helped me a lot. I ran for ages. But then, after that, there weren't no question really," said Danny. "I went straight to the hospital to see my Mum. But she weren't there, they said she'd been discharged ages ago. I didn't know what to do then, so I went round to our house where we lived, but of course I didn't have a key or anything, and so I rang the doorbell and expected to see mum there, but it was some other woman who answered the door. She said she and her husband were living there now, the previous people, that must have been Mum and me, she said they'd moved out months before, and then she went inside and shut the door on me.

I was devastated and didn't really know what to do, so I went down the road to see Mrs. Simkins, she was always friendly with Mum. Anyway, she said Mum had come home from the hospital months ago, and then her mother, that must have been my Gran, had arrived and looked after Mum for a couple of weeks and then they'd moved away. Mrs Simkins thought that Mum had moved away to go and live with gran, so gran could look after her until she was fully better."

"Do you know where your gran lives?" asked Alex.

"Well, no, not really," replied Danny. "I've been there once when I were a little kid, we went there for a holiday just after Dad left. It was up north somewhere. That's all I know. After I said goodbye to Mrs. Simkins, I just kept on the move, away from people, sleeping in barns and such, trying to keep out of the way of Hammond and the others, cos they're sure to have been out looking for me. And then I hid in the front of your boat, to keep out of the rain what was coming."

Alex sat on the grass beside Danny without saying anything, as they watched a couple of ducks noisily swimming along the canal, pecking occasionally at a patch of weed, searching for food, whilst on the other side of the cut a moorhen paddled quietly by, with three or four tiny chicks following obediently behind. Alex felt that there was absolutely nothing that he could say to Danny. The boy had been through a terrible time, but he seemed to be remarkably resilient about all that had happened to him.

Eventually, Alex looked at his watch, and realised that they'd been sitting on the grass beside the boat, talking, all afternoon. It was time to start thinking about some tea. He got up and stretched his arms above his head. "It's time to get some tea, Danny," he said. "How do you fancy chicken pie? And some chips? I've only got a small freezer on board, but I know there's a few chips left in it, enough for us both."

"Cor Mister, that sounds good, don't it," smiled Danny back at him, as he glanced round and looked at the boat, its newly polished paintwork shining in the afternoon sun. "Your boat looks good, don't it? Did well there, didn't we?"

"Yes, " Alex replied. "That's right, we did. We'll do the other side tomorrow, the weather forecast's good again, it should be warm and sunny all day tomorrow."

"How are we going to do that?" asked Danny. "There's all that water on the other side. Do we have to paddle round to do that side? In the water?"

"No," smiled Alex. "Nothing like that. Try again."

"Oh," said Danny, puzzled. "Lay on the top of the boat and reach over?"

"No, not that either. Try again." Alex smiled, as he realised Danny knew he was being teased.

"Turn the boat round?" Danny asked, impatient at not knowing the answer to the riddle Alex had posed.

"No, we can't do that," Alex told him. "Look, the boats longer than the width of the canal. It's not possible to turn the boat here."

"Oh," said Danny, as the expression on his face indicated that he was thinking furiously. "I've got it," he said suddenly, smiling. "We'll just move the boat to the other side of the canal and do it there."

"Well, you're getting warm, but we can't do that either," Alex told him. "You see, the other side of the canal is private land, we'd be trespassing if we moored up there. Usually, we can only moor up to the towpath side."

"Well, I dunno, then," said Danny. "I give up."

"Want a clue?" asked Alex, smiling broadly.

"OK, then, Mister," replied Danny, well intrigued now.

"Well, there's a turnover bridge a bit further up the canal, in the direction we're going, it's about a hour away from here."

"What's that?" asked Danny. "What's a turnover bridge? It ain't a bridge that turns over, is it? Or is a bridge what turns the boat over? How would that work?"

"No," laughed Alex, "let me explain. Further up the canal, the towpath runs on the other side of the water. A turnover bridge is a special design of bridge which, in the olden days when boats were pulled by horses, allowed the horse to easily cross from one side of the canal to the other, so it could stay on the towpath, and not get the towrope snagged on the bridge."

"Ok, then," said Danny, "but how do you know there's that turnover bridge there? Have you been along here before?"

"Well, no I haven't, " said Alex, "but that's easy. It's all in the Nicholson's."

"What's the Nicholson's?" asked Danny, a curious look on his face once again.

"It's a guide book to the canal," Alex told him. "Come on inside and I'll show you."

They went inside the boat, and Alex went to the glass-fronted display cabinet which graced one side of the saloon, and took out one of the Nicholson's guides that sat neatly lined up on the narrow bookshelf at the bottom of the cabinet. He'd bought a full set of the guides, six or seven in all, when he'd first set off in *Jennifer Jo*, and found them invaluable from day one. Alex opened the book at the appropriate page, and handed the book to Danny. "Here, have a look," Alex told him. "They use extracts from the official Ordnance Survey maps, and the canal is shown by this thick blue line. The orange line that you can see beside the blue line shows which side of the canal the towpath is. And, look, here's the turnover bridge which I told you about." Alex pointed the bridge out to Danny, who was eagerly looking at the book in his hand.

"Cor, Mister," exclaimed Danny. "What are all those numbers along the blue line? Look, there's one here – and another one here." He pointed at the map on the open page.

"They're bridge numbers," replied Alex. "See, this symbol here, that marks a bridge. There's one here, and another one a bit further up, here. And every bridge has a number. There should be metal plates on every bridge, one on each side, with that number on it. That's how the boatmen of old could tell whereabouts they were on the canal, and they're still very useful today. But you'll find that some of the number plates have fallen off the bridges, or been stolen. You can also tell if a bridge has been removed, as they don't renumber the ones that are left, so there's a gap in the numbers as you go along the canal."

"So where are we now?" asked Danny.

"We're roughly here," said Alex, pointing out the spot on the map where the boat was. "And look, do you see this black arrow here?"

"Yea, what's that, then ? said Danny, peering closely at the book in Alex's hand.

"That marks where there's a lock," Alex told him. "Each lock has a number, too. Look, this here is the lock I was at yesterday afternoon. It's lock number 12."

"That's really interesting," said Danny. "I never knew anything at all about canals, you know."

"Yes," Alex replied, "it's a very handy little book. You can sit and have a look through it if you like, while I get the tea."

"OK, thanks," said Danny, as he took the book and sat down at the dinette, leafing through it, engrossed, as Alex cooked the chicken pie and chips.

"Not bad, Mister," said Danny, as they finished their meal. "Much better that we got at Grant Hall. Like I said yesterday, you ain't a bad cook. Would you like me to clear up for you?"

"Right-oh, thanks, Danny," Alex replied, "that's very good of you, but if you'd like an apple first for dessert, just help yourself to one, there's plenty there in the bowl. I'll write up my diary while you clear up, and then, perhaps we'll watch some television – if we can get a signal, that is. We can't always get a good enough signal here on the boat, because we don't have a very good aerial, and the canal is pretty low down in the countryside, like most canals are. The canal builders quite often kept to the lower parts of river valleys when they chose their routes – it made for less digging of cuttings and so on. Anyway, what sort of programmes do you like to watch on TV?"

"Any sort of TV would be great," said Danny. We never got to watch TV or anything at Grant Hall, nor at Harding Court. The last time I saw any television was at Mrs. Bradleys, it was really nice there. So, anything really, I don't mind."

"Well, there's a film on tonight, it's a comedy," said Alex. "Do you fancy that?"

"Yea, sure, that'll be fine," Danny replied, grinning in expectation. "I'll clear up now." The boy busied himself in the galley whilst Alex sat and wrote up his diary, and then lit the fire to ward off the evening chill.

They sat and watched the film, and then, after a little channel-hopping, found a repeat of Blackadder, during which Alex was pleased to see Danny laughing uproariously at the funny bits. The boy had had a bad time, and it was nice to see him relax a little. When that was over, Danny stood up, turned to Alex, and said "I'll go to bed now if you don't mind, please, Mister. I'm really tired again now."

"That's OK," Alex replied. "But let me dress your wounds again first."

"Yea thanks, Mister," said Danny, as he pulled off his tee shirt over his head, and Alex attended to Danny's injuries, which seemed to be much the same as they were the day before, but at least, Alex thought, 'they're certainly no worse.' He knew that it would take several days before the first signs of healing would appear.

"There you are, all done," he told Danny as he put the Dettol away, and dropped the cotton wool into the pedal bin in the galley. "All finished. Off you go, now."

"OK, Mister," Danny replied. "G'night."

"Good night, Danny," Alex responded, as the boy disappeared towards his bunk at the rear of the boat.

Alex slipped outside to check the mooring ropes and then turned in himself, but it was a long while before he could get to sleep. He kept thinking about Danny, thinking about what the young boy had been through at Grant Hall. In addition to all the physical abuse, he was being half-starved into the bargain. It was unbelievable that in this day and age such cruelty and brutality could go on, and he felt sure that there must be collusion in high places which allowed it to continue. And the men who came to the Hall at night to abuse the boys there – did they have something to do with it, with suppressing the truth about what was going on? There were so many questions, and as he at last drifted off to a fitful sleep, Alex realised that, to all of those questions, he as yet had none of the answers.

CHAPTER 3

Alex woke at his normal time the next morning, and quickly got dressed and made himself a coffee. Going through the back cabin towards the back of the boat, he saw Danny still fast asleep, curled up in his bunk, his innocent face belying the horrors he'd lived through for the past few months.

As he stepped out onto the rear deck, Alex paused and looked around him. A pair of swans swam slowly past, shepherding their five young cygnets, not more than a few days old, their grey and dull white feathers still downy and fluffy from their recent emergence from their eggs. Alex marvelled at how, in a few months time, these ugly and ungainly young birds would be as beautiful and graceful as were their parents. A clutch of sparrows chirruped noisily in the bushes by the towpath, and on the other side of the water a couple of moorhens busily foraged for their first food of the day amongst the reeds growing there. The sky was blue with hardly a cloud in sight, the birds were singing, and, although the temperature was a little chilly this early in the morning, it was due to climb shortly, as the weather forecast was for another fine day. It was mornings like this that made Alex grateful that he had chosen this way of life to spend his next few years living aboard his boat, travelling the length and breadth of England on the cut, and it was an ever-present source of regret that his Jenny was not there to enjoy it with him.

After casting off the mooring ropes, Alex started the engine, carefully edged the boat away from the bank, and set off along the canal, a procedure he'd carried out many times before. Within a couple of minutes he'd passed a swan's nest on the offside of the canal, newly vacated and surrounded on three sides by high reeds, presumably the nest of the pair he'd seen a few minutes earlier with their young offspring. A good place to have a nest, Alex thought, well hidden away and easy to defend the eggs, and later the young chicks, from predators, of which there were always many along the watercourse.

The boat had only been going for about ten minutes when he heard a faint yelp from inside the boat, followed a few moments later by Danny's head appearing in the hatch from the back cabin, his hair wet, and wearing nothing but a scowl on his face and a towel wrapped around his waist.

"Hey, Mister," he called out. "There's something wrong with your boat!"

"What's that?" asked Alex, having difficulty hiding a smile.

"Well, I just went to have a shower," Danny complained, "and the water's cold. Even Grant Hall had hot water for the showers in the mornings."

"No, Danny," Alex laughed. "There's nothing wrong with the boat, nothing at all. The water's cooled down during the night, and we need to run the engine for a while to get it hot again. I could fire up the gas boiler to heat the water, but it saves on fuel if the waste heat from the engine is used instead. I usually move along for an hour or so in the mornings to get the water hot, before I get myself some breakfast. Get yourself dried off and dressed, grab a cup of coffee if you'd like one, and then come up on the back here, you can have a look at the canal as we go along. There's always something to see."

A few minutes later, Danny re-appeared on the deck and they motored along the canal, the engine running smoothly, pointing out things to each other as they cruised along. It was about an hour later when they rounded a slight bend in the canal and saw a bridge ahead, the last of several that they'd passed under that morning.

"Look, Danny," Alex said, "here's the turnover bridge I was telling you about yesterday. See the special ramps off the towpath on the far side, for the horses to easily get up onto the bridge and go across? The horses would come along the towpath and go under the bridge first, and then turn and cross the canal via the bridge before continuing on their way. That way, the towing rope never got caught up with the bridge."

"Yea, I see now," said Danny admiringly. "Clever, when they built all this, weren't they?"

"Yes," Alex replied, smiling at the boy, who was obviously fascinated in the infrastructure to be found along the canals. "And remember, they didn't have JCB's or mechanical diggers or anything to help them, like we would use nowadays if we were to build the same sort of thing. All this was built by men with picks and shovels, who dug out the canals by hand. That's the origin of the term 'navvy', short for 'navigators', as that's what the workmen were called. And the spoil from the diggings was taken away by horse and cart, and all the bricks and materials needed to build the bridges and locks and so on were brought in the same way. That's why many locks were located adjacent to where bridges were built to carry a road over the canal, so there was a road which they could use to bring the materials in."

"Yes," said Danny, "like what I said, they were really clever."

"Hey, look, Danny," Alex said, raising his hand and pointing to a spot about a hundred yards ahead. "There's a good spot to stop. We'll moor up here and have some breakfast, then we'll clean and polish the other side of the boat. How do you fancy bacon sarnies for breakfast this morning? Would that OK?"

"Yea, sounds great," said Danny, smiling broadly at the thought of another good breakfast, adding "I've had enough porridge to last me for ages." Alex skilfully brought the boat into the side of the cut, and then picked up the loose end of the centre rope secured amidships to the top of the cabin and stepped ashore, gently pulling on the rope to ease the boat the final foot or so towards the bank against the slight breeze which was starting to get up in the morning sunshine, and then mooring up the boat with both fore and aft ropes.

Alex quickly made the sandwiches and a couple of mugs of steaming tea, and brought their breakfasts up to the rear deck where Danny was patiently waiting, perched on the back rail which ran around the rear deck, enjoying the early morning sunshine. Alex sat down on the rail beside Danny. "Here you are, Danny," he said. "Bacon sarnies, nice and crisp inside. There's three, a couple for you, one's sufficient for me."

"Are you sure?" asked Danny. "That ain't really fair, is it?"

"No, it's OK, Danny," Alex replied. "One's sufficient for me, but you're a growing lad, aren't you? You need some good food inside you."

Danny grinned. "Yea, well, OK then, Mister," and reached out for a sandwich from the plate which Alex had set down on top of the gas locker. But as he picked up a sandwich, Alex called out "hang on a minute."

Danny looked at him curiously. "What's up?" he asked.

"Well," said Alex, "can you pick up two at once, please? Just for a moment. One in each hand."

"OK," Danny replied, as he took the other sandwich in his left hand. Alex quickly slipped out his camera and snapped Danny, sitting on the back rail with his sandwiches, the sunlight glinting in his tousled hair, a wide, cheeky grin on his face.

"There you are," said Alex. "I'll caption that 'Danny with a properly balanced meal – a bacon sandwich in each hand.'"

"Yea," Danny laughed. "They're really nice," as he started eating.

"It was the guy who invented the clockwork radio who came up with that phrase about two bacon sarnies, one in each hand, being a balanced meal," said Alex, "and it's always amused me. Trevor Bayliss, his name is. I've got his autobiography down below in the bookshelf, if you'd like to read it sometime. It's quite a good read."

"OK then, thanks, Mister," Danny replied. "Perhaps I will later on.

But I really like looking at the Nicolson's, it's really interesting. Like a road atlas for the waterway."

"Yes," said Alex, "that's exactly right. In fact, some people call the canal 'The Water Road'."

They enjoyed their breakfast and sat together in the sun for a while, and then set to work cleaning the side of the boat which was against the towpath, the opposite side to the one which they had worked on the previous morning. As before, they did not speak or chat as they worked, but kept busy, with Alex washing off the accumulated grime of the last couple of weeks, and Danny following on behind with the polishing. Once again it took them all morning, and then they sat down for a well-earned rest on a bench beside the towpath, a metal plate on it proclaiming it had been provided by the local council 'for the enjoyment of all who pass this way.'

They sat on the bench and had their lunch, a bowl of salad with some chunks of cheese, and followed up by an apple each, watching all the while the wildlife of the canal going about its business along the cut. They spent some time chatting to dog walkers as they exercised their pets, and occasionally waved a cheerful greeting to the crew of a passing boat as it went on its way, a tradition which was well established amongst boaters, and which Alex knew everyone, himself included, really appreciated. It was the ultimate insult not to wave at the crew of another boat. But Alex noticed that Danny always seemed a little nervous whenever anyone was approaching. Perhaps, Alex thought, he was wary in case it might be someone who might recognise him as a fugitive from Grant Hall.

As they at last cleared up their lunch, Alex turned to Danny and asked him, "Danny, will you do something for me please?"

"Yea, what's that Mister?" replied Danny, looking at Alex with a slightly puzzled expression on his face.

"I'd like you to sit inside this afternoon, and write something for me, please Danny," Alex asked.

"Why, can't you write yourself?" Danny riposted, with that cheeky grin which Alex was beginning to see on occasions.

"Well, yes, of course I can write," replied Alex, "I wouldn't have got that teaching job, now, if I hadn't, would I?"

Danny grinned. "Yea, Mister, I suppose you're right," he said. "What do you want me to write?"

"Well, Danny," Alex replied, "I would like you write an account of your life, everything that's happened to you since your mother went into hospital, but especially about your time at Grant Hall."

"Yea, but why do you need me to do that?" asked Danny, still curious.

"Well, Danny." Alex looked carefully at Danny as he answered the boy's question. "It will be evidence. Remember, I took some photos of your injuries the other night, in case they're needed for evidence at some time in the future. Just as your injuries will heal up and fade away in a few weeks time, your memories of those times at Grant Hall will fade away also. Writing it down now will preserve on paper your memories of what you've been through, so that one day, when the time is right, the people who have abused you so much can be brought to justice and punished for what they have done."

"And also, and this is very important, be sure to include your own feelings about how you have been treated. Remember, you may not be at Grant Hall any more, but other boys, some of whom you know well, are still there. You owe it to them, and to others who've not yet been sent to Grant Hall, to try to put a stop to it when the time is right, and let these kids have the sort of childhood they are entitled to, and which they're not getting. There are other people around, like your Mrs. Bradley, who will treat them properly, care for them, and give them a secure home free from abuse. And that's where they should be, not at Grant Hall."

"OK, then," said Danny, albeit a trifle reluctantly, "if you put it like that, then I'll do it."

"That's fine, Danny. Thank you," replied Alex. "Put it all down, just like you told it to me yesterday. But remember, I can't help you at all. It has to all your own work. You do understand why, don't you?"

Danny nodded, and Alex sat him down at the dinette, taking a pad of A4 lined paper out of the drawer below the display unit in the saloon, and handing it to Danny, together with a pen. For some considerable time Danny sat there, writing away, occasionally chewing the end of his pen as he thought of what to write.

Meanwhile, Alex busied himself about the boat, sweeping out the cratch where Danny had hidden a couple of days before, brushing the carpets, and generally making the inside of the boat clean, neat and tidy. Eventually Danny called out "I've finished," and handed Alex the results of his labours, nine sheets of neatly handwritten text.

"Is it OK?" he asked.

"Thanks, Danny," Alex replied, as he quickly scanned the last page, and then handed it back to Danny. "But can you sign it, please, and put the date on it as well."

Danny carefully signed his name at the bottom, together with the date, then Alex took the pen and countersigned as a witness. "That's fine," he thanked the boy again. "I'll read it through later, if you don't mind?"

"Yea, OK, Mister, anything you like," Danny nodded as he flexed his fingers. "My hand aches a bit after all that writing." Alex smiled. It seemed the lad had done well.

After tea, Alex tried to get a TV signal, but, even though they'd moved only a few miles along the cut, there was only snow on the screen. "Hey Danny," he asked, "what do you fancy for tonight? Reading a book? I've got plenty, all sorts. Or, there's some games in the cupboard, if you like."

"Well, I really like looking at the Nicholson's canal book," Danny replied, "but I'll have a look at the games, see if there's anything I like." After a few moments, Danny's head emerged from the cupboard under the television with a chess set. "You've got a set of chessmen," he said. "Shall we play this?"

"You can play chess?" Alex asked.

"Yes, Mister," the boy replied. "My dad taught me the moves some time ago. Apparently he used to play a lot once upon a time, before I was born, I think. And when I was at Mrs. Bradley's, me and her, we played together sometimes."

"Alright then, Danny," Alex agreed. "I haven't played for a while, but at my school I used to play in the chess league there. It ran for the whole of the school year, and although It was mainly for the boys, some of the masters took part as well. It will be nice to play again. There's a board in the back of the cupboard. Set them up, and we'll start."

Danny quickly placed the pieces on the board and the game got under way. Alex expected that he would have an easy victory over the young twelve-year-old, but Danny had drawn white, which gave him a very slender advantage. After the first few moves had been played, Alex realised that Danny represented a worthwhile opponent, as the boy quickly built up a strong position in the centre of the board, whilst Alex countered with a solid defence on the left side. As they played, Alex observed Danny's playing style. The boy studied the board intently, always silent, thinking out his moves carefully, never hesitating once he'd picked up a piece, and once or twice taking four or five minutes before making his move.

As the game progressed, Alex realised that he'd left his right flank somewhat exposed, a weakness which Danny quickly spotted, and exploited to the full. They'd been playing for about an hour and a half when Danny made his final move, lifting his head and speaking for the first time as he did so. "I think that's checkmate, Mister?" he grinned.

"Yes, it is, Danny," Alex said remorsefully. "That was a good game. Well done. I certainly didn't expect you to play so well at your age. I was no mean player myself in the school chess league, I usually managed to come about one-third of the way down from the top of the list. It was a fine win for you, you well deserved it. But tell me, where did you learn to play like that?"

"Well, like I said, it was my dad who first showed me how to play," Danny responded. "But it was Mrs. Bradley, she taught me most of all. You see, after Freddie left, it was just me living there with her, and one night, when there was nothing worth watching on the television, she said let's play a game, and so we did. We had a couple of games, and both of them, she just wiped me off the board in five minutes flat. After the second game, she said 'now, would you like me to teach you how to REALLY play chess?' So I said OK, and she taught me ever so much, like all the standard openings and the proper responses, and loads of stuff like that. You see, she told me that when she was younger, she used to play in competitions and tournaments and she played for her County teams as well. She'd got loads of certificates and medals, and some trophies as well, she showed them to me once. I really liked it at Mrs. Bradley's. She was ever so nice. I wish she'd never moved away, because then I'd never had been sent to Grant Hall."

"Anyway, Mister," he continued. "Do you mind if I go to bed now, please? I'm really tired again. G'night, Mister."

"OK, Danny," Alex replied, still smarting a little from his defeat, "but before you disappear, let's deal with your wounds first. OK?"

Right-oh, Mister," Danny said, as he lifted his tee shirt off and slipped it over his head. As Alex applied the antiseptic cream and Dettol to the wounds, he was pleased to note that small areas of new pink skin were starting to appear around the periphery of the wounds, indicating that the healing process was well under way, on the boys bottom as well as his torso. "They're coming on well, Danny," he told the lad, "I've finished, you can go now."

"Thanks, Mister," Danny replied, G'night then. By the way, where does the Nicholson's belong? I've finished looking at it for the moment. It's really interesting, like I said. But I'll put it away now."

"It belongs on the shelf in the display cabinet, second one in from the left, with all the others, I've got a complete set for all the waterways," Alex replied, as Danny turned and opened the cabinet and placed the book in the right spot on the shelf. But then he called out "hey, what's this?" as he picked up something from inside the cabinet.

"It's a Rubik's cube," Alex told the lad. "Have you never seen one before?"

"No," Danny replied, "but I've heard about them. What do you have to do with it?"

"Oh, that's simple," said Alex, "or at least, simpler said than done. What you have to do is just unscramble it. The sides can be rotated to manipulate the segments, so that each side has all its segments showing all the same colour. That's how it started off when it was given to me, a boy in my House at school gave it to me as a present when I retired. I've spent countless hours trying to solve it, but I've never been able to unscramble it. In the end I just gave up."

"May I have a go with it, please?" Danny asked eagerly.

"Yes, of course you can," Alex told him. "Try it. But I bet you don't have any better luck than I do."

"OK, then," said Danny, "I'll give it a try, anyway. G'night, then."

As Alex tidied up, he thought ruefully about the chess game they'd just played. He certainly hadn't expected the boy to beat him as convincingly as he had, but he realised that he ought to have been forewarned when Danny had said 'you've got a set of chessmen' using the correct terminology, rather than just 'a chess set'. Thinking back to the chess league he'd taken part in at his school, he realised that he shouldn't really have been surprised. There, those at the top of the league had not necessarily been the older boys, nor even the most academically gifted, although those who were good at maths seemed to do better than most. Indeed, it seemed to depend more upon having an analytical mind, and the ability to think ahead. One thing, however, was certain. There was a lot more to this scared, frightened young boy than first met the eye.

As he did every night, Alex slipped outside to check the mooring ropes, but on returning to the saloon, he sat down to read the account of his experiences which Danny had written that afternoon. Alex was pleased to see that it was a very good factual account, covering everything the lad had told him the previous day. Even after just the few days which Danny had spent with him, Alex was beginning to realise It was obvious that Danny was an intelligent and resourceful boy – his neat handwriting, his tidiness, his general polite manner, his good sense of humour, even his ability at chess, they all pointed to the fact that Danny had had a good upbringing, cared for by loving parents. Even though his father had left the family home some years earlier and he'd been through a foster home, followed by a couple of children's homes, the experiences didn't seem to have dampened Danny's appetite for life. After he'd finished reading, Alex sat for a while, somewhat troubled, deep in thought, wondering what on earth he should do about Danny. He was in a real dilemma. But eventually he realised that there were only three options available to him.

He could call the police, and hand Danny over to the authorities. A single phone call would suffice, asking for someone to meet him at a pre-arranged location, where the lad could easily be apprehended. But Alex had promised Danny that there was no secret agenda, and there was no way that Alex was prepared to go back on his word. And that would also mean that Danny would be returned to Grant Hall, and having to endure again the brutality and abuse which this guy Hammond seemed to rejoice in presiding over. And the punishment that would be dished out at Grant Hall to a returned absconder did not bear thinking about. There was no way that Alex was prepared to envisage that, so he turned to consider his next option.

He could just ask the boy to leave the boat. Even after just a couple of days, he'd already learnt that Danny was a resourceful child, and in the summer months that were almost upon them, Danny would probably survive. But eventually, he would of necessity descend into a life of stealing and theft to obtain food. And as the summer drew into Autumn and then into Winter, life would become very harsh, assuming that he managed to stay on the run for so long. He might even be ensnared by a pimp, and forced into male prostitution - a young lad of Danny's age would be an attraction to certain depraved people. And anyway, even if he managed to avoid something like that, and keep on the run, then where would he go to? It seemed that the lad's mother had gone to live with Danny's Gran, and Danny didn't even know where she lived, he had no idea at all. So he would almost certainly, of necessity, become some sort of vagabond and minor criminal, and eventually be picked up by the police for theft or worse, and end up in jail. He knew Danny deserved better than that, and Alex quickly determined that he could not bring himself to turf Danny out to fend for himself.

Alex thought about the third, the remaining, option for some time. He could simply allow Danny to stay aboard the boat with him. He was a likeable lad, and Alex felt sure that the boy would jump at the chance of having somewhere to stay, with food and shelter available. But there were risks attached to this third option, considerable risks. Whilst the first and second options represented risks for Danny, this third option was full of risks for Alex himself.

The boy was just twelve years old, he'd told Alex that he'd celebrated his twelfth birthday just a few weeks before, if celebrated was the right word for a birthday that seemed to have passed almost unnoticed. Should Alex be found by the authorities to be harbouring Danny aboard his boat, regardless of the fact that Danny was free to go at any time, then Alex would have the book thrown at him. He thought for a moment of the possible charges that he might face. Abduction of a minor. False imprisonment. Kidnap. They'd probably try and nail him for child abuse as well, but in fact it was Hammond and the people at Grant Hall who should be facing that sort of charges. Alex vowed that some day, he would do everything he could to bright the perpetrators of that abuse to face the justice they surely deserved.

At last, after a great deal of thought, Alex decided, very reluctantly, that he would talk to Danny in the morning, and tell him that, while there was no compulsion, and he was free to go at any time, he could if he wished stay on the boat with him, for as long as he wanted to. He was sure that Danny would jump at the offer. Alex realised that it would be very strange for him to have someone else living in the boat with him. He and Jenny had decided to spend their retirement together on their narrowboat, but that had turned out not to be. And, in the time since he'd started living aboard on his own, he'd become used to his own company, with the other boaters whom he'd met along the cut providing his social life. And now he was offering to share his home with a young lad, but only because the boy had nowhere else to go, and the only other alternatives were so unpalatable.

Alex went to the dinette and lifted up the seat on one side to gain access to the locker below. He took out his laptop computer and scanner/printer unit, and plugged them all together, finally plugging in his USB modem. Once he'd got his internet connection up and running through the modem, which worked over the mobile phone network, he downloaded his emails and quickly scanned through them. 'Ugh,' he thought, 'my waterways licence is nearly due.' But then, he moved on to surf the net in search of some information about Grant Hall.

The first link he found sent him to Grant Hall's official website. It was not, as he'd supposed, run by the local authority, but instead it was a privately operated children's home, owned and run by a company which contracted its services to various local authorities. The company's Chairman, Managing Director, and General Manager was named as Augustus Hammond. Alex was intrigued to read that Grant Hall claimed to 'specialise in caring specifically for boys who have exhibited behavioural problems, providing a firm environment to enable disturbed youngsters to modify their underlying behaviour to be more in line with accepted norms.'

'Well, what does that mean,' Alex wondered. 'Is that just an effort to excuse the absolute brutality which seems to be going on there?'

But as Alex looked through the website, he gradually became aware of something strange, but at first he could not recognise what it was. Eventually the realisation came to him - there was a complete absence of children in the photographs which were displayed. The parkland, the grounds around the Hall, the main entrance, the dining room, the school rooms, the dormitories, the bathrooms and showers, none of the pictures had any boys in the pictures at all. Alex lingered for a while at the picture of the main entrance hall with its grand, ornate, marble staircase ascending to the upper floors. 'So that,' he thought to himself, 'is where the so-called ball game takes place, where Danny and the other kids get to be dragged semi-naked down the stairs, with their hands tied behind their backs, by a large ball filled with water.' The marble looked really hard. No wonder the kid was covered in bruises.

Alex quickly flicked over to the webpage of his old school, and in nearly all the pictures displayed, there were pictures of happy, smiling youngsters, playing, working at their lessons, playing on the sports fields, playing musical instruments. 'What a difference,' he thought to himself. 'Grant Hall has to be hiding something, and I know what that is.'

He went back to the search page for Grant Hall, and clicked on another link that was displayed there. It was a link to a feature on Grant Hall which had been published by the local newspaper from the town near Grant Hall some nine months before. Alex read it through, and as he worked through it, he became more and more uneasy at what he read. But, just like the Grant Hall website a few minutes before, he at first couldn't place exactly what it was that disturbed him.

Entitled 'What's wrong at Grant Hall', it described how, over the last 5 years, there had been no less than three enquiries into allegations of strange goings-on there. The first investigation had been shelved for lack of evidence. The second had been discontinued after a short while as 'not being in the public interest'. And the third, once again, had been closed for lack of evidence.

Alex read the article through again, slowly and carefully, and then realised what was troubling him. At first glance, each sentence was very straightforward and factual. But, reading between the lines, there was the veiled suggestion of a cover-up. A cover-up orchestrated in high places, by someone with something to hide. Nothing that any person could ever take the newspaper to court for, but the suggestion was there, well hidden, but there all the same. It was a very clever piece of journalism, and Alex looked at the top of the article for the writer's name. Robert Jefferies was the by-line. In his mind, he congratulated Mr. Jefferies for a first-class piece of work. Alex saved the article onto his hard disk as he felt it was worthwhile keeping it for future reference, if he ever was able to follow up his concerns about Grant Hall, and he also printed off a copy.

Alex opened up his scanner, and scanned in Danny's account of Grant Hall which he'd written that afternoon, and then downloaded from his camera the photos he'd taken of the boy's injuries that first night. He printed off a copy of each of the photos, pinned them to Danny's handwritten notes, and together with the printout of the newspaper article, sealed them all into a large A4 envelope he found at the bottom of his stationery drawer, before dismantling his computer equipment, and returning it away to the locker beneath the dinette. The last thing Alex did, before going to bed, was to place the envelope he'd just sealed beneath the mattress in his bedroom. It could stay there, undisturbed, until it was needed. For Alex was certain that one day, the time would come for it to see the light of day once again.

CHAPTER 4

The next morning, as they finished their breakfast together, Alex sat and looked at Danny, sitting opposite him at the dinette. He cradled his mug of tea in his hand and thought again about what he'd decided the previous night. He'd invite Danny to spend some time with him on *Jennifer Jo*, and now seemed to be as good a time as any to broach the subject. "Danny," he said, "I need to talk to you. There's things we need to discuss."

Danny looked up, apprehensive. "Why, what's up, Mister?" he asked.

"I've been thinking about you, Danny," Alex told him. "First, do please remember what I told you the other day, that there is no secret agenda. You have to trust me. I will always be straight with you. Do you understand what I'm saying to you?"

"Yea, right, I understand, that's what you said before," said Danny, his manner still nervous about what he was about to hear.

"That's fine, Danny," Alex replied. "Next, I want you to know that I'm not going to hand you over to the authorities. Instead, I'm prepared to let you stay with me on the boat, on *Jennifer Jo*, for as long as you want to." Alex paused, then asked "How do you feel about that?"

"Well I dunno, really," said Danny. "I were thinking about being on my way tomorrow, moving on."

Alex was really surprised at what Danny had said. "On your way?" he asked. "Still on the run? Fending for yourself out in the open? How long do you think you'll last out there on your own? Having to steal to eat, no warm clothes for when it gets cold or it's raining? It won't be any fun for you, and you'll eventually get caught and they'll return you to Grant Hall, or throw you in jail for stealing."

"No, they won't," said Danny, looking defiantly at Alex. "That's cos I don't do pinching. It ain't right, I know that. I'll be OK, I'll manage. I know I will."

"No, Danny, you won't," said Alex gently, "you've been lucky out there on your own these last few days, but as time goes on it will get more and more tough for you. Especially when you get hungry, really hungry, and there's nothing for you to eat. Or when it's really cold. That tee shirt won't keep you very warm, now, will it? And anyway, where would you go to?" Alex asked him.

"Up north," replied Danny, "that's where my gran lives, and my

Mum's with her, that's what Mrs. Simkins said. I'm going to go and find her and look after her, help her to get better."

"But Danny," Alex said, "you don't even know where your gran lives, do you? Up north is a big place, you know."

"No, I dunno where she lives. But I'll find her, I know I will," Danny replied confidently. "I just know I will. Anyway, if I stay here with you, where are you going to go to in this thing, anyway?"

Alex grimaced slightly, trying hard not to let Danny see the expression on his face. *Jennifer Jo* was his pride and joy, he'd spent well into six figures having the boat built to his exact specifications. And now, here was Danny, with either the innocence of youth or simply the straightforwardness of a child, simply dismissing it as 'this thing'. But Alex ignored it, and carried on talking to the boy sat in front of him.

"I can go anywhere I want," he replied. "I'm what's known as a water gypsy, travelling as and when I want to, going to wherever takes my fancy. Provided, of course, that the canal goes there. Otherwise I have to walk, or take a bus, or hire a car."

"Can you go up north?" asked Danny, a quizzically expression on his face.

"Yes, of course I can," Alex replied. "England has over two thousand miles of canals altogether, and quite a few of them are in the north of England. From here, we can choose from several ways to get there."

"Would you take me up north, then?" asked Danny earnestly. "On the boat, on the canal?"

"Yes, of course I will, if that's what you want," replied Alex. "But don't forget, we don't travel very quickly. It will take a little while to get there. But I'll take you there if you like. I don't mind at all. It's up to you, really."

Alex sat there quietly and looked at Danny, who sat still for a while, his head down, looking at the table top in front of him, his face showing signs of the turmoil going on inside his head. But eventually Danny lifted up his head, looked straight at Alex, and spoke. "OK, Mister, I'll stay with you, as long as you take me up north, OK? But as soon as I find my Mum, then I'm going to go and live with her and my Gran."

That's settled, then," said Alex. "I'm fine with that. I'm very pleased to have you aboard."

"Thanks, Mister. That's very nice of you," Danny grinned, as he finished drinking his tea.

"By the way, Danny," Alex smiled at the lad, "my name's Alex.

Please, you can call me Alex, is that alright? It's so much better than 'Mister'."

"OK, Mister," Danny replied, then suddenly burst out laughing, as did Alex, as they both realised the silliness of what the boy had just said. It took a little while before they'd stopped giggling together.

"Pass me the Nicholson's, can you please, Danny?" Alex asked the lad, and Danny got up and slipped the book onto the table in front of him. Alex sat and studied the canal guide book for a minute or two. "Which way would you like to go, Danny?" he asked, showing the boy the alternative routes that were available. "we can go via Leicester and Nottingham. Or Rugby, Coventry, and Tamworth. Or through Birmingham. Which would you prefer?"

"Well, Mister, I dunno really," Danny replied, after studying the book for a minute or so. "What do you reckon?"

"The cut up to Leicester and Nottingham is quite rural at times," responded Alex. "Birmingham is quite built up, lots of factories and so on. The nicest route is probably the Grand Union canal, through Rugby and Coventry. And then we can go through Fradley junction to the northern canals from there." Alex traced the route out on the map in the Nicholson's. "What do you reckon to that?"

"Seems alright, Mister," Danny nodded. But we will go up north, won't we? You promise?"

"Yes, we will indeed," Alex reassured the lad. "But we'll cruise along for another hour or so now. Then we'll moor up and have a quick lunch, and then go into town, it's there on the map, look."

Danny studied the book for a moment, then asked, "how are we gonna get there then? The canal don't go there, it ain't really near the town. And what are we going there for, anyway?"

"That's simple," replied Alex. "To get there, we'll just walk along the towpath to that bridge, go up onto the road, walk into the village to the bus stop, and catch a bus into town. They're quite frequent along this road." As he spoke, he pointed out the road into the village in the Nicholson's guide.

"Well, I dunno really," said Danny. "Will I be OK there?"

Alex knew exactly what he meant. Danny was still scared of being apprehended and returned to Grant Hall, with all the horrors that would entail.

"Well yes, Danny, I'm pretty sure you'll be OK," Alex replied. "We'll be about thirty miles away from Grant Hall, and you've been away from there for a week now. I reckon they'll have given up and stopped searching for you by now. And we need to go, because we need some supplies for the boat. Food, toilet rolls, bread, milk, some other things as well, just to take care of the essentials. There's one or two places, like Leighton Buzzard, or Rugby, where the canal runs very close to a supermarket, and it's easy to do a large shop and get loads of stuff and restock all the cupboards. But generally, we need to go out a little way and get what we need." He pointed to the open Nicholson's page. "As I said, we can walk into this village here, and there'll be a bus we can catch into town, there's a huge supermarket there. We can get most of what we need for the time being."

"I've made a list of the groceries and other things which we need, but there's some other things we need as well, things for you, since you're going to be staying aboard for a while," Alex told the lad. "We need to get you some clothes. You can't wear those you've got on now all the time, or stay in bed whilst they're being washed. Let's make a list of what you should have."

Alex sat for a minute or so and wrote out a list of the clothes which he thought the boy would need, and when he'd finished, he started reading the list out to Danny.

"Two tee-shirts."
"Two long sleeved polo shirts."
"Two short-sleeved polo shirts."
"Two pairs of jeans."
"Two pairs of shorts."
"Three pairs of white socks."
"Three pairs of black socks."
"One pair of white trainers."
"One pair of black trainers."
"One pullover."
"One anorak or coat."

"How's that?" he asked Danny. "I haven't put waterproofs on the list, as I've got spare waterproofs on board, in case we get caught out in the rain. It's not always practical to stop and moor up every time it rains."

Danny nodded, but there was an anxious look on his face. "We can't do that, Mister," he said. "I ain't got no money to buy no clothes or anything with."

"No, I know that, Danny," Alex told him. "I'll buy them for you. It's OK, I've got a really good pension, and I'm not short of a bob or two."

"I can't let you do that," replied Danny, serious now. "I really can't. It ain't right, you buying me stuff like that."

"Well, if you like, why not consider it a loan," Alex told him, "until you've got some money, later on. You can pay me back then."

"OK, then, Mister," said Danny, "but I will pay you back, I promise."

"Well, If you wish," Alex told him, "but you really don't need to."

"I will," Danny repeated once again. "Just you wait and see. Anyway, ain't you forgotten something?"

"Why, have I?" asked Alex. "What's that?"

"Well, what about some undies, please?" Danny asked. "These ones I've got on now will get a bit smelly if I have to wear them all the time."

"Oh, of course," grinned Alex. "I'm sorry, I clean forgot them. I'll add two packs of briefs to the list, there's usually three in a pack, so that should be sufficient for you," and he added them to the bottom of the list.

"How do you know I don't wear boxers and not briefs?" Danny asked, grinning widely. Alex was starting to realise that Danny liked a good laugh.

"Oh, come on, Danny," Alex replied, "think for a moment. Who washed your clothes the other day, underwear and all?"

"Oh, yea, well, of course," Danny smiled. "Briefs it is, then. And can I have a toothbrush, please? I ain't been able to clean my teeth since I got away from the dentist that day. It ain't very nice having mucky teeth."

"Right-oh," said Alex, as he added a toothbrush to the list. "I'll get several, as I could do with a new one myself, actually. Now, let's get the tape measure, and see what sizes you need."

Once they'd taken all Danny's measurements, Alex smiled at the young boy. "Come on, then, let's get going. Will you clear up whilst we get under way?"

"OK, Mister," Danny smiled at him. "No problem, I'll do the washing up."

They motored along the canal for an hour or so, then moored *Jennifer Jo* just past the bridge which Alex had spotted in the Nicholson's guide. It carried a country lane over the canal, and they set off down the lane to the bus stop in the village. They hadn't been there for more than five minutes when a bus came along, so they got onto the bus and a short while later alighted at the terminal in the town centre. The town was busy, as they made their way through the crowds of shoppers to the supermarket, which they found to be really busy.

Alex first took Danny round to the clothing department, and they selected the clothes Danny needed. Alex noticed that Danny tended to avoid the most expensive items on display, settling instead for clothes which he liked the look of, and would be comfortable for him to wear. Alex could tell that the boy was really excited that someone was buying something for him. 'Poor kid,' he thought, 'he hasn't had much of a life the last few months.' Then they got their groceries and other items, and made their way to the checkouts.

As seemed to be usual these days, there were only about half of the available checkouts in use, the others being unmanned, and there were long queues at every checkout that was in operation. As they joined the end of a queue, awaiting for their turn to unload their trolley onto the conveyor, Danny turned to Alex and said "hey, Mister, I won't be a minute, I need a pee. I'll go and find the customer toilets."

"OK, Danny," Alex replied. "I'll be here at the checkout. It looks like I'll be here quite a while yet, there's such a long queue."

Danny disappeared back into the crowded store amongst the shelves, and Alex waited patiently at the checkout. It irked him a great deal to have to stand and wait his turn, as he felt that it was a complete waste of his valuable time. He'd always thought that supermarkets had missed a trick. How could they be so casual and disinterested about making their customers stand about waiting to pay for the goods they had selected?

Although it didn't affect him now, as he very rarely went to any supermarket by car, many stores had car parks that were too small for the number of customers they were attracting. Surely, the best way to free up more car parking spaces was to get your existing customers out quickly – and that meant opening more checkouts, instead of leaving half of them unused, even at busy times. It wasn't rocket science, Alex thought.

Hex also questioned the need to have checkouts at all. You went round the shelves, selecting the good you needed, and placed them into your trolley, then at the checkout your took them all out again and put them onto the conveyor belt, and then, once the cashier had scanned them, you put them back into your trolley again, albeit inside a carrier bag. What a waste of effort to handle your goods three times. Why couldn't they just give a scanner to each customer and get the customer to scan each item before it was put into the trolley?

Alex realised that it gave an opportunity for theft, as unscrupulous customers could avoid paying for items which they'd taken, simply by not scanning items before placing them into the trolley. But that could be checked by simply weighing the trolley at the payment till – the store's computers could easily be programmed to check the exact weight of each item available on the shelves.

It was a good seven or eight minutes before Alex was wakened from his critical reverie by the cashier calling out "next please," and he realised that it was now his turn, and he was now able to start loading the conveyor. Of Danny there was as yet no sign. As the cashier started to scan his shopping and he packed his purchases into his bags, he saw through the front window of the store a police car arriving and pulling up outside the store, and two officers got out and went inside.

'Oh dear, someone's been caught shoplifting,' he thought, as he slipped his credit card into the card reader and tapped in his PIN. But, as he was putting his card back into his wallet, he happened to glance up across the crowded store, and to his utter dismay he saw Danny, flanked by a police officer on each side of him loosely holding his arms, being walked firmly towards the exit.

Alex could see Danny looked frantically around the store as he was guided away, trying to catch sight of Alex through the crowds of shoppers. He also saw the look of absolute horror and desperation on the boy's face, as he frantically looked around the store, but Danny failed to pick him out from amongst the crowds. Alex quickly thought about what he might be able to do to help Danny, but he soon realised that anything he might be able to do would be pointless and achieve nothing.

But then, Danny suddenly pulled himself free from the grasps of the policemen, and dashed to the customer service desk by the exit. He quickly grabbed the public address system's microphone from an astonished assistant's hand, and yelled into it at the top of his voice "forty-five....forty-five....forty-five," before being grabbed by the policemen and manhandled away, and then being bundled unceremoniously into the waiting police car.

Alex was mortified. How on earth had Danny been picked up? He'd been sure that he would have been alright here. It was a good thirty miles from the area where Grant Hall was located. And worse still, he'd taken great trouble to assure Danny that there was no secret agenda, that he would not be handed over to the authorities, and yet Danny would think that he, Alex, had shopped him and arranged for him to be apprehended.

Alex stood transfixed, rooted to the spot, as he saw Danny being driven away. It was only when he heard a female voice saying "in your own time please," that he realised that he was blocking the checkout, and other customers were waiting behind him to pay for their goods. He apologised, then made his way to the cafe at the rear of the store, where he bought a cup of coffee and sat down at a corner table facing the wall. He wanted to be alone with his thoughts while he considered what had just happened to Danny.

It was unbelievable, what had just taken place. He didn't like to imagine how Danny would be treated once he was returned to Grant Hall. He would certainly be on the receiving end of that guy Hammond's wrath. The punishment that would be meted out to that young boy did not bear thinking about.

Alex's thoughts turned to what he could do next. Should he go to the Social Services people, and tell them what Danny had told him about the regime at Grant Hall? From what Danny had told him, they were having the wool well and truly pulled over their eyes, and very successfully too, from Hammonds point of view. Alex had the photographs of Danny's injuries which he'd taken the night he'd found Danny hiding in the cratch, and he also had the account of life at Grant Hall which he'd got Danny to write the following day. They comprised valuable evidence, although for them to be of any use at all, Danny had to be free to back them up and talk about them. But with Danny back in Grant Hall, where he would be subjected to all manner of intimidation and brutality should he dare to speak out, they were of very little use on their own. And it was pretty certain that the man in charge there, this man Hammond, would use every means at his disposal to ensure that Danny was kept under a very very tight rein indeed.

Also, Alex had his own situation to think about. Well aware that Danny had absconded from Grant Hall, he'd taken in this young boy, given him food and shelter, and not handed him over to the authorities when he would have been expected to do so. And he'd just agreed to let the boy stay on board with him for an indefinite period, and take the boy up north to try to find his mother. Almost certainly the full force of the law would be brought down upon him. He would face charges of abduction of a minor, concealing an absconder, and probably other charges as well. The fact that he did all of this with the best of intentions would be considered immaterial, and the almost-certain resulting verdict of guilty would shatter his reputation as a respected schoolteacher of many years standing. It would be in tatters.

His thoughts turned to what Danny had told him about the strange men in big cars who turned up at Grant Hall late at night. To him, men in large cars equated to people with money. And people with money normally moved in higher social circles. And higher social circles meant well-to-do people with connections and influence. And if, as Danny claimed, they were up to no good with those young boys, then they would exert as much influence as they could to keep their activities well concealed, and suppress any attempt to expose what was going on at Grant

Hall, in case their own part in it came to light. All of which indicated that they would make every effort to ensure that any evidence which he, Alex, put before the authorities would be put on the sidelines and studiously ignored whilst they vigorously pursued charges against him.

Eventually Alex arrived at a decision. It cause him a great deal of heartache, but after a considerable amount of thought, he reluctantly came to the conclusion that there was nothing he could do which would be of any help to Danny and the other boys at Grant Hall. He could only hope that in due course Social Services would realise what the situation there was, and take appropriate action. But Alex had little hope that they would do so, since they had not acted before now. It was a shame, but they were the people whose responsibility it was. If even Robert Jefferies, the newspaper reporter, couldn't bring the goings on at Grant Hall to light, then without a witness such as Danny who could speak freely about his experiences there without fear of intimidation, Alex didn't stand a chance. It hurt Alex a great deal to leave Danny to his fate back at Grant Hall, but he just had to accept that anything he did would be pointless and achieve nothing, except almost certainly lining himself up for arrest and imprisonment.

But the thing that upset Alex most of all was what Danny would be thinking of him right now. 'Trust me,' Alex had said to him many times over the last few days. He'd assured the boy on numerous occasions that there was no hidden agenda. And when he'd been taken into custody, there was no doubt, no doubt at all, that Danny would have felt that it was Alex who had betrayed him. Alex knew full well that he'd played no part whatsoever in Danny's being apprehended, but Danny would almost certainly think the worst, that Alex had somehow contrived the whole affair. And somehow, knowing that Danny would blame him for what had happened to him saddened Alex most of all.

He cast his mind back to when Danny was being taken out of the store by the two policemen. Why had he struggled to get free, then shouted 'forty-five' into the microphone, not just once, but three times in all? Had Danny been trying to say something to him? If so, Alex had no idea of what it might be. However much he thought about it, it just didn't make sense, no sense at all.

Just then, he was aroused from his thoughts by a female voice, one of the cafe's staff. "Oh, you've not touched your coffee at all," she said. "It must be cold by now. Would you like a fresh cup? I'm not supposed to say so, but since you haven't touched a drop, I'll let you have another for no charge, if you like."

"Oh, no thanks," Alex replied. "I really must be going. I have a bus to catch. But thank you anyway." He retrieved his trolley from the secure area by the cafe entrance and started to make his way back to the exit from the store.

As he walked back through the store, Alex looked down at the pile of shopping bags in his trolley. He'd bought a load of clothes for Danny which he no longer needed. It was extremely unlikely that he'd ever see Danny again. The people at Grant Hall would be keeping a very careful eye on him from now on, and it was almost certain that the boy would not be able to abscond again. He went over to the customer service desk and spoke to the assistant, the same young lady who'd been surprised by Danny some time before.

"Hello," she said, with a sweet smile, "how may I help you?"

"I've just bought these boy's clothes, for my grandson," Alex explained, hoping fervently that the assistant wouldn't associate them with the boy who'd just been escorted from the store by the police. "But I've decided that I don't want them after all, I don't think he'll like them. He's very particular about what he wears. Please may I have a refund?"

"We've got a very good returns policy," the assistant told Alex. "Are they faulty? We'll give you a full refund or replacement if they're faulty, whichever you prefer."

"Well, no, they're fine," said Alex. "Nothing wrong with them at all. I've just changed my mind, that's all."

The assistant didn't seem to have heard him, or if she had, she wasn't paying attention. "Are there any minor faults, then?" she asked.

"Well, no," replied Alex. "As I said, they're fine. But I don't want them any longer. Please may I have a refund?"

The assistant still didn't seem to be listening to what Alex had said. "Is there any slight damage or imperfections?" she asked. "Because if there are, if the goods are still fit for purpose, then we can give you a partial refund."

"No," said Alex, who was beginning to wish he hadn't bothered asking. "All I want is a refund, because I don't want them any more. Are you able to help me?"

"No, you can't have a refund if there's nothing wrong with them," said the assistant, a bit frostily. "See over there?" She waved her hand loftily behind her. "We've got twenty eight checkouts. That's because people come here to buy stuff. They're for people to pay for their things before they leave. Now look over here," and she pointed to the entrance. "Do you see any check-ins? For people to sell us stuff when they come in?

No, there aren't any. That's because we don't buy stuff here, we only sell it. If you bought something and now you don't want it, just because you've changed your mind, then I'm sorry, we can't help you. Goodbye. Next please."

Alex felt well and truly put in his place. He realised that the store had a point, he'd freely chosen to buy those items and it wasn't really the store's problem if he'd changed his mind after buying them. But perhaps the assistant he'd spoken to could have shown a little more courtesy, he thought.

Struggling with the six carrier bags containing his shopping, he walked slowly away out of the store and across the car park, and made his way to the bus stop. Alex felt really upset about what had happened to Danny, but he also realised that there was very little which he could have done to help the lad. Had he tried to intervene, then he too would have been taken into custody, and heaven knows what would have happened then. He consoled himself with the thought that he'd given the boy food and shelter for a couple of days, and he hoped that Danny would have appreciated it.

Alex disembarked from the bus and made his way slowly along the lane towards the bridge over the canal. Had Danny still been with him, then carrying the shopping, which of course included the clothes he'd bought for Danny, would have been easy. But as he went along, his six bags of shopping seemed to get heavier and heavier, and he stopped twice to rest his arms, which felt as though they were just about to be pulled from their sockets. But just as he was about to rest for a third time, he was overtaken by a young man, who called out a cheery "hello," and stopped to chat.

"Hello," he said again. "You're off that blue boat down there along the cut, aren't you?"

"Yes," Alex replied, "that's right, my boat's called *Jennifer Jo*."

"I thought so," the man replied, "I'm moored up not far from you with my boat, I saw you walking up to the bridge earlier today. You had a young lad with you."

Alex thought quickly. If Danny was questioned about where he'd been since getting away from his escort at the dentist, he might let slip that he'd been given shelter on a canal boat, aboard *Jennifer Jo* for a couple of days, and then the police might come after him and take him into custody for aiding and abetting an absconder. They might be asking awkward questions of anyone they found on the canal. That would be an outcome he didn't want to have to go through. Whilst he was pleased that he'd been able to help Danny and give him food and shelter, It might be better not to have been associated with Danny, as far as the authorities were concerned. So he decided on a little white lie.

"Yes," he said, "that was my grandson, he's been staying on the boat with me for a couple of days. But he's gone home now, I took him back into town with me when I went to get some shopping. You always need to keep stocked up." And he indicated the six bags of shopping he was struggling with.

"Let me give you a hand," the man said. "My name's Brian, by the way." And he reached out to pick up some of the bags of shopping.

"Thanks," Alex replied, "that's very kind of you. Could you take these please?" He quickly made sure that Brian took the bags of groceries, and none of the bags which contained the clothes he'd bought for Danny. The less Brian knew about Danny, the better. "And I'm Alex," he added.

Brian continued to engage Alex in conversation as they walked across the bridge and down onto the towpath. Normally Alex would have welcomed the chat, as meeting other boaters was one of the attractions of a life afloat. But today, after what had happened to Danny, Alex would have much preferred to have made his way back aboard on his own, and been left alone. "I'd have thought the boy should have been at school," Brian commented. "Half-term was a couple of weeks ago."

"That's right," Alex said, mentally crossing his fingers behind his back as more white lies became necessary. "The roof of his classroom was leaking, and it's taken longer than they expected to fix it, so they gave the class a few days extra holiday. He's back to school tomorrow."

They walked along the towpath until they reached *Jennifer Jo,* and Brian put the bags he was carrying onto the rear deck. "Thanks, Brian," Alex said, "let me know if you need any help at any time." He paused. Whilst he would much rather have been left on his own, courtesy demanded that he should offer some hospitality to Brian, for carrying the shopping back to the boat for him. "Would you like a cuppa while you're here?" he added. "It won't take long to brew up."

"No, thanks," said Brian, "but perhaps we'll chat again tomorrow, OK?"

"Yes, that's fine," replied Alex, heaving a sigh of relief. "And thanks once again." He carried the bags down into the boat, placing those with the clothes he'd bought for Danny onto the bunk in the back cabin where Danny had slept, and then moving forward to the galley, where he put his groceries away in the various cupboards until needed.

Alex spent a miserable evening thinking about what Danny might be going through, now he was back at Grant Hall, and thinking about what punishments were being dispensed to the poor boy because he had absconded. That man Hammond would surely be taking Danny's escape as a personal insult, Alex felt sure of that. Nothing nice would be happening to Danny, Alex felt certain. And why had Danny shouted out 'forty-five' several times as he was being escorted out of the store that afternoon? Surely there wasn't anyone else in the store that Danny knew? Was it meant for him to hear? What message was Danny trying to tell him? There must have been a reason for him to break free from his captors and grab the microphone at the Customer Services desk, but Alex just couldn't think what it was.

Before turning in, Alex did his usual little walk outside to check the mooring ropes, returning into the boat via the back deck and down into the back cabin, where he saw the bags of Danny's clothes which he'd bought that afternoon. He stopped to put them away in the locker beside the boy's bunk, and as he opened the locker he saw the Rubik's cube he'd given Danny the previous night, neatly placed on the shelf at the top of the locker. But, to Alex's surprise and amazement, it was just as it was when Alex had first been given it, fully unscrambled, all the colours of each side the same. Alex marvelled at how Danny had managed to achieve something that he himself had struggled with for many hours before giving up – and here was Danny's handiwork, done in just a few minutes.

Alex lay in his bed that night, thinking about Danny for a long while before getting off to sleep. He realised how much he really hurt for Danny. He hurt for Danny, whose father had walked out of the family home when he was still a young child. He hurt for Danny, whose mother had been, and apparently still was, seriously ill. And he hurt for Danny's miserable life at Grant Hall, and for the abuse he had been subjected to, and would still be receiving there. In the short time that he'd known him, he'd become aware that Danny was a polite and intelligent lad, with a good upbringing and a well-defined sense of right or wrong, and Alex knew that the boy deserved better. But it hurt Alex most of all that there was nothing at all, absolutely nothing, that Alex could do for him now, to help him to a better life.

CHAPTER 5

Alex woke the next morning, after yet another fitful night's sleep, and made his customary cup of coffee. He was just about to set off when Brian appeared from his boat, which was moored just a few yards away from *Jennifer Jo*, and engaged Alex in conversation. In stark contrast to yesterday, when he'd wanted to be on his own, this morning Alex welcomed the chance to chat. It would help him to get the memory of Danny out of his system. It turned out that Brian was an extremely nice, friendly fellow, and it wasn't long before Alex had been invited inside Brian's boat to have a look around, and then they sat together for a while for a chat and another cup of coffee.

Brian insisted on showing Alex all round his boat, of which he was really proud. He'd bought it as a sailaway about 8 years before, with just the engine and windows fitted into the steel shell, with paving slabs laid in the bottom as ballast as was normal practice, and he'd then spent the next 18 months fitting it out himself, having inherited some money from his grandmother, which not only provided the funding to purchase the boat and the materials needed, but also the resources to allow him to take all the time off work to get the job completed.

Alex was impressed with the quality of the workmanship that Brian's handiwork displayed. The interior layout was tidy without being cluttered, and he'd made a good job of the task he'd set himself. An attractive combination of pine woodwork and joinery was nicely set by Brian's choice of light red and orange colours for the soft furnishings of the curtains and upholstery to the seats at the dinette, and a couple of easy chairs in the saloon. It made a nice change from the almost universal choice of black leather seats that seemed to be so popular on many boats along the cut.

But eventually, Alex looked at his watch and realised that the time was almost ten o'clock. He'd been chatting for almost two hours. "I'm really sorry, but I must be getting along," said Alex. "It's been very nice to talk to you, and thank you for letting me see your boat. You've done very well, no wonder you're so proud of it."

"Thanks," said Brian, "let's hope we meet up again sometime along the cut."

"Yes, that would be great," Alex replied, "then you can come and have a look at my *Jennifer Jo*, and I'll make the coffee."

"That's a deal, then," grinned Brian, as they shook hands, "I'll keep an eye open for you."

Alex returned to *Jennifer Jo*, and as it was too late for breakfast, Alex made himself a quick sandwich and decided to dispense with lunch - he could have an early supper to make up for it. As he ate his brunch, he thought about the morning he'd just spent with Brian, and realised how much he had enjoyed the chat, and seeing round Brian's boat, which he was so rightly so proud of. And also, it had helped to take his mind off Danny. Alex wished, when he and Jenny were having *Jennifer Jo* built, that he could have done the same as Brian and fitted out their boat himself, but he'd quickly realised that being a House Master at the school meant that he just wouldn't have been able to spare the time. Also, and perhaps more importantly, he knew that he didn't possess the necessary skills to do that sort of work to the high standard which was required.

Alex finished his lunch, cast off the mooring ropes, and motored up the canal. Gradually the surroundings of the canal changed. Up to now, the canal had been making a course between the villages that were scattered around this part of the countryside, meandering around, passing the outskirts of one village after another, but now the villages fell away, and the cut made its way through open countryside. All that Alex could see were rolling fields and meadows, divided by neatly trimmed hedges, with the occasional tall tree at intervals along their line, and the odd spinney or stand of woodland to break the view. Probably, Alex thought to himself, kept by the landowner to harbour pheasants and other game for when the shooting season started again in the autumn.

But as ever, there was much to see and enjoy along the canal, and as always, Alex took a keen interest in the variety of bridges that spanned the waterway along this stretch. Some were the traditional brick-built hump-back bridges, built two hundred or more years ago, when the line of the newly-constructed canal cut through what passed in those days for a road. Others were simpler structures, built for the local land-owner's access between his fields, consisting of a couple of brick-built support piers situated one at either side of the cut, with a flat bridge deck strung between them. One such bridge he passed under had a timber deck, but on a couple of others the timber deck had been replaced by steel beams, presumably because the wood had rotted over time, and been replaced with a more durable material.

Alex also noticed the bridge plates, secured to each bridge. Each bridge should have displayed two plates, one on each side of the bridge, showing the bridge number. As was not uncommon, some of the plates were missing. Of the remaining, some of the plates were the original cast-iron design, but corroded and gone rusty with the passage of time, and hard to decipher. Others were new plates, of the same design as the originals, but recently made, neatly painted in black with the number picked out in white paint, presumably paid for and fitted by the local canal preservation society. Yet others were made from enamelled steel with black or white numbers on a blue background. Such variety made for an interesting journey along the cut, and helped to give an interesting insight into the heritage of Britain's industrial past.

  As Alex rounded a slight bend in the canal, he saw another bridge coming up ahead, and as he approached it, he, as usual, looked for the bridge number plate, but, on this side of the bridge at least, the plate was missing. As he passed under the bridge, he turned his head back and spotted the number plate fixed above the arch. It was an original cast-iron design, rusty, with all the paint flaked away and difficult to decipher, but before *Jennifer Jo* had drawn too far away to read it, he saw the number – it was bridge 45. Suddenly his heart missed a beat. Forty-five! That was the number Danny had called out in the supermarket yesterday. And for the previous couple of days, Danny had spent a great deal of time poring over the Nicholson's guide to the canals, fascinated by all the information about the canals which it contained. Was Danny trying to tell him something as he was being taken away by the police officers? Was Danny going to try to get away again, try to escape from Grant Hall, and meet him at bridge forty-five?

  Alex looked at his wristwatch. It was nearly five o'clock in the afternoon, so it was time to start thinking about mooring up and getting some supper anyway. On the spur of the moment, Alex decided that it wouldn't hurt for him to stay here for the night. Bridge 45 was in a pleasant, if isolated, spot, and perhaps Danny would turn up, though he realised that the odds were well and truly stacked against the boy ever being able to get away from Grant Hall again. They would be keeping a very close eye on him from now on.

  He throttled back the engine, and, as always, carefully steered *Jennifer Jo* into the side of the canal, bringing the boat to a halt in the centre of a nice gap about one hundred yards long, between a couple of mature oak trees growing in the hedge which lined the towpath, which formed a boundary between the towpath of the canal and the meadows beyond. Taking the centre rope in his hand as he stepped ashore, Alex gently brought the boat to a halt, before quickly stepping back onto the rear deck, where he opened a locker and took out a couple of mooring pins, together with the lump hammer he always carried there. Along this stretch of the canal there was no nice neat steel piling onto which he could secure the ropes to moor *Jennifer Jo*. Instead, he had to make his own secure moorings by hammering the steel pins, each about eighteen inches long, into the ground of the towpath, until only the metal loop welded to the top of each pin was showing above ground level. When both the pins had been satisfactorily hammered into the ground, he passed the ropes through the loops at the top of the pins, tying them back onto the boat round the dollies at the front and the stern.

To finish off his mooring, Alex went back to the rear locker and took a couple of bright fluorescent yellow tennis balls, which in the side of each he'd cut a slit with his craft knife, and placed them over the ends of the mooring pins which protruded above ground level. This would make them easily seen by any walkers or cyclists and any other users of the towpath. The yellow balls made it easy to spot that the pins were there, and hopefully enable people to avoid tripping or falling over them as they made their way along the towpath to wherever they were going.

He returned to the boat, made himself a cup of coffee and took it outside, picking up the Nicholson's guide as he went. He walked along the towpath back to bridge 45. It was a farm accomodation bridge carrying an unmade track between two fields, a typical canal-style hump-backed bridge, built of red brick, with cast-iron rubbing strakes at the front edge of each pier on the towpath side. 'Yet another reminder,' he thought, 'of a bygone age.' The rubbing strakes had numerous grooves worn into their surface, caused by the friction and abrasion of the towing ropes of horse-drawn boats as they'd passed by and rubbed against the structure of the bridge. Without the iron rubbing strakes, the soft red brick of the bridge would have worn away long ago.

In common with many other bridges on the canals, the whole of the brickwork of the bridge was in a poor condition, with signs of impact by passing boats, and a number of cracks in the brickwork indicating that remedial work would be needed before long, otherwise the whole structure would collapse into the water, and possibly onto an unfortunate boater who just happened to be passing under the bridge at the moment of collapse. It was just one more example of the chronic underfunding that the waterways of Britain had been subjected to by various governments over a period of many years. Had it been a bridge over a public road, then it would have been repaired long ago, but public safety on the waterways seemed to have become a prime candidate for neglect.

Alex made his way through a gap in the hedge and up onto the bridge over the canal. From there he could see out over the surrounding countryside. He looked at the relevant page in the Nicholson's. As well as the canal, the guide book showed the surroundings of the canal for a couple of miles on each side of the water, but for this part of the canal, the guide was completely featureless. There was no indication of roads, villages, hamlets or settlements of any kind at all. Many railways had been built a hundred years earlier along much the same route as the canal builders had chosen a hundred years before, but here, unusually, there were no railways to keep company with the canal. Alex looked up from the book and looked around him. Rolling fields made up the view in every direction, with just an occasional hedge or ditch to mark the boundaries between them. The only consistent feature was the line of hedging beside the towpath, showing the route taken by the canal as it meandered away into the distance.

Alex listened for any other signs of life other than himself, but all was soothingly quiet. There was practically no sound at all, apart from the occasional quack of a pair of Mallard ducks splashing about in the water on the far side of the cut, and the occasional chirp, chirp of a couple of sparrows sitting in the hedge beside the towpath.

Unusually, his surroundings were completely silent and still. The only feature at all that was shown in the Nicholson's was the rough, stony, unmade farm track snaking its way towards the canal between the fields, a small low hedge marking its boundary to one side. The track petered out on the offside after it crossed the bridge, which had obviously been provided when the canal was dug, to give access to that part of the field which had been bisected by the construction of the canal.

Alex had chosen a truly isolated spot to stop. He wondered if it was this place which Danny had referred to in the supermarket yesterday. If so, it was an ideal place to go to without being seen by the authorities seeking to apprehend him once again. Provided, he thought, Danny would ever be able to get away from Grant Hall again.

Alex leant against the parapet of the bridge, and thought about Danny for a while. He really wanted to help the lad in any way that he could, but he quickly realised that it might be some time before Danny would be able to get away from Grant Hall again, if ever.

After considering the situation for a while, he resolved to stay there, at bridge forty five, for as long as he possibly could. He had much that he needed to do. The boat needed a good clean inside, and the brass ventilation mushrooms on the top of the boat were becoming tarnished and needed a good polishing. He wished now that he'd spent the extra £100 or so when the boat was being built and had them gold-plated, as some boat owners did. That kept them smart and shiny for ever, and obviated the need for them ever to be polished again. Also, he had emails to answer, bills to pay, and he wanted to return to a major project which he'd been meaning to get to grips with for some time.

On his retirement from teaching, he'd reached agreement with the headmaster and governors of the school that he would write a history of the school – its origins, its move to its present premises in the 1930's, its several building projects to add additional facilities through the years, and perhaps most interesting of all, its staff (himself included, though without being vain) and the achievements of past pupils who'd gone on to great things. He'd made a start and finished some three chapters so far, and he had been lent a wealth of archive material to research through. It was presently all tucked away in a locker beneath one of the dinette seats. All in all, Alex had a great deal to do, and this was perhaps a golden opportunity to get on top of it all, while he waited to see if Danny would turn up.

'Danny, my boy,' he thought to himself, 'I'm here, if this really is where you wanted me to be. I'll be here for as long as I can, waiting for you. The rest, now, is up to you.'

CHAPTER 6

Alex sat back from the table at the dinette and stretched his arms out above his head. He looked at the work he'd just completed, set out on the table in front of him. Since stopping here at bridge 45 almost three-and-a-half weeks ago, he'd been able to press on with his history of the school where he'd taught, and been a House Master for so long. In that time at bridge 45, he'd managed to complete a full couple of chapters on the development of the school, and he felt really proud of what he'd achieved so far. He picked up the pages he'd written that day, and went out onto the rear deck where he could lean against the back rail in the late afternoon sun, and read through the day's work.

Hearing a rustle in the grass on the towpath beside the boat, Alex looked down and was just in time to see a grass snake slithering across the ground, and with a gentle plop launch itself into the water of the canal. Alex watched as it swam strongly across the cut towards a group of moorhens swimming beside the reeds which lined the opposite bank. When they saw the snake swimming towards them they scattered, croaking loudly as they did so. As both snake and moorhens disappeared behind the reeds, Alex wondered whether the snake would have a nice supper, or if the moorhens would survive to fight it out another day. He was seeing nature at its most brutal. Simply put, eat or be eaten.

Alex paused in his reading and looked about him, Unsurprisingly, the surroundings were just as isolated as when he'd stopped there nearly four weeks before. The only company he'd really had in all that time were a few cheerful waves from the crews of other boats as they cruised by. Many boaters seemed to be a trifle reluctant to moor on this stretch of the canal, since there was no convenient steel piling to secure the mooring ropes to. It seemed they preferred to continue on to a spot where there were good moorings, and a reasonable amount of facilities close by.

Many boaters, especially those on holiday, always looked for a pub to moor up near to each night, so they could easily tie up and visit the pub for a meal rather than cook their own. Pubs were very numerous along the cut, many named 'The Navigator' or 'The Navigation' or similar. No doubt they had been built there beside the waterway from the same era as when the canals were being dug out by hand so many years ago, the pubs built to service the needs and demands of the workers, who were known at the time as 'navigators', thus giving rise to the present day word 'navvies'

Only once had a boat moored nearby, and that was to allow the people aboard to walk their dog and have their lunch. And then they had moved on, leaving Alex to the solitude he had chosen, in his decision to wait at bridge 45 in case Danny, against all odds, was going to turn up.

But Danny had not appeared. Alex was well aware that, from the start, it had been a long shot. Whilst the boy seemed very resourceful, perhaps more so that would normally have been expected from someone of such a young age, the people at Grant Hall would have become much more security-conscious than normal after Danny's previous escapade, and they would have made sure that even another visit to the dentist would not have afforded him much opportunity to run off again. It was pretty certain that they would have made sure of that.

Alex returned inside the saloon and put away his books in their normal place under the dinette. He took his diary down from the handy bookshelf where it lived for easy access, and sat down once again to write up his notes for the day. When that was completed, he sat back and considered his situation that he was in. He knew that he had to make a decision, and he didn't like the decision that he was being forced to make.

To a very great extent, whilst living on a boat, one had to be self-sufficient as much as possible. Whether people lived on a boat or in a house ashore, everyone had to go out shopping for food and clothing and other household items, and in a house there was usually plenty of storage space available. But, as Alex had quickly learnt, on a live-aboard boat things were very different.

By the very nature of the design of a narrowboat, there was only a limited amount of storage space, thus restricting how much could be kept aboard the boat at any time. This meant that frequent visits to shops and supermarkets had to become the norm, and when he did get the opportunity to resupply, like everyone else who lived afloat, Alex took full advantage, filling up his cupboards and lockers to the brim. Alex had always been very careful to keep a good stock of food, toiletries, cleaning supplies, and other items aboard *Jennifer Jo*, and, although he was now living out of tins and jars and packets, he had barely enough food to last him for more than a day or two.

After having been at bridge 45 for some five days, Alex had gone on a shopping expedition. He'd locked up the boat, taken his folding bicycle out of the locker on the rear deck, and cycled off down the farm track from the bridge. The winding track had led him between the surrounding fields for about four miles, eventually passing through a farmyard before reaching a road. Alex had then cycled along the road until he came to a village, but on making enquiries of some people waiting at the bus stop in the main street, he'd found that there was no shop there in the village, as the local post office cum shop had closed about eighteen months before.

But he'd also learnt that there was a bus into the nearby town due to arrive within the next few minutes. He was lucky, as a friendly local villager who lived near the bus stop had let him put his cycle in her shed whilst he caught the bus and got himself some shopping. He was limited as to how much he could carry, as he only had a small shoulder bag, but it was big enough for him to get some bacon, bread, milk, and eggs, sufficient to last him a for a week or so. Together with the tinned and packet foods which he always kept on board, it would easily last for another week or more.

The following week, he'd made the same expedition again, but on the way back to the boat along the farm track, the small wheels of his bicycle had become caught in a rut, and he'd lost his balance and fallen off the bike. On picking himself up, more shocked than bruised, Alex was pleased to find that the eggs in his bag were unbroken. But he found that the front wheel of his bike had become badly buckled in the fall and wouldn't turn, and he'd had to walk the rest of the way back to *Jennifer Jo* carrying his food supplies, and dragging his bicycle along the track as he did so. He'd tried to repair the wheel, but he'd eventually given up. The bike was unusable until it could be repaired and have a new wheel fitted. It was much too far for Alex to walk into the village again, and so from then on he'd had to survive on the dwindling stock of provisions he had on board in his cupboards. And now these too were running out.

But Alex was aware that there were other shortages and problems that had been presenting themselves over the last few days. For the last few days, Alex had been unable to do any cooking. He was usually able to choose between the microwave and the gas cooker and hob to heat his food, whichever was more appropriate. But the microwave, to make it work, needed electricity, which was provided by a bank of batteries tucked away in the engine room. He'd been in the habit of running his engine for about an hour or so every morning, to provide hot water for washing and doing the washing up, and at the same time the engine charged the batteries which provided electrical power throughout the boat. Whilst this didn't fully charge the batteries (they needed to have the engine running for about six hours each day to do that) it was sufficient to give enough power to run his laptop for the afternoon, and provide an hour or so of television in the evenings.

Fortunately he had no fresh food left in the fridge, so he'd been able to switch that off as soon as he'd run out of fresh meat and milk, otherwise the engine would have needed to run for the full six hours, as the fridge took a lot of power. Even so, even with all these measures, he was starting to get short of diesel fuel for the engine. There was no contents gauge for the diesel tank, which was located at the rear of the boat. Instead, every few days, he'd dipped the tank using a long piece of wooden dowel, and noted the wet mark on the dowel after withdrawing it from the tank. He had to leave sufficient fuel in the tank to get *Jennifer Jo* the next twenty or so miles along the cut to the next marina, where he would be able to fill up. Alex reckoned that he had enough diesel to get him about thirty miles, and he didn't want to let his safety margin get any lower – it was a complicated job to bleed the fuel system if you ran out of diesel, not to mention the ignominy of having to ask a passing boat for a tow !

The alternative to using the microwave was to use the gas stove. The gas locker at the rear of the boat held two 13 kg cylinders of Calor gas, but one of those had run out the day before he'd found Danny hiding in the cratch, and he'd swapped the connection over to the spare bottle. But since then, he hadn't seen a chandlery or marina to replace the empty bottle, and his gas supply had run out about a week ago. And so he'd been reduced to eating only cold food. The only exception was one evening when it had turned really cold, and he'd lit a fire in the stove to take the evening chill off the boat. He'd decided to try heating a saucepan of soup on the stove, to get something hot inside him. But the stove was much too small to fit even Alex's smallest saucepan on the top, so he'd built a platform of upturned saucepans beside the stove, then placed a baking tray between the top of the stove and the saucepans to conduct some heat from the stove onto the tray, and then put the saucepan of soup on the baking tray. After about 15 minutes, the soup was hot and Alex was able to enjoy a hot supper after all. But ever since then he'd been eating his food cold – not always the most pleasant way to eat, he thought.

But Alex's problems didn't stop there. In a house on dry land, essential supplies and services such as water and sewage disposal were piped to and from the property, usually underground. But on a boat, that was impractical. You had to take those services with you.

Many years ago, it had been prohibited to flush your toilet waste into the water of the canal, and ever since then all boats on the waterways had been fitted with either a cassette toilet, which you could take away and empty at an authorised disposal point, or alternatively, such as was fitted in *Jennifer Jo,* toilet waste was kept hygienically in a holding tank beneath the floor, and for a small fee, boatyards and marinas along the cut could periodically be asked to pump out the tank and properly dispose of its contents into the normal sewerage system. Alex had checked his toilet tank that morning, and found it was almost full. After only two or three more visits, it would be full. And then what would he do? It was not impossible for Alex to answer calls of nature in the hedge beside the towpath, but he was loath to do that – after all, other boats might be passing by at just the wrong moment, and they wouldn't want to see (and smell) the unpleasant evidence of the time he'd spent at this spot on the canal.

But the most pressing problem of all was Alex's supply of fresh water for drinking, washing, and washing his clothes. His fresh water tank held a total of 150 gallons, and he'd filled the tank a few days before Danny had stowed away on *Jennifer Jo,* but this morning Alex had heard the sound he'd been dreading, but expecting, for several days. When running the tap for some drinking water, the pump had spluttered and the flow of water from the tap had ceased.

Alex had known he was getting short of water, for every few days he'd been dipping the tank, using a 6ft long piece of wooden dowel he'd specially bought for the purpose. The wet mark on the bottom of the dowel showed him how much (or rather, how little) water he had left, and yesterday's dip had confirmed what Alex already knew – he was just about out of fresh water. He'd stopped taking showers a couple of weeks before, and instead carried out a strip wash every day, in an effort to conserve his dwindling supply, as Alex had realised that water would be the most serious factor limiting his stay at bridge 45. He always kept a small emergency supply of bottled water at the back of his cupboard in the galley, and he'd been using that since the morning, but there was now only one bottle remaining unopened. And that would be gone by the next morning, and he wouldn't be able to have a wash either. It was strictly for drinking only.

Alex sat and thought for a long, long while. He really wanted to stay there for longer, in case Danny might show up, but his situation was becoming untenable. It was absolutely necessary that he had to move on and get water, fuel, and provisions, and get a pumpout for the toilet tank. He fetched the Nicholson's, and had a look at the page which showed his whereabouts on the canal. There was a marina about a day's cruising up the cut, where he would be able to get most of what he needed, but there was no winding hole or anywhere else to turn the boat round and return to the spot he was at, for another day and a half after that. If he decided to come back, resupplied for, say, another two or three weeks, then it meant that he would be away from bridge 45 for a good five days or so.

And, during that time, Danny could well have arrived, found him not there, and moved on. And then Alex would be sitting there to no avail for the next three weeks or so. All in all, to return and wait for Danny, on the increasingly unlikely event that he would show up, would take about a month, all told. Alex didn't really want to lose that amount of time, he had other places to go to along the cut which he wanted to visit.

Eventually, and not without a great deal of reluctance, Alex decided on the course of action he had to take. He'd only know the boy for two or three days, and he'd felt impelled to help him as much as he could, but there had to come the time to move on. 'I'm sorry, Danny,' he thought to himself, 'but I simply have to go. I'm sorry you couldn't make it here, if indeed this is the place where you wanted me to be waiting for you, but I just can't wait any longer. I wish you well, but I really must move on without you. In the morning, I shall move on and be gone.'

And with that, Alex went inside *Jennifer Jo*, had yet another cold supper, read a book for an hour or so, and then turned in to bed.

CHAPTER 7

Alex woke at his normal time of 7.30 am the next morning, got dressed and had himself some breakfast. 'Nothing to shout about,' he thought, as he sat down to eat – just three digestive biscuits and a glass of water. As soon as they'd disappeared, Alex prepared to move on. After carrying out the daily routine of checking the engine's oil and water levels, he started the engine, untied his mooring ropes, and with a heavy heart and a last look at the towpath behind him for any signs of Danny, he carefully steered *Jennifer Jo* out into the middle of the canal and brought the engine up to its normal cruising speed. He had hoped against hope that Danny would make it through the terrible time which Alex was sure he was having, but regrettably there was nothing more that Alex could do for him.

He'd been going for about 5 minutes, when the boat rounded a bend and revealed a long straight length of canal, stretching away in front of him for almost half a mile, maybe further. Way in the distance, Alex thought he saw a figure walking along the towpath towards him, which he thought to be more than a trifle unusual. After having been stopped at bridge 45 for nearly a month, he'd become aware how isolated this part of the canal really was, with no villages or other human habitation within three or four miles, so to see someone around here really surprised him. The only people he'd seen in all his time there had been people off other canal boats, and there were certainly no boats in the vicinity at the moment.

His attention was distracted momentarily by a couple of ducks engaged in a noisy squabble as he motored past them, and when he looked forward again, whoever he thought he'd seen on the towpath a few moments earlier had disappeared. Probably a rambler out for a long walk, and now walking back home around the margins of the adjoining fields, Alex surmised. He knew how committed ramblers could cover great distances when they set their minds to it.

But as he reached the spot where he'd seen the figure, the tall bushes adjoining the towpath suddenly parted, and a young boy stepped out onto the towpath from where he'd been hiding in the undergrowth. Alex instantly recognised who it was. It was Danny.

"Hey, Mister," Danny called out, his face as cheeky and cheerful as ever. "Bet you didn't think I was coming."

Alex slowly shook his head in amazement, as he throttled back the engine and *Jennifer Jo* drifted to a halt beside the towpath. "You're really lucky, Danny," he replied, "I was just moving on. I've been waiting back there at bridge 45 for nearly four weeks now. And I wasn't going to come back here. You've made it in the nick of time."

"Yea, well," said Danny, his face wreathed in smiles, "I got a bit lost, see, otherwise I'd have been here yesterday."

"I see," said Alex. "You'd better tell me about it later." He paused. "I suppose you'd like some breakfast?"

"Cor, yes please, Mister," said Danny, with a grin. "I've been dreaming about your breakfasts, ever since I got took away, back at the supermarket. You're ain't half a good cook really. Can I have some sausages and bacon and a couple of eggs, please? And some toast to finish? And, have you still got the clothes you bought for me? Cos, while they're cooking, I'll have a shower, I'm feeling a bit grubby."

Alex looked the boy up and down. 'A bit grubby' was the understatement of the year. Danny's tee shirt and jeans were dirty and soiled, torn in several places, and there were several bits of straw on his hair, which looked as though it hadn't seen a comb for some time. His face and hands certainly hadn't seen any soap for quite a while. It was obvious that the boy had been living rough for more than the odd day or two. But it was also immediately apparent that Danny's cheerful disposition hadn't been dulled by what he'd gone through. His spirit was undiminished. It was likely that he'd have preferred to have been living rough, rather than continuing to experience the grim life at Grant Hall.

"Yes, Danny, I've still got all your clothes," Alex told him. "They're in the locker by your bunk. But once again, that's lucky, because after you were taken away at the supermarket, I thought at first that I'd never see you again. So, I tried to hand them back, but they wouldn't accept them. I asked at the customer services desk, but they said that I'd chosen to buy them, and since there was nothing wrong with them, there was no reason for the store to take them back. I suppose they'd got a point, really. But about the shower. I'm sorry, Danny, but it won't be possible for you to have a shower."

"Oh, of course," said Danny, "how silly of me. I forgot. There ain't no hot water, not till we've gone along for a bit. I'll have the shower later, then."

No, Danny, you don't understand," said Alex. "We don't have any water."

" What, no water?" asked Danny, looking a bit disappointed. "None at all?"

"That's right, Danny," replied Alex. "We have no water. None at all. We've run out of fresh water. The water tank is empty. As I said, I've been here for nearly a month now, and I've not been able to get any more. The water tank is at the front of the boat, and it can hold about 150 gallons. Look down there, at the front of the boat, for a moment. Do you see how much the boat is riding high in the water at the front? When the tank is full, we've got about three quarters of a ton of water on board, in the tank in the bow, and then the boat sits level, but as the water is used and the weight goes, then the bow rises up a bit. If I'd gone to fetch more water, I'd have been gone for several days, probably more. And during that time, you might have got here, found me gone, and moved on. I didn't want to risk that. I wanted to stay here for you for as long as possible, in case you turned up."

"Oh, OK then," said Danny, shrugging his shoulders. "I'll just have the breakfast, then. And then we can get moving, and find somewhere to fill up with water."

"No, Danny," Alex told the lad. "The sort of breakfast you've been looking forward to, well, that's just not possible either. I have almost no food left at all. And there's no gas left to heat it with either, that's all gone. And that's assuming we had anything left to heat up."

He turned and smiled at Danny, who looked a bit crestfallen by what he'd just heard. "But," Alex added, "I can rustle up some corned beef, and some baked beans for you, If you like – but they'll be cold."

"OK, then, Mister, that will be fine," Danny smiled. "It'll be loads better than what I had yesterday, anyway."

"So, what did you have yesterday, then?" Alex asked.

"Not much," Danny replied, as he turned and looked at Alex, grinning sheepishly. "Well, nothing, actually."

"Alright, then, Danny," Alex replied. "Get inside, and I'll be there in a moment. I'll just moor up the boat again first. But before I do that can you please tell me, those wounds and injuries which I was treating for you, have they all healed up properly now?"

"Yes, Mister, they have," Danny replied, grinning again. "I made sure I had a hot shower every day after I got back to Grant Hall, and kept them all really clean, as much as I could. By the time I got away again, they'd healed up just fine, which was just as well, because I haven't really been able to have a good wash since then."

"All of them?" Alex asked. "And the ones down below?"

"Yes, Mister, those too," Danny nodded. "But those ones, they took a lot longer to get better. I reckon that was because they were really bad. But that stuff you put on them, that did the trick. You know, when you put that stuff on, whatever it was, you said it might sting a little bit, but it did a lot more than sting. It was like having a chainsaw slicing up my butt, it hurt so much."

It was Alex's turn to smile now. "Yes, Danny," he grinned, "I knew it would. But if I'd told you in advance how much it would hurt, then perhaps you'd never have let me use it. But it's what was needed. I'm really glad that everything is better now. Anyway, you pop down inside while I moor up, then I'll see to what passes for your breakfast today."

Alex quickly banged his mooring pins into the ground and secured the mooring ropes, then went inside and got the boy his breakfast, sitting opposite him at the dinette whilst the boy ate. Once again, Alex noticed how slowly Danny ate his food, savouring every morsel to the full.

When the boy's plate was empty, they quickly cleared away, then went outside, untied the mooring ropes, and set off down the cut, *Jennifer Jo's* engine purring away nicely as they cruised along in the early morning sunshine, with Danny sitting beside Alex on the rear rail. Alex had mixed feeling about the spot where he'd been stopped for the past few weeks; whilst the shortages of fuel, food and water had become quite pressing in the end, he'd quite enjoyed the solitude, being there on his own and getting some more of his project work done. But he was looking forward to meeting other boaters once again, at some of the more popular locations along the canal.

After a while, Alex turned to Danny and asked him, "Danny, please will you tell me what's been happening to you, since we got separated at the supermarket? And, talking about that, there's something really important which I want you to know. I told you before, several times, that there was no secret agenda, and there really wasn't. There never has been, as far as I'm concerned. I want you to understand that I had no hand in what happened to you at the supermarket. It was as much a surprise to me as it was to you."

"I know that," said Danny, turning to Alex with a grin. "I did wonder a little bit at first, you know. But it weren't long before I realised that it was just bad luck, that's all. If I'd thought that you'd had something to do with it, well, then, I wouldn't be here now, would I? And what would you have been thinking of, buying me all those new clothes, if you'd be planning to have me took back to Grant Hall? It's not exactly rocket science, is it?"

Alex smiled. He couldn't fault the boy's logic. There was no way Danny would have returned to stay with someone whom he thought had already arranged for him to be apprehended by the authorities a few weeks previously.

"So what exactly happened to you, then?" asked Alex.

"Well," said Danny. "We were in the supermarket, right? At the checkouts? I went to the toilets, if you remember. I couldn't find the toilets at first, but I did find them eventually. They're right at the back of the store, and you have to go through the restaurant, that's at the back as well, you see, to get to them. So, I walked through the restaurant, it was crowded, really busy, like. I just went straight through the restaurant to the toilet, but when I came out, there was these two store security guards waiting outside the door, they just grabbed me and took me round to the manager's office. That's when I thought it were you what shopped me."

"But there sitting in the manager's office waiting for me was Mr. Prentice, he's one of the Wardens at Grant Hall. The first thing he said to me was 'you're the last person I expected to find here. What a piece of luck!' And that's when I knew it weren't you who'd had told them I was going to be there. You see, it seems that Mr Prentice, well, his Mum lives near the supermarket, and every couple of weeks or so, he drives over from Grant Hall for the twenty miles or so to see her, on his day off, and he takes her to the supermarket to do her shopping and stuff, and then they have a cup of tea and a sticky bun or whatever in the restaurant, before he takes her back home. So Mr. Prentice, he was just sitting there in the restaurant with his Mum, and he spotted me, he sussed it was me, when he saw me going into the toilet. I didn't notice him, you see, cos he was sitting with his back to me when I went through the restaurant."

"And after that, when the police came and took me away, I tried to spot you in the crowds round the checkouts, but I couldn't. That's when I grabbed the microphone from the lady at the desk and shouted 'forty-five'. I didn't even know whether you'd understand what I meant, or even if you'd heard what I'd said, but that was about all that I could do. I daren't say any more, but I just hoped that you'd remember how much time I'd spent looking at the Nicholson's guide, and understand what I was trying to say, that I'd try to get there, to bridge forty-five."

"Then I had to wait at the police station for a bit, they put me into a cell and locked me in, but they did come and give me something to eat and drink so that weren't too bad. Then Hammond arrived and he put me into the back of his car, and drove me back to Grant Hall. When he weren't looking, I tried the door handles to see if I could get out when the car was stopped at traffic lights or something, but the door wouldn't open, I think he must have set the child locks on the car doors. Anyway, eventually I ended up back at Grant Hall, and they put me straight into the Dark Room."

"So, what exactly is the Dark Room, Danny?" Alex asked. "It's real, then, is it? You said before that you'd heard rumours about it, but nobody knew much about it, or if it even existed."

"Oh, yes," Danny replied, "it's real, right enough. I found that out the hard way. When we got back to Grant Hall, we went inside, and then they took me down into the cellars under the main hall. Then they made me take off my clothes, all of them, even my briefs, so that I was completely naked. Then they opened this door and made me go inside this room, and as I went in Hammond said 'welcome to the Dark Room'. That's when I knew that the Dark Room wasn't a rumour after all, it was real, but they obviously only used it for kids who they wanted to punish really severely. There weren't anything in it, nothing at all, just the stone floor and four walls built of stone, and the ceiling, I think that was stone slabs as well."

"I said there weren't nothing in there but actually there was, there was just one thing, that was a bucket in the corner, that was all. Then they shut the door behind me, and I was left on my own. There weren't no windows or lights in that room, nothing at all, it was completely dark in there, and pretty cold at times as well, and there weren't no seat or bench or bed or anything to sit or lie down on. There was just the bucket in the corner for you to pee into, if you could find it in the dark, that is. Then this strange noise started, it was really loud, it were really awful, and it never stopped, it was, like, when your radio goes out of tune, and all you get is this funny hissing noise. It just went on and on, really loud, it made you want to climb up the wall. It was horrible in there, it really was."

Danny stopped talking and was quiet for a while, reflecting no doubt on the time he'd had to spend in the Dark Room.

Alex took the opportunity to say a few words. "They made you strip naked to take away any human dignity you might have had," he told the boy. "Just to demoralise you as much as they could. And I know what the noise was. It's what they call White Noise. The American troops in Iraq and Afghanistan used it, to disorientate prisoners before they were interrogated. I'm told it can be very unpleasant."

"No, Mister." Danny looked round at Alex, an impatient look in his eyes. "I told you, there weren't nothing white in there, it was really dark in there, completely black, all the time. There weren't no lights or anything. You couldn't see a thing." He paused for a moment. "Look here, if you're not going to listen properly, I'm not going to tell you anything else. I'd be just wasting my time."

"OK, Danny, I'm sorry," said Alex with a wry smile. "I'm listening. Please go on. How long were you kept in the Dark Room?"

"Well, the other kids reckoned that I was in the Dark Room for nearly two days," Danny replied. "That's what they thought, anyway, cos they were in the school room when Hammond brought me back in his car, they could see it all out of the window, though they're not supposed to look out while there's lessons or work going on, but it weren't actually lessons, they were doing their evening homework. It weren't very nice in the Dark Room, and there weren't anything to eat or drink in all that while, they didn't give me any food or water at all. And it was really cold in there as well, all of the time I was there, it never got warm at all, cos there was just the stone floor to sit or lie on, and I didn't have any clothes or anything to keep me warm. In fact, it was terrible, I hated being in there. It's no wonder that they use it as a punishment."

"When they let me out it were lunch time, first I had a shower and put some clean clothes on, then they said I could go straight in to the dining room for lunch. When I got there, all the other kids were already in there, sitting down and having their lunch, but as soon as I walked in the door, they started cheering and shouting and banging their plates on the table and stamping their shoes on the floor. It was just like you see on the TV in war films, when escaped soldiers are recaptured and taken back to their prison camps. It was a really wonderful reception what the other kids gave me when I went into the room. You see, I think I was the only kid what had ever got away from Grant Hall. But Hammond, he was furious when all this was going on, he shouted for everyone to shut up and be quiet, but no-one took any notice of him, none at all, they all just carried on banging and stamping their feet, it was really noisy. And the more Hammond shouted at them to be quiet, the more noise they all made."

"I think it were the first time ever at Grant Hall that he'd lost control of the situation, but it didn't last very long, cos he went and closed the door from the dining room into the kitchen, then he got out his keys and locked it, and then he went to the only other door, that's the one that goes into the main hall, and he took a chair and put it by the door. Then he got his cane, and he held it in one hand and kept tapping his other hand with it. The message was obvious, and it went really quiet ever so quick. When the lunch was finished, everyone had to lean over the back of the chair and get a stroke of the cane as they went out of the room. I got two strokes, but then if I'd been Black One then I'd have got loads and loads, my bum would have been in shreds. It were lucky, I was really surprised they didn't make me Black One as soon as I got back, but they didn't, I dunno why. It weren't very nice, everybody getting the cane like that, but afterwards all the kids said it was worth it just to see the expression on Hammond's face, he very nearly lost it. But of course, he won in the end, he always does."

Danny went quiet once again, but after a couple of minutes he gave a cheerful wave to the crew of another boat as it passed them, going in the other direction. "So, what happened after that?" Alex asked.

"Well, it were back into the usual routine for a while," replied Danny. "I kept thinking about ways to get away again. I thought and thought about it for ages, but like what I said to you before, there ain't no way out of Grant Hall, except one. I'm absolutely convinced, the only way out is to walk out of the door."

"But you did get away again," Alex reminded him.

"Yea, that's right," said Danny. "You see, on the Sunday, they put the work rota up on the notice board for the next couple of weeks, and I got a real surprise, cos they'd put me down on the list for gardening duty. I couldn't believe it, but they had."

"So, tell me about the gardening duty then, please," Alex asked Danny, who didn't seem to be taking any notice. He was waving furiously at a young girl, about the same age as himself, walking her dog along the towpath with her parents. "If, that is, you can tear yourself away from the scenery," Alex added, with a wry smile.

Danny grinned as he was rewarded with a nice smile from the girl, and a friendly wave in reply. Alex really liked the pleasant atmosphere that existed on the cut, the way boaters and towpath users all waved and acknowledged each other– a wave was a friendly gesture, and the absence of some sort of a greeting was considered to be a bit of a mild insult. And Danny seemed to be wholeheartedly entering into the spirit of things, especially where young girls were concerned.

"Gardening duty, then?" Alex reminded Danny, who was still looking back at his newfound friend as she disappeared along the towpath as *Jennifer Jo* rounded a slight bend in the canal.

"Oh, yea," said Danny at last, "gardening duty. Well, there's a work rota goes up on the notice board every fortnight, and there's about a dozen kids put down for gardening duty, then at the end of the two weeks, it all changes round, cos there's a new rota goes up, and you might end up on kitchen duty, or in the school room for lessons, or cleaning and decorating, or whatever else they want you to do. You just don't know till the rota goes up on the board. If you're on gardening duty, a couple of kids have to do the grounds round the hall, but the gate out of the grounds into the park is always kept locked, so they can't get out, there's no way they could do that. The rest have to go down the kitchen garden, you go out of the gate and through into the park, that's about 15 minutes walk to get there, but we normally do it in about ten minutes, cos we get marched there and back, as if we're in the Army. Although some of the kids are allowed to walk, cos they're carrying the boxes, it's one box between two of us, cos they're quite heavy really, even when they're empty."

"What are those boxes, then, Danny?" asked Alex, intrigued.

"It's wooden boxes, what they bring the produce back in, from the kitchen garden, when you've finished every day, bringing the stuff they've harvested back to the Hall. They get took back to the kitchen garden empty, except for a couple of the boxes, cos they've got the lunches in. You know, the sandwiches and the apples, cos once you get to the garden you're not allowed out again, until it's time to go back to the Hall in the late afternoon. The kitchen garden, I think, it was made when there was posh people lived in Grant Hall a hundred years ago. It's on a south-facing slope so it gets the sun, and its completely surrounded by this big high red brick wall, it's about 11 or 12 feet high. When you get there, to the garden, they unlock the gate and let you in, there's only one gate, you see, and then once you're in they lock the gate again until it's time to go back to the Hall, that's when they unlock the gate again and let you out, and you get marched back, but this time of course, some of us have to carry the boxes of spuds and cabbages and carrots and stuff, for them to put in the stew for the suppers."

"The kitchen garden, It's huge, it really is, it takes you a couple of minutes, maybe more, to walk from one end to the other. Apparently it was really overgrown and run down, it hadn't been used for years and years, but about nine months ago they started getting the kids to sort it out, and about half of it is sorted now, and growing crops and stuff. There's some old guy from the village what comes in on his bike three of four times a week for an hour or so in the mornings, and he tells the Wardens what he wants done. Then he goes off home and leaves us to it, to do all the work, while the Wardens, well they just stand about and watch and make sure we're not slacking nor anything."

"There ain't no chance to get away when we're being marched down to the garden, or back again afterwards, cos usually Hammond is there with Brutus. If you made a run for it, then the Rottie would get you, no messing, he'd take your leg off with one bite, and probably he'd eat it as well, before Hammond could pull him off. Sometimes Hammond stays there all day, but quite often he goes after a bit, and then he comes back in the afternoon to make sure we've done all the work what the old guy wanted doing, and escort us all back to the Hall."

"There's all sorts of veggies growing there, spuds, carrots, cabbages, and so on, and there's some fruit bushes as well, like raspberries and blackcurrants and blackberries, and there's some strawberry plants too. But when it's the fruit that's ready to be picked, the Wardens watch you like hawks, you're not allowed to eat any while you're picking them, if you do then Hammond gets told and you get a couple of strokes of the lash or the cane. And when they get taken back to the Hall, you don't get to eat them, cos the Wardens, they get to have them all, lucky sods. We do all the work in the garden and they get to eat all the best stuff, it's not fair, but that's like what it is at Grant Hall."

"Down in the kitchen garden, they put me and a couple of the others on clearing out some of the overgrown parts. They were digging out the weeds and stuff, and I had to load up the wheelbarrow with all the stuff they dug out, then take it round to the compost heap behind the greenhouse, and fork it onto the top of the heap, it's quite high, there's no end of stuff been dug out. It's hard work down there in the veggie garden, you have to work all the time without a break. Except at lunch time, you get twenty minutes to sit and have your lunch, otherwise you've got to keep going all the time."

"But you're allowed to have a drink of water any time you want, there's a tap beside the greenhouse when you can get a drink if you bend down and stick your mouth underneath it. Once or twice, when Hammond weren't there, it was a really hot day, and it was Mr. Prentice in charge, he's really nice, he'd let you put the hose onto the tap and one of the kids could spray the others with cold water, and you could have a little run around, and try to dodge the water. That was fun, but then one time we were doing that and Hammond came back early and caught us doing it. There was a right row, he was really cross with Mr. Prentice, and he weren't allowed to be in charge, down at the veggie garden, after that."

As Danny paused again, Alex reflected on how Danny referred to the various Wardens who were in charge at Grant Hall. It was always Mr. Prentice or Mr. Whoever, but never Mr. Hammond. It was always just 'Hammond'. It showed, Alex thought, that the boy had respect for some of the staff there, but none at all for this guy Hammond.

"You didn't like this Hammond guy, did you?" Alex asked.

"No, nobody did," the lad replied. "Would you? One or two of the Wardens, like Mr. Prentice, well, they were really nice. So was Mr. Wilkins, who I gave the slip to at the dentist's the other week. A few others were

OK, but most of them just took their lead from Hammond, and some of them, they seemed to really enjoy being nasty to us all. It weren't very nice at Grant Hall, not very pleasant at all."

"There ain't no way to get out of the kitchen garden, I looked and looked for a way out, but there ain't none, the walls are too high. There's some new young fruit trees what they've had us plant out, tied right up against the wall, they're being trained to run along the wall, you know, with these wires, what are fixed to the wall with nails, but the trees ain't strong enough yet for anyone to climb up. If you did try to climb up them, they'd break really easily, and the nails aren't long enough to give you a foothold, I looked at them. There ain't no chance of climbing up the walls to get over."

"So, if you couldn't get away when you're all going to or from the kitchen garden, and you couldn't get out from inside the garden, why was it so good to be put on gardening duty?" Alex asked. "After all, you said it was hard work in there, and you only got a short break at lunchtimes. How did you manage to get away? Was it from the Hall, or from the kitchen garden? Or somehow else?"

Danny turned to look at Alex, with a wide grin stretching from ear to ear. "I got out of the kitchen garden," he said triumphantly. "That weren't bad, was it? They never thought anyone could get out of there. But I did. That taught them. I bet Hammond was furious when he found out how I got out."

"So, how did you manage it?" Alex asked. He was itching to know how the boy had managed to get away, to do what on the face of it seemed to be impossible.

"I aren't telling you," replied Danny, with a mischievous grin. "But I might, if you let me choose what we have for supper."

"Well," Alex replied, "if we don't get to the shop at the marina before it closes, then it will have to be just baked beans again. Cold. But we're making good progress, we should be there in a hour or so. there may not be a very wide choice at the shop, there never is at these small places. They usually only have the essentials like bread, butter, cheese, milk, eggs, possibly some bacon if we're lucky, but there'll certainly be some tins as well, tinned meat, tinned fruit, that sort of thing. But it will be sufficient to keep us going, until we find a supermarket to properly stock up again."

"So, go on, please," Alex continued. "I'll cook you a really great supper if you tell me how you escaped. You can certainly choose what we have, from what we've been able to buy at the shop."

"OK," Danny said, still smiling. "It were like this." He paused again, just to tease Alex, who gave him a mild nudge in the ribs to get him going.

"Like I said, I had to take the weeds and stuff round to the compost heap, round the back of the greenhouse. Well, I told you about the wooden boxes, what we take the produce back to the hall in, well, there's this big pile of boxes round behind the greenhouse, just near the compost heap. The boxes are supposed to be stacked neat and tidy, like, but they aren't. They're just piled up higgledy-piggledy in a big heap."

"So, every time I went round to the compost heap with the wheelbarrow, that's every quarter of an hour or so, I rearranged some of the boxes, just two or three at a time, only a few at a time, so no one else would notice. After about three or four days, I'd managed to make a small hiding place, like a cave, inside the pile of boxes. It was well hidden, you had to know what boxes to pull out to see the hiding place I'd made inside, and if you pulled the wrong ones out, well then the whole pile would have collapsed and the hiding place would have been destroyed, and I'd have had to start all over again. I had to be really careful when I moved the boxes about, you see, I couldn't move any of the boxes when there was anyone else there, but like I said, after about a week it was all done and ready."

"I couldn't do anything else, not until till I knew that Hammond weren't going to be there at the garden, cos if I'd hidden in the den I'd made inside the pile of boxes when he was going to be there with Brutus, well the Rottie would have smelt me out in a moment. But one night, it was when I'd got called out of the dorm for me to do the ball game for them, I heard Hammond talking to one of the other Wardens. He said he'd got to go down to London for a couple of days for some conference or other, and he'd be staying in a hotel for the night. So I knew that would be my best chance of getting away, with Hammond out of the picture for a couple of days, it was going to be my best chance."

"The first day he was away, it were Mr. Prentice and Mr. McCall who took us down to the garden. I worked normally during the morning, and at lunchtime when they handed out the sandwiches and apples and did the roll call, I was there, and made sure that everyone could see me, just like as if it was a normal day. But after lunch was over, I decided that I was definitely going to go that day, cos the weather was nice and looked like it should stay that way for several days. I was going to get out and get away, and this time try to keep out of Hammonds' clutches."

"But I needed some help, though, so I asked a couple of the kids, they were Jamie Blanchard and Johnny Raeburn, if they'd help me. They was really good about it, they said I was nuts to try, but as soon as I told them what I wanted them to do, they said OK. Once they'd agreed to it, I chose my moment when no-one else was looking, and left my wheelbarrow half full where we was clearing out the weeds, and went behind the greenhouse to have a pee. There ain't a toilet in the garden, you see, everyone goes behind the greenhouse and pees into the compost heap, they reckon it helps the stuff to rot down quicker, but I don't really know if that's true or not."

"Anyway, when I'd had a pee, there weren't no-one else about, so I pulled out a couple of the boxes, and crawled inside the pile, into the little sort of cave I'd made earlier, and then I pulled the boxes in behind me. So I just lay there under the boxes, and no-one else knew I was there, except Johnny and Jamie, and they weren't going to tell, cos I trusted them to help me get away."

"It was about an hour before anyone missed me, and then I heard Mr. Prentice asking if anyone had seen me, and all the other kids said no. But that's where John and Jamie had to do their bit, they said that they'd seen me climbing up the apple trees what were growing by the wall, and climb over the wall and jump down the other side. It was really good of them to say that, because they knew that they'd get the cane off Hammond when he found out that they'd seen me getting over the wall and not told anyone, not told the Wardens or anything. But I needed them to do that, so it would put the Wardens and everyone else off the scent, cos if they'd thought that I might still be in the garden, then they'd have made a really good search, and probably found me hiding inside the pile of wooden boxes."

"Even though I was inside the pile of boxes, I could hear what was going on, and well, Mr. Prentice and Mr. McCall, they were in a right stew then. I could hear them talking about what to do, and after a little while they decided to get everyone back to the Hall, and phone Hammond. So they all went back to the Hall, and I heard them locking the gate, and then I was all alone in the garden, hidden inside the pile of boxes in the garden, behind the greenhouse."

"I stayed there for ages, until it was almost dark, and then I thought it would be safe to come out, so I crawled out, and my muscles all ached from having to lie still for so long in my cave, but I was OK after a little while. I went into the greenhouse and lay down on a couple of sacks underneath one of the benches, and tried to get some sleep, I think I did for a bit, but not much. But after a while, the moon came out and it was time for me to get out of the garden."

"So, how did you do that, Danny?" asked Alex. "You said it wasn't possible to climb the walls and get over."

"No, Mister, it were easy, really easy, once I was there on my own." Danny turned to Alex and grinned. "I just got some of the wooden boxes and stacked them upside down against the wall, they're really quite strong, strong enough for you to stand on. I started off with just one, then beside it I put two, one on top of the other, then next to that I put three, again with them all on top of each other, then a pile of four boxes beside that, and so on until they reached almost to the top of the wall. I made a big pile, really neat, it must have taken me about half an hour altogether."

"I had a bit of a rest then, I just sat on the grass for a couple of minutes and admired my stairway to freedom which I'd just built. Then I just climbed up the boxes and when I got to the top of the wall, I checked there weren't no-one about, and there weren't, I mean it was really late, so then I climbed over, and jumped down onto the grass the other side."

" And I was free!" Danny shouted loudly. He got up from the rear rail for a moment, and jumped up and down, waving his arms in the air. He turned and looked at Alex. "You don't know what it's like to be out of that place," he said, "to be free again. I know Hammond would half kill me if I got caught again, because that was the second time I'd got away in less than a month, he'd take it as a personal insult, so I had to make sure I didn't get caught this time."

Alex had to hand it to Danny. He'd thought up a cunning plan to get away from Grant Hall, and against all the odds he'd succeeded. If he'd not been put on gardening duty, then he might have been there still. But, as it was, here he was on *Jennifer Jo*, cruising up the canal and every minute being taken just that little bit further away from Grant Hall, hopefully never to go back to the dismal life that seemed to be the norm for the youngsters who had to live there. As far as Alex was concerned, he was determined that he would do all that he could to help and support the lad. There was no doubt that Danny deserved a better life than he'd been getting for some time past.

"So, what did you do, once you'd got over the wall?" asked Alex. He had to hand it to the boy, he'd shown some real ingenuity in devising a plan to get out of the garden, and away from Grant Hall. But he still might have been caught; there would have been a thorough search taking place for him, once the authorities had realised that he had gone missing.

"I just ran," said Danny. "I ran and ran and ran. And when I couldn't run any further, I ran some more." Alex smiled at the way Danny had put it, as the boy continued, "Not fast, but a fair trot, I suppose you'd call it. All that running round the grounds of the Hall three times a week must have done me some good after all." He turned to Alex and grinned once again. "I ran and ran until it started to get light again, then I decided I'd better hide up somewhere and wait till the evening again, cos I knew they'd all be out searching for me, during the daytime."

"How long ago was this, when you got away, Danny?" Alex asked. "How long have you been on the run?"

"I think it must have been a couple of weeks ago, when I went over the wall," Danny replied, serious for a moment. "It's difficult to keep track of the days when you're living rough like I was. Because I had to hide up for most of the day-time, I didn't get very far each day. And some nights there wasn't any moon or anything, so I couldn't really see to go anywhere anyway. I just had to hide up and wait for the clouds to go and the moon to come out, or something like that."

"So, where did you hide up, then?" asked Alex. "Did you find a farmer's barn in a field, or something like that? I suppose that's just about the best place to hide in?"

"Well, actually, no, it's not," replied Danny. "A barn's pretty good, but the thing is, a barn is the sort of place they'd look in first, when they're looking for you. There's a much better place to hide than that, and I was lucky, really lucky, cos I found what probably was the very best place of all to hide in, for that first day."

"Tell me, then, where did you hide?" Alex enquired, his curiosity aroused now.

"I found a stack," said Danny. "That's the best place of all to hide in. It's almost impossible for anyone to find you there."

"What do you mean, a stack?" Alex asked him, a bit puzzled.

"A straw stack," Danny replied. "You know, when the farmer's had the combine harvester in the field, to cut the barley or wheat or whatever, the straw is all thrown out the back, and then they come along with a baler or something, it gathers up all the straw into big rectangular bales, and then they build all the straw bales into a big stack, that's the best place of all to hide in."

"So how do you hide in a stack," asked Alex, still puzzled. "I mean, it's solid straw, isn't it?"

"Well, yes," Danny replied, "but there's places to hide in it, really good places, as long as you know where to hide."

"Where, then?" asked Alex.

"Well, what you do is this." Danny paused again, enjoying the teasing he was dishing out to Alex. "First, you break off two or three stout sticks from the hedge," he went on, "and then you climb up the stack. It's really easy, you can use the red string what they wrap round the bales, you know, when they come out of the baling machine, to use as hand holds, it's really strong, you know, and you can shove your feet into the joints between the bales."

"Then, you climb up the stack, right up onto the top, but you've got to take the sticks with you, of course, what you've just got out of the hedge. When you're on the top, you lift out one of the bales, they're really heavy but I managed it alright, and then you lift out a second one from directly underneath where the first one was. So now, you've got a bit of a hole in the top of the stack, it's the size and shape of one single bale, but of course, it's two bales deep. Then you can wedge the sticks what you've brought up with you, into the joints across the gap you've made, so they're one bale above the floor of the hole, the hiding place you've made. Then, you can get inside the hole, and pull one of the bales down over you, and the sticks what you've put in, in between the bales, they keep it off you."

"It's really nice in there, it's like a little nest inside the stack. It's nice and warm when it's cold, and dry if it rains, and no-one on the ground knows that you're there. Even if they've got a helicopter up looking for you, all it will see is one odd bale on the top of the stack, and if you put that neatly lined up with all the others, no-one would think that there's anything wrong. The only other thing you've got to do, is, when you leave, is to put all the bales back properly, so no-one will ever know you've been there. Otherwise, if they sussed it out, you wouldn't be able to use that sort of hiding place again in the future, cos they'd be on the lookout for it."

Alex had to hand it to the lad. Once again, he'd displayed a remarkable talent for improvising. Hiding inside a straw stack, like Danny had done, would never have occurred to Alex, not in a million years.

"Well, Danny, where else did you hide, then?" asked Alex.

"Well, barns, of course, like you said. There's only a few straw stacks about now, cos it's nearly harvest time again, and they've used most of the straw to bed the cattle down when they bring them in over the winter, into the barns. I hid in the woods sometimes as well, you can build a bit of a shelter out of fallen branches and so on. I managed. After all, its summer, and I was moving most nights, and hiding up during the daytime. It weren't really difficult, if you want to hide up and not be caught, there's plenty of places, if you look around and try to make use of what's available."

"What about food?" Alex asked. "It can't have been easy getting something to eat every day."

"Well, actually, I didn't eat every day," Danny said. "Some days, I didn't have anything to eat at all. The first day I didn't have anything, but the next day, I came across this field of carrots, it was huge, you couldn't see one side of the field from the other. So I ate a load of carrots, they filled me up, but It didn't really stop me from being hungry. I suppose it was pinching really, and I don't do pinching, but I was really hungry, and I'm sure the farmer wouldn't miss a few, like what I said, the field was huge, there must have been millions of carrots in there."

"Then, a couple of days later, I had some hot potatoes," Danny exclaimed proudly. "Hot potatoes, would you believe that?"

"Well, actually, now that I know you a little bit now, I suppose I would," replied Alex. "But, just how did you manage to get hot potatoes? Did some little old lady in an isolated cottage somewhere take pity on you and feed you up?"

"Oh, no, it weren't like that at all," Danny replied. "I was hiding in these woods, right, and there was this big potato field next to the woods. And on the other side of the potato field, there was these blokes working, they were cutting back the hedges, they were really overgrown. They were saving all the big bits, cutting them up into logs and sticks, for firewood and kindling I suppose, and all the smaller bits, the twigs and branches and stuff, well they'd got a bonfire going, and they were burning them. But after a bit, later on, they all went home for the night, so I pulled out some potatoes from the field, and put them in the embers to cook. They were really nice. But after I'd eaten them, I was still a bit hungry, so I went and got some more, and did another load. Then I went back again and got some more and had a third helping. And then I cooked some more still, but those I wrapped them in my hankie and took them with me, and I had them later on."

"And then, couple of days later, I had some cake, washed down with a bottle of milk!" Danny proclaimed, proud of his prowess in fending for himself. "And I didn't really pinch them either, Mum always taught me never to pinch anything. I'm sorry about the carrots and potatoes, but I was really hungry then."

"Well, as you said, there were plenty in the field," said Alex, "but, tell me about the cakes and milk. Was there some little old lady who took pity on you after all?"

"Well, it were like this, Mister," Danny told him. "I was having a kip in this bus shelter one morning, on the outskirts of some village. I was lying down on the bench in the bus shelter, and I saw this one pound coin on the floor, right tucked up in the corner it was. I reckon someone had dropped it and couldn't find, it, cos I only managed to see it cos I was lying down, if you'd been sitting on the bench or standing up, you'd never have seen it. So I picked it up and put it in my pocket. I mean, it had been lost, and it had been there for ages, it was really dirty. That weren't really pinching, was it?"

Alex shook his head. "No, Danny, I would say that was alright," he reassured the boy. "Please go on, tell me about the cakes and milk."

"Ok, then, Mister. Then I went into the village, it was really early in the morning, there weren't no-one about. But I reckon It must have been dustbin day, cos all the wheelie bins, they'd must have been put out the night before, cos they were all lined up along the road, on both sides, like soldiers at a military parade or something like that, it was really funny. So I had a look inside the bins as I went along, cos I was hungry, see, and there, in the top of one of the bins, was this packet of cakes, fancy cakes they were, you know little sponge cakes, with the knob of cream on the top, and all covered with icing, you know, yellow, pink, or brown icing– that's chocolate flavour, isn't it?"

Danny didn't stop for Alex to reply. "They were still in the packet," he went on. "I thought they'd been slung out cos they were out of date, I looked on the box, but they were only a day or so over the 'best by' date, so I reckoned it was OK to eat them. And just as I was getting the cakes out of the box, this milkman came along, delivering milk, he was. I hid behind a hedge while he went past. Then, I thought, well, I've got this pound coin, so I took a bottle of milk off one of the doorsteps and left the pound coin there to pay for it. That weren't pinching, Mister, was it?" Danny asked, anxious for Alex's approval.

"I suppose not, no, if you paid for it, I reckon that would have been OK," 'Alex reassured the lad. "Although, probably, the person who lived there might have been a little bit peeved that they hadn't got all the milk they'd ordered. But, did you enjoy the cake, and the milk?"

"Yea, I did," said Danny with a grin. "They were really nice. But I didn't have much to eat really, all the time I was on the run. But it was almost as much as they gave you at Grant Hall, actually. Not a patch on what you fed me, when I was here on your boat with you last time."

"I'll feed you up now, don't you worry about that," Alex said. "You won't go hungry again, not whilst you're with me, anyway. But first, we've got to get to the marina in time, if we're going to eat tonight. But it shouldn't be long now."

"Yea, that's great," Danny replied, grinning again. "Remember, I'm choosing?"

"Yes OK, Danny." Alex turned and smiled back at Danny, who was obviously looking forward to his first decent meal in days. "It's your choice. But, tell me, when you were on the run, what about drink, you've got to have water, or something else to drink, as well as food, a single bottle of milk in over a week isn't enough."

"No Mister, drinking's easy," Danny replied. "It's easier than finding food to eat, actually. Its summer, right, and there's lots of houses have an outside tap, what you can go and have a drink at, and if you only turn the tap on a little so the water don't make a noise in the pipes, it won't disturb anyone inside. And, there's hoses at the petrol stations, which they use to wash the cars with, and also, there's garden sprinklers left on the lawns of some of the houses overnight. No, water's not a problem, I never had to drink water out of a ditch or stream or anything. I mean, you never know what bugs and stuff you're drinking with the water, when you get some water from a ditch or whatever."

"So you eventually made your way to the canal, then?" asked Alex.

"Yea, well," replied Danny, "I knew roughly in what direction to go, but I didn't know how far it was, and I lost my bearings a bit, cos I didn't have a map or anything."

"But you found it in the end," Alex said.

"Yes," Danny grinned. "Like I just said, I knew roughly what direction to go in, and eventually I found the canal, but then I had a sort of problem, cos the part of the canal what I got to, I didn't know what direction to go in to get to bridge 45, should I go right or left along the towpath?"

"In the end, I went left along the towpath, but it was ages before I got to a bridge, and it were bridge number 39. But that still didn't help me, cos I still didn't know, if I carried on in the same direction, if I'd get to bridge 38 or bridge 40, so I just carried on the way I was going. It took ages to get to another bridge, and that didn't have a number on it at all. I knew to look on both sides of the bridge to find the number, but the plates what should have been there were missing, you could see where they used to be."

"So I had to go on even further, and eventually I got to the next bridge, and that was bridge 37, so then I had to turn round and go back all the way I'd come, and then on some more, and eventually I knew I was getting close to bridge 45. But when I heard a boat coming, I didn't know who it was, so that's why I hid in the hedge. But when I recognised that it was *Jennifer Jo*, that's when I came out and shouted to you."

"I'm really glad you did," Alex replied. "I've been very worried about you, wondering about how you were getting on. But I'm glad you're back aboard with me now. As I said, we're just about out of provisions, food, fuels, everything. I couldn't have stayed there at bridge 45 any longer. I just HAD to go."

" Yea, I understand," said Danny. "But it don't matter now, cos I'm here."

"That's right Danny." Alex replied, smiling at the lad, who seemed to be pleased that he'd found his way back to *Jennifer Jo*. "I'm glad you made it. But there's one thing I want to ask you, if I can, please?"

"What's that, Mister?" asked Danny, curious now.

"Well, while you were back in Grant Hall, were those men you told me about, you know, the ones who came to the Hall late at night in those big cars, were they still coming to the Hall? And were some of the boys still being called down to be with them?"

"Oh, yea, they still came," Danny replied, scowling as he spoke. "Every Tuesday night, and sometimes other nights as well. But we started doing like what you suggested."

"What's that then," Alex asked, enquiringly. "I don't remember suggesting anything to you."

"Well, you asked did we know who they were, or did we get their car numbers or anything, didn't you?"

"Yes that's right, I did," replied Alex.

"Well, we started spotting the car numbers and writing them down, and we put down the dates when they came as well, and the names of whoever it was got called down. Sometimes it was someone from our dorm, and sometimes it was someone from one of the other dorms, but we found out the next morning who it was, and it all got written down. We used a bit of a code, so no-one else would know what it meant, except one of us, that is. And we hid the piece of paper so no- one could find it, unless they knew where it was, cos if Hammond or any of the others had found out about it, then we'd have been for it, no question about that."

"Where did you hide it then?" asked Alex.

"Well Mr. McCall, you see, he's a smoker, he makes his own fags, rollups, and when one of his tobacco tins is empty, he puts it in one of the rubbish baskets, so we found one and fished it out of the basket and used the tin to put the paper in, inside the tin. And then we hid the tin under one of the floorboards in the dorm, under Stevie Anson's locker it was, we found the loose floorboard a couple of months ago when we had to paint the floorboards in the dorm, but normally Stevie's locker is over it, we had to move it to do the painting, see? Otherwise, the locker never gets moved, no-one else apart from us kids in the dorm know about it, no-one else would know where to look."

"That seems as good a place as any, doesn't it, Danny?" Alex replied. "Let's hope it will be safe there."

"Yea," Danny was quiet for a moment. "It should be OK. But I don't know if they'll keep on taking the numbers and so on, now I'm not there any more."

"Well, let's hope so," said Alex. "They might come in useful at some time in the future. But look, there's the marina, just appearing round the bend up ahead. We're in good time, so we'll be able to get all the things we need there."

As Alex deftly brought *Jennifer Jo* in to the bank right by the servicing area, and moored her up, an attendant appeared from out of the adjacent workshop. "Hello," he said, "what can I do for you?"

"Well," replied Alex, "can we have some diesel, a full tank please, and also, two bottle of gas, and a pump-out for the toilet. And, while you're doing that for us, Danny here will be getting some water sorted out."

"That's fine, I'll see to you right away," the attendant replied, adding "the water tap's over there, young man," as he looked at Danny.

"OK," said Danny. Turning to Alex, he asked, "hey Mister, what do I need to do for the water?"

"That's easy, Danny," Alex replied. "If you slip down into the saloon, then pull back the steps which lead up to the cratch, you'll gain access to the storage locker underneath the floor of the cratch. In there, you'll see a reel of water hose. Fish it out, and connect one end to the tap over there, it screws on, so it'll be no problem, and then put the other end into the water filler on the boat, and off you go. But since the tank is empty, it will take about 45 minutes to fill it up. That will give me time to get everything else sorted out."

"Yes, but where's the water filler?" asked Danny. "Where do I put the water in?"

"It's near the bow, just in front of the front cratchboard," Alex replied. "But you'll need a special key to get the cap off. It's a funny curvy metal key. That's kept on the shelf in the galley, beside the clock. Have a look, you'll soon find it. And, after you've connected the hose, run the tap into the canal for about half-a-minute before you start filling the tank. That will get any stale water which was left in the hose from the last time it was used, out of the system."

"OK Mister," said Danny with his usual trademark grin, "leave it to me, I'll find it and sort it for you."

"Right-oh," replied Alex, "and while it's filling, there's several bags of rubbish to get rid of in the galley, ask the guy doing the diesel, he'll tell you where the bins are. And when you've done that, and I've sorted out all the other things, we'll pay a visit to the shop."

It was almost an hour later before Danny came up to Alex. "Hey, Mister, the tank's full now, and I've done the bins like you said. Shall I put the hose back in the locker under the cratch?"

"No, not yet, Danny," Alex replied. "We need to try and make sure there's no water left in the hose, otherwise it tends to get stale, like I told you before. Here, I'll show you how it's done." They rolled out the full length of the hose along the concrete beside the boat, and then Alex held the hose reel up high while turning the handle, allowing the water left in the hose to drain away from the free end as it was wound back onto the reel. "Right, Danny," Alex said, "that's a good job done. Would you like to pop the hose back into the locker now, and then let's get to the shop, they'll be closing shortly."

"OK, Mister," Danny said, adding with a grin, "remember, I'm choosing, right?"

"Yes, that's right, that was the bargain," replied Alex. He was beginning to like the boy's cheerful humour. "You can choose, but they'll only have a small selection, because it's only a small shop, but we should be able to get all the essentials. Let's see what they have, first."

Alex made his way to the shop, where Danny joined him a few moments later. It wasn't long before they were making their way back to *Jennifer Jo*, each bearing two carrier bags of provisions. As they were walking back to the boat, Alex turned to Danny and asked "well, Danny, have you decided yet what we're having for supper?"

"Yes, I have," said Danny, yet another grin on his face. "Fish and chips, please."

"But, Danny, we haven't got any fish, nor any chips either," said Alex, slightly bemused. "They didn't have any in the freezer, remember?"

"Yea, that's right, they didn't, Mister," Danny said. "But look over there," and he pointed to the gate of the marina which led out to the road. There, just pulling up outside the gate, was a mobile fish and chip van, its steaming chimney sending a delicious aroma wafting towards them. A small knot of people who'd been waiting patiently by the gate moved forwards to the van, as the attendant started serving his customers. "Didn't you see the notice in the shop?" Danny asked. "It says the fish and chip van comes here every Tuesday and Thursday at 5 o'clock. I checked the clock on the wall in the shop just now."

"Well, fish and chips it is, Danny." It was Alex's turn to grin. "A good choice. Well spotted." Taking a ten-pound note from his wallet, he added "here, go get the supper, I'll go and put the kettle on. And we've got the last apple pie they had in the shop, how do you fancy that for afters?"

"Sounds good to me," replied Danny, taking the money. "Back in a mo."

Alex and Danny sat at the dinette and enjoyed their meal. "That was pretty good, Mister, weren't it?" smiled Danny. "It's the best fish and chips I've had for ages. And the apple pie just now weren't bad either."

"I'm glad you enjoyed it," replied Alex. "I did too. It makes a change, because there's not much chance to get fresh fish and chips when you're afloat."

"We didn't get nothing like that at Grant Hall," Danny commented sadly. "It were stew all the time."

"No, I'm sure you didn't," said Alex. "But, before we clear up, there's some things I want to talk to you about."

A cautious, almost scared, look instantly appeared on Danny's face. "What's that, then?" he asked nervously. Alex realised that the boy was still feeling very insecure, and was perhaps a little unsure as to whether Alex would let him stay in his new found home.

"Oh, it's nothing serious," Alex replied. "Just some things you ought to know."

"Like what?" asked Danny, still looking a bit worried.

"Well, first of all, relax," replied Alex. "Like I said before, there is absolutely no hidden agenda whilst you're here with me. I want you to know that you're welcome to stay with me here, on board *Jennifer Jo,* for as long as you want. You need to understand that I really mean that."

"You're sure ?" Danny asked, smiling again. "Really?"

"Yes." Alex replied. "This can be your home now." Alex had thought long and hard about giving Danny a permanent home with him on *Jennifer Jo*, but had come to the same conclusion which he'd reached a few weeks previously. The boy had nowhere else to go to, and returning him to the further misery that would be inflicted upon him at Grant Hall was out of the question. Should the authorities catch up with them, then Alex would be for the high jump, but he'd decided that with his exemplary record as a schoolteacher and later as a house master for all of his adult years, would stand him on good stead, should any prosecution arise for abduction of a minor, or whatever.

But Danny was smiling again. "Thanks, Mister," he said, "that's really nice of you. But I'll only going to stay until I find my Mum, cos as soon as I find her, then I'm going to go and live with her and look after her and help her get better."

"Yes, Danny," Alex replied, "I understand that. You must care for your mother once you find her. It's right that your family, that is, yourself, your mother, and your Gran, should be together again." But, deep within his mind, Alex had real doubts as to whether or not Danny would ever find his mother. 'Up North' was a big place, and Danny had no idea, no idea at all, as to where his mother might be. 'Talk about finding a needle in a haystack, Danny my boy,' he thought, 'you've got a real search on your hands here. I wonder, do you really have any idea of how difficult it's going to be to find your mother?'

The other thing Alex had considered was that Danny, being unable to find his mother, would stay on the boat with him for many years to come. Alex had thought long and hard about that eventuality, too. But his past experience of many of the boys who'd left his school and then come back visiting years later, was that expectations and aspirations change. Danny was only just 12 years old, and Alex was certain that, in a few years' time, as he reached maturity, the boy's horizons would widen considerably.

Unlike Alex, now in the autumn of his years, as Danny grew older he would not be satisfied with a life afloat, forever meandering around the countryside on *Jennifer Jo*. He would want to spread his wings, widen his horizons, and move ashore, to a conventional, permanent home, and build a more settled future. But in the meantime, being on board *Jennifer Jo* with Alex would provide a secure environment in which Danny could grow up through his teenage years. And for himself, Alex would welcome and enjoy the company that having the lad on board would provide. It was, in fact, a win-win situation for them both.

"Also, Danny," Alex went on, "I'd like you to help me working *Jennifer Jo*. You very kindly helped me to clean her the other week, and there's no end to the work that needs to be done to keep her smart and shiny. And if you can help me work her through the locks, that would be great. Doing the locks single handed is a real pain and quite time-consuming, and two people working together make life really easy. And that brings me on to the next thing." Alex paused.

"There's more?" asked Danny, looking a bit fearful as to what might be coming next.

"Yes," replied Alex. "And this is really important."

"Go on , then," said Danny. "I'm ready." But Alex noticed that he still looked a little bit wary of what might be coming next. He paused for a few moments before continuing.

"Canals are perhaps the safest form of boating that there is," Alex went on. "Think of the three fours."

"What are they, then?" asked Danny, looking a bit puzzled.

"Well, firstly, generally speaking, you're never more than four yards from dry land. Then, you never go along faster than about four miles per hour. And thirdly, the water is usually never more than about four feet deep. But even so, it's not without its dangers. If you were to fall into the water off the back of the boat whilst the propeller is turning, then you'd very quickly be sucked into the propeller, and they'd end up fishing you out of the canal in little pieces. That's not a very nice thought, is it?"

Danny shook his head in agreement.

"Also," Alex went on, "if you jump off the boat across a largish gap and you miss your footing and fall, then you're very likely to cut yourself to pieces if you fall onto the sharp edge of the steel piling which lines the edge of the towpath in many places. That won't be very nice either."

Once again, Danny shook his head.

"And at the locks, well, they're perhaps the most hazardous places of all. There are no guard rails or anything along the edge of the locks. If the lock is full of water, then the water will be very deep. And if the lock is empty, it's a long drop down into the water, or there may be a boat in the lock which you fall onto, and you'd dent the top of the boat and probably break some bones as well. If you ever need to cross the lock, always be sure to use the footbridge, if there is one. If there isn't a bridge, and you have to cross the lock by walking over the gates, then always hold on to the handrails."

"If you're aware of the dangers, and follow these sensible rules, then you'll be fine. As I said, it's the safest form of getting afloat that I know of. And finally, one more thing. There must be no mucking about, or doing anything silly. Do you know what I mean, do you understand?"

"Yea I do," said Danny, with a smile. "I won't misbehave or anything, I've seen what can go wrong when you mess about. Back at Grant Hall, a couple of the kids were messing about once, having a mock swordfight down the kitchen garden, round the back of the greenhouse, when Hammond weren't looking. They were using garden canes as swords, and one of them slipped and he cut the other kid's arm wide open with the pointed end of the cane. He had to go to the hospital to get it stitched up, and he's still got a big scar there now. Hammond, he were furious. He gave them four lashes every night for a week, both of them, even the kid who's arm got cut open, as a lesson to everyone else. They didn't do it again. And I won't either, Mister, you can rely on me. Just you see."

"That's fine, Danny," Alex replied. "I'm sure I can rely on you. The only other thing is, like I think I told you before, there's lots of nasty bugs in the water, so if you do have the misfortune to fall in, be sure to have a shower and get cleaned up straight away. And if you have any cuts or grazes, always have a plaster on them, to make sure that they're covered up against any canal water getting into the wound and giving you an infection."

"OK, Mister, that'll be fine," said Danny, smiling once more.

"On the good side," Alex went on, "there's plenty of companionship around the canals. If we're doing a lock, it's normal to help another boat, either if it's following us in the same direction as we're going, or if it's coming in the opposite direction. It's a chance to assist, and chat to the crews of the other boats as well. Everyone's really friendly."

"I think I'm going to like it here on your boat with you," Danny replied. It seems like it's really good."

"Yes, it is, Danny, really good," replied Alex. "And I hope you enjoy it, I really do. And I'm sure you'll soon get used to the routine I keep aboard *Jennifer Jo.* Normally, in the morning, I get up and make a quick cup of coffee, and then move the boat along for a hour or so, till the water is hot, and then I stop for a while to get some breakfast, and a shower. After that, we'll knock along again until it's lunchtime, and find a spot to stop for the rest of the day, and where we can stay until the next morning. Afternoons is maintenance time, cleaning the boat, or getting water, or going shopping. But if it's raining, we generally won't move the boat unless it's really necessary. There's no real fun in getting wet just for the sake of it, if it's going to be OK to stay wherever we are for another day or so. Evenings after tea is free time, to do as you want, watching tv or reading, or maybe a game or something together. You'll soon get used to it."

"Sounds good," opined Danny. "I'll certainly help with looking after the boat, and cleaning and stuff, of course I will. There ain't no problems there."

"Thanks, Danny, that's great," replied Alex, "but now, let's clear up the supper things. Then how about a game of chess? I think it's my turn to win."

"Yea, so it may be," agreed Danny, with a grin. "But that don't mean nothing. You're playing against me, remember? You ain't got no chance. Just you wait and see."

And Danny was right. Once again, he quickly gained the upper hand and wiped Alex off the board, taking less than an hour and forty minutes to do so.

CHAPTER 8

"OK, Mister, you can bring her out now," called out Danny, as he swung open the top gate of the lock, at the same time beckoning with his hand. Alex gently nudged *Jennifer Jo* into gear, and eased her forward, clear of the lock gate, bringing the boat to a halt just by the tail of the lock, an easy position for Danny to step aboard once he'd closed the gate. But Danny had gone back to the bottom end of the lock, and was busy winding up the paddle to empty the lock once more, ready for the boat which they'd both spotted following them along the canal.

Alex watched as he saw Danny lingering by the bottom of the lock for a while, and then he saw what the attraction was. Two young girls, aged about thirteen, wearing similar light blue tops and dark blue shorts, had appeared from below the lock, windlasses in hand, ready to work the lock. By the look of them, they were twins, identical twins. Soon, Danny was hard in conversation with the two girls as their boat worked its way through the lock, and it was a full five minutes before he returned to the top of the lock and stepped aboard the rear deck of the boat. Putting the engine into gear and drawing away from the lock, Alex remarked on the delay. He liked to tease Danny when the opportunity arose.

"We're in no hurry, Danny," he said. "In your own time. Taking in the scenery, were you?"

"Yea, that's OK, Mister," Danny replied, sporting another of his mischievous grins. "I'm ready now. Did you see those girls? They're really nice. They're called Alice and Alison, and they're twins, would you believe that? I couldn't tell the two of them apart. They live in Basingstoke, and they're on holiday on their boat, it's a hire boat, for a couple of weeks with their parents. They've got an older brother, but he's away at university at the moment, although he's going to join them on the boat at the weekend. They said that if they're moored up near us tonight, they'll come and see me and we can have a good chat and get to know each other better." And Danny smiled once more, obviously taken with his brief encounter with the fairer sex.

"That's fine, Danny," Alex replied, "someone for you to talk to, perhaps. But it's a wonder you haven't got their phone number already," he teased the boy.

"Well, I have, they did give it to me," Danny replied, another grin lighting up his face. "But I ain't got a phone, and anyway I didn't have nothing to write it down with. I've forgotten what it was, now, anyway."

As the boy spoke, he picked up the pair of binoculars which Alex made sure always lived within easy reach on the top of the gas locker, and studied the couple walking their dog along the towpath. Alex had noticed that Danny was never far away from the binoculars whilst they were cruising along. At first he'd thought that the boy was keeping a lookout for anyone from Grant Hall, who by a sheer coincidence might be beside the canal, similar to what had happened at the supermarket a couple of months previously. As the weeks had passed, however, Alex had become aware that that possibility had become more and more distant.

Now, Alex had realised, Danny was not looking for anyone who might apprehend him. More than that, he was keeping a lookout on all passersby, just in case one of them might be his mother or his Gran. Alex hadn't talked to Danny about how remote the chance was of finding his relatives along the cut, but Danny was full of hope, and Alex did not wish to dampen the boy's spirits in any way. Time would do that in its own due course.

They cruised along the canal for about an hour before mooring up for lunch in a pleasant spot, sheltered from the wind by the hedge which lined the towpath and separated it from the adjacent field. There was a nice view across the canal to a field of ripening barley on the offside, waving gently in the freshening wind. It was a lovely summer's afternoon, the sort of day which Alex enjoyed the most.

After their lunch, Alex said to Danny, "there's nothing much to do to keep *Jennifer Jo* neat and clean and tidy, so it's free time this afternoon. I'll clear up the lunch things, if you want to read or anything."

"OK, Mister, thanks, "Danny replied. "I'll take a book and go and sit on the towpath and have a read, if that's alright?"

"Yes, of course, Danny, that's fine," Alex replied "I'll just finish off here, and then I'll come and join you."

Danny disappeared up onto the rear deck, while Alex washed up the few lunch things, and then took the Nicholson's guide and his own book and went up out of the boat onto the towpath. He'd had a quick look through the Nicholson's the night before, and he was aware that a decision was looming, which they'd have to address the next day. For up ahead, about two hours' cruising away from where they were now, was a canal junction. That presented a choice of which way to go. Normally, on his own, Alex would just go wherever way the fancy took him, but now he had Danny with him, and he knew that the boy wanted to go 'up north'. Both routes eventually led in that direction, but Alex felt that it was right for Danny to be able to choose which way they asked *Jennifer Jo* to take them.

Alex looked around, both up and down the canal, but to his alarm Danny was nowhere to be seen. Alex was immediately worried. It seemed that over the last few weeks Danny had settled well into life afloat, but he was still only a relatively young child, and whilst he seemed to be a resilient and self-reliant youngster, there could be much that Danny was holding back and not telling Alex about. Alex walked forward a few paces, but the canal ahead was long and straight, and of Danny there was no sign. Alex then turned round, and ran back along the towpath, retracing the route along the canal which they'd come along that morning on *Jennifer Jo*. After a few minutes, he gave a sigh of relief as he rounded a bend and saw Danny in the far distance, sitting on the grassy bank by the towpath. His knees were drawn up to his chest, with his hands stretched around his legs, and he was just staring into the distance, his book lying unopened on the grass besides him.

It worried Alex to see him like this – the boy was obviously brooding and upset about something. Was it something he'd done, he wondered, some inadvertent comment, or whatever, that had unsettled the boy? Alex fervently hoped not. He'd thought that he and Danny had been getting along well together, but maybe Danny had been hiding his thoughts and keeping them to himself. Whatever it was, from his years as a teacher and housemaster at his old school, Alex knew that it was important that he had to talk to the boy, and try to gain his confidence.

Alex slowed down to a walk to get his breath back, and as he reached Danny he sat down beside the boy, saying gently, "may I sit with you, please, Danny?"

The boy didn't answer, but merely nodded his head in silent agreement. They sat there together, the ex-teacher Alex, now in his late fifties, and Danny, the troubled twelve-year-old, for about five minutes, before Alex asked quietly "what's the matter, Danny? What's troubling you?"

Danny didn't reply straight away, and Alex knew not to press him. If he was going to talk, and Alex very much hoped that he would, then he was aware that Danny would do so in his own time. And after a while he did start to speak, very softly, but still staring all the while at the meadow across the cut. "You wouldn't understand, Mister," he said.

Alex considered his reply carefully, eventually answering "I might understand, Danny. Remember, I've spent most of my life looking after young boys much the same age as yourself. You'd be surprised at the things I've helped sort out for them. Try me. If I can help you, then I will. But it does concern me that you're upset about something. Talk to me, please, Danny. It always helps to talk about something that's troubling you."

Danny didn't answer. Alex waited patiently, for he knew that an answer would be forthcoming in due course. And, eventually, after a long pause Danny started talking, although he still kept staring into the distance across the cut.

"Well, Mister," he said, "please don't think I don't like being with you on the boat, because I do, I really do. It's nice, really nice. In fact, it's great. And I know it's very good of you to take me in like you have, and look after me. But..........." Danny's voice tailed off to nothing.

After a while he started speaking again. "It's just that, ever since Mum was taken ill, I've never really been on my own. When I was with Mrs Bradley, there was little Freddie there with me all the time. Don't get me wrong, he was a lovely kid, especially once I got him talking again, after what he'd been through. And then at Harding Court, you was always with loads of other kids, in the dining room, or the common room, or the dormitory or whatever, or at church, like they made us go to all the time. And after that, at Grant Hall, there was always loads of other kids about. It's just that sometimes I want to be alone, and I never have been, not for ages, not since Mum was took into hospital and they took me into care."

"And your boat's really nice. As canal boats go it's pretty big, I realise that now, but it's quite small really. I'm always with you. You're always about, all the time. Don't get me wrong, I think you're a really nice guy. If you'd been in charge at Grant Hall it would have been great there. But I'm sorry, it's just that sometimes I feel I just want to be alone. I can't really explain it any more than that." Danny turned and looked at Alex with an impassioned look, and with more than a trace of tears in his eyes.

Alex waited for a while before he answered. "Yes, Danny, I do understand," he said. "I really do understand how you feel. Don't be sorry about it. It's quite a normal reaction to the situation you've found yourself in, after everything that's happened to you, especially at Grant Hall. I understand that you want your own space. That's quite a human response to what you've had to go through. And you're right, the boat is small and a bit cramped, and we're on top of each other much of the time. And while you do have your own bunk in the back cabin, that too is pretty cramped. I'll try to make sure you have some time to yourself, to be by yourself, from now on, whenever you like. But I need to ask just one thing of you in exchange."

"What's that, then, Mister?" asked Danny, turning to look at Alex with an enquiring glance.

"Well, Danny, if you do go away from the boat to have some solitude, that's quite alright with me, but please, please, stay within sight of me, can you please? After all, someone might have come along and grabbed hold of you and taken you back to Grant Hall, and then I'd never even have known about it, would I?"

"S'pose not," Danny replied with a slight grin, "I wouldn't want that to happen. Grant Hall was awful, it really was."

"Yes Danny, I can imagine," Alex replied quietly. "It can't have been very pleasant for you, nor for any of the other boys who were there. From what you've told me, I know that all of you boys all stuck up for each other and looked out for each other, but even so, it must have been very difficult to keep your spirits up."

"Yea, all the kids at Grant Hall, well, we all looked after each other," Danny replied. "We especially looked out for the younger ones, there was one or two who were only eight or nine, or maybe even younger than that."

Alex waited for a moment before speaking again. "Whilst we're talking, Danny, there's something else which I need to talk to you about."

"What's that, Mister? What you wanna talk about?" Danny asked, turning and looking at Alex, the customary grin temporarily gone. It brought it home to Alex that Danny's insecurity was never very far below the surface.

"Well, Danny." Alex paused for a moment. "There's plenty of free time for you here on *Jennifer Jo*, especially in the afternoons after we've moved the boat and done all the chores. Do you find that all the free time hangs heavily sometimes, especially when it's raining and you can't get outside?"

"Well, actually, yes, I do," Danny replied. "It's easy to get a little bored sometimes. I mean, being on the boat is great, do you remember when we saw that fox in the long grass the other day, that was great! And a couple of days later, there was this bat flying along the towpath just as it got dark, it kept going backwards and forwards for ages besides the bushes before it flew off. Isn't that wonderful, to see things like that? But, while there's always something different to see, there's not always a lot to do some afternoons. Especially, as you said, when its wet outside."

"That's right, Danny," Alex agreed. "But I've got a fix for that. I hope you're going to like it."

"Come on, then, tell me," said Danny, fixing Alex with another of his grins. Alex liked the way Danny nearly always had a grin on his face. Apart from the solitude which he'd just told Alex he sometimes sought, it was apparent that he was enjoying life on *Jennifer Jo,* and he seemed to have settled down well to his new way of life after the misery he'd had to endure at Grant Hall.

"Well, Danny," said Alex, "we're coming up to September, and most other kids your age will be thinking of going back to school after their summer holidays. At Grant Hall they gave you lessons, didn't they?"

"Yes, that's right," said Danny, "they had teachers come in, weekdays during term-time. They were very strict about that, about you doing your school work. And they made you do exams too, at the end of term. And if you didn't do very well in the exams, well, there was Hammond who sorted you out. And no-one ever dared to mess about in class, like some of the kids did at my other schools, Hammond would have soon seen to that as well."

"Well, Danny," Alex continued. "I'm sure you realise that you too should be going to school as well, and getting an education, to prepare you for the time when you'll go out into the world and get a job to support yourself. It's not possible for you to go to a normal school, as we're moving along on the boat nearly every day. But, if you remember, I was a schoolteacher. What I propose is that I give you lessons, here on *Jennifer Jo,* every afternoon, for five days every week. And some homework too, for you to do on your own, in the evenings." Alex paused for a moment, to let the news sink in, then continued "How do you feel about that?"

Danny was quiet and serious for a moment before he replied. Then his usual grin returned as he turned to Alex and said, "that's a great idea, Mister," he said, "I bet you're a great teacher."

It was Alex's turn to grin. "Well, I did have my moments," he replied. "But look, what I suggest is this. There'll be 3 hours a day, weekday afternoons, from 2.00 to 5.00 pm. Four lessons each afternoon, of forty minutes each, with a 20- minute break half way through. There will be English and Maths, probably four sessions a week of each, because they are the most important subjects, and they are what potential employers will be looking for above anything else."

"I'm a traditional teacher, and believe in giving a wide-ranging education, so there will also be Geography, History, a foreign language (probably French), General Science, and a couple of extras for just one session a week each."

"What will they be, then, Mister?" enquired Danny. "These extras?"

"There will be Current Affairs," replied Alex, "just talking about what's been happening on the television news or wherever. Politics, perhaps. Or what's happening elsewhere in the world. And the other subject, I'm pretty certain, will surprise you. It's Latin."

"What, Latin," exclaimed Danny. "That's a dead language, ain't it? Only dead people spoke that."

"Well," said Alex, "Apart from the Vatican City, where it's their normal language, it's not spoken nowadays in any country, except perhaps in Italy, where Italian is derived from the original roman Latin. But the benefit of Latin is that it's a very firmly structured language. Learning Latin gives you a good insight into the use of English, and how to express yourself clearly in conversation, or in writing. It will be very worthwhile to you, even though it may not seem to be so at first."

"Well, OK, Mister, if you say so," Danny replied quietly.

"Yes, Danny," Alex said. "Remember, it is important that you get some schooling, even though you're afloat with me. I'll put together a timetable for you, and we'll stick to that as much as possible. And we can get some textbooks and some exercise books for you next week when we go through that large town you saw in the Nicholson's yesterday, there's sure to be a suitable bookshop there. And we'll see how it goes from there."

"That's fine, Mister," Danny replied. "I always used to like school. I think I'll enjoy having you as my teacher."

"And I think you'll be a good pupil, Danny," Alex responded. "But I'll make you stick to it, you know, and make sure that you work hard at your lessons. There's no point in it if you don't, no point at all."

Danny just grinned once again, and nodded. "I'll be OK," he said, "I won't let you down. Just you wait and see."

"And, Danny," Alex continued, "there's something else I think you might appreciate getting to know about." Maybe a couple of things, actually."

"What's that, Mister?" asked Danny, apprehensive once more. "What else have you got in mind for me?"

"Well," said Alex, smiling. "How about me giving you a few lessons about cooking. Would you like me to teach you a little about that?"

"I can do cooking," said Danny, a little defiantly. "I can make a good breakfast."

"Can you?" said Alex, with an enquiring look.

"Yes," replied Danny proudly. "I can do cornflakes, and milk. And toast, with butter and jam."

"Anything else?" asked Alex. "Scrambled eggs, perhaps? Or fried bacon?"

"Well." Danny looked a bit sheepish. "Not really, Mister. Perhaps you'd better teach me after all, hadn't you? I'm OK with a few things, but not much. But that apple pie you made the other day was really nice, could you teach me how to do that sort of thing?"

"Yes, of course," replied Alex. "But that will be outside your academic timetable, if that's OK. We can't let that slip at all."

"Yea alright then, Mister," said Danny. "That will be OK, I'll do the sessions like what you said. And the homework."

"That's fine Danny, then. That's what we'll do. And I'll also teach you some basic diesel engine maintenance too. We have to look after our engine on a regular basis, like changing the filters and things like that. You can help me with that too, I think you'll find it interesting. And there's often other things to be attended to on the boat as well. We can do them together."

"Fine, Mister," said Danny, with yet another grin. That's just fine."

"Come on then, Danny," Alex said, sitting up. "Let's get back to the boat, and we'll have a cup of tea. If you still want to sit on your own for a bit, then that's alright by me. But please stay within sight, where I can see you, will you please?"

"Alright, thanks, Mister," Danny turned and smiled. "Like what I said just now, you ain't a bad bloke are you? And I don't need to sit on my own any more, I feel alright about things now. it was right what you said, it does help to talk when you're upset about something." They stood up and walked slowly together along the towpath back to *Jennifer Jo*, Alex's hand on the shoulder of the young lad.

Alex put the kettle on and made the tea, and then he and Danny sat together on the towpath and had a cup of tea together. Danny had slipped off his tee-shirt in the warm afternoon sun, and Alex noticed that the signs of under-nourishment which he'd noticed when he'd first met Danny had all but disappeared. A couple of months of decent meals and proper food had worked wonders on the twelve year old.

Alex showed Danny the Nicholson's, and pointed out the choice of routes to go 'up North' and, after a little deliberation, Danny made his choice. Alex knew that it was somewhat academic, as, in this case, 'all roads lead to Rome.' They would eventually cover all the canals in the system as they traversed the country in their search for Danny's mother, fruitless though it almost certainly would be. But Danny's conviction that he would ultimately find her was as absolute now as it ever had been. Alex had not yet tried to tell Danny that it was a hopeless task – the time for that would eventually arrive, and he wanted Danny to come to that conclusion of his own accord, and in his own time. He would talk to Danny about it when the time came, but only after Danny had broached the subject first.

They sat there on the towpath for some time, chatting idly about nothing in particular, and then a boat rounded the corner of the canal behind them and gradually made its way towards them. Sitting in the front of the boat were the two girls whom Danny had been chatting to at the lock earlier in the day. "There he is," cried one of the girls, standing up and turning to her father, who was at the back of the boat, steering it along the cut. "Can we stop here for the night, please Dad?" she called out. "Please?"

The girls' father simply smiled and nodded, as he eased off the throttle and brought the boat to a halt about 50 yards ahead of where *Jennifer Jo* was moored. As he did so, Danny jumped to his feet, and ran along the towpath, deftly catching the rope that was thrown to him, and holding the boat still whilst the girls' parents made their moorings fast. Once the boat was safely moored, Alex watched with amusement as Danny immediately went and sat on the front of the boat and started chatting to the girls, no doubt picking up from where he'd left off earlier at the lock.

The girls' father walked back to *Jennifer Jo* and started talking to Alex. "Hello," he said. "My name's George, George Perkin. And those are my two girls, Alice and Alison, up the front there with your lad." Alex shook hands with George and introduced himself.

"Is this is your own boat?" George asked, indicating *Jennifer Jo*.

"Yes, that's right," Alex replied.

"It's very nice," commented George. "We've hired our boat for a couple of week's holiday. He paused for a moment, looking at the front of his boat where Danny was busy chatting to his two daughters. "Your lad's well interested in my two girls. Is he your grandson?"

Alex was now in a bit of a quandary. He couldn't really say the truth, that he'd picked up Danny along the cut a few weeks before, and had befriended him and given him a temporary home until he managed to find his mother, however remote that possibility seemed to be. It might in the end lead to Danny being taken back to Grant Hall, and Alex was determined not to allow that to happen, as long as he, Alex, could do anything to prevent it. So he decided upon a little white lie. "Yes," he replied, "that's my Grandson. His name's Danny. He's staying on the boat with me for a few weeks."

"He seems a nice lad," the man replied.

"Yes, he is," said Alex. "He's had a bit of a bad time recently, but he's OK now. Are you enjoying your holiday?"

"Yes, we are," was the response. "It's great. The girls sit together up at the front of the boat, talking all day about, well, girlie things, I suppose, and Barbara and I keep at the back and just put the world to rights, whilst we sit and watch the world go by.   It's very quiet and peaceful. And the girls help with handling the boat and doing the locks, and they do the washing up for us every night after we've had a meal. But what about you? Do you live on your boat all the time?"

"Yes, I do," replied Alex. "For the past few months, I have, anyway. Almost a year now, actually."

Alex carried on chatting to the man and his wife Barbara, who'd just joined them, but eventually they said their goodbyes and returned to their boat, while Alex went inside and got the supper ready. With a keen nose for whenever there was food in the offing, Danny returned just as their supper was ready, and they sat and enjoyed their meal, chatting together as they did so.

"Well, Danny," Alex asked, with a teasing smile, "how did you get on with the girls this afternoon? You seemed to be well in there?"

"Yes, Mister," Danny replied, "they're really nice. You know, they're twins, but I can't tell them apart, I just can't, even though they told me what differences to look out for. And, they gave me their phone number again, they wrote it down for me this time. I don't suppose I'll ever use it though. And, by the way, there's something I've got to tell you ....."

"Yes?" asked Alex, as Danny's voice tailed off.

"Well, I said you were my Grandad. They kept asking about us, and I didn't know what else to say. I hope that was alright?"

"Yes, Danny, that's fine," replied Alex. "Actually, I told the girls' father that you were my grandson, so we both got it right, didn't we?"

Danny laughed and smiled. "Not bad, Mister," he said. "We do get on well together, don't we?"

"Yes we do," said Alex. "If anyone else asks, that's what we'll stick to, if you can remember that."

"I will," replied Danny. "No problem."

Alex nodded in silent agreement. "But tonight, I'm going to upset you. Not much, mind, but just a little bit," he added.

"How's that ?" asked Danny, a little puzzled. He now knew that Alex would do nothing that would really upset him.

"I'm going to beat you at chess, that's how, " said Alex, with another smile.

"Fat chance," Danny grinned back. "Remember, like I said before, it's me you're playing against. You don't have a chance."

Alex put together a strong position, and for a time seemed to have the upper hand, but eventually Danny broke through his defence and seized the advantage. It seemed Alex was always going to be doomed to failure at chess, as once again Danny wiped him off the board.

CHAPTER 9

"OK, Mister, you can bring her in now," Danny called out, as he swung open the bottom gate of the lock. Alex allowed himself a wry smile. Over the last few weeks, It had become a now-familiar routine at every lock. Danny went ashore and worked the lock, whilst Alex drove *Jennifer Jo* into and out of the lock. It was always the same call from Danny as soon as the lock was ready. And, In a few minutes, when the lock had filled, Alex knew that Danny would open the top gate and call out 'OK Mister, you can bring her out now.' Whenever Danny called that out, It was really stating the obvious, but Alex didn't mind – if it helped to make Danny feel a full part of their team aboard *Jennifer Jo*, then that was all to the good.

Danny now appeared to have settled down well into his new life afloat, and seemed to enjoy operating the locks as they slowly worked the boat northwards. They only covered just a few miles every day, and sometimes not at all if it were raining, unless they needed supplies of food, fuel, or water, or any of the other myriad things that were needed to keep *Jennifer Jo* in good working condition.

Alex had also become familiar was the way in which Danny socialised and conversed with other boaters waiting to use the locks they traversed, or with dog walkers or families enjoying a walk along the towpath. Especially, Alex thought, if there were young females around of much the same age as Danny himself. It was only nature starting to get hold of the boy, Alex, realised, and puberty starting to take control of his hormones. He'd seen it happen many times before, to the boys in his house at the school where he'd taught for many years. Danny was starting to experience a strong attraction to young girls; they seemed to exert a strong magnetism on the lad, and he appeared to really enjoy their company, even though it was usually for a only a few minutes or so at a lock before he jumped aboard *Jennifer Jo* once again, and they set off on their way along the canal.

It was nearly three weeks now since they had started working to the new routine which Alex had outlined to Danny, of boating or boat maintenance in the mornings, and schooling in the afternoon, for five days a week. The weekends were kept clear of school work, to allow Danny some time to himself, and he'd often go and sit a little way along the towpath, usually with a book, for he had become an avid reader, or occasionally just sitting watching the boats go by, or chatting to walkers on the towpath.

Much to Danny's surprise, Alex had started off the teaching lessons with a few examinations, so that he could ascertain how much Danny had learnt from his previous schooling, before he'd come to live aboard *Jennifer Jo* with Alex. It would have been a waste of time to cover the same ground again, and it helped Alex to assess what sort of intellect lay hidden inside Danny's mind. He'd been pleasantly surprised to find that Danny appeared to be quite a bright lad. He'd performed well in the examinations where he knew the subject matter, and in the instances where he hadn't yet been taught the material, he'd made a good attempt at answering all the questions which Alex had set. It had made Alex's task in putting together a good schedule of lessons much easier.

Not once had Danny complained about the loss of free time, and he'd applied himself with enthusiasm to the lessons Alex had been giving him. Even Latin, about which Danny had expressed some surprise when Alex first mentioned it, was receiving Danny's full attention. The boy's handwriting was very neat and tidy, and the sketches and illustrations which he produced to accompany his written work hinted at a real artistic talent hidden away somewhere.

And in the evenings, Danny, without being told or reminded, had sat down at the dinette and applied himself to his homework, whilst Alex cleared away their supper things, and then sat down opposite the lad to write up his daily diary. Once or twice whilst doing his homework, he'd asked Alex for guidance, but Alex had politely declined to give any assistance. 'No, Danny,' he'd told the boy, 'homework is for you, and you alone. If you get it wrong, then so be it – it will tell me where we need to go over the material again, to help you get a better understanding of the principles involved.' And Danny had understood, and seemed to be happy to do the best he could.

Some of Alex's time had been spent in marking Danny's work, and preparing for the next day's or week's lessons, but in general Danny's education was proceeding well. He really sparkled at maths, and his English was good, both in comprehension and creative writing, and Alex found it easy to read Danny's neat handwriting. Very soon after Danny had been taken in by Alex and taken up residence on *Jennifer Jo*, Alex had realised that Danny's spoken English needed a lot of work, and at least one English lesson per week was devoted to improving Danny's spoken grammar.

As Alex sat on the back rail and waited whilst the lock gradually filled with water, Alex decided that it was time for him to ensure that Danny felt himself to be a 100% part of Alex's life afloat, a full member of the team aboard *Jennifer Jo*. As they'd cruised along the waterways, never once had Danny expressed any wish to drive the boat. In fact, Alex always drove the boat, at all times. Danny had always been content to sit beside Alex on the back rail, looking at the scenery and the wildlife as they cruised along, always with the binoculars to hand, ready to focus on a distant subject of interest, and always to look closely at anyone walking the towpath. Alex knew that Danny was always checking to see if it might be his mother walking along, and he still hadn't plucked up the courage to talk to Danny about this, and how remote that possibility might be. For his part, Danny seemed just as convinced as ever that some day he would find his mother, and Alex knew that the time to tell Danny that it almost certainly would never happen was still well away into the future.

Alex had checked out the Nicholson's the previous evening, and he knew that just after the bend in the canal which he could just see in the distance, the canal, most unusually, went straight and true for almost a mile – just perfect for what he had in mind. There was a slight breeze blowing, and if the trees that surrounded the lock thinned out and gave way to hedges on either side of the cut, then that would be ideal for his purpose. Then there came the familiar call from Danny which Alex had been expecting.

"OK Mister, you can bring her out now." Alex smiled as Danny pulled open the top gate of the lock, and then walked round to the ground paddle to close off the water supply into the lock and leave it ready for the next boat. Alex nudged the engine into gear for a few moments, just enough to give *Jennifer Jo* a slow forward motion, and then moved the control lever back into neutral to allow the boat to come to a halt at the toe of the lock, and enable Danny to step aboard.

Danny jumped onto the rear deck and stowed the windlass back into the locker, as Alex put the engine into gear again and *Jennifer Jo* slowly drew away from the lock.

Danny turned to Alex. "That was easy, Mister," he said, "those gates and paddles were really easy to move, they must have attended to them recently. Some locks are really difficult, but not that one."

"Yes, Danny," Alex replied, as they rounded the bend in the canal, "I think you're right. It's a shame they're not all like that."

"Yea, Mister, you're right there," Danny replied with a grin as he settled back to sit on the rail beside Alex.

"Hey Danny," Alex called out after about half a minute or so. "Would you like to take her?"

"What do you mean Mister?" Danny exclaimed, with a surprised expression. "Do you mean you're gonna let me drive *Jay-Jay*? Really?"

Alex smiled. Recently, instead of calling his boat 'your boat' or 'the boat' or '*Jennifer Jo*', Danny had taken to referring to it as '*Jay-Jay*', and Alex had to admit it was a neat little nickname for the vessel that was his pride and joy, and more than that, his home.

"Yes, Danny, you have a go. It's about time you got to drive her." Alex turned to Danny and nodded as he smiled encouragingly.

"If you're sure, Mister," Danny replied. "I'd love to. I'll be ever so careful, I promise."

"That's fine, Danny, I know you will," Alex assured the youngster. "But before you start, there's a few things for you to remember, which will help you as you go along. You've probably noticed some of them already as you've watched me drive the boat, but it won't hurt for me to mention them to you."

"Firstly, the boat will always move in the direction of wherever it's pointing towards. But when turning, she will always pivot around her centre point. It's not noticeable when you're going along at normal cruising speed, but when you're manoeuvring at low speeds, it's something you need to be aware of and to watch out for. For example, if you're turning the boat to the left, the back end of the boat will swing out to the right, and that may catch you unawares. And of course, to turn the boat to the left you must push the tiller over to the right. It seems counter-intuitive at first, but it's something that you'll get used to very quickly."

"Another thing is that you only have control of your steering whilst the propeller is pushing water over the rudder. If you're approaching a situation where you need to be going very slowly, it's much better to put the engine down to tick-over speed well in advance, and then motor slowly up to it, rather than put the engine out of gear and coast along, with no control over your steering."

"And talking about steering, you have no steering control at all when the boat is going backwards. There are ways and means of controlling where the boat is going when it's in reverse, but we can leave that for another day."

Danny looked at Alex dubiously. "That's a lot to remember, Mister, aint it?" he exclaimed. "Are you sure you're happy for me to drive her?"

"Yes, go ahead," Alex replied, smiling slightly. "Here, off you go."

Alex took his hand off the tiller and moved to one side. Danny stepped forward, taking the tiller firmly in his right hand, standing proudly on the rear deck, his gaze fixed rigidly ahead. Alex sat back quietly on the back rail and waited.

As he had anticipated, the trees around the lock had given way to low hedges on either side of the canal, and the breeze coming over the meadows on the offside had now become quite strong. Alex knew exactly what was going to happen. The only thing in question was just how long it would take. It was a shame, but there was only one way for Danny to learn how to drive the boat properly, and unfortunately that involved making mistakes. 'After all,' Alex thought, 'you can learn a lot from your mistakes.'

At first, Danny did quite well, keeping *Jennifer Jo* on a good straight course, but gradually she drifted off the line Danny had been holding along the middle of the waterway. The boat started to develop a zig-zag course, with the zigzags gradually getting more and more pronounced as Danny tried in vain to hold the straight line he was aiming for. The zigs and zags became ever more pronounced, until eventually Danny lost control altogether and *Jennifer Jo* buried her nose in the reeds on the offside of the cut and ground to a halt, the front of the boat rising up slightly as she ran out of water beneath her bow and rode up onto the mud and clay on the bed of the canal.

Danny pulled the control lever back to neutral, and turned round to face Alex. But he couldn't bring himself to look Alex in the face. Instead, deeply disappointed with his first performance at steering the boat, he kept his gaze firmly fixed on the deck just in front of this feet, a stance Alex had only seen from Danny once before, that very first time he'd come across Danny, after he'd found the boy hiding in the cratch that day by the lock several months ago.

"I'm sorry, Mister. I've run her aground," he said sheepishly, so very quiet that Alex could hardly hear him. "I'm really sorry. I dunno how it happened, I really don't. I don't s'pose you'll ever let me drive her again."

Alex reached out his hand and put it under the boy's chin, lifting up his head till he could see his face. There were tears in Danny eyes, and Alex realised just how disappointed Danny must be feeling at this very moment. He'd wanted do to do so well driving *Jennifer Jo*, and he'd ended up putting her into the bank instead, and running aground into the bargain.

"I'm really sorry, Mister," he said once again, looking down at the deck once more. And just then, to add insult to injury, a sudden gust of wind caught the boat and pushed it round broadside to the canal, coming to rest with the bow stuck firmly in the reeds and mud on the offside, and with the stern against the towpath side. And to add even further embarrassment to Danny's predicament, a couple of cyclists came into view riding along the towpath, stopping to watch, and wondering exactly how Alex and Danny would extricate themselves from the unfortunate situation which Danny had got them into.

"That's alright, Danny," Alex told the lad, as he lifted up the boy's head again and fixing him with a cheering smile. "It happens to everyone. Believe it or not, it's happened to me once or twice, when I was first starting out on the boat. It's not a problem, really it's not."

"Are you sure ?" asked Danny tearfully.

"Yes, I'm sure," replied Alex. "Absolutely sure. It's no problem at all."

"But we're aground," wailed Danny. "And stuck across the canal. How on earth are we gonna get off the mud, and get going again?"

"Oh, that's easy," replied Alex. "Here's what to do."

Danny looked up, a little more cheerful now. "What's that?" he asked.

"Well, Danny, do you see that wooden pole on the top of the boat, on the upstands there?" asked Alex. Danny nodded silently, still looking rather miserable.

"Well, go up on the roof and fetch it, Danny, and then come back here." Alex told him. "Then use it to push against the bank. The back end of the boat will swing round as you push, and at the same time, I'll use reverse gear to get the engine to pull us off the mud."

"Alright, Mister, whatever you say," Danny replied, as he climbed up onto the roof of the boat and fetched the brightly painted pole Alex had pointed out to him. "I often wondered what that pole was for."

"That's it," said Alex. "Now get over here, and when I say push, push. Push against the bank to start with, then when the boat starts swinging away, move the end of the pole into the water and push again, against the bottom of the canal."

"OK, Mister said Danny. "When you're ready."

"Right, Danny, now! PUSH!" exclaimed Alex, as he put the engine into reverse gear and gently opened the throttle a little way. Danny put the pole against the towpath bank and pushed with all his strength, and slowly *Jennifer Jo* swung around away from the bank. Alex opened up the throttle a bit more and, as the propeller churned up the water beneath the hull, *Jennifer Jo's* bow slid off the mud, slowly at first, then faster and faster as the sticky mud released its grip. Deftly, Alex slipped the control into forward gear and swung the tiller around, and within 15 seconds or so they were making a straight line along the canal once again.

"Gosh, Mister, that was a close thing," exclaimed Danny, "I thought we'd be stuck there for ever."

"No," replied Alex, smiling. "This sort of thing can happen quite frequently until you become accustomed to steering the boat. It's not often that we can't get off the mud. There's other ways and means as well, if this didn't work."

"What about the pole?" asked Danny. "It's all dirty, and just look at all that gloop stuck around the other end. It's all on the top of the roof now, as well, now I've put the pole back on the supports."

Alex smiled. 'Gloop' was a good term for the sticky grey mud and clay that had become enslimed around the end of the pole. "Yes, you can't help that. But leave it for the moment, Danny," he said. "Guess who's going to be doing a bit of cleaning tonight, though."

"I suppose that's me," Danny sighed, much relieved at them having been able to extricate themselves from their predicament, at the same time waving at the cyclists who'd been watching them, as they mounted their machines and continued on their way.

"Yes, you're right there," Alex replied, adding "how did you guess?" Danny laughed, with a wry smile. Alex knew that Danny would set to with the cleaning equipment as soon as the opportunity arose, probably after lunch before his afternoon lessons started.

"Come on, Danny," Alex told him. "Here, have another go."

"Are you sure, Mister?" asked Danny, looking anxiously at Alex. "After what happened last time?"

"Yes, I'm sure," replied Alex. "Go on, give it a go. You have to learn. Remember, I need someone I can rely on to drive the boat, besides me doing it all the time."

"All right then." Danny took hold of the tiller, a little nervously, and started steering the boat once again. But gradually the boat once more developed a zig-zag path along the canal, and eventually *Jennifer Jo* buried her bow once again in the reeds on the offside. Danny was heartbroken.

"Hey, Mister," he said. "I just can't do it, I dunno why. She just won't behave herself when I'm steering."

"Don't worry, Danny," Alex responded. "It's alright. That's all part of learning," he added, as he nudged the engine into reverse and opened the throttle. Water boiled under *Jennifer Jo's* stern as the propeller responded, but unlike the previous time, she refused to budge.

"Oh dear! What are we gonna do now?" exclaimed Danny. "I've got us well and truly stuck this time!"

"Don't worry, Danny," Alex replied calmly. "Hop up on the roof and take the pole to the front of the boat. lay it on the roof there. Then come back here, go through the boat to the cratch at the front, and you can use the pole to push us off."

"Oh. OK then," said Danny, as he did what Alex had asked. "Ready now," he called when he was in position with the pole at the front of the boat.

"Right, Danny, PUSH," called out Alex, as he opened up the throttle once again. But *Jennifer Jo* refused to shift.

"She's not moving," called out Danny. "I'm pushing as hard as I can!"

"Keep pushing, Danny," replied Alex, as he opened up the throttle even further, at the same time moving swiftly from one side of the boat to the other. The shifting weight caused the boat to develop a rocking motion in the water, and this extra effort suddenly enabled *Jennifer Jo* to free herself from the mud and slide backwards into deeper water.

"Well done, Mister," called out Danny as he returned to the rear deck and retrieved the pole. I thought we were gonna be stuck there for ever!"

"No way," smiled Alex. "If the worst happened, we'd flag down a passing boat and pass them a rope and ask them to help pull us off. That almost always works. Now, have another go with the tiller."

"No, Mister, I don't think so," said Danny glumly. "I've messed things up twice already."

"Don't be silly, Danny," replied Alex. "Here, I'll help you. And I'll talk you through it as we go." Alex took Danny's hand and placed it on the tiller, and then put his hand on top of Danny's, so they were both keeping hold of the tiller. Danny didn't speak, but looked up at Alex and nodded with a smile, as if to say 'thanks, Mister.'

As they went along, Alex told Danny the secrets of how to achieve a straight course along the canal. "Danny, what you need to realise is that the answer to driving and steering the boat can be summed up as 'little and often.' Be sure to always make small, gentle corrections with the tiller, very frequently. Your trouble was that, when she drifted off the line you wanted, you waited too long before correcting it, and when you did make a correction, it was too much. You were over-compensating all the time. That's why you ended up doing a zigzag along the cut, and eventually ending up aground. Just keep a careful watch on where we're going, all the time, and compensate for it as soon as you can, but only in small amounts. And remember, the wind can blow you off course very quickly indeed."

Danny looked up momentarily. "OK, Mister, I'll do that," he said, with a weak smile. Alex took his hand off the tiller, and let Danny have full control once again, but every so often taking hold of the tiller once again for just a few seconds, helping Danny to correct their course, but only when Alex felt he needed a little guidance. But as the morning drew on, Alex found that he needed to help Danny less and less. Gradually he was getting the gist of how to steer the boat. Just as with his school lessons, Danny was a quick learner.

"Hey, Mister," Danny exclaimed suddenly. "There's a bridge coming up. What do I do now?"

"Simple," Alex told him. "Just proceed as normal – but be careful, remember you don't aim for the middle of the arch."

"Why ever not?" asked Danny. It's slap bang in the middle of the bridge, isn't it?"

"Well, so it may be," replied Alex. "But it's not in the middle of the water, now, is it? Don't forget that the towpath runs under the bridge as well. Aim to give yourself about a couple of feet away from the bridge wall on the offside, then that will give you sufficient space to miss the towpath side as well."

"OK Mister," said Danny, and a wide smile gradually appeared on his face as he successfully steered the boat through the bridge.

"Hey, there's another boat coming now," called out Danny after a minute or so. "What do I do now?"

"Again, that's simple," Alex told him. "Move the boat over to the right a little bit, to allow him to come past on your left side. Don't go too far over so we're in the reeds again, but make sure that the other boat has sufficient room between us and the other side of the water."

"OK, Mister," Danny replied, as he moved the tiller over, and *Jennifer Jo* obediently moved off the centre line of the canal and allowed the other boat to pass. Alex allowed himself a brief smile as he watched Danny gave the people on the other boat a proud wave, as if to say, 'hey, look at me, I'm driving this boat.'

"Now, we've got another bridge," said Danny. "I'll aim same as before, right? Just off to one side?"

"Well, be careful, Danny," Alex told the lad, as they approached the bridge. "This one is a blind bridge."

"What do you mean ?" Danny asked, incredulously. "Do you mean the other bridges can see?"

"Well, not really," Alex laughed. "It's just that, at the other bridge, we could see if there were any other boats coming towards us, because the canal on the other side of the bridge was fairly straight, and we could see what was coming towards us. But, if you look, directly after this bridge, there's a sharp bend. The bridge abutments obstruct the view of the canal ahead. It happens quite often. We can't see if there's another boat coming towards us or not, and of course, the bridge is only wide enough for one boat to go under at a time."

"So what do we do now, then?" asked Danny, a little nervously.

"That's easy," replied Alex. "Just slow down to a tick-over on the throttle and sound your horn. That way, any other boat coming towards us can hear us before they see us. And, because we'll have slowed down, it will be a lot easier to avoid a collision with the other boat if it suddenly comes into view as we go through the bridge."

Danny slowed the engine and pushed the horn button on the engine control panel, and the horn at the front of the boat sounded for a few seconds. To their surprise, they heard another horn answer in reply.

"There's another boat coming!" Danny exclaimed.

"That's right, Danny," Alex replied. "Now remember what I told you just now. Use reverse gear, and slow the boat down to a gentle crawl. And keep the boat over to the right-hand side, to give him room as he comes past you."

Danny did as Alex told him, and they coasted to a halt just before the bridge. Just a few moments later, a boat came into view round the bend and passed under the bridge. The man and woman on the back waved cheerfully at Danny and Alex as they passed, calling out "thank you, there's nothing behind us."

Danny waved back. "Thank you," he said in reply. And Alex nodded. "It was nice of them to say there's nothing behind," he told Danny. "Sometimes, you let an oncoming boat through the bridge, and then just as you're going through yourself, another boat comes along, close behind the first one."

"I s'pose that could be interesting," grinned Danny.

"Yes, it is sometimes," Alex replied. "But we usually manage somehow. Everyone tries to avoid hitting another boat if at all possible, people can get quite upset if you do. Especially if you cause some damage to their paintwork. Most people take a lot of pride in their boats, and how well they're turned out."

As the morning wore on, Alex found that, just as with his schooling, Danny learned quickly, needing Alex's help less and less. But, eventually, Alex looked at his watch. "It's time to moor up now, Danny," he told the boy. "How's about over there, just past those trees?"

"OK, Mister," said Danny. "But I'll let you take her in, if you don't mind. I don't want to hit the bank."

"That's alright, Danny, I'll take her," Alex told him, as he moved over and took the tiller. "We can practice mooring up tomorrow. And moving off as well, there's special techniques for both manoeuvres, which you'll need to know and learn. Locks as well. And tunnels. And winding holes. But practice makes perfect, as I'm sure you'll agree."

Danny just nodded, and smiled once again. "What's a winding hole, Mister?" he asked, puzzled once more.

"It's a special, short place along the canal, which is wider than normal, cut out of the offside, where you can turn a boat round. You see, most boats are much longer than the canal is wide, so they can't be turned round wherever you like. You have to find a winding hole to do that."

"But why on earth is it called a winding hole?" asked Danny.

"Well," replied Alex with another smile, "in the old days, when boats didn't have engines and were pulled by horses, it was really difficult to turn a boat around. So what they did, they drove the boat into the winding hole, and allowed the wind to push the other end of the boat around. As you'll remember from your experience this morning, the wind can play a big part in where exactly the boat is going. When you're turning the boat round, then you can use the wind to help you, for once. Hence the term 'winding hole'."

Danny nodded in silence, then added, "There's more to it than you first realise, ain't there? There's an awful lot to know." Alex just nodded in reply.

Later, as they sat at the dinette eating their lunch, Danny asked "How did I do, Mister, was I alright? Driving *Jay-Jay*? After the first disasters, of course?"

Alex smiled back at the boy. "Yes, Danny you did quite well, once you got the hang of it. And disasters like yours are part of boating, remember. It's not easy controlling a boat the size of *Jennifer Jo*. But there's some other, important, things that you must be aware of."

"What are they, then, Mister?" Danny asked, eagerly.

"Well, firstly, and perhaps the most important lesson of all. Never forget that when you're driving the boat, you're in charge of 18 tonnes of moving machinery. And the only brakes you have are applied by putting the engine into reverse. And that's not very effective, at the best of times - the design of the hull below the water is optimised for making the boat go forwards, not backwards. And as I said earlier, she won't respond to the tiller when you're reversing, it will hardly steer at all. There are ways to get round that, but that lesson is for another time."

"The other important thing is to remember that when you're driving the boat, then it is you who is in charge. No-one else. You are responsible for the safety of the boat and her crew, as well as everyone else around the boat, whether on board or not, around locks, on other boats, or walking or cycling along the towpath, fishermen on the bank, everyone. It's a big responsibility. And when you're in charge, all your crew should do whatever you tell them. You always do for me, and I'm very thankful for that, and when you're driving *Jennifer Jo,* then I'll always do whatever you tell me. When I'm on the bank or at a lock, remember that I can't control the boat – you do. Don't be afraid to give out orders, especially in situations which may develop into something hazardous. Think ahead, and anticipate what may happen, what might go wrong. Be in control of yourself, the boat, and your crew, at all times. And always strive to have *Jennifer Jo* in the right place, at the right speed, at the right time. And never ever chase anyone else coming towards you for a bridge – if they're closer to the bridge than you are, then it's their bridge, so you should slow down and let them come through first."

"And finally, be sure that you never, ever, take any unnecessary risks. There are dangers to being on the canals, especially around the locks, so always strive to be aware of whatever risks may be present, and do your very best to avoid them. That way, you, and your crew, will stay safe on the water at all times."

"That's a bit much to remember, ain't it, Mister?" Danny said, with a worried frown.

"Well yes it is, at first," replied Alex. "But you'll get used to it in no time. Don't worry, I'll always be here to guide you. But that's enough for today. Would you like to clear up the lunch things while I sort out your lessons for this afternoon?"

"Right-oh, Mister, I'll do the washing up," Danny said. "And after lessons shall I wash the boat and the pole, while you get the tea?

"That's a bargain," grinned Alex. "Sounds good to me."

CHAPTER 10

"OK, Danny, you can bring her in now," Alex called out, beckoning the lad to bring the boat into the lock. As he did so, he allowed himself a wry smile. By now, it had become a bit of a ritual, a game almost, for whoever was working the lock to give that call. Danny had started it, making that same call every time they went through a lock, ever since he'd starting living aboard with Alex, the call to bring *Jennifer Jo* into or out of whichever lock they were working through. And now, whenever Danny was taking his turn driving the boat, Alex had continued in the same vein. They both knew that it was merely stating the obvious, and totally unnecessary, but neither of them wished to spoil It - it was another little part of the bond that had developed between them, a small piece of ritual that they both enjoyed.

A small crowd of about 2 dozen people, with a number of children, had gathered round the lock from the adjacent pub garden to watch *Jennifer Jo* being worked through the lock. The part of the canal system where they were now was not heavily used, and a boat using the lock was almost guaranteed to create a stir of interest, especially when there was a busy pub nearby.

Alex sat on the balance beam of the bottom lock gate and watched approvingly as Danny pushed the rear end of *Jennifer Jo* away from the bank, and engaged reverse gear for a few seconds to pull the boat away from the bank. He then swung the tiller hard over as he engaged forward gear, steered the boat into the middle of the canal, and then, keeping the engine at tick-over, carefully guided *Jennifer* Jo towards the lock.

Alex was proud of how well Danny had learnt the navigation skills needed to control the boat, since Alex had first suggested he take the helm just three weeks before, and now Alex felt comfortable that Danny could handle almost anything that occurred. And what reinforced his view was the fact that Danny recognised there were occasional instances when a situation occurred which he felt less than comfortable with, and then asking Alex to take control once again. It pleased Alex to find that Danny wasn't too proud to admit that he was still learning the tricks of the trade, as it were.

As the boat approached the lock, Danny turned to look at a woman, a short, extremely fat, lady wearing a floral print dress, who was walking her dog on the towpath. Suddenly, the dog, a brown and white King Charles spaniel with long floppy ears, stopped and lowered its rear end, and then started defecating onto the towpath, right in the middle of the path where people would be walking. The woman stood proudly by whilst the dog finished its business, then gave a tug on its lead and started walking away along the towpath.

Alex watched as Danny's face creased into a frown. He knew that Danny had developed a strong aversion to dogs' mess on the towpath, and unfortunately there was lot of it about. Many people who lived near the canal brought their dogs for exercise along the towpath - after all, it made for a very pleasant walk, and there was always the chance of seeing the odd boat pass by. A few of them cleared up after their dogs, but there were very many more who did not. Danny had told Alex on more than one occasion how disgusting he thought it was, and he'd several times had to clean his shoes after inadvertently stepping in some foul deposit or other. But he'd never before seen the dirty deed being done, never actually caught a dog owner leaving the scene without clearing up after their pet.

Alex had thought that he'd got to know Danny quite well in the several months since he'd come to live with Alex on *Jennifer Jo,* but what happened next really surprised him. Danny cut the engine, and turned to face the dog owner.

"Hey you," he called out angrily. "Aren't you gonna clear up your dog's mess?"

The woman stopped walking for a moment, and stared at Danny without saying a word, then started walking away again. For Danny, that was it. He started shouting at her at the top of his voice.

"Now you look here," he called out. "We live on this boat, it's our boat, and it's our home. For us, wherever we go, wherever we are, the towpath is our garden. We don't want your dogs mess in our garden. How would you like it if I came and crapped in your garden? Hey?"

By now, the gongoozlers who'd gathered around the lock to watch *Jennifer Jo* being worked through were all watching this exchange with interest. The woman stopped walking, turned to Danny, and shouted back at him. "Mind your own business, you little runt," she yelled. "Leave me and my dog alone."

That seemed to infuriate Danny even more. "Look here, you clear up that mess, right now," he shouted. "If you don't, I'll gather it up and follow you home, and post it through your letter box. How would you like that?"

The woman just started at Danny, momentarily lost for words, then she shouted back at the boy. "I'm not clearing it up," she shouted. "Why should I? It's just nature for dogs to relieve themselves."

"Yes, but not in our garden, it ain't," Danny called out, as he put the engine into reverse to draw the boat backwards and stay abreast of the unfortunate woman. "I suppose you're too damned fat to bend over," he yelled. "But you ain't gonna leave it here. NOW PICK IT UP!" he screamed at the top of his voice.

The woman hesitated as her face turned a bright shade of red, and, embarrassed now, looked around at all the people watching. Then, weakly, she said "I can't. I haven't got anything to pick it up with."

"Well then, use your handkerchief," Danny yelled. "Go on, pick it up NOW!""

The woman blushed, muttering to herself, and looked around once again at all the people watching. Then, very slowly and reluctantly, she pulled out a handkerchief from her pocket, and with some difficulty bent down and picked up the dog's excreta.

"That's better, I should think so. Thank you," yelled Danny. "Probably the best thing you've done this week, if not this year."

The woman moved to the water's edge and made to deposit the handkerchief and its contents into the water. Danny watched in fury.

"No you don't," he yelled. "Take your dog's mess home. We don't want it here, fouling and polluting the water. It's dirty enough as it is."

Her face still red, the woman turned away and hurried off down the towpath, still holding the handkerchief in her hand, muttering to herself and tugging at the dogs lead as she went.

"I should think so too," Danny shouted after her. "Don't ever come back here again, will you! We'll be watching you if you do!" as he put the engine into gear and steered the boat towards the lock once again.

"Well done, lad," one of the onlookers called out. "She needed telling. She's always along here, always letting her dog foul the towpath. We often see her about here, along the canal."

"Yes, that's right," called out another. "My kids get that muck on their shoes no end of times. It's just not good enough. It needed saying."

Someone else called out "good for you, boy." It was Danny's turn for his face to go a mild shade of red, as, embarrassed now, he turned to the task in hand and carefully guided the boat into the lock, bringing her to a gentle halt midway along the 75ft length of the lock, and then staring fixedly at the roof of the boat just in front of him, his gaze not wavering as he waited patiently for Alex to close the gate and open the paddles to allow the lock to fill.

Once safely in the confines of the lock, Danny kept his head down, staring at the deck, a pose which Alex had only seen a few times before, a pose which Alex recognised Danny adopted whenever he felt embarrassed or depressed. Alex swung the bottom gate of the lock closed, walked to the top end of the lock, and cracked open the top paddle part of the way, to allow the water from the upper pound to slowly fill the lock. Once the lock was two-thirds full, Alex would open the paddle to its fullest extent, but he knew that if the paddle was opened before then, a rush of water would develop which would cause *Jennifer Jo* to be forced forward uncontrollably onto the cill, or sent crashing uncontrollably into the top gate. Much better to take a minute or two more to work the lock, than risk any damage to the lock mechanism, or to *Jennifer Jo*.

The lock was one of the deepest Alex had yet encountered on the system, having a rise of almost 12 feet, and only one paddle was working properly, so the water was taking a long time to flow into the lock and fill it. Whilst Alex sat on the balance beam and waited patiently, he looked around at the assembled crowd watching the proceedings. Suddenly there was the musical sound of a mobile phone ringing. Everyone looked around at each other, grinning, wondering whose it was, with several taking their mobiles out of their pockets to check that it wasn't theirs.

Suddenly, on the other side of the lock to where he was resting, Alex spotted a woman in the crowd, aged about thirty, with long unkempt hair and scruffy clothes, who was pushing a little girl in a buggy. She looked around and smiled apologetically, put the brake on the pushchair, and pulled out her mobile phone from the bag hanging on the back of the buggy. She then turned her back and walked away, deep in her private conversation, leaving the buggy unattended at the side of the lock. But even as Alex watched, the child, certainly no more than about two years old, wriggled out of the buggy and started walking along near the top wall of the lock, right close to the edge, just above the bubbling, boiling water in the lock below, unaware of the lurking danger.

Alex was horrified, but it seemed no-one else was taking any notice, or if they had noticed, they didn't dare to do anything, an unwanted by-product perhaps of the law of unintended consequences. Touch someone else's child these days, even to wipe its nose or to pick it up if it fell and hurt itself, and most likely you'd be in court charged with child abduction, or assault, or paedophile intentions. And so it was nowadays that people just tended to ignore any duty of care that they might once upon a time have felt towards someone else's child.

And then, the inevitable happened. Whilst the child's mother was still stood talking into her mobile, with her back to the lock, Alex was horrified to see the child trip and tumble over, and fall into the lock. It all seemed to happen in slow-motion, and Alex was unable to do anything except cry out – but by them it was too late, and the little girl was falling, ever so slowly it seemed, down into the lock, towards the water where, if she wasn't trapped and crushed between the boat and the lock wall, she would enter the water and almost certainly drown.

But Alex had reckoned without Danny, sitting on the back rail at the rear of *Jennifer Jo*. He'd been patiently sitting there, waiting for the lock to fill, but still staring at the deck after his earlier encounter with the lady and her dog. But on hearing Alex's shout, Danny looked up, instantly assessed the situation, and leapt into action. He immediately jumped up onto the gas locker, and then up onto the roof of the boat, dashing forwards towards the girl as she fell down towards the water. With a start, Alex realised that however fast Danny ran along the top of the boat, he would not make it in time to catch the child.

But once again, Danny surprised Alex by the speed of his reactions. As he neared the girl, he lunged forward, as if making a rugby tackle, and stretched out his right hand. As the full length of his body came to rest on the top deck of the boat, by some sort of miracle his hand caught under the girl's dress just before she hit the water. Very slowly, he managed to drag her up onto the deck, as she cried her eyes out with fear. Danny sat up on the deck, and drew the child to him, hugging her tightly and cuddling her, all the time murmuring into her ear, and slowly stroking her hair. And as he did so, she stopped crying and smiled at Danny, as if to say thank you.

Alex suddenly remembered what Danny had told him about the young boy, Freddie, whom he'd been with when he was being fostered by Mrs. Bradley. Back then, over the course of weeks and months, Danny had comforted the child and helped him come to terms with the terrible scenes he'd witnessed when he'd seen his father attack and kill his mother. And now Danny was exhibiting the same technique here with this young girl. There was no doubt that Danny had a way with young, distressed children.

By now, the boat had risen almost to the top of the lock, and *Jennifer Jo's* roof was just about level with the ground beside the lock. Alex looked over at the child's mother as, just then, she finished her phone call. Looking around, she walked swiftly over to the lock, where she was astonished to find her buggy empty, with Danny still sat on the roof cuddling the young girl whom he'd saved from almost certain death a few moments before.

"What do you think you're doing with Susan?" she screamed. "You pervert! Give her back here this minute," she went on, as she rushed forward, ready to take the child and put her back into the buggy. "I'm going to report you to the police," she screamed, "you're a pedophile, that's what you are, taking my kid, and right in front of all these people too." She looked round at the crowd. "Why didn't you lot stop him taking my Susan?" she shouted accusingly.

Danny looked at the woman, not speaking, as she continued her rant. "Have you no shame?" she asked loudly. "Someone as young as you, you should be ashamed of yourself. You're like all those people you read about in the papers. They should put you in prison, so they should."

Danny's face contorted into a fierce scowl as he resisted the temptation to respond. Once again his face became a bright shade of red as he put the child back on the ground by the lock and scrambled back down onto the rear deck and resumed staring at the roof of the boat directly in front of him. His gaze didn't waver as he stood there silently, gripping the tiller ever-so-tightly in his right hand, his left hand resting equally tightly on the gear lever, ready to set *Jennifer Jo* moving off as soon as he could. It was obvious that he didn't like being falsely accused like that, just a few moments after he'd saved the woman's child from near death. Alex could tell that the boy was extremely angry at what the woman had just said to him, but he continued to remain quiet and tight-lipped.

"Leave the boy alone," a small, neatly dressed woman called out. "He saved your kid's life, you know. She fell into the lock while your back was turned, and he caught her, just in time. You should be thanking him now, not having a go at him like that."

"Mind your own business, you," the mother shouted back. "Keep your nose out of it."

"She's right," commented an elderly man in a smart jacket and trousers who was standing nearby with his wife. "Don't you think you'd better leave? It would be best for everyone if you didn't say anything else."

"Oh, leave me alone," the mother shouted. "Why don't you lot mind your own sodding business?" Sensing the crowd's hostility towards her, and scowling nastily at anyone who came into her gaze, she rushed off, pushing the buggy before her.

"The lad saved that kid's life," shouted another onlooker. "Give him some encouragement, why don't we? Well done, boy!" He started clapping, and the other onlookers joined in, as another round of applause swept around the lock.

Danny continued to say nothing, with just a small inclination of his head acknowledging the applause, as he looked up only just enough to take *Jennifer Jo* out of the lock, bringing her to a halt to allow Alex to step aboard. As he did so, the boy left the tiller for Alex to take, went forward a couple of steps, turned his back on Alex and sat on the deck with his knees drawn up to his chest, hands clasped around his legs. He stared out fixedly at the offside bank of the canal, rocking slowly back and forth, as Alex put the engine into gear and the boat slowly gathered forward way once again and moved away from the lock and its crowds of onlookers.

Alex steered the boat along the canal for another half-hour or so, then moved the boat into the bank and moored up. Unusually, Danny didn't help as usual, but without saying a word, he stepped off the boat, and made his way along the towpath for about 100 yards. Alex watched anxiously as Danny sat down on the grass, staring out over the cut, with his knees drawn up to his chest and his hands clasped around his knees once more. Alex was worried. He'd only seen Danny like this a few times before, and he knew that something was troubling the boy. But he knew Danny well enough to know that, at times like this, Danny simply wanted to be alone.

Alex went inside to the galley and made a couple of plates of sandwiches for lunch. Putting them on a tray with a couple of glasses of squash and some apples, he went out onto the towpath and walked slowly up to Danny, who was still sitting there morosely, staring out over the cut.

"Here's some lunch," Alex said. "May I join you?"

Danny silently reached out, and took a plate of sandwiches and a drink. "May I join you, please?" Alex repeated.

Danny slowly shook his head, as he started eating his lunch, still staring out over the meadow on the off side of the canal.

Alex knew better than to argue with Danny when he was upset about something, as he certainly seemed to be now. He went back to *Jennifer Jo* and sat in the cratch to eat his lunch, making sure that he could see Danny in the distance. He wondered what was troubling the boy. Admittedly, he'd had a shouting match with the woman whose dog had fouled the towpath. But he'd saved the life of that young girl who'd fallen into the lock. It was something that Danny should have been celebrating, not sitting morosely on the grass staring out across the cut at the moment.

In all the time that they'd been together on *Jennifer Jo,* it was a side of Danny which Alex had never ever seen before, a side of his personality which Danny had kept well hidden. To Alex, Danny was defined by his lively demeanour and his trademark grin, which never seemed to be very far away. It troubled Alex a great deal to see Danny so much out of his normal character.

Alex waited for Danny to return to the boat for the afternoon's lessons, but the young boy remained sitting on the towpath all afternoon, staring out at the countryside, occasionally picking off a long stem of grass to chew and spit out. It wasn't until early evening, when Alex called out to him to say that supper was ready, that the boy returned to the boat. He came in and sat at the dinette, in his usual spot opposite Alex, and ate his meal. But the whole of the meal was spent in silence, Danny not once responding to Alex's attempts to start a conversation, a big departure from their normal meals when Danny would chat with Alex about anything that caught their fancy.

Immediately after tea, Danny went straight to his berth in the back cabin, and once again Alex knew better than to disturb him. At their usual time of around 9 o'clock, Alex made an evening drink, and took Danny's through to him. This time, Danny spoke. "Thanks, Mister," he said, as he smiled weakly.

"May I sit and talk to you, please?" Alex asked. Danny nodded.

Alex perched on the vacant bunk opposite and looked at him. His complexion seemed a bit pale compared to his usual tan.

"What is it Danny?" Alex asked. "I don't like to see you like this. What's wrong? Talk to me please. Like I told you that first week you were with me, it really does help to talk about anything that may be troubling you."

Danny sat in his bunk, staring down at the duvet. It was a full two minutes before he spoke, as Alex waited patiently.

"I'm sorry," he said quietly. "Really sorry."

"Sorry?" exclaimed Alex. "What on earth for? You haven't done anything to be sorry about."

The boy turned and looked up at Alex with an anguished expression. "Yes I have, Mister," he said. I'm ever so sorry."

"I don't understand, Danny," Alex said quietly. "You'd better explain, please."

"I let you down," the boy replied slowly. "Really badly. I don't know how I can persuade you to forgive me. You might not want to let me stay with you any more. I don't want to have to go on the run again, it wouldn't be very nice now that it's coming up to winter now. I like being here on your boat with you, it's really nice."

Alex noticed tears forming in the corners of Danny's eyes. He felt shocked by what Danny had just said. He hastened to reassure the boy. "Danny, do you remember what I told you some time ago?" he asked. "I told you that you could stay here with me on *Jennifer Jo* for as long as you wanted to. I really did mean what I said. Nothing has changed that, nothing at all. And I'm not aware that you let me down at all. What makes you think that you have?"

"That woman with the dog," he said. "I shouted at her. Said some nasty things to her what I never should have said. I shouldn't ever have spoken to her like that. With all those people watching as well. I was really cross, seeing her dog doing its mess on the towpath, and I just lost it. I lost my self-control completely. I really let myself down. And you see, everyone watching knew I was with you, of course. And because you're the adult, you're sort of responsible for me, for what I do, for what I say, it reflects badly, really badly, on you too. I'm ever so sorry."

"Danny, listen to me," Alex reassured the troubled youngster. "You have nothing to apologise about. You know that I feel the same way about dogs fouling the towpath as you do. And what you said to that woman needed saying. I'm sure that she'll pick up after her dog in future. Everyone gets a bit worked up at times, about all sorts of things. There's lots of worse things which you could have said to her, but you didn't. So you didn't lose it much at all. You didn't let me down, or yourself, at all. Don't worry about it. I certainly won't. And remember, the people at the lock supported you as well. Forget about it, please. It's nothing."

"Are you sure?" Danny asked tearfully, looking up.

"Yes, Danny, I'm sure," Alex replied. "And remember, you saved that little girl's life a few minutes later. You should be really proud of that. If you hadn't caught her when you did, she'd almost certainly have been killed. Well done."

Danny shook his head, more miserable than ever.

"No, Mister," he said. "It was an accident," he said, very quietly. "An accident."

"Of course it was," Alex replied. "The girl fell off the edge of the lock wall. She would have gone into the water, or been crushed by the boat, if you hadn't caught her. Everyone knows it was an accident. You saved her life. You should be very proud."

Danny shook his head. "No, Mister," he said. "It were an accident."

"What do you mean, an accident, Danny?" Alex asked. "What are you talking about?"

"That girl," he said. "it were an accident that I saved her. You see, when you shouted out, I saw her trip up at the top of the lock wall, I could see she were gonna fall into the lock. But I knew she were too far away for me to get to her in time."

"It's just like when we're going along the canal, and we go round a bend and there's a narrow bridge ahead, only wide enough for one boat to go through, and there's another boat on the other side of the bridge, coming towards us. You can tell instantly whose bridge it is, which boat is the closest. It was just like that back there with that little girl. As soon as I saw her trip up, I just knew that by the time I'd got up on the roof of the boat, and run along to where she was, and then crouched down and stuck my hand out, well, she'd have been in the water by then. I just knew I wasn't going to be able to save her. But I just had to try, didn't I?"

"Yes, you did very well," replied Alex, "But you did save her, didn't you?"

"Yea, but only by accident," Danny replied, morosely. "I knew even before I started climbing up onto the roof of the boat that I was too far away, that I wouldn't get to her in time, even though I was going to run as fast as I could. It was just too far." Danny stopped talking and was quiet again. So Alex asked, eventually, "go on, please, Danny. Tell me what you mean?"

"Well you see, it were an accident, an accident that I saved her," he said. "Like I said, I ran as fast as I could, even though I knew I weren't going to get to her in time. And then I tripped. My foot caught against the upstand for the gangplank. That's what made me lunge forwards, falling forwards onto the roof of the boat like that. But I didn't do it on purpose. I only caught her 'cos I fell over, and stretched out my hand at just the right time. I didn't really save her. It was just luck. I ain't no hero or nothing. I didn't deserve all that applause and stuff. I only got her by accident."

"Well, never mind, Danny," Alex replied. "However you managed it, you did save that child's life. You still have much to be proud of."

"No, I don't think so," Danny responded, glumly. "But at least the kid's alive. She's really sweet, ain't she? I suppose we gotta be thankful for that."

"Yes, we have," said Alex. "And so should the girls' mother, even though she may not be the best mother in the world. You could have said a lot to her, when she started shouting at you like she did. I thought you showed a great deal of self-control. It was very good of you to say nothing, not to start shouting back at her, like you did with that dog woman earlier."

"Yea," Danny replied sadly. "I told her didn't I, that woman with the dog? But I shouldn't have done, should I? I just lost it. Lost it completely. My Mum and Dad always taught me to be nice to people, even if I didn't like them. I should never have spoken like that, said what I did. I really let myself down today, and you as well. Now, I'm really ashamed of what I said. It weren't right to talk like that, to anyone, however much they deserved it."

"Yes, Danny." Alex spoke softly and gently. "The lady with the dog did deserve it. She needed telling. But do you know why people don't speak out, and say things that should be said, like you did today?"

Danny looked up at Alex, shaking his head.

"People don't speak out, and say what should be said, because they know that very often, the truth hurts. Sometimes the truth can hurt a lot, very much indeed. It's out of kindness that people keep quiet, and don't say what should be said, out of consideration for the other person's feelings. In a way, it's unkind to be kind, because quite often, people should be told things which they don't realise for themselves. But it's not an easy decision to make, and the more one thinks about speaking out, then the more difficult it becomes to say what needs to be said. Quite often, speaking off the cuff, like you did today, is a kindness in itself, even though at the time it may hurt, hurt very much. And of course, whatever you say might well be ignored anyway."

Alex paused for a moment, and then continued. "Danny, you have nothing to be ashamed of, about anything that happened today. And, as I said before, you can be very proud that you saved that girl's life, however the circumstance in which you managed it. And, I'd like you to remember that I'm proud of you too. And your mother would have been too, had she been here. Very proud indeed."

Danny looked up again and nodded. Alex took the lad's hand and gave it a gentle squeeze, and saw Danny smile back in return. "I'll leave you to it," he added. "Come through to watch a bit of TV if you like."

Danny shook his head. "No thanks, Mister," he said. "I'm ok here for the moment, and I'm gonna settle down soon. I'm rather tired after everything that happened today."

"That's alright, Danny," Alex replied, "as you wish." He returned to the saloon to enjoy his own cup of tea, and see what was worth watching on the television. But there was nothing which he really felt was worth watching. Instead, he sat in the saloon and thought about Danny. Rarely, if ever, had he seen the boy so upset, for upset he surely was.

Alex realised that beneath Danny's cheerful exterior there lay a deeply troubled child, a troubled and insecure child, a part of his personality which remained well hidden for most of the time. Danny had experienced far more than his fair share of bad fortune. His father had left the family home whilst Danny was still young. His mother had been taken into hospital, and the boy had been left home alone for some time. Then through a foster home, and a children's home, before ending up at Grant

Hall. 'How on earth,' Alex thought, 'could any young child remain unaffected by those experiences?' Alex realised that Danny's usually lively personality concealed a child with a lot of grief within, a lot of grief which had yet to be discharged over the course of time.

Alex thought for a long while about how he could help Danny, but in the end he came to the conclusion that there was nothing more that he could do for him, nothing which he wasn't already doing. He was providing a secure home environment for the boy, albeit a slightly unusual one, and generally Danny had responded well. The boy's only unsettled item was finding Danny's mother, a goal Danny had never once given up on, and Alex knew that the time to talk about the absolute impossibility of finding his mother was still a long way off. When the boy was sixteen or seventeen, and mature enough to cope with the thought that he might never see his mother again, then that would be the time. But without any doubt at all, the time to talk about that was not now.

It was about half an hour later, as Alex started tidying up in the saloon, that he heard the water pump running, and heard Danny moving around in the bathroom.

Suddenly Alex heard a movement behind him, and turned to find Danny standing behind him. "Hey, Mister," he said quietly.

"Yes, Danny, what is it?" Alex asked.

Danny remained silent as he lifted up his tee shirt to reveal a huge bruise on the right side of his chest, just above the bottom of his ribcage. It was a deep purple, and stretched in a long line across his ribs and across his abdomen.

"How did you do that, Danny?" Alex asked.

"It was when I fell. Catching that little girl, " he said. "Like I said, I tripped. When I fell, I fell onto the handrail along the edge of the roof. That's how it happened."

"It looks awful," Alex said, "but bruises often do. Does it hurt?"

Danny nodded, without saying anything.

"Come here, let's have a look," Alex instructed the boy, who stepped closer, as Alex stretched out his hand and gently felt around the bruise. Several times, Danny winced with pain, but he didn't cry out.

"I think you may have broken some ribs," Alex said. "Go and lie down, and I'll have a look in my first aid book."

After a minute or so, Alex returned to Danny's berth in the back cabin. "Danny," he asked, "do you have any of the following symptoms? Severe shortness of breath? Coughing blood? Confusion or dizziness? General weakness? Blood in your urine?"

"No, Mister," Danny replied, after a moment spent thinking about what Alex had asked him. "It just hurts, when I breath heavy."

Alex looked at his watch. It was gone 10 o'clock in the evening. It was at times like this that he missed the easy availability of transport, such as he'd had for many years at the school, with his car just around the corner in its garage.

"OK, Danny," Alex said. "What we'll do, is, in the morning we'll get you to hospital, to have it checked over. And no arguing about that, please. But for now, try to get some sleep. Would you like a couple of aspirins, to help with the pain?"

Danny nodded. "Yea, please, Mister," he said. "That would be nice."

Alex fetched the tablets from his first aid box, and a glass of water, and sat and watched whilst Danny swallowed them down. "Thanks, Mister," he said again. "G'night."

"Goodnight, Danny," Alex replied. "If it gets worse during the night, come and wake me, do you understand? You must. Don't be afraid to come and see me, OK?"

Danny nodded. "I will, Mister," he said, "but I'll try not to, unless it's really bad."

"OK, Danny," Alex replied, as the lad got up to go. "But be sure to do so if you need to."

The next morning, Alex took *Jennifer Jo* along the cut for about half an hour, until they reached a canal-side pub with a main road running nearby. Danny had remained in his bunk, not eating any of the breakfast which Alex had taken in to him. Alex moored up the boat, and walked the short distance to the pub. Trying the door, he found it locked. He went round to the back, and found a young man stacking empty barrels in the pub yard.

"Excuse me, please, can you help me?" Alex asked.

"Yes? What do you want? We're closed." the man replied.

"Can you help me with the phone number for a taxi, please?" Alex asked. "My boy on the boat has hurt himself. I need to call a taxi and get him to a hospital."

The man straightened up and smiled briefly. "Yes, that's OK, then," he replied. "Come with me, follow me." Alex followed him into the bar, and the man pointed to a payphone mounted on the wall near the front entrance door. Tucked into the bottom of the booth were several cards from taxi firms. Alex pulled out his notebook from his pocket and noted down some of the numbers.

"Thank you," he said, "thank you very much," as he left the pub and walked the short distance back to the boat. The first number he tried was not a success, giving the unobtainable tone, but Alex did better with the second number. The person on the other end of the phone agreed to have a taxi there at the pub within the next ten minutes. Alex went down inside the boat, and went through into the back cabin.

"Come on, then, Danny, get up please," he said. "There's a taxi coming for us. You've got ten minutes to get showered and dressed. Do you want anything to eat?"

Danny shook his head. "I won't shower today," he replied. "It still hurts quite a bit. I'll have a quick wash instead."

Alex nodded. "OK, Danny, that's fine." Come up outside when you're ready."

The taxi arrived just as Danny made an appearance on the back deck of *Jennifer Jo*. "Just in time," Alex smiled to him as they clambered into the back of the car.

"Where to, please?" the driver asked.

"Hospital, please," Alex replied, "the nearest one with an A & E department."

"No problem," the driver replied. "Be there in about 20 minutes."

Alex sat with Danny in the back of the taxi, neither of them speaking until they reached the hospital. "Thank you," Alex said to the driver as he paid the fare. "Please give me your card and I'll ring you when we're ready to go back." Alex took the card the driver offered, and then took Danny into the A & E department of the hospital.

Danny walked through to the waiting area and sat down, whilst Alex went to the reception desk.

"Yes, can I help you?" the lady behind the desk asked, a middle aged lady with a big bosom and a smile to match.

"Yes, please," Alex replied. "It's the young boy sitting over there. His name's Daniel Marshall. He's sustained some sort of injuries to his chest."

"Right," said the reception nurse. "What relation are you to him?" she asked, looking over Alex's shoulder at Danny, sitting quietly in the waiting area. "He's my grandson," Alex replied, crossing his fingers behind his back as he did so. The little white lie they used to conceal their true relationship, that they were not related to each other in any way at all, was being used more and more.

"Right," said the nurse, as she wrote it down, and started filling out a form. "Now, what address, please?"

Alex was stymied for a moment. "Narrowboat *Jennifer Jo*, on the canal," he said after a short pause.

"No, I mean your permanent address," she said, huffily. The smile had disappeared, replaced with a slight frown.

"This is our permanent address," Alex told her. "We live on our boat."

"Well, shall I put you down as 'no fixed abode,' then?" asked the reception nurse. "No permanent address?"

"Well, that's not strictly true," replied Alex. "We do have a permanent abode. Like I said, our boat is our permanent address. It's just that it moves around. On the canal."

"Is there no other way we can get in touch with you?" asked the nurse, getting more and more frustrated by the minute.

"Well, I've got an email address," Alex told her. "And a mobile phone number. The email works over the mobile phone network. But they don't always work, because, a lot of time on the canal, since the route of the canal keeps to the low ground, mobile reception is quite often very poor, and we can't get a signal. That's the best I can do for you. Will that be sufficient?"

"I suppose it will have to," the nurse said, scowling at Alex as she did so, and then writing down the details Alex gave her. "Please take a seat," she said eventually, the scowl now replaced by a slight smile, "and you'll be seen shortly."

Alex went and sat down beside Danny, who was watching the wide-screen TV set high up on the wall in the waiting area, above a large placard proclaiming that the TV had been provided free of charge by a local electrical company.

Less than five minutes had passed when another nurse appeared, small with fair hair tied up in a bun at the back of her head beneath her little cap, and called out 'Daniel Marshall, please.' Alex looked round at Danny, who was still sitting there, eyes glued to the TV. Alex gave him a nudge.

"That's you, Danny," he said, as the nurse called out his name once again.

"Oh, yea," Danny replied. "Thanks, Mister. I ain't used to being called Daniel. Everyone always calls me Danny." He got up and started to walk towards the nurse, then paused and turned to Alex, still sitting on the seat behind him. "Aren't you coming in too?" he asked.

Alex shook his head. "No, Danny," he replied. "You go in on your own. You're a big boy now, remember," he smiled. "They'll look after you really well without my being there."

Danny nodded and went into the treatment area with the nurse, but re-appeared just a couple of minutes later, and sat down by Alex once again. "That weren't much," Danny told him. "They just had a quick look, and then said I'd gotta come out and sit down again. Do we go now?"

"No, Danny, we don't go yet, "Alex told him. "That's just the triage nurse."

"So, what's that?" asked Danny, curiously.

"Well," Alex replied, "whenever anyone arrives at A & E, first of all they have a quick look, and determine the severity of the patient's injuries. The ones that are serious are always looked at first. Others, which aren't so serious, have to wait until all the more urgent cases have been seen. That way, those with the most pressing clinical needs are attended to first."

"Well, I s'pose that's a good idea," said Danny. "It hurts quite a bit, but I don't think it's life-threatening. So they'll look at me more closely in a little while?"

Alex smiled. "Yes, they will, they'll call you in again soon. This first examination, it's called triage," he said. "Don't ask me why."

"I told them you were my granddad," Danny replied. "And that we lived on the boat, on *Jay-Jay*. Was that OK?"

"Yes, that was fine," Alex told the lad. "That's exactly what I said too."

It was about 20 minutes before Danny was called in again, Danny giving Alex a wry smile as he walked back into the treatment area once again. Alex settled down in front of the TV to watch whatever was being shown. The sound was turned off, but subtitles appeared on the bottom of the screen to enable anyone who was watching to read the dialogue which was being spoken. Alex settled down to a long wait. He knew that the medical staff would make sure Danny was alright, and that their diagnosis and treatment wouldn't be rushed.

After about an hour, a nurse appeared and called out "Anyone with Daniel Marshall, please?" Alex got up and went into a side room with the nurse, and sat down on one of the chairs as she closed the door behind them, leaving just the two of them in the room.

"Now," the nurse said, "I'm a senior nursing practitioner here. Can you please tell me how Daniel got his injuries?"

Alex nodded, and recounted the events of the previous day, including his praise for the boy in saving the little girl who'd fallen into the lock.

"Right," said the nurse when he'd finished, "that's all for now, thank you. Please can you go back to the waiting area. We've nearly finished with Daniel now, he'll be with you shortly."

Alex went and sat down once again, but he'd only been there a couple of minutes when he was called into the treatment area. There on a bed sat Danny, surrounded by a couple of nurses and a doctor in a white coat.

"Right," said the doctor. "Daniel here has sustained severe bruising to his chest, and especially to his lower ribs on the right-hand side. We've X-rayed the suspect area, and think there's nothing serious, but it's possible that there's a hairline fracture to one of his ribs. We can't be exactly sure, as the X-ray isn't too clear. There's not a lot we can do for him, except to advise that he does very little strenuous exercise for about 6 weeks, and to take things easy, very easy, in the meantime. The pain he's experiencing is mostly caused by the bruising, especially to the bones, and it will wear off after a couple of weeks or so, but maybe a little longer, it's difficult to tell at this stage. We've given him some painkillers to take when he feels the need for them, but please make sure that he doesn't ever take more than one tablet at a time. Otherwise, that's about all. You may go now."

"Thank you, thank you very much," said Alex, as he shook hands with the doctor, nodded to the nurses, returned back to the reception area with Danny, and then out of the hospital into the bright sunshine. Taking out his mobile, he phoned the taxi service which had brought them to the hospital, and arranged for a pickup, which he was told would be within the next 15 minutes. Whilst they waited, Alex and Danny sat on a bench in the bright sunshine, and enjoyed the view over the well-kept grounds of the hospital.

"That wasn't too bad, Danny, was it?" asked Alex.

"No," replied Danny. "There's some nice nurses in there, ain't there?" Alex laughed. It seemed that, even with his injuries, Danny had not missed the opportunity to eye up the ladies.

"There was one funny thing, though," Danny continued. "There was this nurse, she asked me how I did it, then a bit later, there was this other guy, with a white coat, he came and asked me how it happened, and then after the X-rays had been done, there was this other nurse came and asked me the same question. And they all wrote it down, what I said."

"What did you tell them, then?" asked Alex.

"Well, I told them what happened, just like it was, that's all," replied Danny. "I dunno why they wanted three different people to ask the same questions."

"That's easy," Alex told the lad. "As far as they're concerned, you're still a child. They always look at injuries to children very carefully, in case the child in question has been abused by his family, or friends. They came and asked me as well. Don't worry about it. If they'd been really concerned, then they would have called in the police. But look, here's our taxi. Let's get back to the boat and have some lunch."

As they rode back to *Jennifer Jo*, Danny suddenly turned to Alex. "Hey, Mister," he said, "I've just thought. How are you going to handle *Jay-Jay* on your own? If I'm not allowed to help you with pulling her in to the side and mooring up and doing the locks? Will you be able to manage her alright?"

"Don't worry about that, Danny," Alex replied. "I reckon you should still be able to drive the boat, the tiller's not heavy at all. I can do the locks and the heavy stuff. And, don't forget, I used to handle her on my own, before I found a stowaway one evening a few months ago."

Danny grinned. "Well oh yea, then, I suppose so," he sighed. "But I'll help as much as I can."

"Yes, I know you will," said Alex. "But if there's anything you're doing that hurts your chest, then you must stop, at once. That's an order. Do you understand?"

Danny nodded and grinned. "If you say so, Mister," he said.

"But that won't stop you doing the washing up, now, Danny will it?" Alex turned and smiled.

"No, spose not," Danny sighed. "It's never ending isn't it? But it comes with having to eat, don't it?"

Alex smiled again, and nodded. He was pleased to see Danny's sense of humour was as good as ever.

CHAPTER 11

"There it is, Mister," Danny called out, as they rounded yet another bend of the canal. "I think that's it, up there on the offside, just past that long line of poplar trees."

Alex picked up the binoculars and looked ahead up the canal. "Yes, Danny, I think you're right," he replied. "Throttle down a bit and we'll take it easy, till we find out if this is the right place."

Danny did as Alex had suggested, and *Jennifer Jo* gradually slowed down to a crawl. A heavy boat, she always took a long while to stop. Thinking ahead when at the helm of the boat would always be the name of the game.

As they drew closer, Alex was able to see that Danny was right. It was indeed the place they'd been looking for since they started out earlier that morning, the morning of Christmas Eve. He'd booked *Jennifer Jo* into a short-term berth at a marina over Christmas, just for a period of a fortnight. There would be electrical power available on the pontoon for their shoreline, so there would be no need to run the engine to keep the boat's batteries charged, and the electric immersion heater would provide plenty of hot water. They'd got plenty of coal for the stove, too, and it was very likely that the marina would hold a stock of coal should they need more. During the winter months, Alex always tried to keep the stove alight through the night, and he had a thermally powered electric fan which he placed on top of the stove every evening, to circulate the warm air coming off the stove around the interior of the boat.

He'd spotted the marina's advert in one of the canal magazines a few weeks before – 'temporary berths available over the Christmas break – good rates and good company. Phone for details.' And since they weren't that far away, he'd phoned in, confirmed the price and availability, and made the booking straight away. It was lucky that he'd done so when he did, the guy on the other end of the phone had told him, 'you've got the last berth – every other one has gone already. So now we're fully booked.'

There were other advantages too, to being in the marina. They would be secure in there during the two weeks of the year when the hours of daylight would be at their least, and a bout of extremely cold weather was forecast, with heavy frosts and perhaps the chance of snow a little later on. Alex didn't worry about taking *Jennifer Jo* along in the cold, as both he and Danny had good outdoor clothing, and it was always nicely warm inside, but he'd felt that a couple of weeks without moving over

Christmas would make a welcome change for them both. And, if there were other boaters around, then there would be the chance to have a chat and maybe visit other boats and generally socialise and get to know the people from the other boats.

Danny brought the boat to a gentle halt at the side of the canal by the marina's jetty, then Alex stepped off onto the pontoon and took the mooring ropes whilst Danny stopped the engine.

"You moor up temporarily, will you please, Danny," he asked, "while I go and check in, and find out which is our berth." Danny nodded in agreement, with a slight grin. Nothing seemed to faze Danny any more. His injuries which he'd sustained from falling onto the top of the boat had healed up well, with no ill effects, and he'd once again become a full working member of *Jennifer Jo's* crew.

As he walked to the office, Alex looked around him. The marina was obviously brand new. The concrete he was walking on was still a virgin white, obviously freshly laid just a few weeks before. The pontoons jutting out into the water were constructed from hardwood, still with their original colour. Alex knew that after a year or two, they would fade away to a dull grey, as did most wood, but at the moment their colour proclaimed their newness to all who would look at them. About six of the twelve or so berths were already occupied, all end-on to the canal, with most of the boats having slim wisps of wood smoke curling up from their chimneys. Keeping a stove alight during the cold winter months was just about an essential for all boaters.

Alex went into the small office at the side of the marina, and introduced himself.

"Hello," the man behind the counter said. "My name's David," adding with a smile, "I'm the boss round here. *Jennifer Jo's* is the berth on the end, number 12. Plug your electric cable into that blue pillar on the pontoon. It's metered, and I'll give you the bill before you leave. There's water at the pillar as well, but that's not metered, it's included in your mooring fee, and of course you paid that by credit card when you made your booking. But please remember to run the water for about 30 seconds to start with, before you start filling up your tank, to get any stale water out of the system."

Alex nodded. That was standard practice anyway, but it certainly didn't hurt to be reminded of simple facts like that.

Pointing out of the window at a small compound surrounded by a wire fence, David added, "we've just got our stock of gas in, we're lucky as it only arrived yesterday, so if you need it, no problem. And there's some coal, in plastic sacks, round the back, as well, should you run out. And If you find there's anything else you want, just let me know. If I'm not here in the office, then I'll probably be on my boat. That's mine, at the other end, berth no. 1. It's called *Vagabond*. But I won't be out cruising much now, with the marina to get up and running."

Alex nodded. "Thank you," he said. "We'll go and get into the berth, and hook up."

"That's fine," David replied. "And, don't forget, we've got a welcome meeting later this afternoon, at 4.30. In the chandlery next door," and he pointed through a door to a large room beyond.

'Welcome meeting? I wonder what that will be about?' Alex thought, as he looked through the glass panel in the door at the side of the office. He saw an empty room, with just a few shelves and some cardboard boxes stacked against one wall, ready to be installed. "Chandlery?" he asked.

"Yes, well, it will be," David smiled, "once we get it all fixed up, and the stock arrives. It's all on order, but it's not due to be delivered until the New Year. Come along at half past four and I'll explain."

"OK," Alex replied. "We'll be there." And he turned to go out of the door, and return to Danny and walk back to *Jennifer Jo*.

"Oh, by the way," David called after him. "I've got three parcels here for you. They came a couple of weeks ago. Would you like to take them now?"

"No, thanks," Alex replied, looking out of the window at Danny, patiently standing beside the boat, holding the mooring ropes in his hand. He didn't want Danny to see that he'd got some parcels. "I've got the boy waiting outside. Is it alright," he asked, gesturing towards Danny, "if I collect them later, after we've moored up?"

"Yes, that will be fine," was the reply. David smiled and nodded. He knew exactly what Alex meant. "If I'm not here, then just tap on the window of my boat, Vagabond, and I'll slip out and see to you."

"Thanks, David. I'll be along later on," replied Alex, as David nodded and smiled warmly, and they shook hands once again.

Alex returned to *Jennifer Jo* and he and Danny carefully manoeuvred her into their berth, backing in gently, with Danny pulling on the ropes to guide her in and avoid her hitting the pontoon as she crept slowly backwards. When she was in position, Alex moored up, whilst Danny hooked up the electric cable, and then together they refilled their fresh water tank. It was wise to do that straight away – if the temperature dropped, then the water in the pipes along the pontoon might freeze, and then they would have to carry all the water they needed in cans from the tap in the toilet block. Then Alex did some minor checks on the engine, before they retired into the saloon and had a cup of tea together.

"Before we put the boat to bed for a couple of weeks, Danny, I need to refill the stern tube greaser," Alex said to Danny as they finished their tea. "Want to come up and keep me company?"

Danny nodded. "Yea, OK, then, Mister," he replied. "While you put your overalls on, I'll grab my coat, it's a bit parky out there."

Alex nodded in reply, and went up onto the rear deck, where he lifted one of the deck covers to reveal the greaser tube, and started the messy task of refilling the tube with grease. Danny sat nearby on the rear rail, and they chatted together whilst Alex attended to the greaser. The grease came in 200ml tins, and Alex had always found it difficult to get the grease into the tube without it going every else as well. He'd got Danny to do it a couple of times previously, but, whilst he tried his best, Danny's efforts turned out to be even worse than Alex's. In the end, they'd agreed that in future Alex would do it, while Danny would look on, learn, and observe. But, just as Alex was finishing, Danny looked up. "Hey, Mister," he said, "there's another boat coming in. I'll go and give them a hand to moor up. It's really difficult to get in, isn't it?"

"Yes, Danny, that's fine. Off you go. I've nearly finished here anyway. I'll get cleaned up and then start thinking about getting some supper ready."

It took Alex only a few minutes more before the greaser was sorted, and just as Alex was replacing the deck cover and stepping out of his overalls, Danny returned. "All moored up , then?" Alex asked him.

"Yes, fine, they thanked me for helping them," Danny replied, then adding "I'll go and have a walk round and get some sticks for the fire now, if you like."

"But, Danny, we've got plenty of sticks," Alex told the lad. "We collected a couple of full bags the other day. Don't you remember?"

"Yes, well, you can never have too many, now, can you?" Danny grinned as he disappeared inside *Jennifer Jo,* returning a few moments later with a handful of plastic carrier bags. "If I go now, then I'll be able to get plenty of sticks and be back before it gets too dark." And with that parting comment, Danny disappeared off along the pontoon at the side of the marina.

Alex watched him from the back of *Jennifer Jo,* partly hidden by the cabin of the boat lying beside them in the marina. What was Danny up to? They both knew that there were plenty of sticks in the saloon, and the boxes in the engine room were just about full as well. During the winter, they kept the fire in all the time if they could, and so sticks were only needed when the fire needed relighting, if it had gone out overnight.

But as Alex watched Danny hurry up the pontoon, it all became clear. Danny walked up the pontoon to the boat which had just arrived, and tapped gently on the saloon window. At once, the sliding hatch at the rear opened and a young girl, about the same age as Danny, climbed out of the hatch. Danny took her hand and together they walked off along the pontoon and into the woods at the back of the marina, carrier bags in hand.

'So that's it, Danny,' Alex smiled to himself. 'You are a fast worker, aren't you? I'll tease you about this when you get back. But whilst you're socialising, Danny my boy, I can go and fetch the parcels that are waiting for me in the office.' He replaced the deck cover and stepped out of his overalls, before slipping inside the boat to wash his hands, and then walked over to the office to collect his parcels. As soon as he'd made the booking for the marina and known where he'd be spending Christmas, he'd ordered the items the parcels contained on the internet one evening when Danny had turned in early. Come to think of it, Danny had been going to bed early for several weeks now. Alex had asked the lad if he was feeling alright, but Danny had said he was fine, but just a little bit tired.

Alex quickly walked over to the office and collected his parcels, one in a large jiffy bag, one in a slightly smaller jiffy bag, and a small carton about 8" square. Whilst Danny was off collecting sticks with his new friend, it was an ideal opportunity to get the parcels on board, and conceal them away from prying eyes until tomorrow, Christmas Day. He stowed them away in the lockers beneath the dinette seats, and had just started peeling the potatoes for supper when Danny returned. Alex walked through to the engine room where Danny was busy emptying four bags full of sticks into the boxes beside the engine.

"You've got a lot there, Danny," Alex commented. "it didn't take you long to get all those, did it, all on your own?"

"No," Danny replied sheepishly. "There were plenty laying around. Really easy, all you've got to do is just pick them up and pop them into the bags. They should do us for some time now." There was no mention, Alex noted, of the young assistant he'd managed to find to help him get the sticks, as he'd made his way along the pontoon a few minutes before.

Alex finished the potatoes, and then they put on their coats and made their way across to the office for David's welcome meeting. As they walked along the pontoon, Alex casually said to Danny "it's getting colder, there might be a frost tonight."

"Yes, Mister," Danny replied, "the wind's getting up too."

"Yes, Danny, that's right. I think it might be a quite a hard frost," Ales responded, then adding casually, "by the way, what's her name?"

"She's called Margaret, she's staying on the................" he tailed off, realising belatedly that Alex had twigged his little secret. If it hadn't been dark, Alex would have been able to see Danny's face blush a pale red colour for a few moments.

"It's all right, Danny," Alex told him. "I just couldn't resist teasing you. You always manage to find the girls, don't you?"

Danny didn't answer. But Alex guessed that he was smiling in the dark.

"Anyway," Alex continued, "it's nice for you to have someone your own age to be with, especially as we're here for the next couple of weeks."

"Yea, I suppose so," Danny responded. "She's really nice. It's her Uncle and Aunt's boat, it's called *Andante*, that's Latin ain't it? It means 'slowly', doesn't it? You see, I do pay attention in my Latin lessons, don't I?"

Alex smiled at Danny and nodded. Yes, Danny, that's right. Well done."

"They're live-aboards, just like us," Danny continued. "Her dad works for the government and he's abroad lots of the time, and her mum's usually with him as well, so she's at boarding school, but she spends her holidays on the boat with them, they're her Uncle and Aunt, see? She really likes it. But she don't like steering the boat, not at all. She's scared she'll put it into the bank. That's quite easy to do, really, aint it?"

Alex could see Danny's smile in the light from the office as they drew near. 'Good to see Danny's sense of humour was as sharp as ever,' Alex thought. Danny obviously hadn't forgotten his own first attempts at steering *Jennifer Jo*.

They went into the marina office, and then through into the room which would shortly become the new chandlery. There were several people already there, including a couple whom Alex had met about a year before, so Alex went over and re-introduced himself, introducing Danny as his grandson. The little white lie was being perpetuated once again. Over the next few minutes, the room gradually filled, with Danny's new friend Margaret coming over to stand beside him. Suddenly, the door from the office opened, and David came in and stood on a small stool.

"Can you all hear me alright?" he asked, looking around the room. "That's fine," he added, as he saw the assembled throng nodding their heads, adding, as he looked around the room, "I think you're all here."

"Well, firstly," he continued, "I want to welcome you to our small marina. I'm David, but I'm sure most of you know that already. I'm the boss round here, so the buck stops with me. If there's anything you want or need, please do come along and ask. If I'm not in the office, then I'll most likely be aboard my boat, that's *Vagabond*, over there in berth no. 1. We've got three other berths occupied on a long term basis, the rest of you are here just for the 14 days Christmas break."

"It occurred to me that, instead of just sitting in our boats all over Christmas, we ought to get together and have a bit of fun. Nothing too serious, mind, just some social activities to add to the festive cheer. This room we're standing in now will become the chandlery once we've got it fixed up, we'll be doing that during January. But in the meantime, I thought we could use it as a sort of social club. It's got heating and lighting, but not many chairs, so you'll have to bring your own. I'll arrange a couple of tables and some glasses, so that if you want to bring a bottle or two to share, then that will be fine. But please remember we can't sell alcohol, as we don't have a licence for that."

"What I'm going to suggest is that we each of us organise an activity, one for each free day. It could be morning, afternoon, or evening, it's up to you. It could be indoors, here, or outdoors somewhere, within easy walking distance of the marina. I've prepared some envelopes with some dates inside, but for obvious reasons, I've left out Christmas Day, and New Year's Eve. Otherwise all the dates are up for grabs. So if you'd like to join in and organise something, then please come and take an envelope, and see what day you've got. If it clashes with a date you've got arranged for visitors or whatever, then ask the people next to you to swap dates. But of course, your visitors can join in as well if they want – the more the merrier. And remember, it's all voluntary – if you don't want to join in, then please don't feel that you're obliged to. But I'm sure it will be much more fun for everyone if you do. Now, who's going to take an envelope?"

Danny turned to Alex. "What do you think, Mister?" he asked. "Shall we go for it?"

"I think it's a great idea," replied Alex. "It might be a bit of fun."

"Shall I go and get an envelope, then?" Danny asked.

"Yes, sure," Alex told him. "Off you go." Danny walked over to David and took one of the envelopes he was handing out. When they'd all been taken, David spoke again.

"When you've decided what you'd like to arrange, please come and tell me so that I can put it down on this piece of paper," he said. "Then I'll print up the list when it's complete and let you all have a copy."

Danny opened the envelope he'd collected a few moments before, "We've got Tuesday. That's the very last day, before we leave. Is that OK?" he asked.

Alex nodded in agreement. "Yes, that's fine," he replied. "I mean, we've got nothing else on, have we?"

Danny grinned as he shook his head. "No, we ain't, not really."

"So, Danny, what shall we do, then. Any ideas? We've taken the envelope, so now we've got to think of something to do to entertain everyone."

"Well, what about a quiz?" asked Danny. "We've got all those school books you're teaching me with, to get the questions from, and you used to be a teacher. You must know lots of stuff."

"Yes what a good idea," Alex responded. "Go and tell David we'll do a quiz in the evening, Tuesday evening, here in the chandlery – or should I say Social Club?"

Danny grinned again as he walked over to David, who wrote his choice down on the paper secured onto the clipboard he was holding. Gradually his paper filled up until it was full – a complete social programme for the next fortnight had been arranged in as little as five minutes. Alex had to admire David's organising skills. There was little doubt that his new marina would be a success.

David started speaking again. "That's fine," he said. "Thank you to everyone for taking part. I'll put the list round later tonight. But now, I've got to confess to a little cheating. I've already bagged Boxing Day for myself. I'll take you all out to a place of interest not far from here, to walk off your Christmas pudding or whatever. Until then, may I wish all of you a very enjoyable Christmas, and hope to see you all here, with your outdoor clothes on, at 10.30 am on Boxing Day. Thank you and good night to you all." And with that, he stepped down from his stool and left, smiling at everyone as he did so.

Alex and Danny walked back to *Jennifer Jo* together. "What are we going to do about this quiz, then, Mister?" asked Danny.

"Nothing," replied Alex.

"But we can't do nothing!" exclaimed Danny, as he turned to Alex in surprise. "We said we'd do it, and we've got to do it now. We can't let David down now."

"Yes, Danny, I know," Alex replied. "But tomorrow is Christmas Day. Had you forgotten? And after that, we've got a week to get the quiz ready. That will help to keep us occupied during the times when we're not taking part in the activities David's got everyone arranging, or when we want a rest from watching the television or whatever. It will give us something to do. And, by the way, I think it was a great idea of yours to do a quiz. I'm sure we'll do it well, the two of us together."

Danny smiled. "OK, then, Mister," he said. "We'll make a start right after Christmas, OK?"

"Yes, Danny, that will be fine," Alex replied. "Now, come on, let's get inside and get some supper ready."

The next morning, Alex woke at his usual time. 'But,' he thought, 'it's Christmas Day today. No need to go anywhere today. I'll have a little lie in'. So he turned over in the bed and lay there, dozing gently. He hardly noticed Danny slipping quietly past the bed into the galley. But a few minutes later, Danny came back, bearing a tray.

"Come on, Mister," he said. "Here's your Christmas breakfast," and he placed the tray on the small cabinet beside the bed. On the tray was a glass of orange juice, a bowl of cornflakes, and a small jug of milk. "Eat up," he commanded. "Bacon and eggs coming up shortly."

" Thanks, Danny," Alex smiled. "This is very nice. Perhaps we should have Christmas Day every day, then?" He enjoyed teasing the boy on occasion.

"Well, I dunno about that," Danny retorted, with a sly grin. "Don't push your luck, now." And he disappeared back to the galley. Alex sat up in bed and ate his cereal, finishing just in time as Danny reappeared with a plate of sausages, eggs, and bacon and a slice of fried bread. "Here you are, then, Mister," he said, "toast and marmalade is on its way in a mo." And the toast and marmalade duly appeared a few minutes later.

"That's really nice, Danny," Alex said, as he spread his marmalade on the toast. "I haven't had breakfast in bed for ages and ages. Thank you for thinking of it. And, it's nice to know that my cooking lessons haven't been entirely wasted. You've done this really well."

"Yes, Mister, well, like I said, don't get too used to it," Danny replied. "You only got it cos its a special day today. Christmas Day don't come every day, remember?"

Alex nodded and smiled again. He hadn't expected to have been given such a treat. "Get up when you like," Danny told him, "I'll wash these things up and have something to eat myself, and then I'll see to the fire, it's gone out. I think it's choked up with ash, so I'll sort that out while you have a bit more lie in."

"No, Danny, it's time for me to get up now," Alex replied. "I'll have a quick shower whilst you do the fire."

After all the chores were done, Alex sat with Danny at the dinette. "So, shall we start doing the quiz now, then, Mister?" Danny asked.

"Oh, no, not on Christmas Day," replied Alex. "I told you before, there's plenty of time yet. But as its Christmas, I have something for you. A little present for you. And he reached into the locker under the dinette seat and brought out a small parcel, one of those which he'd collected from David in the office the previous afternoon.

"Here, Danny, this is for you," Alex told him. "Happy Christmas. I think it's something you both want and need." Danny took the parcel and carefully unwrapped it. Inside was a battery-powered electric shaver, complete with a recharging lead.

"Cor, Mister, thanks ever so much," Danny exclaimed. "You're right, It's just what I need," sheepishly adding "I got few whiskers growing now. Dunno why." And Danny grinned his usual cheerful grin. He lowered his voice a little before continuing, "actually, Mister, I been using yours once or twice now. Gotta get rid of them somehow. Hope you don't mind."

"Yes, I know you have," Alex replied. "I can tell you've been using my shaver."

"How ?" Danny asked, his eyebrows raised slightly.

"I can hear it," Alex smiled. "It makes a small buzz, and the partitions around the bathroom aren't very thick. But it doesn't matter. You've got your own now. Remember to keep it clean and charge it up regularly, there's a power point in your back cabin for when you need to."

"OK Mister, I will," Danny promised. "I'm really pleased with it. Thanks once again. Thanks ever so much."

"That's all right, Danny," Alex told him. "I'm glad you like it. "But I've got something else for you as well."

"Have you? Really?" Danny asked. "I didn't expect any presents at all, let alone two."

"Yes, I've got another one for you. Here it is." Alex smiled as he reached into the locker once again and drew out a second parcel wrapped in brown paper, and passed it over to Danny, who carefully unwrapped it. Inside he found a pile of blue clothing, which one by one he unfolded and examined.

"Here's a tee-shirt," he exclaimed. "Its blue, just the same colour as *Jay-Jay*. And," he shouted out excitedly, "it's got the name of the boat embroidered on it, *Jennifer Jo*, in gold colour, with a brown rope twisted underneath. That's really nice. And here's a polo shirt, the same. And a sweatshirt to match. And a fleece. All with the boat's name on. That's lovely. Are they really all for me?"

"Yes Danny, they are," Alex told the excited young boy. "You're part of the crew, so you'll really look the part now."

"Yes, I will," Danny replied. "They're ever so nice, thanks, and thanks again. I'll really feel I belong on *Jay-Jay* now. Everyone will know what boat I'm off. There ain't many other people with the names of their boats on their tops, is there?"

"No, Danny, there isn't," Alex replied. "But actually, I thought since you're going to display the name of our boat on your tops, then I might as well join you. And it was his turn to grin at Danny as he reached into the locker yet again, and withdrew the last of the parcels which he'd collected from David's office the day before. "Whilst I was ordering your clothing, I thought I may as well order myself a set as well!" And he unwrapped the parcel to show Danny a full set of clothing to match the one he'd just given to Danny.

Danny started laughing, giggling even. "Cor, Mister," he exclaimed, "we'll make a right pair now, won't we?"

"Yes, Danny," Alex laughed. "They'll see us coming alright. But, why not? Why not be proud of our home?"

Danny nodded, and then suddenly he stopped giggling and became serious again. "I'm sorry, Mister," he said. "I nearly forgot in all the excitement. I've got something for you too. Hang on a minute." And he disappeared off to the back cabin, returning after a few moments with a large A3-sized brown envelope. Alex recognised it as one that had been languishing at the bottom of his stationery drawer for ages. He'd had no need for it, and hadn't missed its disappearance. Danny handed the envelope to Alex, saying shyly as he did so, "here you are, Mister. I made this for you. I did it all myself. I hope you like it."

Alex opened the envelope and drew out a large piece of A3 card, which Alex recognised as also coming from *Jennifer Jo's* stationery drawer. It was blank, but as Alex turned it over, he was amazed by what he saw on the other side.

On the card Danny had drawn a picture of a canal scene, carefully executed in the style of an etching, and drawn with a very fine pencil, and then coloured in with a faint wash of colour pencil. Alex sat and studied it carefully. It showed a narrowboat, moored at the side of the canal, in front of a long stretch of poplar trees which lined the canal on the far side of the towpath. Alex instantly recognised the boat as *Jennifer Jo,* even before he read the name which Danny had inscribed in miniscule writing on the bow of the boat. Just beyond *Jennifer Jo* was a lock, in the familiar waterways colours of black and white, in sharp contrast to the blue of *Jennifer* Jo and the various shades of greens of the trees and grass and low shrubs at ground level.

Just beyond the lock could be seen a bridge over the canal, constructed in the traditional style of hump-backed bridge dating back 200 years or so. The figure of a man stood on the towpath by the back of the boat, talking to a couple walking their dog, and at the front there was a young lad, holding a mooring rope, talking to a young girl standing astride a bicycle. 'Yes, Danny,' Alex thought, "you've got me and you in there, just right. Just like you to be taking to a young lady!'

The whole picture was greatly enhanced by the light application of colour which Danny had carefully added over the pencil drawing. Alex was amazed at how well Danny had been able to capture the scene. As he studied the huge amount of detail which Danny had managed to include, his thoughts were interrupted by Danny. "You don't like it?" he asked, a disappointed look spreading across his face.

Alex looked up at Danny and shook his head. "No, Danny. I like it very much. I like it very much indeed. I think this is very very good." Danny's worried look was replaced by a broad smile.

"I really am very impressed with what you've done here," Alex continued. "You should be congratulated on how well you've put this together. It must have taken you ages to do. And I never even knew that you were doing it. You kept it well hidden. How on earth did you manage that?"

"Well," Danny replied. "Sometimes lately, two or three times, I've said you could go to the shops on your own, remember? I told you a few little fibs, saying I was a bit tired. Well, that was so I could stay here and work on the picture. And sometimes I turned in and went to bed early, and did a little bit every now and then like that, before I went to sleep. I kept it under the mattress in my bunk In the back cabin. But I only finished it last week. There were times when I thought I wouldn't finish it in time."

"Danny, you should be very proud of this," Alex congratulated the boy. "Because, I certainly am. I'm going to get it framed, and put it up on the wall in the saloon. There's an unused patch over the television cabinet. It will go well there, don't you think?"

Danny nodded. "That would be nice," he said. "I'm really glad you like it. I wanted to get you something for Christmas, but there weren't anything I could buy for you, cos I don't have no money, see? So I hit on the idea of drawing you a picture. I was sort of hoping that you'd like it. I couldn't think of anything else to do, and I wanted to give you something."

"I do like it, Danny," Alex responded. "I like it very much. It's worth more to me that anything you could have bought, because it's something which you've done and made all on your own. That's worth a great deal." Danny just nodded and smiled. "Thanks, Mister," he said.

"And whilst we're handing out envelopes, Danny," Alex added, "I nearly forgot. I've got an envelope for you, too." And Alex dived into the locker beneath the dinette seat once more, and brought out a brown A4 envelope which he handed to Danny. "What's this, then, Mister?" he asked anxiously. Alex just smiled. Danny soon displayed a bit of nervousness whenever something occurred that was outside of his normal comfort zone. 'Perhaps,' Alex thought, it's result of his experiences at Grant Hall, or whatever.' It showed that beneath Danny's happy cheerful exterior there still lay, deeply hidden for most of the time, a basic sense of insecurity. Alex knew that whilst he had done his very best to provide a safe and secure home for Danny on *Jennifer Jo*, life as a water gypsy, always moving on every day or two, was no real substitute for having a permanent home, and attending a normal school with other children of his own age.

"Don't worry, Danny. You'll like it," Alex told him. "Open it and see."

Danny opened the envelope and drew out a half a dozen sheets of neatly-printed A4 paper. "What's all this, then, Mister?" he asked.

"It's your school report," Alex told him. "Every good school produces a report on each pupil's work every term. There's no need for this school you're learning at, with me, to be any different."

Danny sat and started reading, carefully working through the report, right to the end. "This extra- mural activities, what's that mean?" he asked at one point.

"Well, Danny, it covers things which aren't on the normal academic syllabus. Things you've learnt outside of the normal school subjects. Mainly, in your case, boat handling, diesel engine maintenance, and cooking, or catering to give it it's proper name."

Danny nodded quietly, and carried on reading. Suddenly, he started reading out loud the summary which Alex had included at the end. "Danny has worked well this term," he read, "given the somewhat unusual circumstances of his schooling. He has applied himself well to most subjects, although he sometimes needs to pay more attention to detail, and avoid jumping to conclusions. His written work is well presented, especially the accompanying sketches and drawings. Spoken English is improving but still remains weak. But all told, a good term's work."

"That's really nice, Mister," Danny added. "Have I really done as well as all that, like what you said?"

"Yes, Danny, you have," Alex replied. "I wouldn't have put it down if it wasn't true, now would I? You surely know me better than that?"

"Yes, of course, sure," Danny smiled again. "Thanks, Mister. You've been a great teacher. I bet all the kids at your school really liked you."

"Well, I had my moments," Alex smiled. "But all that's in the past now. Anyway, it's gone 12 o'clock. What shall we have for lunch?"

"Leave that to me," Danny responded. "I'm doing the catering today, remember?" Alex smiled at the lad. "Yes, Danny, breakfast was fine. Let's see how you do for lunch. And are you going to do supper as well? We've got a turkey roast in the fridge for our Christmas Meal, do you remember?"

"Yes," Danny said, "I was with you when we bought it, remember? I'll do the supper as well, no problem, no problem at all." And Danny did indeed prepare a nice Christmas meal, with Christmas pudding and custard for dessert.

The next morning, Boxing Day, Alex and Danny went over to the social club at 10.30, and joined in the walk which was being led by David. Nearly everyone off the boats had decided to come along, so there was a good crowd to talk to as they walked along, Danny walking beside with his new friend Margaret, chatting earnestly all the while. After about half-an hour, David stopped and turned to face the crowd.

"We're just about here now," he said. "Just round the corner is an old earthwork. It's a Motte and Bailey castle. It dates from the 11th century. Originally it had a wooden palisade around the top, with a castle, constructed from wood, inside it, but of course that has all disappeared now. But the earthworks still remain, with the hill at the centre, and the defensive ditches around the perimeter, much as they were hundreds of years ago. They're really well preserved. Come and have a look." As he finished speaking, David turned and walked swiftly along, and very soon the remains of the castle came into view.

Alex was pleasantly surprised to find how well preserved the ancient earthwork was. Obviously whoever was responsible for its maintenance and upkeep had taken their responsibilities very seriously. He tagged along as David took his group around the site, talking all the while about its history, and the artefacts that had been found during some excavations which had been carried out some years ago by the local archaeological society, of which he was a member. Alex and most of the other adults in the group politely declined his invitation to climb to the top of the mound some 60 feet above them, but Danny and Margaret had other ideas.

"Come on, Margaret," Danny exclaimed excitedly, "I'll race you to the top."

"Alright then, see you there. I'll be at the top, waiting for you when you get there," she replied cheerily, as she dashed off and started clambering up the mound, leaving Danny well behind. But as they neared the top of the mound, she flagged a little, and Danny caught her up, and they crested the top of the rise together, hand in hand.

"Cooeee," they called out together, as they waved at the rest of the group. Alex and a few others waved back, and then he watched as they carefully clambered down again to rejoin the group.

After about half an hour, David called the group together and started speaking again. "If you've all seen enough," he said, "I think it's time to move on. It's a bit cold to be standing around for too long, isn't it? Follow me. We'll go back a different way." And he walked swiftly off, followed by his little group. After about five minutes or so, they came to a pub. "We'll go in here," David said, wearing a broad smile. "We can have something here to warm us up." He led them through the main door into the bar, which was almost full with Boxing Day customers, and then through to a private room at the back. "This is reserved for us," he said, "there's hot sausage rolls and mince pies coming up, it's my treat to you all for being my first customers at the marina."

"Thanks, David," said Alex, "that's very nice of you." David nodded in response. "But, please can you all buy your own booze," he added, as he looked around. "I can't run to that as well. Thank you." And David smiled when he saw everyone's heads nodding.

After a pleasant hour or so in the pub, everyone gradually drifted back to the marina. As Alex and Danny settled down, back aboard *Jennifer Jo*, Danny turned to Alex. "That was really interesting," he said. "It's just like what you taught me in that history lesson a couple of months ago. Being there and seeing the real thing makes it all come to life, sort of, doesn't it?"

Alex nodded. "Yes, Danny," he replied, "it does. A field trip like that is always worthwhile. What was the view like from the top of mound?"

"You could see for miles," Danny replied. "The ground around here is pretty flat generally, so any one attacking the castle would have been spotted long before they actually got there. The defenders would have been able to get ready well before the attackers arrived. And climbing the mound was quite a struggle. I bet there were some fierce battles there once upon a time."

"Yes, I guess you're right," replied Alex. "It can't have been a very pleasant time to be living in."

Danny nodded. "So, what shall we do this afternoon?" he asked.

"Well, we could start getting the quiz ready," Alex suggested.

"Yes, that's great. Let's do that." Danny paused. "But, I really don't know how we go about it! Do you?"

"Yes, actually, Danny, I do," Alex replied. "We used to have a quiz club at my school. Each school house would pick a team and the various teams would play in a league, every fortnight there was a quiz, and at the end of term there was a small trophy and prizes for the winning team. We could have a team off each boat. How does that sound?"

"That's good," Danny responded. "But how about setting the questions?"

"Well," Alex smiled. "We'll have two sessions of questions, of forty questions in each session, with a break in between, to allow people to get some refreshments and have a rest. Then, while the second set of questions are being asked, I'll sit in the corner and start marking the first set."

"That sounds like a good arrangement," Danny replied. "I'll help you with the marking, alright? But who will we get to ask the questions? Shall we ask David? He'd do it quite well, don't you think?"

"Well yes, I'm sure he would," Alex replied, "but he's not going to do it. We're not going to ask him."

"Why not ? Who is asking the questions, then?" asked Danny.

Well who's idea was it for us to do a quiz in the first place?" Alex asked.

"Well, mine, I suppose," Danny replied, not yet realising what this was leading to.

"That's right," Alex replied. "And since it was your idea, I think that you should be the one asking the questions."

"What, me?" asked Danny, his face suddenly showing a shadow of uncertainty.

"Yes, Danny, you," Alex responded. "You'll do it well. All you need to do is to read out the questions, speaking out loudly and clearly, and giving everyone sufficient time to write their answers down, before moving on to the next one. And at the end of each session, ask if anyone would like to have any question repeated, and then give them another few minutes more to think about their answers, before they hand in their answer sheets. I can create those and print them off on the computer beforehand. It should be a good evening for everyone."

"Well, OK. then," replied Danny, a little reluctantly. "If you say so, Mister."

"Yes, you'll be fine," Alex reassured to lad. "We can have a practice session here, beforehand, if you like, so you're quite comfortable with it."

"Alright then, Mister." Danny's face lit up. "I'll give it a go, like you said."

Alex smiled. "That's fine, Danny," he replied. "I'm sure you'll do it well." He settled down at the dinette opposite Danny, in their usual seats. "Now, about the questions," he continued. "To have a successful quiz, we need to grade the questions, or grade them roughly, at least."

"What do you mean, grade them, exactly?" enquired Danny, a quizzical look upon his face.

"Well, Danny, just think about it," Alex replied. "If we're going to have eighty questions in total, and nobody gets more than about ten or twelve right, then everyone will be well disappointed. And likewise, if everyone gets seventy or more right, then they'll say it was too easy, and on top of that, we'll probably get a tie for top score, and then we'll have to have a tiebreak or something. So, to avoid either of those things happening, we need to grade the questions and try to ensure that everyone gets a good score. But, we'll also make sure there's some difficult questions as well, and some in between for good measure. That should sort it out OK, because there's sure to be some people who have specialist knowledge about a particular subject. I'm always surprised about things like that."

"So, what we'll do," Alex continued, warming to the theme, "is to have eight rounds in each session. Each round will containing five questions on a particular topic, such as history, pop music, politics, geography, celebrities, and so on. And, we'll arrange the questions so that around 40 percent of them are what we would rate as easy, another 40 percent we'll rate as medium, and the other 20 percent will be the more difficult ones. That should sort it out well. And we can spread the easy, medium, and difficult questions across the different rounds, as well. It should be an interesting evening, if we get it right."

Danny nodded. I'll get the textbooks out, then, and start getting some questions together, shall I?"

"Yes Danny, please do," Alex replied. "And I'll do the same. And then we'll review each other's work. And also, and this is very important, we'll have to make sure that all of our answers are correct. We don't want any arguments now, do we?"

Danny grinned. "Well, no, we don't," he smiled in reply, adding, "Like it said in my school report yesterday, I'm quite good at geography, so I'll start with that, shall I?"

"Right-oh," Alex agreed. "And I'll start with politics. Let's get to it, Danny. Let's see who thinks up the best questions, right?"

Danny nodded, with his characteristic grin. "OK, Mister," he replied. "It should pass the rest of the day, shouldn't it?"

"That's right, Danny," said Alex, as he picked up his pencil. "It probably will."

CHAPTER 12

"After you, Danny." Alex unlocked the sliding hatch and pushed it back, motioning to Danny to step inside *Jennifer Jo*. Danny climbed down the three steps from the rear deck and made his way through the boat to the saloon, as Alex secured the hatch and followed him through. "A cup of tea, while we wind down before we turn in?" he asked. Danny nodded. "Yes, please, Mister," he replied.

"So, that went really well, didn't it?" Alex asked, as he filled the kettle and set it on the stove. "You made a really good quizmaster, didn't you? A little bit hesitant at first, perhaps, but after a few minutes you really got into your stride. I told you it would be easy."

"Yea," Danny acknowledged, with his usual grin. "I was a little bit nervous at first, but as you say, once I got started, it was alright. And when they all clapped me at the end, well, I was quite proud actually. And," he added, "you were right about grading the questions, weren't you? I mean, the winner got 69 out of 80, and the lowest score was 58, so that made it a good contest, didn't it?"

"Yes, Danny, it did." Alex paused for a moment. "It was a good end to our Christmas break, wasn't it? And we had quite a few other interesting evenings as well, didn't we? It was a good idea to invite the people off each boat to host an evening's entertainment each. It made for a wide variety of activities to do. It really helped to pass the time."

"Yes," Danny exclaimed. "The Beetle Drive was better than I thought it would be, even though it was quite a simple thing to do. But I didn't go much on the Line Dancing. I really struggled with that. You were alright at it, though, weren't you?"

"Yes, Danny," Alex laughed. "You seemed to have two left feet at times. I bet Margaret had a few bruises on her toes after that evening. What else did you like?"

"Well, the talent show weren't bad either," Danny responded. "I didn't know you could play the clarinet like that. I wondered what was in that little box you were carrying as we went over to the clubroom that night."

Alex smiled. "Yes," he replied, "the music teacher at my school used to give me a few lessons, now and again, a few years ago. And I took some music exams too – the boys taking their own exams were really surprised to see me in the waiting room with them. I passed all the exams I took, and got as far as Grade 5, which is quite a respectable level of achievement, especially at the age I was when I took that one. But, talking about the talent show, you did really well too."

"Do you think so?" asked Danny, a shy grin spreading across his face.

"Oh, yes," said Alex. He'd seen yet another side to this young lad, a side which he'd never seen before. "You'd make a good stand-up comic, any time. You had some really good jokes, and a few superb one-liners. And your put-down to that guy in the corner, who was making some snide comments about you, was first-class. I think he must have been a bit drunk, actually, to have shouted out at you like that. But like I said, your put-down was really good. Something like that always sets the tone for the rest of the act, and it got the audience on your side, early on. After that, you carried them with you all the way through, no problem at all."

"Well, Mister," replied Danny, "I used to tell funny jokes and stories when I was at Grant Hall, you know, to keep the other kids amused and cheer them up when things were a bit bad and everyone was getting a bit depressed. Actually, I know quite a few more jokes which I didn't use, but they're a little bit rude, or even worse. Alright for us kids, but in the end I thought it weren't right to tell them to that sort of audience."

"No, that was quite right," Alex told the lad. "You'd only be letting yourself down. Keep it clean and keep it simple, that's always the best bet. What else did you like, though?"

"The nature ramble was quite good," Danny exclaimed. "I never realised there was so much to see outdoors during the winter. It was really interesting. And it was lucky that the weather was good for it, too."

"Yes, Danny, the sun shone on us that day," Alex replied. "That made it a good afternoon out. It was a bit cold out of the sun, but the stop in the pub on the way back helped a lot, to get us all warmed up again. So, all round, it's been a good Christmas break for us, hasn't it?"

Yes, Mister," Danny replied, "it has. It's been the best Christmas I've had, ever since my dad le...le..lef...left...home..............." And suddenly, Danny's face crumpled up and he burst out crying, his shoulders heaving as he hung his head and staring at the floor. Alex stretched out his arms and drew the boy to him, as Danny buried his face onto Alex's chest, his young body shaking as he sobbed his heart out.

It was getting on for a minute before the young lad's tears subsided and he pushed himself away from Alex, rubbing his eyes as he did so. "I'm sorry, Mister," he mumbled. "You must think I'm a right cry-baby. I'll turn in now." And he made to make his way to his berth in the back cabin.

"No, wait," Alex called out after him. "Come and sit down here, please. I need to talk to you." And he gestured to Danny's usual seat at the dinette. Danny turned and sat down, while Alex set a couple of mugs of tea onto the table, then took his normal seat opposite him. Danny just sat there quietly, staring down resolutely at the table, occasionally rubbing his red eyes.

"Now, listen to me, Danny," Alex began. "You've nothing to be ashamed of, nothing at all. You've been through a lot in the last few years. Your father walking out of the family home, leaving you and your mother on your own. Then your mother being taken ill, and you being left to fend for yourself on your own for a while. And then being fostered, after that being placed in a children's home, and eventually ending up at Grant Hall."

"That's more than enough grief for anyone, let alone a youngster like you. And ever since you've been here, on *Jennifer Jo* with me, you've bottled up your inner feelings about it all. They had to come out sometime. The big surprise is that it's taken so long. It just shows your strength of character that it hasn't happened before now. But eventually it has to come out. Having a good cry is just a way of releasing your sadness and grief. It's not a sign of weakness. It's quite normal. I certainly don't think any less of you for it. And tomorrow you'll feel much better about yourself, for having got it off your mind. Just you wait and see."

"You really think so, Mister?" Danny asked, still staring resolutely at the table.

"Yes, Danny, I do," Alex continued. "Everyone has their ups and downs. Sometimes they feel that they just can't cope with what life has thrown at them. But, even though it's not easy, they manage to put it behind them, whatever it is that's been worrying them, and move forward. It will be the same with you. I've seen it before at the school where I was a House Master for so many years. Some of the boys, especially the younger ones, had difficulty settling in. They found boarding school to be a very different environment to the home life they had been used to. But before long they became accustomed to the life of the school, and joined in all the activities which were available, and quite soon, they ended up really enjoying their time with us. I certainly can't offer you the same facilities as we had there. But I hope you're finding life on the cut interesting."

"Well, yes, Mister, I am," Danny replied, as he looked up at Alex with a weak smile. "It's great being here on *Jay-Jay*. There's something different to see every day as we go along the cut. And I'm getting some good schooling as well, aren't I? And when I find my Mum then I'll be back to normal altogether," he added, in a matter-of-fact manner.

Alex sighed quietly to himself. Danny never gave up hope that he would one day find his mother and be reunited with her. Alex knew there was so little chance of that happening. But now was not the time to disillusion the boy.

"Yes, Danny," he reassured him. "That will be nice for you, and for your mother as well. I wish I could tell you when we'll find her for you, but you must know I can't. We just have to keep looking. And we will, for as long as it takes." Alex was happy to make that promise to Danny. He was quite content to cruise the waterways in *Jennifer Jo*. After all, that was the way of life he'd chosen, and it didn't matter to him at all that they kept to the northern parts of the waterway system, in the vain hope that Danny would find his mother. The time would come when he would have to sit down with Danny and discuss the futility of their search with him, but that time was several years away yet.

"Yes, Mister," Danny smiled again. "Thanks ever so. But you won't tell her, will you? Tell my Mum, I mean, when we find her? About what happened just now?"

"No, of course not, Danny," Alex exclaimed, with a slight grin. "That's just between us, the two of us, and that's how it will remain. You really didn't need to ask that, now, did you? You must surely know me well enough by now. As far as I'm concerned, this is over. Is that alright?"

"Well, yes. Thanks, Mister." Danny picked up his mug of tea and drained it. "I'll turn in now, if you don't mind."

"Alright, Danny," Alex replied. "I'll clear up and see to the fire while you go to the bathroom. But will you please come back here when you've finished in the bathroom. We need to talk about our plans for the next couple of weeks. There's something I want to talk to you about, and it will help to take your mind of what happened just now."

It was only a few minutes before Alex and Danny were sat back in their usual places at the dinette. "What is it, then, Mister?" Danny asked. "What's up?"

"Well, Danny, Alex replied. "I'm thinking of having our bottom blacked."

Immediately, a worried expression flitted across Danny's face. It was Danny's normal reaction to anything out of the ordinary, anything that was new to him, anything out of his comfort zone. Alex knew that it indicated Danny's deep-seated sense of insecurity. He knew that he was doing the very best he could for Danny, but he also knew that the lad would never be fully relaxed and at ease with the world until he was reunited with his mother, in a secure home environment.

"What do you mean, Mister?" Danny asked nervously.

"Well, Danny," Alex explained, "you may have noticed that the lower part of *Jennifer Jo's* hull, the part that's near the water line, and in fact all the way down below the surface of the water, right down to the bottom plate, is painted black. The paint protects the metalwork of the hull from corrosion and damage, but it doesn't last for ever. It's time for it to be re-done. The boat's been in the water now for a couple of years, and the blacking, as it's called, needs to be cleaned up and repainted."

"Oh." Danny's relief was self-evident as his worried frown disappeared, and was replaced with his usual grin. "I thought for a minute that you wanted to do something kinky with a tin of black shoe polish," he exclaimed.

Alex smiled at the young boy, whose wry sense of humour never ceased to amuse him.

"So how do we do that, then?" Danny asked, curiously.

"Actually, Danny, that's quite easy," Alex explained. "We have the boat lifted out of the water, and then we clean down the black area and repaint it. I've been looking at the Nicholson's guide. There's a boatyard just along the cut, about 2or 3 days cruising away, where there's a crane. I'll phone them in the morning and see if we can use their facilities for a few days. We can buy everything we need there."

"Alright, Mister," Danny agreed. "That sounds like a good idea."

"Right-oh, then," Alex said. "I'll sort it in the morning. You turn in now, then. Goodnight."

"G'night, Mister," Danny replied, as he made his way to his berth in the back cabin.

Alex himself turned in a few minutes later, but it was a long time before he drifted off to sleep. He lay there, thinking about Danny, and what had happened earlier that evening. He'd often marvelled and wondered at how Danny had managed to cope with all the trials and travails that had befallen him. There had been a big burden for the young lad to carry on his shoulders. Alex had been well aware that it had all been bottled up inside the boy, suppressed deep down in his mind. But now the dam had broken. The grief had been released. And Alex knew that Danny would be much the better for it, in the days and weeks to come.

Danny was late up the next morning. By the time he appeared, Alex had already finished his own breakfast, peeled the potatoes for supper, and was starting to see to the fire.

"Hi Danny," Alex called out over his shoulder as he knelt in front of the fire. "We're all set for the blacking. I phoned the boatyard a little while ago, and they've got a vacancy on their hard-standing for a whole week, starting on Monday. How's that?"

"Not bad Mister," Danny replied. "Let's hope the weather holds for us."

"Yes, I've looked at the forecast," Alex reassured him. "It's going to turn quite mild, well, relatively so, for the next week or more, and there's no rain forecast. And the work will keep us warm. So we should be able to get the blacking done without any problems."

Just after lunchtime a couple of days later, *Jennifer Jo* arrived at the boatyard. "Can you make a temporary mooring here, please Danny," Alex asked, "while I go to the office and see about what arrangements they've made for us?"

"Alright, Mister, leave her with me," Danny replied, as he jumped ashore and quickly made the boat fast at bow and stern, then sitting on the back rail in the weak sunlight as he waited for Alex to return. He only had to wait a few minutes before he spotted Alex walking back to the boat.

"It's all arranged, Danny," Alex told the young lad. "If we move her forward about 100 yards, they'll bring the crane over for us." Danny nodded and united the ropes, and then he and Alex gently pulled on the ropes to move the craft forward, walking slowly along the jetty as they did so. Just as they arrived at the correct spot, a large crawler-mounted crane appeared from behind some buildings and made its way to the waters' edge.

The driver stepped down from his cab and came over to speak to them. "I'm Bruce," he said, shaking Alex by the hand. "We're all ready for you. Earlier today, I set those railways sleepers over there out ready for your boat," he added, waving his hand at two stacks of wooden railway sleepers, each about 3 feet high, set up on a an area of concrete a little way back from the canal. "I'll drop these slings into the water, and then if you can pull her forward a little way further, over the slings, I'll do the lift, then we can swing her round, and drop her onto the sleepers. Is that alright?"

"Don't drop her please," Danny exclaimed anxiously. "Lower her gently, won't you? It's our boat you're talking about. It's where we live, you know!"

"This is my grandson, Danny," Alex interrupted, as he introducing the boy to Bruce. He needed to perpetuate the myth about being the boy's grandfather, in order to avoid any awkward questions being asked about why a young boy was alone on a boat with a much older man.

Bruce turned to face Danny, smiling broadly. "Don't worry, lad," he replied with a smile. "Just a figure of speech. Your boat will be fine. Trust me.'

Alex gently manoeuvred *Jennifer Jo* over the slings which Bruce had lowered into the water with the crane, and stopped the engine. "Please can you both get off the boat," Bruce called out. "No-one's allowed on the boat while it's being lifted. Health and Safety, you know," he added with a sly wink. "Can't upset them can we? And stand well back while I'm lifting, please. Our insurance company won't be too pleased if I drop the boat with you two underneath, now, will they? And, can you bring both the front and back ropes off with you, please, then while I lift her, you can help to steady her with the ropes as she swings round, and make sure she sits on the sleepers properly."

Alex took Danny to one side, and they stood together and watched as the crane slowly lifted *Jennifer Jo* out of the water. Then, very slowly, the crane gently swung the boat round and settled her onto the sleepers while Alex carefully guided the boat using the bow rope, with Danny taking the rope from the stern. The whole process had taken less than ten minutes from start to finish.

Bruce got out of the crane's cab and walked round the boat, carefully checking that it was properly positioned onto the sleepers and would not shift unexpectedly. "I'll leave it with you now," he said, "but if you need anything else and there's no-one else around, just come and knock me up. I live on that boat moored over there, in the marina. I'm the marina warden, amongst other things. And my wife's the grounds-woman for the site. You'll probably see her doing odds and ends from time to time while you're here, picking up litter and cigarette ends and that sort of thing. Mind you, there's not much for her to do at this time of year. But she's much busier in the summer, what with all the grass to cut and everything." With that, he shook Alex and Danny by the hand, and then climbed back into his cab and drove the crane away.

"Hey, Mister," Danny called out. "I've just thought of something."

"What's that, Danny?" Alex asked. "What's the matter?"

"Well," Danny replied. "Where are we going to live while *Jay-Jay's* up there? We're down here on the ground, and all our clothes and food and stuff's up there on the boat!"

"Yes, that's right," Alex replied. "But that's not a problem. We'll continue to live on the boat, just like we usually do."

"But it's far too high for us to get into," Danny exclaimed. "There's no way we can climb up onto her from here."

"That's right, Danny," Alex smiled. "But, like I said, it's not a problem." He pointed to a corner of the boatyard. "If you look over there, you'll see a metal stairway. It's on wheels. That's what everyone uses to get onto their boat while its being blacked. Living aboard while the boat's on dry land may seem a bit strange, but it isn't a problem, as long as we don't run our engine. We can hook up our electrics to the boatyard power supply, there's sure to be a power point somewhere we can plug into. And we've got gas for cooking, just like we always have. We've got the stove for heating, as usual. And, don't forget we've got a gas boiler for hot water as well, although we haven't needed to use it for ages, because the engine usually gives us all the hot water we need. And if we need to top up our water tank, then that's no problem, there's a water tap just over there, behind you. The boatyard has all the facilities we need. And of course, we can use their toilet as well."

"Now," Alex continued, "why don't you pull that stairway over and set it against the boat, near the stern, while I go to the office and see about getting our paint organised?"

"Alright, Mister," Danny replied, a little dubiously. "I'll see if I can manage it."

"Thanks, Danny," Alex said. "I'll be back shortly. Why don't you see about some lunch after that, while I'm over at the office?" Danny nodded, and set out to fetch the stairway while Alex made his way over to the office.

After they'd had their lunch, Alex and Danny climbed down the stairway and had a walk round *Jennifer Jo*. Alex was pleased with the general condition of the hull, but it was indeed due for a cleanup and blacking. "We'll start work tomorrow morning, Danny," Alex told the boy. "We'll get everything ready today, then we can start first thing after breakfast."

Danny nodded in agreement. "Alright, Mister," he said. "The work will keep us warm if it gets colder, won't it? And I'll work hard with you to get it done."

"I know you will, Danny," Alex smiled. "I never had any doubts about that. The first thing we need to do is clean off all the weed and encrusted growth which has taken hold along the waterline. It needs to be scraped off by hand, then washed down. We'll do that with their jet-washer, which the boatyard will let us use. With any luck, we'll be able to get one side done tomorrow, and the other side the next day. After that, the painting will take another couple of days, again one day each side. That will take us up to Sunday, when we can have a rest day, because Bruce, the crane driver, won't want to lift us back into the water until Monday. And then we can be on our way again."

"OK, Mister," Danny replied. "No problem. Let's do it. By the way, what are those funny white things stuck on the side of the hull there? There's three along this side, and another three along the other side as well."

"Ah, yes," Alex responded. "They're anodes, or to be more correct, sacrificial anodes. They've been on the hull all the time, Danny, but you've never seen them before, as they're usually hidden well below the waterline."

"So what are they for, then?" Danny asked. "Do we have to have them?"

"Well, yes, we do, Danny," Alex replied. "When two boats are moored near each other, there's very often minute electric currents running between them through the water. The currents are very small, but over time they can cause corrosion of the metalwork of the hull. So, to stop that, these anodes are fitted to the hull of the boat. They're made of magnesium, or sometimes zinc, which if you can remember from your science lessons a few months ago, are elements in the periodic table. Another element in the periodic table is iron, which is the main constituent of the steel which is used to make the hull. Because magnesium is lower in the periodic table than iron, the electric currents will attack the magnesium instead of the iron, thus protecting the hull of the boat from corrosion. They're called sacrificial anodes because they are sacrificed instead of the iron, and eventually they will get eaten away, and must be replaced. You can see that our anodes are a bit ragged, but it looks as though there's a good lot of life left in them yet. There's no need to have them replaced for quite a while."

Danny looked up at Alex and grinned. "That's really clever!" he said. "All that stuff you're teaching me is worthwhile after all, isn't it?"

Alex nodded. "Yes, Danny," he replied. "That's education for you. But now, let's go over to the chandlery and get kitted out for tomorrow. We need some overalls, to start with. They should have paper ones, disposable after we've finished with them. We'll need some safety glasses as well, to protect our eyes from the spray off the jetwasher, and from the paint as well, and we'll also get a couple of hard-hats, to protect our heads whilst we're working. And a pair of baseball caps as well, to keep our hair clean, we can wear them under the hard-hats. They'll keep our heads warm at the same time. And we mustn't forget the paintbrushes, and a couple of scrapers too."

"OK, Mister," Danny replied. I hope they've got my size in overalls. I'm not as big as you are."

"We'll see," laughed Alex. "They almost certainly will." And they walked over to the chandlery together.

Walking back towards *Jennifer Jo* with their purchases a few minutes later, they saw a forklift truck approach the boat and place a pallet onto the ground beside the boat, and then turn round and disappear behind one of the boatyard's buildings at the back of the yard. Taking off the tarpaulin from the pallet, they found a stack of large blue plastic drums.

"Ah, said Alex. "Here's our paint."

There's rather a lot, isn't there?" asked Danny. "There's no end of it here. Six drums altogether. We're never going use all that, are we?"

"Well, yes, we will, I think," replied Alex. "That's why I ordered so much. It's a special bituminous paint. It's very thick, like treacle. It's specially made for blacking boats with. We'll almost certainly use most of it."

"Anyway, Mister, you've been fiddled!" Danny exclaimed, looking closely at the drums of paint. "This drum here, it's been opened. It's only half full. You can tell, look."

"No, don't worry, Danny," Alex replied. "It's part of the arrangement they have here for blacking. You see, I've ordered and paid for five drums of paint. And we've got five, right?"

Danny nodded. "So, why the extra half-used one then?" he asked.

"Well," Alex said. "It's simple really. The boatyard will take back any unopened drums of paint which we don't use, and they'll refund me the money I paid for it, in full. But they won't take back unopened drums of paint. It's the same for everyone who does their blacking here. So, this half-used drum is left over from whoever was the previous person to do their blacking here. It's been left here by whoever it was, for use by the next person to do their blacking. We'll use that one first, and then if we've got any half-used drums left when we've finished, then we'll leave it for the next person after us. After all, we don't want to take it with us, we won't need it any more, and we really don't have the space to store it anyway. Once the blacking is done, we'll have no further use for it. So we may as well leave it for someone else to use. Simple, right?"

"Yes, Mister, I hadn't thought of that. It's a good idea, really, isn't it?" replied Danny. "They've got it all worked out, haven't they?"

Alex nodded. "Yes, they have. But it's starting to get dark now. Let's get the electrics hooked up, we haven't done that yet, there's a blue cable for that in the locker in the engine room, it connects into that socket on the rear deck, behind the door. And then we can start thinking about tea."

"Sound good, Mister," Danny responded. "I'll cook tonight, shall

I?"

"That sounds good to me, too," replied Alex. Your choice as to what we'll have, OK?"

Danny nodded. "Leave it to me," he smiled.

The next morning, after an early breakfast, Alex and Danny donned their overalls, caps, and safety glasses, and set to work. "Would you like to start on the scraping, please, Danny?" Alex asked, "then I'll come along behind you with the jet-washer. And after a bit, we can swap over."

"OK Mister," Danny replied, "I'll give it a go. Tell me if I'm not doing it right, won't you?" Alex nodded, as Danny picked up the scraper and set to scraping off the weeds and marine growth which had attached itself to *Jennifer Jo's* hull around the water line. As Alex watched, he saw that Danny was making a thorough job of it - there was no need to make any comment. As with most things, Danny was a willing worker, keen to help. Danny gradually progressed along the length of the boat, with Alex following along with the jet-washer, leaving the hull nice and clean, ready for the application of the blacking paint later in the week.

After about an hour, Danny put down his scraper and turned to Alex. "Hey, Mister," he exclaimed, "my arms are aching a bit. Can I have a rest, please?"

"Yes, of course, Danny, of course you can," Alex replied. "You've been doing really well. Why don't you nip up into the boat and make a couple of mugs of coffee, and bring them down to us, then we can have a rest whilst we have some refreshment. Then I'll do the scraping while you can jet-wash. And, as a special treat, there's some chocolate bars in the cupboard, bring a couple of them down as well, can you?"

"Sure thing, Mister," Danny replied, with his usual trademark grin. "No problem. Two coffees and two bars of chocolate coming up. Or should I say coming down?" he added with a smile, as he climbed up the stairway onto *Jennifer Jo* and disappeared inside the boat.

They sat on a nearby packing case and enjoyed their snack in the weak winter sunshine, and then Alex picked up the scraper. "Here, Danny," he said. "You use the jet washer, OK? But be careful, because it could cause an injury if someone gets caught by the jet. So be careful, please."

"It's alright, Mister," Danny replied. I will. You can trust me."

"Yes, I know I can, Danny. That's fine," said Alex. "I just wanted you to be aware, that's all," he added, as he started working with the scraper. Danny stood back and waited a few minutes before he started up the jet-washer, cleaning off the muck and grime from the normally-submerged metalwork of the boat.

It was just after midday when Alex put down his scraper and stood back as Danny jet-washed the last few areas of the hull, then bent down and switched it off. "Well done, Danny," Alex exclaimed. "We've done really well today. That's one side finished already. We'll stop for lunch now, and then rest up this afternoon, ready to tackle the other side tomorrow. It's not worth starting it today, it will be getting dark well before we've finished. What do you reckon to that?"

"Sounds good, Mister," Danny replied. "It's hard work, isn't it? I think we've earned a rest, don't you?"

We sure have, Danny," replied Alex. "We have indeed. Come on, let's get these overalls off and clean ourselves up, and have some lunch." And he beckoned Danny up the stairway, following the lad closely behind.

By the early afternoon the next day, they'd finished the other side of the boat, and the stern and rudder of the boat as well. "We've done well, Danny," Alex told the lad. "If we allow another two days to do the painting, then we'll get it all finished before the weather turns nasty again. It's forecast to be really cold with some snow as well, at the end of the week."

"We'll get it done, don't you worry, Mister," Danny replied. "We'll work really hard to finish it in time." Alex nodded in agreement. "That's right, Danny. We will," he smiled.

The next morning, Alex and Danny got to work with the paint. "Remember, Danny," Alex told him, "put it on nice and thick. And leave the anodes bare, we don't want any paint on them."

"That's right, Mister, Danny replied. "They won't work if they're covered with paint, will they?"

"No, Danny. That's right. I'm glad you remembered what I told you about them."

Danny just grinned and set to work. They'd worked their way about half-way along the side of the boat when Danny suddenly stopped. "Hey, Mister," he called out. You've forgotten something!"

"What's that, Danny," asked Alex. "Coffee time?"

"Well, that as well, if we've got time to stop," the boy replied. "But, about the painting. We haven't cleaned off the underside of the boat, or sorted out about how we're going to paint that!"

"No, Danny," we haven't," Alex told tim. "But we don't need to paint the bottom. No-one ever does paint the bottom of their boats."

"Why on earth not?" asked Danny, curiously.

"Well," Alex told him. "Can you remember your science lessons? What are the essentials required for metal to rust? We only did it a few weeks ago."

"Let's see," Danny thought for a moment. "Water, of course. And air?"

"That's right, Danny," Alex agreed. "But it's actually the oxygen in the air which is needed for metal to go rusty. Then the metal will degrade into iron oxide. But underneath the boat, which of course is submerged under the water, there's very little air or oxygen. So that part of the hull doesn't rust. And if it doesn't rust, then it's not necessary to paint it. Also, don't forget that sometimes we go aground, and then the paint would get scraped off anyway."

"Yes, I suppose so," replied Danny, nodding, as he picked up his paintbrush and set to work again, while Alex went inside *Jennifer Jo* and brewed up two cups of coffee.

The pair worked hard all that day and the next, and by the early afternoon the job had been finished. "That's a job well done, Danny," Alex exclaimed. "Thanks for helping me with it. You've made the job a lot easier for me than it would have been had I been doing it on my own."

"That's alright. Mister," replied Danny. "I suppose you could say I've been working my passage, so to speak."

"Yes, you've certainly done that," Alex said with a smile. "But as you know, you're welcome to stay with me on *Jennifer Jo* for as long as you want."

"Yes Mister, I know," Danny responded. But I might as well stay with you. I haven't got anywhere else to go, have I? And I haven't found my Mum yet, have I?"

Alex managed a wry smile, and stifled his response. Now was not the time to talk to Danny about that. It was something still far off in the future. Changing the subject, Alex spoke again. "As a special treat, Danny, we'll go out for a meal tonight, shall we? There's a good pub about ten minutes walk away, the people in the marina office recommended it to me the other day. I think we've both earned a rest from cooking for one night at least, after all the hard work we've done."

"Good idea, Mister. That sound great," Danny replied. "I don't think I've ever been into a pub before."

"Well then, Danny, that will be a new experience for you, won't it? I hope you enjoy the meal. You've certainly earned it. And tomorrow, we'll arrange for the boat to be put back into the water, and then we can go on our way."

It was a dull start to the day the next morning. Danny and Alex stood and watched as the crane arrived and carefully lifted *Jennifer Jo* back into the water. Alex started the engine, gently moved the boat away from the crane area, and then moored up again.

"Hey, Mister, what have we stopped here for?" enquired Danny. "I thought we were moving on?"

"Well, yes we are," replied Alex. "But there's just a few things to sort out before we go. Look, here's some supplies coming now." Danny looked over Alex's shoulder and saw one of the marina staff approaching, pulling a pallet trolley behind him. On the pallet were a dozen sacks of coal. "We need some coal, Danny," Alex continued, "because it's going to be really cold from now on. We've got room for some of it in the cratch lockers, but the rest we'll have to put on the roof of the boat. I don't like doing that, as it's rather untidy, but if the water in the canal freezes, then we won't be able to move and get any more until a thaw sets in. This will keep us nice and warm till we can move again. As I said, it's untidy to store stuff on the top, but we'll soon use it up."

They'd just finished stacking the coal onto the boat when a large van painted in the livery of a local supermarket arrived, and drove up to the boat. "Is this *Jennifer Jo*?" asked the driver, as he got out of the cab.

"Yes, that's right," Danny said. "What do you want?"

"Well, I've got a delivery for you," the driver replied. "Where do you want it?"

"What is it?" asked Danny.

"Groceries and stuff," the driver replied. "It was ordered on the internet a couple of days ago, for delivery to here, this morning. To a narrowboat called *Jennifer Jo*. Is this it?"

"Yes, that's us," Danny responded. "Shall I give you a hand to unload?"

"Yes, please," the driver replied, as Danny helped the driver unload over a dozen bags from the van, signed the driver's delivery ticket, and then took them down inside the boat. "I didn't know you'd ordered anything, Mister?" asked Danny.

"No,, Danny, I forgot to tell you," Alex replied. "I did it online after you'd turned in the other night. If we can't move the boat because of the frost, and the water in the canal is frozen solid, then at least we'll have plenty of food to eat, until we can get moving again. I've just about run out of food and water once before, if you remember, and I don't want that to happen again."

"That's a good idea, Mister," replied Danny. "There's always something to think of, isn't there? But we manage alright, don't we?"

Alex nodded. "Yes, Danny, we do, we certainly do," he replied.

"But let's move on now, shall we, and see how we get on?" he added, as he started the engine, waited for Danny to untie the mooring ropes, and as Danny stepped aboard, carefully steered *Jennifer Jo* out into the canal once more.

CHAPTER 13

Alex eased the tiller over and expertly steered *Jennifer Jo* around the bend in the canal. After a dull start to the day, it had turned out to be a nice Spring morning, a welcome change, Alex thought, from the hard winter which now, thankfully, lay behind them. Pleasant enough, in fact, for Danny to have slipped off his tee shirt to enjoy the warm, bright, sunlight. As the boat drew round the bend, they entered a long straight stretch of canal, with the next lock, their first that morning, coming into view in the far distance.

"Looks like there's a bit of a queue, Mister," Danny exclaimed, as he picked up the binoculars from their usual place on the gas locker to have a closer look. "There's five or six boats by the lock, waiting their turn, by the look of it. There's a pub right by the lock, I think it's called The Navigation, just like loads of the pubs by the canal. But I don't think the people off the boats are at the pub, they wouldn't moor up there if they were, they'd be in the way of boats waiting for the lock, they'd be much further back than that."

"That's alright, Danny," Alex replied. "We'll just pull in behind the last one, then I'll pop inside and make a couple of cups of coffee, whilst you can slip up to the lock and see what's going on."

Alex carefully steered *Jennifer Jo* towards the bank, as Danny stepped off and made fast the ropes at bow and stern. "I'll go and see what's happening," he said, "I'll be back in a minute, it shouldn't take long." Alex nodded, and went inside to make the coffee. He was just coming up the stairway onto the rear deck with the two mugs of coffee as Danny returned. "So, what's up, Danny?" he asked, handing Danny his coffee as he did so.

"Well, Mister," Danny replied. "The lock's taking twice as long to fill as it should do, and it s a deep lock, really deep, so it's taking a long time to fill. The offside paddle gear's not working."

"Why's that, then?" enquired Alex.

"The paddle gear's broken," Danny answered. "The second intermediate pinion is broken, it's lying on the ground in three or four pieces, that's why. You can't lift the paddle at all. There's a notice beside it, saying that it will be fixed tomorrow, the maintenance men have had to go and fetch some new parts."

Alex sipped his coffee whilst he digested what Danny had just said. He was particularly pleased to note the wording Danny had used. Not 'the gearwheel', nor 'the cogwheel'. He'd used the correct terminology, precisely identifying the broken part as the 'second intermediate pinion'. That showed that Danny was really taking in the school lessons which Alex had been giving him, every afternoon, Monday to Friday.

Ever since he'd first become a teacher many years ago, Alex had always tried hard to make his lessons interesting and relevant, and he saw no reason not to continue that, just because he and Danny lived on a canal boat. In Danny's science lessons, for instance, they'd examined the paddle gear at the locks, counting the number of teeth on each part of the mechanism, and calculated the Mechanical Advantage which the gearing offered. And for homework one day, he'd set Danny the task of drawing the paddle gear and labelling up its constituent parts. Danny had spent some time at the lock, and produced a neat and elegant picture of the paddle gear, with the constituent parts all properly labelled and identified. There was no doubt that Danny had a particular aptitude for drawing. Reflecting their historic heritage, different parts of the canal system utilised differing styles of paddle gear, and they'd studied them all as they came across them, and found and noted down the difference between them.

Danny's topical lessons had not stopped at the paddle gear, either. Also in science, they'd studied levers, and Alex had tasked Danny to measuring the length of the balance beams on the lock gates, and calculate the Mechanical Advantage which they provided to the boaters. And in maths, they'd measured the length of the locks, and the rise and fall of the water by counting how many bricks were covered and uncovered as the level rose and fell. They'd measured the length of the lock gates, and, taking into account the fact that the lock gates were at an angle to the side of the lock, and to each other, used trigonometry to calculate the width of the lock. Thus they'd been able to calculate the volume of water required to fill a lock, and they'd used a watch to time how long it took to fill and empty a lock, and calculated the average flow rate in gallons per minute.

They'd also timed how long it took for each brick in the lock wall to be uncovered as the lock emptied, and from that information he'd had Danny draw a graph showing how long it took to reveal each brick. And from that, he'd asked Danny to draw another graph showing how the rate of emptying decreased as the water level in the lock became lower and lower. 'That's really interesting, Mister,' he recalled Danny had commented, as he'd handed in his homework to be marked later that evening. 'You never know how much you can find out with just a few simple measurements, do you?'

Alex had just smiled and nodded. 'That's right, Danny,' he'd replied. 'Mathematics can be a very powerful tool, if you use it in the right way. You will see, as we progress your lessons, just how powerful it can be.' Although Danny didn't realise it, the work he'd done was effectively calculating the first and second differentials of the water flow, thus laying the foundations for the introduction to differential calculus which Alex planned to start teaching to Danny in about a year's time. He was really pleased that Danny was making such good progress in his lessons.

All of this and more, Danny had tackled with enthusiasm, making neat sketches and drawings, and writing up his notes in his exercise books. It seemed that Danny really enjoyed the teaching which Alex had been giving him. He'd always been attentive, asking questions if something wasn't quite clear to him. He'd been diligent with his homework, too. Alex considered Danny to be a real pleasure to teach.

Just then, Alex was awoken from his reverie by Danny calling out "hey, Mister, the lock's just opened and there's a boat coming out. We're all moving up."

Alex nodded, and made ready to step ashore and pull *Jennifer Jo* forward a few yards. It wasn't difficult to pull the boat on the ropes for a short while, and it certainly wasn't worthwhile starting the engine for such a short distance. But instead of Danny helping him, the boy stepped off and made his way to the boat next to them in the queue. "The boat in front of us is a holiday boat," he called out over his shoulder. "There's six Girl Guides on it, and a couple of Leaders too. I'll go and see if they need a hand moving their boat."

"Alright, Danny, that's fine," Alex called after him, smiling as he did so. He too had spotted the Girl Guides. And he'd been wondering how long it would be before Danny found some excuse to go and socialise with them. Alex was acutely aware that, living on a boat, travelling and moving on almost every day, Danny had only limited opportunities to socialise with other people, especially young people of his own age. He knew that Danny was well aware that six girls and two adults were easily capable of moving their boat just a few yards, and Danny's going to help them would leave Alex to move *Jennifer Jo* on his own. But Alex was used to handling his boat single-handed, and was well capable of such tasks. He'd managed his boat on his own for some time before he'd taken in Danny to come and live with him on *Jennifer Jo*, and it pleased him to see Danny chatting away, surrounded by a gaggle of young girls. 'So, Danny,' he thought, 'go and chat by all means.'

The boating community was always very friendly, it was normal to give a friendly wave to other boaters as they passed by, to walkers on the towpath as well, and fishermen too. If fact, it was considered to be a bit of an insult NOT to wave and extend a greeting. When moored up in the evenings, it was common to walk along the towpath, talking to other boaters about their boats, their pets (many live-aboard boaters had a dog aboard with them), and almost anything else that came up in the course of conversation. But the people they spoke to were mainly adults, many of whom either lived aboard their boats all the year round, or were retired people who spent a lot of their time boating. Except during school holiday times, few children of Danny's age were about on the canals. It was at the locks, working through in company with other boats, that the best opportunity to chat and socialise presented itself. But generally, he and Danny spent most of their time together, with no-one else for company.

Every fifteen minutes or so, the lock gates opened and another boat exited the lock, cruising slowly past the waiting line of boats. Then the boat at the front of the queue manoeuvred into the lock, the crew closed the gates, and the rest of the queue move up a space nearer the lock.

But as Alex sat on the rail at the back of *Jennifer Jo*, watching Danny chatting excitedly to the Girl Guides, he suddenly realised that the Danny he was looking at now was not the same Danny as he'd taken in some twelve months before. Then, he'd been a scared and frightened child, on the run after absconding from the children's home where he'd suffered appalling abuse. He'd been terrified of being sent back to whatever retribution would have awaited him there, with starvation rations and yet more physical and mental abuse. Alex remembered the weals and bruises all over his body, and how skinny Danny had been, well underweight, with his stick-thin arms, and his ribs showing through the tightly-stretched skin on his chest, indications of being undernourished, underfed almost to the point of mild starvation. The boy, then just turned 12, had barely been the size of a skinny ten-year old.

But now, a few weeks after they had celebrated Danny's thirteenth birthday with a meal at a local canalside restaurant, and with 12 months of proper food and a varied diet behind him, Danny had changed considerably. The thin arms and scraggy chest had filled out, a gradual change which had started to become apparent after just a few weeks. And now, a year later, it was noticeable how other changes had been taking place also. The boy's shoulders had broadened, he'd grown noticeably taller and his voice had deepened. And he was now shaving every couple of days, using the shaver which Alex had bought him for Christmas. He was in the iron grip of puberty, that dramatic period in his life when, within the space of just a few short months, he would make the transformation from a boy into a young man, an adolescent.

Danny's mental state had changed too. Initially scared and frightened, unsure as to whether or not he could trust Alex, he'd gradually come to accept that Alex was happy for him to stay with him on *Jennifer Jo* for as long as he wished. Whilst moving along the canal every day or two on *Jennifer Jo* was not ideal, it was the closest thing to a stable home environment that Alex could provide for the lad. And Danny had gradually relaxed, and appeared to have become comfortable with his situation, happy to spend this part of his life with Alex on *Jennifer Jo*.

He recalled the times in the past when, even though he had his own space on board in the back cabin, Danny would frequently walk up the towpath, to be away from Alex, away from the boat, and sit down on the grass, wanting to be alone, slowly chewing on a blade of grass whilst staring into the water, with just his thoughts for company. But these episodes had gradually occurred less and less often, and ever since that day just after Christmas when Danny had broken down and cried in Alex's arms, they had stopped altogether.

That indicated to Alex that Danny had accepted his way of life for the time being, and had come to enjoy his time with Alex on *Jennifer Jo*. Looking at Danny now, happily chatting away with the Girl Guides on the boat in front, Alex felt more than a little proud of what he had achieved, and what he had been able to do for Danny. The boy was pleasant company, he always behaved himself, he helped around the boat at every opportunity, and he'd shown a keen interest in his lessons and applied himself to all of them with eagerness and enthusiasm, never once complaining about having to do his homework in the evenings.

But one thing above all others permeated Danny's outlook on life. He was absolutely certain that he would somehow find his mother, and be reunited with her. However, Alex had recently come to realise that Danny's conviction, that he would some day find his mother, was the anchor by which he was able to live his life, to get through each day as it happened. It was the means by which he was able to face an uncertain future. It was something to hang on to, something he could look forward to, something to pin his hopes on. Perhaps, Alex thought, Danny too realised that finding his mother was an impossibility, but by not admitting it to himself, and not accepting the inevitable, he was able to put all other scenarios out of his mind.

Alex had always been aware that finding Danny's mother would be all but impossible, but he'd not discussed it with Danny at all. Now was not the time to dash his hopes. He knew that eventually, at some time in the future, Danny and he would part company, and he did not look forward to talking to Danny about it when the time came, even though that moment was still several years away. But recently Alex had become aware that, as Danny began to mature into an older teenager, it was likely that the boy would probably decide for himself when it was right for him to leave *Jennifer Jo* and make his way in the world on his own.

At last it was the turn of the boat in front of *Jennifer Jo*, with Danny's newly-befriended Girl Guides aboard, to move forward and enter the lock. Alex watched as Danny helped the girls through the lock, then as he waited for the lock to empty again, stand and waved goodbye to the departing Girl Guides. Eventually Danny opened the lock's bottom gate, and beckoned Alex forward. "You can bring her in now, Mister," he called out, then collapsed with laughter, giggling at their standing joke, oblivious to the curious look of a dog walker passing by at that moment.

Alex carefully brought *Jennifer Jo* to a halt in the lock and waited whilst Danny closed the bottom gates. As Danny had remarked earlier, it was a deep lock, one of the deepest in the entire canal system, with a rise of over 11 feet. Like all the locks on this stretch of canal, it was a narrow lock too, only just wide enough for *Jennifer Jo* to squeeze into, with a couple of inches to spare at each side of the boat. Once in the lock, Alex could only see the grey slime-encrusted brickwork of the lock walls, still dripping water, and a rectangle of blue sky far above him. Danny cracked open the nearside top paddle, the only one which was working, and the boat slowly rose up the lock, inch by inch, as the water level rose. Alex was pleased that Danny always followed what he'd been told, at the very first lock he'd encountered with Danny on board, to initially raise the paddle just a quarter of the way, to avoid the boat being thrown about in the lock by the inrushing water, and then wait until the lock was half-full before fully opening the paddle.

As the lock became half-full, Alex waited patiently for Danny to open the paddle the rest of the way, but nothing happened. For some reason Danny had left the paddle just a quarter open, and not opened it any further. Eventually, however, Alex's head came above the brickwork of the lock as the boat gradually rose, and he looked around to spot Danny and ask him why he'd not opened the paddle fully.

But Danny was nowhere to be seen. His windlass, easily identified by the blue ring of paint Alex had marked it with some years ago to signify that it came from *Jennifer Jo*, was lying on the ground beside the paddle gear, its shaft neatly aligned parallel to the walls of the lock, in the manner Danny always used whenever he put down his windlass for whatever reason. Alex scanned the area between the lock and the pub garden, whose grass came all the way down to the lock, separated from it by a low white-painted picket fence, just a couple of feet high, presumably to keep young children away from the ever-present dangers around the lock and its surroundings. There were about ten or twelve picnic tables spread around on the grass, with customers from the pub starting to sit down with their drinks, no doubt waiting for the serving staff to bring out their lunches from the kitchens. But of Danny there was no sign.

Alex stepped off the boat and walked along the lock-side to wind up the paddle, allowing the lock to fill to its maximum, then he opened the top gate and carefully steered *Jennifer Jo* away from the lock, mooring up about fifty yards further along the canal, to allow space at the lock landing for other boats to stop whilst they waited to use the lock. Maybe even six months ago, he would have been worried that Danny wasn't about, possibly apprehended once again to be returned to Grant Hall. But the chances of that happening now were negligible. They were over two hundred miles away from Grant Hall, and now no one would be looking for a boy who'd absconded a considerable time ago. And with the changes that were taking place within Danny, his appearance would be somewhat dissimilar to any photographs of him that may have been circulated at the time. Alex knew that Danny would return in his own good time.

But after some 45 minutes had elapsed, Alex started to began to become a little bit anxious. Danny had never before been away from *Jennifer Jo,* out of sight, for so long. So it was with a gentle sigh of relief that he suddenly saw Danny, half-walking, half trotting, coming across the grass towards him. But this was a completely different Danny to all the Dannys he'd ever seen before. He'd seen Danny in many different moods. On occasions he'd seen the boy sad, morose, frightened, and miserable, but more usually the lady had been reasonably happy and contented. But now, Danny seemed hyper, bubbling over with excitement as he rushed over to the boat.

"Hey Mister, come with me," he called out, grinning broadly from ear to ear, as he took Alex's hand, tugging it eagerly. "You'll never believe what I've got to show you."

"Hold on a minute, Danny, please," Alex exclaimed. "Let me lock up first, then I'll be ready. Wait just a minute." As Alex locked the boat, he looked at Danny, who was fidgeting eagerly from one foot to the other, like a cat on a hot tin roof.

"Come on, Mister," Danny called out, "quick." Alex stepped off the boat and followed Danny, who'd grabbed his hand once again and was tugging him towards the pub. But as he got nearer, he turned to the right, and Alex saw another large lawn with yet more picnic tables spread around over the grass. This part of the pub garden was hidden from the lock and the canal by a dense screen of bushes. Danny dragged him towards one of the tables, where Alex saw there were two women sitting down with their backs to them, just finishing eating their lunch.

Danny wheeled Alex around the table to face the women as they sat eating. "Hey, Mister," he said, excitedly. "This is my Mum. And over there, that's my Gran." Alex was stunned.

"Are you sure, Danny?" he managed to ask, dumbfounded, as his mouth dropped open in astonishment. But Danny's body language said it all. He'd gone to sit down beside his mother, who'd put her arm around him and hugged him tightly to her. And Danny had cuddled up to his mother, resting his head on her, grinning broadly all the while.

"Oh, I'm sorry, how silly of me," Alex apologised, as he hurriedly tried to gather his thoughts. There was no doubt about it, no doubt at all. Almost unbelievably, amazingly and against all the odds, Danny had found his mother. Alex extended his hand and shook hands with Danny's mother, as he racked his brain to remember Danny's surname. It came to him just in time. "Hello, Mrs. Marshall," he said. "It's nice to meet you. And your mother too," shaking hands with Danny's gran also.

Alex sat down opposite Danny and his mother as Danny started chattering away excitedly, nineteen to the dozen. "Hey, Mister, what do you think of this?" he asked, still very excited. "I nearly missed them, you know. I'd let you into the lock, and then lifted the paddle a little way, like I always do, then I decided I needed to have a pee. But the boat was down in the lock, and I couldn't go in the bushes, there were too many people about. So I decided to go into the pub and use the toilet there. But it was really busy in there, I had to wait a little while before there was a space free. And when I came back across the grass to go back to the lock, there was my mum and my gran just starting to sit down. If I hadn't had to wait in the toilet, I'd have missed them!"

Alex smiled to see Danny so excited, and obviously deliriously happy at finding his mother at long last. But Danny's mother had started speaking. "It's really strange," she said. "We'd been to the garden centre down the road to get some bedding plants for the garden, and we were planning to have our lunch in the restaurant there. But the kitchen was out of action, I think they were having some new equipment installed. So we came here instead. We'd been to the garden centre several times, but we've never been here to this pub before, and we didn't even know that there was a canal at the bottom of the garden. But you can't even see the canal from where we're sitting here."

"Yes, what a coincidence that you've met here, quite by chance," Alex replied. "Danny's been really looking forward to finding you again."

"Yes, I can believe that," Mrs. Marshall added. "You know, after I got over my illness, I spent ages trying to find Daniel too, but all the leads we had came to a dead end. Mother and I spent ages looking, trying to track him down. We knew that he'd been placed with a foster mother after I was taken ill, because she used to bring Daniel to see me every week whilst I was in hospital."

"That's right," Danny interjected. "That was Mrs. Bradley. She was ever so nice. I liked it when I was living with her. But then she moved away and I was put in this religious place, Harding Court, it was called. I wasn't allowed out to go and see Mum after that. But I did manage to nip out to see her a few times, anyway."

"Yes, you did," Danny's mother continued. "But then the visits stopped altogether, I don't know why. After that, I didn't see Daniel any more. No-one told me where he was, and nobody seemed to care about helping me find out where he was, or why he wasn't coming to see me. After I was discharged from hospital, I was still very weak, and our house where we used to live had been re-let, so I came up here to convalesce and live with my mother, and recover and build up my strength again."

At that point Danny interrupted again. "I did come to see you in the hospital, one more time," he said. "But you weren't there any more."

"I never knew that!" his mother responded, looking surprised.

"They told me you'd been allowed to go home a couple of weeks before," Danny added. "But they didn't tell me where you were or anything."

"They probably didn't know," his mother replied. "And if they had known, then probably they're not allowed to say. Patient confidentiality and that sort of thing, I suppose. But from then on, no-one wanted to help us. I did eventually manage to get in touch with the religious sect who used to run Harding Court, they'd moved to a different location after the Court was burnt down. Apparently someone had left some damp clothing over a heater in the office and then forgotten about it, and it was there all night, and caught fire. The place burnt down and all their old records in their archive, next door to the office, were destroyed.

But I think that Daniel had moved on from there before the fire. Because all the archive records had been lost, it was impossible to find any trace of what happened to any of the children who'd been living there before then. I was ever so upset, because I thought I'd never see my son again. But I never gave up hope, and here he is! Isn't it wonderful?" And she beamed at Alex, so obviously really happy at being reunited with Danny at last.

"Yes, it is," Alex replied. "Danny never gave up hope either. It's been the one thing he's never wavered from."

Mrs. Marshall smiled and nodded in response, then, turning to Danny, she said "Daniel, we need to be on our way soon. Alright?"

"Yes, Mum," Danny replied. Turning to Alex, he added, "I'm going to live with my Mum now, Mister," he said. "Is it alright if I go and collect my stuff? Clothes and things?"

"Yes, of course, Danny," Alex replied. "You go ahead. I'll be along shortly." Danny nodded as, still grinning hugely, he disappeared in the direction of the lock and the canal.

Mrs. Marshall started speaking again. "Daniel tells me he's been living with you for a little while?" she asked. "On your canal boat? I do hope he hasn't been a nuisance to you, or anything?"

"No, not at all," Alex responded. "He's a great lad. He had a bit of a difficult time before I met him, but he's well over that now. He's been really pleasant company."

"How did you meet him?" she asked. Alex paused for a moment. He didn't want too many awkward questions being asked about the circumstances surrounding his decision to take in Danny and give him a home. He was acutely aware that he could still be in trouble for child abduction or worse. In the worst scenario, he might even end up in jail.

"Well, I was working my boat through a lock, and Danny was there watching, and he needed somewhere to stop for the night, and since I had a spare berth, I let him stay on board my boat overnight," he replied. It was near enough to the truth to pass muster. "And he's been with me ever since. He'll tell you all about it in due course, I'm sure."

Alex continued chatting to Danny's mother and his gran for about twenty minutes, then, getting up, he said, "I'd better go and see how Danny's getting on. It's been every so nice to meet you both. And I'm really pleased for you all, and especially for Danny, that you're all together again. He's really had his heart set on it, on finding you again. It's been the one thing which has held him together ever since you were parted. I'm sure that it will be strange for him at first, but I do think he's enjoyed being with me. So I'll say goodbye now, then."

"Goodbye, Alex," Danny's mother said. "Thank you so much for looking after Daniel like you have. From what he's said, he seems to have enjoyed being with you."

"That's nice to know," Alex smiled. "I've tried to look after him as best I can. But it's been a pleasure to have him aboard with me. He's helped me with the boat, and he's learnt to drive it along and work the locks too. And he's learnt a lot about the canals and their history, too."

After shaking hands with both of the ladies, Alex said his goodbyes and made his way back to *Jennifer Jo*. As he approached, he could see a pile of five or six carrier bags stacked on the back deck, and as he stepped onto the boat, Danny's arm appeared out of the hatch and deposited yet another bag beside them. "I didn't know you'd got so much stuff, Danny," he said as he stepped aboard. "It's surprising how it adds up, isn't it?"

Danny climbed up the stairway and stood beside him on the deck. "Yes, Mister," he said. "it's lucky there's enough carrier bags in the cupboard. But I'm done now, that's the lot. By the way, I've got the special tee shirts and sweatshirts and stuff with the boat's name on, is it alright for me to keep them? It will remind me of my time here on *Jay-Jay* with you."

"Yes, that's fine, Danny," Alex replied. "I'll have no need for them. After all, they won't fit me, will they? And at the rate you're growing, they won't fit you for very much longer, anyway, will they?" Danny didn't answer, as he just nodded and grinned his usual trademark smile.

"So, you've got everything, now, then?" Alex enquired. "What about your school books. You'll need them to show your teachers at your new school."

"Oh, no, I forgot them," Danny replied. "I'll go and get them. The textbooks as well?"

"No, not them," Alex told the lad. "Your new school will have their own, and they'll almost certainly be different to the ones we've been using. Better leave them here."

"Ok Mister," Danny replied, as he ducked back into *Jennifer Jo* and returned a few moments later with his exercise books, tucking them into one of the carrier bags.

"Well, that's it," he said, as he bent over and picked up all his carrier bags and then stood there for a moment or two, hands full, suddenly unsure of himself once again. "Goodbye, then, Mister," he said awkwardly, staring at the deck and avoiding Alex's gaze. Then, suddenly, without another word, he stepped off the boat and hesitantly walked away across the grass, towards where his mother and grandmother were waiting for him.

Alex stood and watched as Danny covered perhaps a couple of dozen steps, before he suddenly dropped the carrier bags onto the ground, spun round, and ran back, arms outstretched, to the back of the boat where Alex was standing. Reaching Alex, he flung his arms round him and buried his head in Alex's chest. Alex embraced the boy and pulled him close, hugging him tight, and they stood there together for some 30 seconds or so, ignoring the curious glances of the passers-by and the pub customers sitting at the tables nearby.

Eventually they disentangled themselves, and Danny looked up at Alex, with tears in his eyes.

"I'm sorry I'm crying, Mister," he apologised. "I never cried, even once, all the time I was at Grant Hall, but loads of the other kids did. Some of them cried every night. And here I am crying now. I'm really sorry, but I just can't help it."

"It's alright, Danny," Alex comforted the boy. "It's nothing to be ashamed of. There's no need to apologise. These are tears of joy, not of sadness. It's because you've found your mother at last. It's what you've been looking forward to, ever since you first came onto *Jennifer Jo*."

"Yes, Mister, I know," said Danny, wiping his eyes. "I always knew I'd find her some day. But you never thought I would, did you? You never admitted it, but I could tell."

Alex was a bit taken aback by what Danny had said. Admittedly, he'd tried to dampen Danny's hopes on several occasions, and told him that it wouldn't be easy to find his mother, but the boy had read his mind much better than he'd given him credit for. But he quickly collected his thoughts, and spoke to Danny again. "Well, I was aware that it was going to be a difficult search," he said. But I'm so glad for you now, I really am. It's a really good result, isn't it?"

Danny nodded. "Yes, Mister, it is," he said, adding, "but I'd better say goodbye now. It's been great here on *Jay-Jay* with you, really nice. I never thought it would be as good as it has been. And to think that at first, on that first night, when you found me hiding in the cratch, I really thought you might be a pedo. I was only going to stay the one night, until the weather cleared up, but you made me a really nice breakfast, and washed my clothes for me, and with all those pictures you showed me, of you at your school with all those other kids, all happy and smiling and that, so I decided to stay on and see how things turned out. I'm glad I did, because you weren't a pedo after all. I'm really sorry now, that I could ever think that about you. You're actually one of the nicest guys I've ever met."

Alex hugged the boy again. "I told you that you were quite safe with me, Danny, if you can remember." Danny nodded, as Alex continued "but I can understand you being a bit wary. Unfortunately, there are some strange people about. And their improper behaviour towards youngsters causes everyone to be tarred with the same brush of suspicion, by those who really should know better. But, thank you for placing your trust in me. I hope you feel it was well placed."

Danny nodded in agreement. "Yes. Like I said, Mister, you're OK. It really has been nice, being on *Jay-Jay* with you," he went on. "I don't really want to leave."

"That's understandable, Danny," Alex responded. "But your rightful place is with your mother now. It's what you've been looking forward to ever since you came aboard."

"Yes, I know," replied Danny. "It'll be strange at first, living in a new house and all that, and a new school as well."

"Yes, it will," Alex reassured the lad. "But you'll soon get used to it. Now, are you sure you've got everything?"

"Yes, I think so," Danny added. "But I'd better go, Mum's waiting for me." Danny turned and stepped off the boat, but as he did so, Alex remembered something and called him back. "Wait a minute, please, Danny," he called out. "There's something else you should have."

"What's that, then?" asked Danny.

"Hang on, I'll go and fetch it," Alex replied. "Please wait just a moment." Danny nodded, while Alex went inside the boat and went to his bedroom, where he lifted up the mattress, pulling out the large A4 envelope which he'd put there a year ago, just a couple of days after he'd found a frightened Danny hiding in the cratch at the front of the boat, shivering in the cold.

Taking the envelope back on deck, he handed it to Danny. "What is it, Mister?" Danny asked once again. "What's in here?"

"This, Danny, is unfinished business," Alex told him, placing his hands firmly on the boys shoulders and giving them a gentle squeeze as he looked him squarely in the face. "It's a big responsibility to be placing on your young shoulders, but it's something which has to be dealt with. And you're probably the only person who can do so. You, and no-one else, although of course once you do decide to finish it, there should be other people who can help you to bring it to a satisfactory conclusion. But they won't be able to do it without you. And it needs to be done, it really does. You're old enough now, I'm sure, to know what you have to do. But leave it for a while. Don't worry about it for now. Wait until you've become used to living with your mother once again, and become settled in at your new school. Then look at it and talk it through with your mother. She'll help you with it."

"Alright, Mister," Danny replied, taking the envelope. "I'll look at it later. But my mum's waiting for me, I've really got to go. Goodbye once again."

"Goodbye, Danny," Alex said quietly. "I like to think that I've been able to help you in the last twelve months or so since you came aboard. I hope you do too. And be sure to work hard at school. You've done really well with me. Have you got the school reports I prepared?"

" Yes, Mister, I put them in when I got my exercise books. And I will work hard, I promise you," said Danny. "You've been a good teacher. You've made the lessons really interesting."

"Thank you, Danny," Alex smiled. "Teaching is what I did for all my working life, so I suppose I've picked up a few hints and such along the way." Alex paused before continuing. "Now, Danny, here's something really serious for you to consider. In times to come, whenever you think back about the time you've spent with me, above all else remember what I tell you now. It's really important."

"Remember always that your life is not a rehearsal, it's the real thing, and you'll only ever get one chance at it. You will have to make many choices as you go through life, and hopefully you will always make the right ones. We all make mistakes from time to time, and with hindsight, you may find that some of the choices you have made may turn out not to have been the best ones. But do try to learn from your mistakes, and always be sure to be pleasant to the people around you, even those that may upset you. And lastly, be sure to always strive to do your best at whatever you attempt."

"I will, Mister, I promise," Danny nodded.

"I've enjoyed having you aboard *Jennifer Jo*, and I hope that you've enjoyed being with me," Alex went on. "It's been nice to have some company with me, and help working the boat." He paused for a moment. "But you'd better be on your way now. Remember that I wish you well in all that you do, and above all, for you to be happy in your life. Goodbye, and take care of yourself, won't you? And look after your mother and your gran, too. I'm sure they're overjoyed at finding you again."

"Yes, Mister, they are," the boy responded. "And thank you for looking after me and letting me stay with you on your boat. Like what I said just now, it's been really nice." Alex gave him a final hug, then stood and watched as Danny walked over to where he'd left his bags, tucking the envelope Alex had just given him into one of them. Then, picking them up and with his head held high, he proudly walked quickly towards where his mother and gran stood watching and waiting. As Danny turned and gave

Alex a final wave, the three of them walked round the pub garden till they were out of sight.

Alex started the engine, then untied the mooring ropes and navigated out into the canal. He cruised along for about half an hour before mooring up for the night, and preparing his evening meal. Sitting at the dinette, he found it strange to be eating his meal on his own, with Danny not seated in his usual place opposite, chatting together as they ate. After clearing up after his meal, Alex sat down to write up his diary, something he'd done every day ever since he'd first stepped aboard *Jennifer Jo* and cast off for the first time to become a live-aboard boater.

He wrote for about fifteen minutes, giving a full account of Danny's departure, and once he'd finished, he leafed through the dairy, looking a the various previous entries, especially those he'd made since Danny had first come aboard.

He knew that he would miss Danny. He would miss him quite a bit at first, but from his previous experience as a teacher, with boys whom he'd got to really know well moving away from his school every year after spending six or seven years there, Alex knew that he would gradually get used to Danny not being with him on *Jennifer Jo*, and to being on his own once again.

He sat and thought for a while about Danny, and especially about Danny's future. The boy seemed to have successfully put the horrors of Grant Hall behind him, but Alex well knew that those memories would remain deep within his subconscious for ever. Experiences like that could never be fully forgotten, and if Danny did what Alex hoped and expected him to do, to go to the authorities and tell them about how life had been, and almost certainly still was, at Grant Hall, then he would have to relive them all over again. And, in court, he would no doubt have to face cross-examination from hostile defence lawyers.

But, with Danny's firm understanding and conviction of what was right and wrong, Alex was sure that this was something that Danny would be able to handle. He'd shown that he was resourceful and self-reliant even before then, living hand-to mouth for ten days or so while he was on the run from Grant Hall, and since he'd come to live with Alex on *Jennifer Jo* he'd matured a great deal, in mind as well as body. His intrinsic self-assured, outgoing personality, subdued at first by his experiences at Grant Hall, had gradually come to the fore. Certainly, in Alex's opinion, there was, without doubt, an adult head resting firmly on Danny's young shoulders.

And the boy was intelligent, there was no doubt about that. If he continued to work at school as hard as he had at his lessons with Alex, then he should be able to make a good life for himself. But Alex also knew that school lessons in a class with thirty other children were quite different to the one-to-one lessons he'd been giving Danny. But Danny seemed keen to learn, and took a great interest in what he was being taught. He should be able to achieve some good examination results at the end of his schooling. And, with luck, that should set him up well for whatever career he chose to follow.

But suddenly, Alex clenched his fist and brought it down on the table with a loud bang. A terrible thought had just come to him. In all the excitement of Danny finding his mother and leaving *Jennifer Jo* to go and live with her and his gran, Alex had forgotten one important thing. He'd completely forgotten to ask where Danny would be living. He had no address, no telephone number, or anything. There was no way that he would be able to keep in touch with Danny in future, to hear how he was, and he was getting on in life.

Alex realised that the chances of finding Danny again were just about non-existent. Going back to the pub the next day, or cruising up and down the canal in the forlorn hope of finding him again, would be fruitless. The young boy who had so suddenly come into his life a year ago, lived with him for a year, and then just as suddenly departed, had effectively disappeared completely and without trace. There was absolutely no way that Alex would be able to keep in touch with him. 'How could I have not remembered to find out something more about where Danny was going to be?' Alex angrily chided himself. He was mightily annoyed at having neglected such a simple task which he should have done before Danny left.

Alex found it really difficult to get out of his mind how careless he'd been in not getting any address for Danny. But trying to putting that thought aside, Alex sat and considered his plans for the next few months. He'd spent a good year cruising the northern waterways with Danny, looking for the boy's mother. But now that task had come to a successful conclusion, he decided he would make his way back south again, for a change of scenery. Also, there were two new canals to be explored, canals that had fallen into disuse and been abandoned many years ago, but just recently fully restored and reopened after many years of fundraising and hard work by local canal societies. And with no Danny to give lessons to, he would be able to take up once again his unfinished project, the history of his school which he'd been working on, which he'd had to put to one side when Danny came onto the scene. With that, and of course with the daily routine of working his boat along the canals and through the locks,

Alex would, as always, have plenty to occupy his time.

The next morning, Alex went through to the back of the boat to set off, and, passing through the back cabin, he noticed Danny's berth, neatly made up as usual from the previous morning, but not slept in, now that Danny was no longer living on *Jennifer Jo*. Alex stripped the bed, ready to put the bedding into the washing machine, but was surprised to find, tucked away and hidden under the mattress, a large unsealed A3-sized envelope. He sat down on the bunk and carefully withdrew the contents to study them. What he saw amazed him.

It was another of Danny's drawings. It showed Alex and Danny sitting side by side on the balance beam of a lock gate, looking at each other and laughing, with *Jennifer Jo* in the lock behind them. There was a white-painted lock cottage in the background, and, adjacent to the canal as it stretched away into the distance, a line of upright poplar trees on the offside, their branches gently swaying in the breeze as they pointed towards a few fluffy white clouds moving across the sky. It had been very carefully drawn, with a huge amount of detail, and then delicately coloured in.

Alex was aware that Danny knew that it was Alex's birthday coming up soon, just a couple of months after Danny's own, when he'd turned thirteen, and this must have been the birthday present that Danny had made for him. Danny had already given him one drawing, at Christmas, and this one was equally as good, maybe even better. Without a doubt, Alex thought, Danny has a real talent for drawing, and it would be a waste if he did not pursue his talent and develop his drawing abilities. Hopefully there would be a good art department at his new school, where his skills in this field could be developed and encouraged.

Alex sat and studied the drawing for some time, but eventually he replaced it into the envelope and carefully stored it away in the saloon. He would scan it into his computer that evening, and use it as his desktop background. It would be a permanent reminder, as if he needed one, of the young lad who'd stayed with him on *Jennifer Jo* for the past year, and then moved on to continue his life with his mother. But Alex needed to move on too, in more ways than one. He started the engine, untied his mooring ropes, and set off to make his way along the canal in the bright spring morning sunshine.

CHAPTER 14

Alex leaned back on the dinette seat and carefully read through the text he'd just finished typing into his laptop. His work on his school's history was coming together nicely. In the nine months or so since Danny had left *Jennifer Jo*, he'd been able to spend quite a bit of time on his project, especially during the dark winter days, and he reckoned that in about three or four months time, it would be finished, and he'd be able to send it to one of his ex-colleagues for review.

He closed down all his files and set the laptop to shut down, and while it did so, for the umpteenth time Alex studied the desktop background on the screen, Danny's drawing of himself and Alex at the lockside with *Jennifer Jo* in the lock behind them, the drawing which he'd found under the boy's mattress the day after he'd left to go and live with his mother. He never ceased to marvel at the intricate details which Danny had incorporated into his work, something which he knew was really difficult to achieve, but a technique which Danny had managed to master so well at such a young age.

Whilst the computer busied itself closing down, Alex sat back and thought about Danny, something he'd done frequently over the last nine months since Danny had said goodbye and gone to live with his mother. With the two of them having lived in such close proximity within the confines of *Jennifer Jo* for almost a year, the boy had made a lasting impression on Alex. He often wondered how Danny was getting on in life. Alex deeply regretted not being able to keep in touch with Danny, and he was still mightily annoyed with himself for forgetting to enquire about his new address at the time. Now, all he could do was to wonder about the boy, and how he was getting on in life. Was he working hard at school? Was he looking after his mother and his gran properly? There was no way that Alex could find out, and he just had to live with his lack of forethought at the time.

Suddenly, Alex looked at his watch and realised that he might just catch the weather forecast at the end of the news, so he switched on the television sitting on the cabinet in the corner of the saloon to see what lay in store for him tomorrow. Long ago, he'd adopted the routine of not moving *Jennifer Jo* whilst it was raining, as he was never in a hurry to get anywhere, and, even though he'd got good waterproof clothing there seemed to be little point in being out in the wet if there was no need to be there. If it was going to be wet tomorrow, he'd stay put, as he was moored in a pleasant spot with nice views over the surrounding countryside.

As the television sprang into life, Alex took the remote and selected the channel where he knew the early evening news bulletin was about to end. He was just in time, as the news was just finishing. The screen showed one of the news reporters standing in front of two large wrought-iron gates set in a high brick wall, and through the gates in the background could be seen a large country house. Alex was just able to hear his closing words as he rounded off his piece to camera:

". . . . . thought that the Hall will now be sold. And now, back to the studio, where I think Anne will have the weather forecast for you."

Alex watched the weather forecast with his usual interest. It would be dull the next day with some drizzle at times, although quite warm, as a depression moved away to the East. A good day to stay put, he decided. But as he put his laptop away the locker under the seat, something was niggling him in his mind, although he couldn't quite determine what exactly it was that was troubling him. It was a good twenty minutes, as he worked in the galley preparing his evening meal, before he realised what it was. The scrap of the item he'd managed to catch at the end of the news bulletin, and especially the picture of the gates set in the high wall behind the news reporter reminded him of how Danny had described Grant Hall.

He tried to recall what exactly Danny had said when he'd been talking about his experiences there, and how he'd described the Hall itself. 'Set in a nice park,' the lad had said. 'Tall brick walls round the Hall, with just a single pair of high gates which were always kept locked, except for access into or out of the Hall.'

Alex sat at the dinette and ate his meal, thinking about how well the few brief moments he'd seen on the television news fitted Danny's description of Grant Hall. Curious, he put down his knife and fork and picked up the remote once again, and tuned in to the 24-hour news channel from the broadcaster whose news bulletin he'd been watching earlier. Perhaps they'd run that story again.

Becoming more and more impatient, he had to wait as the presenters worked their way through the running order set by the producers. Trouble in the Middle East, yet more MP's fiddling their expenses, further calls for Britain to withdraw from Europe, economic stagnation in America, and other well-aired issues were covered in detail. 'Nothing much changes,' Alex thought, 'they could have run a bulletin from six months ago and it would have been just as true today as it was then.'

But eventually, they arrived at the piece Alex was waiting for. He sat and listened eagerly as the newsreader started the story:

"A fifty-two year old man was today sentenced to 6 years in prison for abusing young boys entrusted to his care. Our reporter Austin James has the details...."

The picture then cut to a view of pleasant parkland, with oak and cedar trees dotted around. As the camera slowly panned round, it showed sheep grazing in the meadows, with further trees and woodland in the distance. Gradually, as the reporter Austin James, a familiar figure on the news bulletins on this channel came into view, standing beside the high gates in the wall which Alex had seen in the earlier snippet, he started speaking....

"These lovely surroundings would at first glance seem an ideal place for a children's home. But at Grant Hall, behind me here, things were very different. Augustus Hammond, an ex-army career officer, used his army gratuity and some money left to him by his father to buy Grant Hall when he retired from the army eight years ago. He ran the Hall as a children's home for difficult-to-control boys aged between ten and sixteen who, and here I quote from the Hall's website, have exhibited behavioural difficulties."

As the reporter was speaking, the screen switched to a picture of Hammond. Alex instantly recognise him as the man dressed all in black, whom he'd met at the lock the day Danny had stowed away on his boat all that time ago.

Alex remembered that he hadn't much like Hammond then. His first impressions on meeting someone quite often proved, with hindsight, to have been correct. The screen switched to various pictures which Alex remembered having seen before on the Hall's website. As Alex had noted at the time, the pictures showed the interior of the building, but in none of them were there any children. The reporter continued....

"Grant Hall provided accommodation for seventy-two boys, and as soon as it was opened, it quickly became popular with several local authorities, as they were able to send disruptive boys there, and it was very often full with a waiting list. But it seemed that inside Grant Hall, Hammond presided over a reign of terror in which discipline was achieved by the continuous application of physical abuse towards the boys in his

charge. Apparently constant canings and applications of the lash were the order of the day."

"The abuse came to light when a thirteen-year-old boy walked into a police station in the North of England accompanied by his mother, and made allegations of abuse against Hammond and most of the other staff who worked at Grant Hall. It appears that the boy, who cannot be named for legal reasons, was previously in care in a childrens' home at nearby Harding Court before it was destroyed by fire, but was sent to Grant Hall about two-and-a-half years ago. After about six months there he absconded, but was apprehended after a couple of days. However, the boy absconded again a few weeks later, and despite a widespread search, he was not found, and eventually the search was abandoned."

"It appears that the boy had been living with his mother for about three months before he made the allegations to the local police. How he managed to travel from Grant Hall, which is located in the south of the country, to his mother's home in the North of England, and his whereabouts during the year that elapsed between his absconding from Grant Hall and starting to live with his mother, are something of a mystery, as despite repeated questioning, both the boy and his mother have consistently refused to give any details. The boy certainly did not live with his father, whom it appears was separated from the boy's mother, as the father was indeed questioned by police investigating the boy's story."

"It does seems that someone must have taken the boy in and provided him with food and shelter, as the boy enrolled at the local school immediately upon starting to live with his mother and grandmother, and the school records show that he was fit and healthy, and the staff at the school had no concerns nor worries about the state of the boy's health."

Alex leaned forward a trifle and listened intently as the reporter continued......

"The case against Hammond revolved around a written account of the conditions inside Grant Hall, with full details of the abuse being suffered by the boys there. It appears that this account, in the boy's own handwriting, had been written just a day or two after the boy had absconded for the first time. It was accompanied by photographs of the boy's injuries, which had been taken at the same time."

"Instead of handing the case over to the local police in whose area Grant Hall falls, the North of England police placed the case with the new PNCU, the Police National Children's Unit. This, you may remember, was set up last autumn to enable a nationwide response to complaints of child abuse, relieving local police forces of that role. The PNCU's first task was to ensure that all of the sixty-nine boys currently living at Grant Hall at the time of the allegations were rehomed in alternative accommodation within a few days, and then Grant Hall was closed pending further investigation."

"The PNCU spent some time questioning these children, but they all refused to confirm the allegations. It is believed that Hammond had threatened them with yet further abuse should they be returned to the Hall at a later date. So the case against Hammond rested solely on the boy's evidence."

"The trial lasted a total of four days, of which the boy spent two whole days in the witness box. Apparently he had refused the offer of being able to give evidence via video link, saying that he wanted Hammond to see that he was no longer afraid of him. When the photographs of the boy's injuries were passed around the court, some of the jurors were visibly shocked by what they saw."

"Despite repeated and sometimes aggressive questioning by Hammond's counsel, the boy's spoken evidence in court was always fully consistent with what had been recorded in the written account of his experiences, which was also passed around the court. He described how the Hall seemed to be like a prison, with bars on the dormitory windows, which were on the first floor, and with the main gate from the Hall out into the surrounding park always being kept securely locked, except for access. He also stated that he was singled out by Hammond for special punishment, as he refused to be cowed by Hammond, fixing him with a silent stare instead of crying, as many of the other boys did. Throughout his evidence, the boy appeared to be confident and self-assured."

"When Hammond took the witness box and was asked to explain the boy's injuries shown in the photographs, he claimed that the boy never tied up his shoelaces, and thus often tripped and fell, often falling all the way down the large marble staircase in the grand entrance lobby at Grant Hall. He said that the bars on the windows were for the boys' own protection, to avoid any possibility of them climbing out of the windows, missing their footing, and falling onto the concrete below. And as for the main gates always being kept locked, he claimed that that too was for the boys' protection, to keep out any perverts or paedophiles who might seek to prey on the young boys living at the Hall. He painted the boy as persistently unruly and aggressive, with a disrespectful attitude towards any form of authority, and claimed that the allegations against him were completely false, motivated by the boy's resentment at having to knuckle down to the *strict routine in force at the Hall."*

On hearing that, Alex shook his head in amazement. He knew the real Danny, and knew that the words that Hammond had used to describe the boy in court were a travesty of the truth. But the reporter was speaking again....

"Hammond consistently denied using any form of physical abuse against any of the boys in his charge. His barrister presented a very skilful defence, suggesting that all of the boys placed at Grant Hall had a previous history of being unruly and difficult to control, and that a small amount of firm discipline was necessary for the smooth running of the home, but that neither Hammond nor any of the staff there had ever used violence against any of the boys. He used very persuasive arguments to suggest that the jury should not believe the words of a young boy motivated by spite, against the testimony of an ex-soldier who had served his country with honour and distinction. With the only evidence against Hammond being the boys' written account and evidence from the witness box, as the trial drew to a close it did appear that the case against Hammond would be not proven, and that he would be acquitted. However, in a dramatic turn of events, the prosecuting counsel suddenly asked for an adjournment, claiming that new evidence had come to light."

"When the trial resumed after a break of about ten days, the prosecution produced a number of new witnesses, mainly young men in their late teens or early twenties. They had all at one time or another been in care and resident at Grant Hall whilst they were in their early teenage years, but upon reaching the age of sixteen, had been allowed to leave the Hall and make their lives elsewhere. They had been prompted to come forward after reading accounts of the trial in the local newspaper. All of these new witnesses confirmed and corroborated the boy's statements and written account of life at Grant Hall, and in the face of what was now overwhelming evidence, the jury took only six hours to reach a unanimous verdict of guilty as charged."

"In mitigation, Hammond's counsel stated that he had been an exemplary soldier in the Army, serving his country with distinction in a number of theatres. His last position with the Army had been in charge of an Army corrective centre, and that perhaps he had let his enthusiasm for training and rehabilitating misbehaving soldiers spill over into his civilian life after he had left the Army. However, the judge did not assign a lot of weight to this argument, and sentenced Hammond to six years in jail. A

number of other defendants, all of whom worked or had worked at Grant Hall, were also found guilty and received lesser sentences. A further four defendants were found not guilty and acquitted."

"With me now is Robert Jefferies, who is the senior reporter with the local newspaper."

At this point, the camera swung round to reveal another man standing beside the reporter. Alex instantly recalled the name. When Danny had first stowed away on *Jennifer Jo*, Alex had searched the internet for information about Grant Hall, and found an article on the newspaper's website with Robert Jefferies' name as the by-line under the headline. But the reporter was speaking again.......

"Mr. Jefferies, your newspaper gave a lot of coverage to Hammond's trial. It could be said that without your coverage, the fresh witnesses would not have come forward, and Hammond might well have been acquitted."

"That's probably right," said Jefferies. "I've had my worries about what might have been happening at Grant Hall for some time. There's been no less three enquiries in the last six years or so, but all of them came to nothing. None of them could find any evidence of any mistreatment of the kids there. But I just knew that something wasn't right. The local authority had been making regular inspections every six months or so, and I was actually invited by Augustus Hammond to accompany the inspectors on one of their visits. That was so that he could rebut an article I'd published about Grant Hall a few weeks before which said that there might have been something wrong with the way they were looking after the kids."

"That visit convinced me even more that things weren't right there, even though the inspectors didn't suspect anything. It was the body language of the boys, really, which confirmed my suspicions. For example, we were taken into the school room, and there were all these boys sitting there in rows on these benches beside these long tables, really quiet, not saying a word. Normally, in any other school you go into, it's quite different. I go into some of the local schools occasionally, to give the kids a talk about a career in journalism or printing, and as soon as the teacher turns to speak to me, the kids are laughing and grinning and chatting quietly amongst themselves, really happy."

"But these kids, they were different, sitting there all quiet, with sullen expressions on their faces, all of them. When any of them were asked a question, they all had a quick glance at Hammond before they said anything, nothing more than just a brief eye contact really. But unless you were really looking for it, you could easily have missed it. And the answer, when it came, was usually either a 'yes' or a 'no', nothing more. It was really difficult to get them to say anything else. It would have been easier to squeeze blood out of a stone than get them to say much more at all. There was no doubt in my mind, no doubt at all, that they were all scared of Hammond, really scared. I don't think the food could have been that good, either, as lots of the kids seemed to be a bit on the skinny side. The lunch he gave for the inspectors was pretty good, but we never saw what the kids had to eat."

"The only good impression I came away with from that visit, was that all the kids were clean and well-presented in clean clothes, with neat haircuts, although they'd probably been especially spruced up for the inspection. Apparently the kids had to have a shower every couple of days, that's part of the routine there, and they all have a locker beside their beds in the dormitories for what few personal possessions they're allowed. But I think I'd have hated to have had to live there when I was a kid."

The camera then switched back to the reporter, Austin James, who took up the commentary...

"Thank you, Mr. Jefferies," he continued. "So tonight, Hammond starts his sentence of six years in jail, and hopefully the boys who were here at Grant Hall are more comfortable in their new accommodation elsewhere than they ever were here. Before bringing the trial to a close, the judge congratulated the boy on the way he gave his evidence, and on his courage in coming forward in the first place. He said that without his determination to bring the situation at Grant Hall to the attention of the police, the abuse which had been taking place there might well still be continuing. It is thought that the Hall will now be sold. And now, back to the studio, where I think Anne will have the weather forecast for you."

Alex picked up the remote and switched off the television, and then sat back, thinking about what he'd just heard. So Danny had done it. Alex's heart went out to the lad. He felt a huge outpouring of respect and admiration for him. Danny's strong sense of right and wrong had impelled him to come forward, as Alex had obliquely suggested he should when he'd handed Danny that envelope the day he'd left *Jennifer Jo*, saying that it was unfinished business which only he could bring to an end. It was that envelope which held his account of his time at Grant Hall, together with the pictures of his injuries. It seemed that Danny had performed well in court, facing hostile questioning with equanimity. And it was very brave of him to choose to give evidence in open court, facing Hammond across the courtroom, rather than from a separate room via a video link.

Alex fervently hoped that Danny was as well pleased with the end result as he himself was. At last, the unfinished business was indeed finished and could now be put to rest, and Danny could get on with his life, hopefully leaving his memories of Grant Hall behind him.

But as the evening wore on, there was a niggling thought in the back of Alex's mind, something about the news of Hammond's trial and guilty verdict. It was a thought which he just couldn't place, a thought which just wouldn't go away. There was something not quite right about what he'd heard on the television news. And it worried Alex a good deal that he was unable to determine exactly what it was. He just couldn't place it.

Alex turned in to bed at his usual time, but unusually, he didn't fall asleep within a few minutes, as he usually did. He kept thinking about the news about Hammond and Grant Hall. And then, suddenly, after about an hour spent tossing and turning in his berth, unable to settle down, it came to him.

The trial, and Hammond's subsequent conviction, had all been about the physical abuse dished out to the boys living at Grant Hall. The canings, the lash, the general atmosphere of fear which seemed to have pervaded every aspect of life there. But of the large cars which Danny had told him about, the cars which arrived late at night, and of the boys being called down from the dormitories for sexual abuse by whomsoever was in these cars, of this there had been no mention, no mention at all.

Alex's euphoria at the news of Grant Hall being closed, and of Hammonds subsequent conviction, swiftly evaporated as he took in the import of what he'd just realised. A short while earlier, he'd imagined that what he'd described to Danny as unfinished business, was at last finished. But now he realised that the unfinished business still remained unfinished. How and why it remained unfinished, Alex could only wonder and conjecture. And Alex realised, with a considerable degree of sadness, that there was nothing that he could possibly do about it. But he vowed to himself that, if the opportunity ever arose, he would do all he could to bring that whole unsavoury business to a satisfactory conclusion, and ensure that those responsible were held to account for what they had done. And with that thought to satisfy himself, Alex at last dropped off to a fitful sleep.

PART TWO

CHAPTER 15

Alex finished clearing away his breakfast things, and peered out of the window. The drizzle which had been drifting down from the dull grey clouds ever since he got up had just about stopped, and the sky was beginning to clear, with a few light blue patches starting to show through between the breaks in the cloud. It was forecast to be a fine summer's day after a dull start, and Alex decided to wait a little while and check his emails before moving off. He took his laptop out of the locker beneath the dinette seat, plugged it in, and waited patiently for the machine to boot up. As it did so, Alex regarded once again the picture he used as his desktop background, Danny's drawing of the two of them by the lock, the drawing he'd found under the boy's mattress the day after he'd left *Jennifer Jo,* now a full seven years ago.

In those intervening seven years, Alex had kept himself busy. He'd finished his book about the history of the school where he used to teach and had been a House Master, with his wife as Matron. He'd written a second book, about some of the amusing incidents which had happened during his time at the school. The mischief that some of the boys got up to had never ceased to amuse him. Alex had always allowed himself to be mildly tolerant of such antics, provided that they weren't maliciously directed against any of the other boys. After all, he'd often thought, boys will be boys, and they needed to be able to let off a little bit of steam occasionally, confined as they were into a relatively strict school routine. And a third book, about some of the interesting people he'd met during his travels along the cut, and the amusing happenings he'd come across whilst cruising the 2000 miles of the inland canal network, had been published a few months ago.

All three of his books were selling, albeit in small but steady numbers. And now he'd started working on his fourth book, a collection of fictional short stories. He'd found that he enjoyed writing, and it helped to pass the time, especially during the long dark winter evenings. Since his first book had been published, he'd received numerous congratulations on his easygoing writing style. He thanked the school he'd attended as a child for that, as whilst there he'd been required to study Latin. Although he hadn't appreciated it at the time, he'd realised since that it had given him a good command of the English language, a skill which was standing him in good stead now that he'd become a writer. He'd made sure, too, whilst he'd been teaching Danny, that Latin was part of the boy's studies. And over the 12 months that Danny had been with him, Alex had noticed how much Danny's use of English as a language had improved.

With his laptop now up and running, Alex checked his emails. There was only one, from his publisher, detailing his royalty payments for the previous quarter. Alex had assigned the royalties from all of his books to his school's Foundation, an organisation established a few years ago to bridge the gap between the school and its old boys' network, and to foster closer ties between the two. The Foundation also undertook fundraising, with a special emphasis on raising money from the previous pupils of the school to help finance developments and improvements to the school which could not be afforded from its normal income.

However, Alex had insisted that all of his royalties went to the Foundation's Bursaries fund, money especially set aside to assist with the school fees for boys who would benefit from the education the school provided but whose parents, for whatever reason, couldn't afford the full fees. He'd been prompted to do this by his time with Danny, as he'd realised that Danny would have benefited greatly from the education which the school could have offered him. Alex wanted other boys to have the same opportunity, regardless of their background and the ability of their parents to pay the school fees. Previously, the school had been full with the boys whose parents were in the diplomatic service on overseas postings, but recently the school's traditional catchment had declined somewhat, and the school had now broadened its intake to include any boy who was able to pass the school's stiff entrance exam.

Alex looked out of the window once again, and saw that the earlier clouds had cleared away completely. It was time to get moving. *Jennifer Jo* was moored in a pleasant spot, out in the countryside, and Alex wondered to himself why he'd not cruised the canals of the North more often. It was the first time he'd returned to this canal, the same canal he'd been on when Danny had left *Jennifer Jo* seven years previously. A couple of weeks before, he'd worked the boat through the lock beside the pub where Danny had found his mother all those years ago. After working the lock, he'd moored up and walked around the pub garden, and inside the pub as well, in the forlorn hope that by some terrific coincidence Danny might be around, but of course, unsurprisingly, he was not there.

Alex shut down his computer and tucked it away into the locker, then went up onto the deck and made ready to cast off and be on his way. But before he could do so, the lady on the boat moored up behind him walked forward and engaged him in conversation. Like Alex, she was a live-aboard, boating on her own, after her husband had died the year before, and Alex suspected that she was a little lonely. That was the greatest thing about boating on the canals – you were part of a community and with very few exceptions, everyone was helpful and friendly to each other. It was a good half-hour before he was able to finally untie his ropes and be on his way.

As the canal approached the outskirts of the nearby town, whose lights he'd seen in the distance the evening before, Alex noticed how much the canal environment had changed since his previous visit along here seven years ago. Then, the canal had appeared to have been badly neglected, with a bumpy, overgrown grassy track for a towpath, with trees and branches overhanging the canal, and various items of rubbish strewn around. In the water there had been an assortment of shopping trolleys, bicycles, and even a discarded sofa lying on the offside bank, with an assortment of plastic bags floating around or blowing in the wind.

But now, it seemed that the local council had at last recognised that, with a bit of care and attention, the canal could become an asset for the local community, a green lung through the town. All the rubbish had gone, the canal had been dredged and the shopping trolleys and bicycles removed. The trees had been cut back, and the towpath had been levelled and resurfaced, with the grass beside it neatly mown. It was now a really pleasant place to be. And the local townspeople appeared to have taken the canal to their heart. Various groups of people were walking the towpath, and looking at the brightly-painted boats as they passed slowly by. There were families with young children running around, and older couples walking along more slowly as they took the air, talking quietly to each other, and teenagers riding their bicycles too, ringing their bells as they carefully avoided the other towpath users.

As Alex rounded a tight bend in the canal, he had to pull the tiller hard over to avoid another boat which came round the blind corner rather too fast. Unsurprisingly, it was a hire boat, probably fresh out from its base earlier that morning, or perhaps the previous afternoon. Until they became used to the slow pace of life on the cut, new hirers often went a little too fast.

It was a source of annoyance to seasoned boaters, because a boat travelling too fast created a lot of wash in the shallow waters of the canal, and this caused moored boats to be pulled away from the bank, and then thrown back again, often hitting against the steel piling with a fair degree of force. Sometimes this was sufficiently severe to dislodge and break valuable items inside the boat. Nonetheless, Alex gave the steerer a friendly wave, as was his custom, and the young woman on the back of the other boat responded in like manner. However, she suddenly started shouting something at Alex, but Alex was unable to hear what was being said over the noise of the two boats' engines purring loudly as they powered the boats along.

Alex shrugged his shoulders and spread out his hands, to indicate that he couldn't make out what was being said. Acknowledging this gesture with another wave, the girl just pointed behind Alex, and smiled sweetly. Alex turned round, and saw a young man running along the towpath, pushing a buggy with a young child inside, waving to Alex and shouting something unintelligible as he did so. Alex couldn't hear what the man was saying, so he once again shrugged his shoulders and spread his hand out. The man nodded and stopped shouting, instead pointing further up the canal. Alex waved in response, as he turned and looked ahead, but there was another bend coming up, and he couldn't see very far along the canal at that point. Alex had no idea what the man was trying to say to him, so he decided to continue on his way regardless.

On rounding the next bend, Alex saw that there was a canalside pub just a little further along, on the towpath side of the canal. Perhaps the man who'd been shouting at him wanted him to stop there, but for what reason Alex had no idea. However, it was nearly lunchtime, so Alex motored past the pub for about a hundred yards, and then brought *Jennifer Jo* gently into the bank to moor up, so that he could get himself something to eat. A ham sandwich and a cup of tea seemed a nice idea, Alex thought to himself.

He was kneeling down on the grass, securing his mooring rope to the steel piling which lined this section of the canal, when a shadow fell across the grass beside him. Looking up, he saw a man standing above him, the man who'd been shouting at him a minute or so earlier. The man's face was in the shade from the bright sunlight, but it seemed vaguely familiar, although Alex couldn't place him. It wasn't until the man spoke that Alex recognised the voice.

"Hello, Mister," the man said. "Do you remember me?"

Alex stood up and looked at the man, immediately recognising who it was. If Alex had needed any hints as to whom It might be, the trademark grin on the man's face gave it away. It was Danny. A very different Danny, of course, to the young boy who'd left *Jennifer Jo* seven years earlier, but an adult Danny, with broad shoulders, and now maybe even a touch taller than Alex was himself. Alex had always remembered Danny as the young thirteen-year-old whom he'd last seen striding confidently across the grass towards his mother, but in the intervening years, it seemed that Danny had matured into a fine, handsome young adult. In many ways he'd changed as he'd matured, but there was no doubt that this was the same Danny as he'd always known.

"I never thought I'd see you again, Danny," Alex exclaimed, as they embraced tightly. "I'm so glad we've come across each other again. What a lovely coincidence. I'm so very pleased that we've met again. I never ever thought we would. Ever since you left *Jennifer Jo* to live with your mother, I've been kicking myself that I never thought, before you left, to ask how to keep in touch with you."

"Me too," said Danny, smiling as he did so. "It was a couple of days afterwards that I realised that I probably wouldn't ever be able to see you again. I was a bit upset about that. But I got over it in the end. And we won't make that mistake again, will we?"

Alex shook his head. "No, we certainly won't," he replied. "What's your address? And phone number? And are you on email?"

"I'll tell you before we go," said Danny, still grinning broadly. "But we're about to have some lunch at the pub. Why don't you come and join us?"

"Are you sure, Danny?" Alex asked. "I don't want to intrude on your lunch. I presume you're with someone else?"

"No, come on, it'll be alright," Danny said, nodding as he did so. "You'll be welcome, very welcome. Come over and I'll introduce you to the family."

"Alright then," agreed Alex. "Just hang on a moment while I lock up, and I'll be along." Danny waited patiently beside the boat as Alex locked the doors, and then they walked together back down the towpath to the pub. Walking up a couple of steps into the pub garden, Danny led the way to a couple of picnic tables, where a group of people were sitting down studying the menu.

Danny introduced Alex to his family. "Hey Mister, here's my mum and my gran, you've met them before, haven't you?" he asked. "And sitting opposite them here, they're Sophie's mum and dad. It's his birthday today," he added, turning to Alex with another grin. "But don't ask how old!" Then Danny turned to the other table, where sat a young woman about Danny's age. "And here's my wife Sophie," he added proudly. Finally, as he bent over the buggy and lifted the child out, he added, more proudly than ever, "and this is our little baby girl."

That's wonderful, Danny," Alex exclaimed. "You're married, and you're a father as well! Many congratulations to you both."

"Thanks, Mister," Danny nodded, as he sat down with Sophie,

placing his daughter on the table in front of him. "Here, sit down with us. Isn't she lovely?" he added, as he started cuddling and playing with the baby.

"Yes, she certainly is," Alex replied. "How old is she?"

"She's about nine months now," Sophie replied. "Getting bigger every day now, too."

"Yes they do, don't they?" Alex agreed with a smile. Then, turning to Danny, he asked, "so, Danny, what are you doing with yourself now, then?"

Well, I did really well at school," he said. "And now I'm about halfway through an apprenticeship, with Smart Brothers. They're a big building firm, they employ around two hundred people. They do all the large building contracts round here. I'm doing carpentry and joinery. I'm in the joinery workshop at the moment. You know, making doors and window frames and kitchen cabinets, that sort of thing. I really like it. And I've got a bit of a sideline as well."

What's that, then, Danny?" enquired Alex, a little curious now.

"I do drawings for people, coloured drawings," Danny replied. "You know, portraits. Family groups. Children, pets, that sort of thing."

"How did you get into that, Danny?" asked Alex. He remembered that Danny had shown a real talent for that sort of thing whilst he was living on *Jennifer Jo* with Alex.

"Well, it was like this," Danny continued. "I did one for Sophie's parents last Christmas, you know. It was of me and her and the baby. It was their Christmas present from us all. And after Christmas they took it into the art shop in town to get it framed. But then Sophie's mum wasn't well for a couple of weeks, and she couldn't collect it. So the shop, they put it on display in their window until she came in for it. And the next thing they knew, they had loads of people coming into the shop asking about who'd done it, and where they could get one done like it."

"So, me and the guy who owns the shop, we came to an agreement. They put the people in touch with me, and we arrange for them to come into the shop and sit for me while I make some rough sketches, and usually I take a few photos as well. Then I go home and do the drawing and colour it, during the week, and when it's finished I take it back. The customer gets charged £100, and the shop give me £85 of that, and they keep the rest."

"It doesn't seem much for the shop to have," suggested Alex, "considering the overheads they must have to meet to run the shop."

"Ah, Mister, but it doesn't stop there, does it?" Danny was grinning broadly. "Most people, you see, well, when they come and collect the picture, they're really pleased with it, and they want to have it framed, don't they? So, the guy who runs the shop, he makes a frame for them, and he charges them another £50 for that. That's where he makes his money, really. He's ever so quick, he can do the mount and everything, cut the wood and the glass, and make a really good frame, all in about ten minutes. He does a lot of framing work. He can knock out four or five frames every hour, once he gets going. We've got a good thing going there, between us. I usually do about one picture a week. I could do more, but they take quite a lot of time to do properly, and I want to make sure I do them properly, and of course I need to have some time to myself, with Sophie and the baby as well. So I usually stick to doing about one a week."

"And the money I get for doing the pictures, well, we're putting that aside, so that we can use it for the deposit on a house, once we've got enough. We've got a nice house to live in at the moment, and it's not too far from where mum and gran live, so I can pop round every week and see that they're both alright. The neighbours are great, too, but we'd like to have our own place eventually."

Alex nodded, as, suddenly, Danny bent down to the baby sitting on the table in front of him, and wrinkled up his nose. "I think, young lady, you've filled your nappy," he said, grinning at Alex. "Let's go and get you cleaned up, shall we?" And he stood up, picking up the baby as he did so, grabbed the baby bag off the back of the buggy, and disappeared off into the pub to see to his daughter.

"Danny's very proud of his daughter, isn't he?" commented Alex.

Sophie smiled again. "Yes," she agreed. "I stopped work when she was born, to look after her, but as soon as Danny comes home from work, he does everything for her. He won't let me do a thing. He's great, he really is."

"Danny seems to like his work, too," Alex said.

"Yes," replied Sophie. "He certainly does. You know, he wouldn't tell you this, but there were almost two hundred kids applied that year for just four apprenticeships at Smarts. He was really lucky to get one. And he's doing really well there. He's been apprentice of the year twice."

"That's good," said Alex. "And, he's always been able to draw well, really well, too."

"Yes," said Sophie. "You've seen some of his pictures, then?"

"Yes, he did a couple for me a few years ago," Alex replied. "They're really really good. I'm very proud of them."

Sophie nodded in agreement, then paused for a moment. "So,

Alex," she asked, " how do you know Danny, then?"

Alex thought for a moment before replying. He didn't want to say too much. He didn't know how much Sophie knew about Danny's past, so he was deliberately a little bit evasive with his answer. "Oh, our paths crossed for a while, some time ago," he said eventually. Changing the subject slightly, he added, "but what about you? How did you come to meet Danny?"

"Well, we were at school together," she said. "Danny and I, we were in the same class. It was a bit unusual, because Danny started at the school in mid-term, not like most people who start at the beginning of a term. Apparently he used to live down south somewhere, but he moved up here to live with his mother. I think she'd moved up here about a year before that, so his gran could look after his mum while she recuperated. She'd been seriously ill for some time, you see, but she's much better now."

"Anyway, I was being bullied at school. Some of the other girls in our class, they'd follow me home after school, calling me names and throwing stones at me. But as soon as Danny heard about it, he insisted on walking me home every afternoon after school, even though I lived on the other side of town from where he did. When I got home, he had to walk all the way back across town to get to his house. But he said he didn't mind, he wasn't going to allow me to be upset by those others like that."

"After a few weeks, we were going home one afternoon when I tripped and stumbled, and I would have fallen over and hurt myself, but Danny grabbed my hand and stopped me. When I got my balance back, I didn't let go of his hand, and nor did he let go of mine, and after that we always walked home holding hands together."

"And as time went on," she continued, "I began to realise what a wonderful person Danny was. Basically, we fell in love with each other. I felt really lucky, because there were loads of other girls after him, they all wanted to have him as their boyfriend, but he wanted me. I felt really lucky, because he felt the same way about me as I did about him."

Sophie leant forward, speaking more quietly now. "I shouldn't tell you this, I suppose, but as soon as I was sixteen, I wanted him to ...to ...to ..." here Sophie paused for a moment , searching to get the right words. "...I wanted him to lay with me, but he wouldn't. He said that it wasn't right, not until we were married."

Alex nodded. This was the Danny he knew, always with a firm dividing line between right and wrong. But Sophie was speaking again. "We got married as soon as we could, when we were both eighteen, and could afford to have a place of our own. Danny got a large bonus when he won the apprentice of the year, and his pay went up a lot as well, so we could afford to rent a house after that. And it went up again the following year, when he was the best apprentice again. And then a year after we got married, the baby was born. Danny was so proud."

"Yes, I forgot to ask you," Alex interjected. "I never asked you what the baby's name is."

"Well, that's really strange." Sophie reflected for a moment. "Ever since we started going out together, Danny was always happy to let me decide on everything. You know, where to go, what to buy, where to live, what colours to paint the walls, everything. Danny's always been happy to let me choose whatever I want, all the time. But when we found out that I was expecting, he insisted that he'd choose the baby's name. Whether it was going to be a boy or a girl, and we didn't know in advance, we chose not to be told, he said that he'd choose the name. He was quite definite about that. He said he'd already decided what the name would be. Boy or girl, he'd got a name for either. Of course, I didn't mind. He always lets me choose everything usually, so I was happy to let him name the baby whatever he wanted."

"So what is your daughter's name, then?" asked Alex once again.

"It's Jenny," Sophie replied. "But that's what we call her for short. Her real name is Jennifer. Actually, Jennifer Jo. I asked Danny why he'd chosen those names, and all he said was that it was about something really good which happened to him a few years ago, before he came up here to live with his mother. It's funny, you know, but he never says anything about his life before he came here. Whenever I ask him, and I've asked him loads of times, he just says he doesn't want to talk about it. I think something really bad happened to him, something really unpleasant, but he just won't say. Do you know what it was?"

Alex's heart skipped a beat as he listened to what Sophie was saying. Danny had named his baby daughter the same as the name of the narrowboat where he'd spent a year with Alex after getting away from Grant Hall. Alex had often wondered how Danny had felt about being on *Jennifer Jo* with him, cruising around the canal network, never staying in the same place for more than a day or two, with no permanent place to put down roots and call home. When it was first built, Alex had named his boat after his wife, and now the name would continue with Danny's daughter for many years to come. Alex felt very proud that Danny had indicated in such a positive way how much he'd appreciated what Alex had been able to do for him.

Alex looked across the table at Sophie. "I'm sure he'll tell you one day," he said, neatly avoiding the question, as Danny reappeared with baby Jennifer on his arm.

"Here we are," Danny exclaimed, "all clean and nice now. Until the next time, that is." And he grinned once again, laughing as he did so.

Alex enjoyed a pleasant lunch at the pub, chatting to Danny and Sophie. Danny was keen to tell Alex everything about what had happened to him since leaving *Jenifer Jo*, and Alex listened with interest. The boy, or rather young man as he now was, had done well for himself, and Alex was very pleased for him. But eventually Danny stood up. "I'll go and pay the bill now," he said.

"Here, Danny, let me pay for mine," Alex offered.

"No Mister, this is my treat," responded Danny. "It's Sophie's dad's birthday, and I'm paying. And as far as you're concerned, I reckon it's my turn now, don't you?"

Alex nodded as he agreed to let Danny pay for his lunch. "Alright," he said. "If you insist. Thank you very much."

"I do insist," Danny responded. "That's settled then." And he went off to pay the bill.

As they all walked down the steps back onto the towpath, Alex asked Danny something. "Danny, please can you come back to the boat with me for a moment? I need to take your contact details. I don't want to lose touch with you again."

"Alright, Mister," Danny replied, turning to Sophie as he did so. "Here, Sophie, can you take the buggy please. I'll catch you up in a minute," and he then turned and walked back to *Jennifer Jo* with Alex.

Danny climbed down the rear stairway and walked past the berth he used to occupy in the back cabin, and then on through the boat to the saloon, where he sat down in what used to be his usual place at the dinette. "It's much smaller than I remember, Mister," he exclaimed.

"Perhaps, Danny," Alex laughed, "but remember, you've grown quite a bit since you were last here. You're a great deal bigger yourself now."

"Yes, I suppose so," was the rejoinder, as Alex sat down at the dinette opposite Danny, who took the pen and paper which Alex offered him, and wrote out his address and phone numbers and email details in his familiar neat handwriting. In return, Alex wrote down his phone number and passed it over to Danny.

"I'm afraid there's no postal address, Danny," he apologised. "Water gypsies like me don't have such things. But, before you go, there's a couple of things I'd like to talk to you about."

"What are they, then, Mister?" Danny asked.

"Well, Danny," Alex replied. "Firstly, very many congratulations on getting married, and becoming a father. I'm really very pleased for you."

"Thanks, Mister," said Danny, smiling. "Sophie's wonderful, isn't she? And Jenny, too? I couldn't want for anything more. We're really happy together. It's great, it really is."

"You did very well to get an apprenticeship, too," Alex continued, "they don't give them out very much these days."

"No, I know, that's right," Danny replied. "I did really well at school after I left *Jay-Jay*, and I managed to get some really good exam results. I think it was the lessons which you gave me when I was living here on *Jay-Jay* that really helped me along."

Alex nodded. "I tried my best," he said. "Next, very very well done for going to the police and telling them about what happened to you at Grant Hall. It was the right thing to do, and I'm glad that you had the courage to do it. I'm really proud of you."

"Well," Danny replied. "I'd been home a few weeks, before I showed mum that envelope you gave me when I left *Jennifer Jo,* and asked her what I should do. She said that it was up to me, to make up my own mind. I wasn't sure at first, but after a while I kept thinking about the kids who were still there, at Grant Hall, getting caned every day, and I realised that I just had to do it. Because I knew that as long as Hammond was there, then it would keep going on until someone stopped it. And those photos you took, and the report that you made me write, I was sure that would be enough evidence to convict Hammond."

"And it was very brave of you to give your evidence in open court, as I remember it, rather than via a video link," Alex added. "It can't have been easy. That must have taken some doing, standing there with everyone looking at you, especially Hammond."

Danny shook his head. "No," he said. "The police I went to, the police station near where I lived, they handed the case over to the PNCU, that's the Police National Children's Unit, straight away. And they assigned me a CLO, that's a Child Liaison Officer, to keep in touch with me, right from the start, from when I first went to the police station with my mum. And when they were setting up the trial, he said to use the video link. But I said no, I wouldn't. I wanted to see Hammond, and to see how he reacted when I told everyone about what had been going on at Grant Hall and how they treated all the kids there. I just stood there and stared at him the whole time, just like I used to when I was at Grant Hall. You could tell that it un-nerved him, because whenever we made eye contact, he just looked away, very quickly."

"Me, before I went into the witness box, I asked Martin, he was my CLO, what I should say when they asked me questions and the like, and he said that he couldn't tell me what to say. He said to just tell the truth about everything that had happened, and to let the facts speak for themselves. So that's what I did."

"Hammond nearly got off, though. If it wasn't for those other people coming forward, then he might have got away with it. A couple of them, I knew them, they were at Grant Hall the same time as me. One of them was Johnnie Raeburn, I managed to have a chat with him after the trial had ended. He said he'd got four strokes of the cane, that day I got away from the kitchen garden, because he hadn't told the wardens that I'd gone over the wall until I was being missed and they were all asking where I was, although actually he didn't know that I was still hiding in the pile of boxes at the time. But Johnnie Raeburn, he said it was worth every one of them, and all the others as well, to see Hammond being sent down."

"I suppose Hammond's out now, though, he only got six years. And he'd probably have been let out early anyway, like most prisoners are now. But Mr Wilkins, I'm glad he was found not guilty. He was alright, he was. It was him who I got away from the first time, you know, when he took me to the dentist. He must have got into a lot of trouble from Hammond about that."

Alex nodded again. "Danny," he asked, "there was something about the trial which I didn't quite understand. Of course, I only know what I saw on the television news that night, but it seems that the trial was only concerned with the physical abuse and violence which you all had to endure. You told me once about the people in big posh cars, men who arrived late at night, and some of the boys being called down to be with them, to be interfered with and to be subjected to sexual abuse. Yet there was no mention of that at the trial, nothing at all. Didn't you tell the police and your CLO about all that?"

"Oh, yes, Mister, of course I did," Danny replied. "It was in that account about Grant Hall which you got me to write, you know, the day after I first hid up on *JayJay*. And Martin, every time he met with me and told me how things were going, well I kept asking him about the men with the cars and that, and he said that there wasn't any progress on that, none at all."

"You see, he said that while the PNCU were in charge of the investigation, they had to rely on the local police force to do a lot of the spadework on the ground, you know, interviewing people and that sort of thing. And every time he asked them about the cars and those strange men who came late at night, they just said that they were concentrating on the physical abuse which Hammond had been dishing out."

"Apparently, they kept saying it was a low priority as there was no evidence, because when they interviewed Hammond about it, he denied knowing anything about it. He said that nothing like that ever happened, and it was just me making all up and trying to make things worse for him. Once or twice, Martin said in the end that he suspected the local police were being un-cooperative about that, and more than a little obstructive at times and not wanting to follow it up, he didn't know why."

"But Danny," Alex interjected, "don't you remember that I said that you should keep a record of who came, to take down the numbers of the cars and the dates they came, and who got called out to go downstairs to be with them? You did that, didn't you? Didn't you tell the police that you'd done that, and hidden the information away somewhere?"

"Actually, Mister, no, I didn't." Danny looked up at Alex, smiling broadly. "And I'm really glad I didn't. You see, we did do that, like you suggested. But I forgot about it to start with, because all the questioning and such which they kept asking me, well it was all about Hammond and getting the lash and being caned, and the like. And when Martin said that he felt that the local police were being obstructive, well I began to smell a rat."

"You see, those men, they could have been high up police officers, couldn't they? Or being shielded by their friends in the police. I figured out that if I told them about what we'd done, and where we'd hidden the tobacco tin which we put the information in under the floorboards, then perhaps they'd go and find it and it would miraculously disappear, and they'd come back and say they'd looked and didn't find anything. I think they might have wanted to do a cover-up."

"So, Danny, do you reckon that the tobacco tin is still there?" Alex asked. "Hidden away still?"

Danny nodded. "Yes, Mister. I'm sure of it. I don't think anyone would be able to find it, unless they knew where to look, unless they ripped up all the floorboards in our dorm."

Alex paused for a moment. "Danny," he said eventually, "when I heard that Hammond and some of the other wardens had been found guilty and been sent to prison, I thought that what I once told you was unfinished business, had been brought to an end. But it seems that it hasn't. It's still unfinished business, in my book. How do you feel about it?"

Danny nodded again. "Yes, Mister, you're right," he agreed. "It's definitely unfinished business, but how we can do anything more about it now? I just don't know."

"No, neither do I, Danny," Alex replied. "But I'd sure like to see it finished, if it ever can be. And I don't know how, either. But if we can, together, possibly do anything about it, then I think that we should. Don't you?"

Danny looked at Alex, his smile replaced for once by a more serious expression. "Yes, I do," he said. "It was one of the worst things to happen to me and the others at Grant Hall, worse even than getting the lash or being caned by Hammond all the time. You don't know what it's like to be lying in bed chatting to the other kids after lights out, when were supposed to be asleep, and then hearing the cars arriving, hearing the crunch of the tyres on the gravel outside."

"We'd all get out of bed and nip to the window to have a quick look, to see who it was. And then, when we heard the footsteps in the corridor, we'd all skip back into bed, hoping that the footsteps would go past our door. Sometimes they did, and sometimes they didn't. And if it was our door that was opened, we'd all just lie still, with our eyes closed, pretending to be asleep, and hoping that the footsteps would go past our bed to someone else's. And then you'd get the poke in the ribs from Hammond's stick, and you'd be told to go downstairs with him, where he'd hand you over to one of those horrid men. It was awful. Really it was. And as for what happened after that, well.........."

Danny paused for a moment, and Alex thought that he could detect the trace of a tear in Danny's eyes. "It's not right what they did, Mister, not right at all," he continued. "They should be in jail, all of them. If there's any way that I can help to put them there, then I will."

"Thank you, Danny," Alex replied quietly. "We'll just have to see what transpires, wont we? But I mustn't keep you any longer. Your family will be wondering where you've got to."

Alex accompanied Danny up onto the rear deck, where they said their goodbyes. "I'm really glad that we've met up again, Mister," Danny said. "I'll keep in touch with you now, I promise," he added, as they shook hands and embraced briefly once again, before Danny turned and walked off along the towpath to where his wife and family were waiting for him in the far distance. Alex stood and watched him as he walked along, thinking about how much Danny had changed from the frightened young child who'd stowed away on *Jennifer Jo* all those years ago.

Alex well knew that the pathway from childhood to adult was

tricky, twisty, and difficult, made even more so for Danny by what he had experienced at Grant Hall. But there was no doubt that Danny had successfully reached the end of that particular journey, and come out the other side a well-balanced young man. Now married with a child of his own, whom he obviously adored, he had a good job which he really enjoyed, with excellent prospects, and a bright future to look forward to. Alex felt so pleased for him, how he'd been able to rebuild his life, with perhaps a little help from Alex himself.

Alex also considered what he could do about the unfinished business of Grant Hall. However much he thought about it, he always came up with the same conclusion - there seemed to be little that he could do. But he vowed to himself that wouldn't stop him from trying.

He decided to make his way down south again, to the area near to Grant Hall, where he'd first come across Danny, and see what possible leads, if any, he could find to investigate.

CHAPTER 16

Alex carefully read through the text he'd just typed into his laptop and, satisfied with what he'd written, clicked on the 'send' button on the screen to send the email across to Danny. Since parting with Danny six months before, Danny had been as good as his word. Every fortnight or so, Danny would send Alex a chatty, friendly message, all about what he'd been doing and how things were going for himself and his young family. There was usually a photo attachment as well, usually of his daughter Jenny or his wife Sophie, or a picture showing some project he'd just finished at his place of work of which he was really proud. The latest picture had been of an oak cabinet he'd been required to make as part of his apprenticeships exams, and Danny had proudly recounted how Smarts had been so pleased with it that it had been placed on display in the company's main reception area at their offices.

And Alex, in return, had sent regular messages back to Danny, about where his current location was on the 2000 miles of the canal system, and recounting various amusing incidents that had occurred on the cut. It had taken Alex nearly all the time since he'd parted with Danny to gradually make his way back down south again. But he was now not far from the area where Danny had hidden on *Jennifer Jo* all those years ago.

He closed down his laptop and put it away in the locker in its usual place under the dinette seat, and put on his outdoor shoes. He needed to do some shopping for provisions, and he knew that there was a village shop not far away.

Alex locked the door of the boat, and walked along the towpath for about 5 minutes, enjoying the early morning sunshine, till he reached a road bridge which passed over the canal at that point. He made his way up the track onto the road, where he turned left and walked along the footpath beside the road into the nearby village.

At the village shop, he bought some bread, milk, a packet of bacon, a box of breakfast cereal, and a few other items. As he came out of the shop, he noticed that a mobile barber's van, emblazoned with the words 'Barry the Mobile Barber' on the outside in large red lettering, had just arrived and parked up outside the shop while he was inside. Alex put his hand to his head and felt his hair. It was getting a bit long, especially at the back and around his ears. He decided it was time to have a trim, and it would support the barber into the bargain. He was well aware that small traders such as this deserved all the support they could muster.

He opened the door and stepped inside the van. There he found the barber just starting work on an elderly gentleman who was sitting in the chair in front of a mirror, with a smock around him. "Can you manage a trim for me please?" Alex asked. The barber, a young man in his late twenties, paused from his cutting and turned round, giving Alex a welcoming smile as he did so. "Yes, of course," he said. "I won't be long with Harry here. Would you like to take a seat over there? There's some newspapers to have a look at while you're waiting."

"That's fine, thank you," Alex replied, as he sat down in the small waiting area and picked up one of the newspapers lying on the table in the corner and started to scan through it. He very rarely bought a newspaper to read, getting most of his news from the television bulletins, so he liked to have a look at a newspaper when the opportunity arose. The paper he picked up was a local daily paper, and, turning to one of the inside pages, he was surprised to find a headline which read:

"GRANT HALL SOLD – work to start soon."

Alex had been thinking about Grant Hall and how to move forward with what they'd discussed and agreed, ever since he'd met up with Danny, but was saddened to admit that so far he'd not come up with any sort of plan whatsoever. He read on with interest:

'Nearby Grant Hall has been sold to Gordon Brothers, a developer of care homes for retired people. The sale was agreed some time ago, but was conditional upon planning permission being granted for the necessary conversion work to make it suitable for its new use. The appropriate permission was confirmed at a full meeting of the Council last week.'

'The Hall was previously used as a residential care home for boys who had exhibited behavioural difficulties, but was closed some seven years ago after a high profile court case alleging extreme physical abuse of the boys living there. Augustus Hammond, who owned and was in charge of Grant Hall, was convicted and sentenced to six years imprisonment for his part in the abuse, but was released after serving just four years of his sentence. It is believed he now lives abroad.'

'Builders have already moved onto the site to carry out preparatory work, and a workforce of about 40 people will be engaged on the project, which is expected to take about four months to complete.'

The article was accompanied by a photograph of Grant Hall,

showing the Hall through the tall wrought iron gates set into a high wall, the scene Alex remembered seeing on television when news of Hammond's conviction had broken all those years ago, the location where the interviewer had spoken with the local newspaper reporter. Alex looked at the article once again, and saw the same reporter's by-line below the headline – Robert Jefferies.

Alex sat and thought once again about how he might put this news to good use, but his train of thought was interrupted by the barber, who was now standing beside him, saying "next please."

"Oh, I'm sorry," Alex said meekly, "I was miles away." He put down the newspaper he'd been reading, and sat down in the barber's chair as the barber drew a smock around him, and started snipping behind Alex's ears.

"You're not one of my regulars," the barber said in conversation. "I'm Barry, by the way. Just moved in around here somewhere, have you?"

"Well, yes and no," Alex replied. "I'm off a canal boat. It's moored not far away, just down the road, not far from where the road crosses the canal. I live on my boat, all year round. Most people describe people like me as water gypsies, because we move around all the time and don't have a permanent location. I was doing some shopping, saw your van, and decided I needed a trim."

"I didn't realise there was a canal anywhere near here," remarked Barry.

"No?" asked Alex. "There's lots of people who aren't aware that they've got a canal practically on their doorstep, so to speak." Barry nodded, and Alex spent the next ten minutes, while Barry was cutting his hair, talking about his boat and how he travelled all round the country on the canal network. Barry was very interested, asking numerous questions, and before long Alex 's hair was finished. Alex paid for his trim and went to leave the van, but as he did so, he turned and asked, "excuse me, Barry, but do you think I could have that paper I was looking at? There was something in it which I'd like to read through again, if you don't mind."

"Yes, of course," Barry replied. "No problem, help yourself. It's several days old now, anyway. The shop here gives me all their unsold papers at the end of the day. Several other shops do the same, when I'm by there. Help yourself."

"Thank you," Alex said gratefully. "Much appreciated." He picked up the newspaper, tucked it into his bag with his shopping, and made his way back to *Jennifer Jo*, thinking all the while about what he'd read. Back on the boat, he had a quick lunch and while he did so, he checked on the map and found that Grant Hall was only about 6 miles from where he was moored on the canal. Then the solution suddenly came to him. He would go to Grant Hall and see it for himself, and then maybe find the means of moving forward on the project he and Danny had set themselves.

He cleared away his lunch things, then locked up the boat and took his folding bicycle out of the locker where it was stored. Unfolding the bike and clamping it into its normal riding position, he set off along the towpath, and thence onto the road where he'd walked back from the shop and the barber's van less than an hour before. At the next road junction, he took out his map and checked which way to go. It was a nice sunny afternoon, and the miles soon went by, and less than an hour later he was outside the main gates of Grant Hall, where the road to the Hall led off the public road and through pleasant parkland towards the Hall.

Alex stood for a while and surveyed the scene. A large sign reading *"Gordon Brothers"* had been erected beside the gates, announcing to the world that they had been appointed main contractors for the conversion project. Beside it was a another display sign with a number of spaces for the long rectangular boards advertising the various sub-contractors working there also. As he watched, a large lorry laden with building materials turned into the gates and proceeded along the long straight driveway through the park. Alex mounted his bicycle and followed the lorry towards the Hall.

Approaching the Hall itself, Alex dismounted, stood in the shade beneath a large oak tree, and looked around. A number of site huts had been placed in a compound near the main entrance gates in the high wall which surrounded the Hall. Some of them were obviously for storage, Alex saw, whilst others served as offices, with a couple more providing amenity facilities for the workers. A digger was busy excavating a trench leading away from one of the amenity cabins, presumably to lay a temporary sewage outfall. Another worker was using a diesel powered hand roller to flatten some recently laid aggregates, which would serve as a parking area for the staff's cars and vans. And other men were busy erecting temporary fencing to create a secure storage compound for building materials.

As Alex watched, the lorry he'd followed into the park backed up, manoeuvred into a position beside the compound and started offloading its load of materials. Alex noted that a small cabin had been placed beside the gates in the high wall leading to the Hall itself, and a man ensconced in the cabin was checking staff into and out of the Hall and its immediate environs inside the wall. There were a couple of workers being checked in, and Alex saw one of them being turned away, only to return a moment or two later wearing a hard hat, which he hadn't had on his head earlier. Health and Safety, Alex thought, you can't get away from it these days. The builders must be strictly enforcing a rule that no-one is allowed on site unless they are wearing a hard hat, and rightly so.

Alex decided to walk round the Hall, outside the wall, to see just how big were the Hall's immediate grounds. He leant his bicycle against the tree and set off, thinking as he went about how Danny had described the hall's situation. As he finished his walk round and returned to his bicycle, he realised that Danny had been right when he'd said that the only way out was through the big high gates at the front. There was no other gate in the wall at all, not even for deliveries to the kitchen or other facilities or service areas. Surveying the scene, he began to appreciate how much like a prison it must have seemed to the boys who lived there.

Ales took out his mobile phone and took a number of pictures of the scene, taking care not to be spotted by any of staff who were all busy at work. Then he mounted his bicycle again and rode back to the main gates, where he found a small white van had just arrived. Each side of the van bore a colourful logo painted on it, and beneath it were the words 'Ewington David – Quantity Surveyors'.

The driver nodded to Alex as he got out of the van, took a long rectangular sign out of the back of the van, and started to fix it on the display board beside all the other sub-contractor's signs. Alex walked over to him and engaged him in conversation. "Hello," he said, "your firm's got the contract here, then?"

"Yes, that's right," the driver replied. "Mr. David, that's George David, our senior partner, is starting here on Monday, he's got another job to finish first, that will take two or three days to wrap up. After that, he'll be busy here. But me, I'm just the odd job man, I've been asked to put up the sign, that's all. Nice day, isn't it?"

"Yes, it is," Alex replied, "nice to talk to you," as the driver got back into his van and drove off. Alex took out his camera phone again and took some more photographs, with a few special close-up views of the signboards, before retrieving his bicycle and returning to *Jennifer Jo*. As he rode along, he thought about what he'd seen at Grant Hall, and the beginnings of an idea started to take shape in his mind.

After having his tea, Alex decided to have a word with Danny. Usually they were content to communicate using email, as their messages were seldom of high importance, but this was urgent. The opportunity to get inside Grant Hall might not last very long. He waited till it was gone seven o'clock, as he knew that Danny would be busy until then bathing his daughter and putting her to bed, so he was pleased when Danny answered his call straight away.

"Hello, Danny," Alex greeted him. "How are you?"

"I'm fine, thanks, Mister," Danny replied over the phone. "And Sophie, and Jenny, too. You?"

"Yes, Danny, I'm fine, thanks." Alex paused a moment before continuing. "Danny, I'm moored up not far from Grant Hall, in fact, it's only about five or six miles away. I went to have a look at it this afternoon. I think there's a chance that we can move forward on our unfinished business, if you know what I mean. We've talked about it quite a bit in the past, haven't we? Is it possible for you to come down here, as soon as you're free, but preferably tomorrow and Friday?"

"What do you mean, move forward, Mister?" Danny asked. "How, exactly?"

"Well," Alex told him. "It will need a bit of subterfuge, but I think there's a good chance that we can get into the Hall, and see if the tobacco tin with the car numbers and so on, which you told me was hidden under the floorboards in your dormitory, to see if it's still there. If so, we can retrieve it, get the information inside it, and decide how to take it further from there."

"That's a good idea," said Danny. "But how are we going to get in there and get the tin, even if it's still there?"

"I'll tell you when you get here," replied Alex. "Do you think you can make it?"

"Well yes, you're in luck," said Danny, "I'm on holiday from work all this week. I've got a few things to do tomorrow morning, but I could get a train down there later in the afternoon. Is that all right?"

"That's fine, Danny," Alex said. "Thank you very much. Email me what time your train arrives, and I'll pick you up from the train station. Is that alright?"

"Sure is," Danny acknowledged. "It will be great to see you again, anyway."

"One more thing, Danny," Alex asked. "You'll need a smart suit. Can you remember to bring one with you, please?"

"Of course I can," Danny replied, laughing. "I've only got one, so I'll bring that. See you tomorrow, then. Bye."

"Yes, Danny. And you. Goodbye." Alex put down his phone, and took out his laptop and fired it up. He had a lot of work to do before Danny arrived, to be certain that he'd got everything ready for Friday.

At about half-past-six the next evening, Alex was waiting outside the train station as Danny came out amongst the crowds of people disembarking from the train. They greeted each other warmly and shook hands, then Alex led the way across the car park to a smart, newish looking car parked in a corner.

"Hey, Mister, "nice motor you've got here!" Danny exclaimed. "Coming up in the world, are we?" he added with his usual trademark grin, a grin which hadn't altered one bit since the day Alex had first met him.

"Well, no, actually," Alex replied, smiling. "It's not mine. I've just hired it for a few days. It's all to do with image and presentation. We'll need all of that tomorrow."

Alex drove back to the canal near where *Jennifer Jo* was moored, and drew into the car park of a canal-side pub. "They've very kindly let me park here," he explained, "in exchange for my buying a few beers last night. But come on, the boat's just along here." He led the way along the towpath, and they soon came to *Jennifer Jo*. "I've made up your old berth in the back cabin for you, Danny," Alex told him. "I hope it will be alright for you."

"Well, Mister," Danny smiled. "It did me alright for a year, so I suppose another few days will seem like old times, won't they?"

Alex nodded. "Come and sit down," he said, "we can chat while I get the supper. Tell me, how's Sophie? And young Jenny? And your mum and gran?"

"Sophie's fine," replied Danny. "And Jenny, well she's wonderful, she really is. She's growing up really fast. And mum and gran are OK too, although gran's started to slow down a bit now, but she's still quite active. I slip round to see them at least once a week, and sometimes more often. I've told mum to phone me if she ever wants me round there. We don't live far away so it's no problem, no problem at all."

"That's good, Danny," Alex told him. "Be sure to look after your mum and gran, won't you."

Danny nodded in agreement as Alex busied himself in the galley, while Danny sat at the dinette. Alex got him to talk some more about his family and his young daughter, and how he was progressing at his work. It was very obvious how proud Danny was of young Jenny, who it seemed was growing up fast, and he was really enjoying his job at Smart Brothers, the building firm.

But as they sat and ate their meal and continued to chat, Alex began to sense that there was something wrong. On the face of it, Danny was the same Danny as Alex had always known, but Danny had lived with Alex on *Jennifer Jo* for a year, and Alex had got to know all of Danny's moods really well. After clearing away their supper things and doing the washing up, Alex made a couple of mugs of coffee, and setting one down in front of Danny, he sat down opposite him at the dinette. "What's the matter, Danny?" he asked quietly. "There's something wrong, I know."

Danny just continued to sit there, saying nothing, just staring at his coffee mug cradled in his hands, turning it round and round and round, just like the thoughts rushing through his head. Alex knew better than to push him, as he knew that Danny would open up eventually, and it was a good minute before he spoke.

"It's my dad, Mister," he said eventually, still staring at his mug as he did so.

"Your father, Danny?" Alex asked. "I thought you hadn't been in touch with him for years, not since he left the family home when you were quite young."

"Well, yes Mister. And, no," Danny replied quietly.

"You'd better explain, Danny," Alex told him. "I don't understand. Please tell me what's been happening."

Once again, Danny sat quietly, saying nothing, but at last he started to tell Alex about his father. "You're right, Mister," he said, "I'll never forget that day I came home from school and dad was there, that was rather strange, because he was usually out at work when I got in, you see. He told me that he loved us both, very much, but he didn't want to live there with us any more, then he picked up his bags and opened the door and gave the key to mum, and then he went out of the door and closed it behind him, and that was the last time I saw him."

"I was really upset because I thought he was a great dad, we'd had loads of fun together, and I just kept wondering what I'd done wrong to make him not want to be with us any longer. You see, I thought it was all my fault that he'd moved out. And mum, she wouldn't talk about him any more after that. She just said that we'd got to get used to living there without him."

Danny fell silent again, as Alex digested what Danny had just told him. He knew that Danny had spent several years growing up without his father, before his mother had become ill and Danny had been taken into care, but Danny had never before said that he blamed himself for what had happened. Taken together with Danny's experiences of Grant Hall, Alex could well understand the turmoil that had been going on inside the boy's head when he'd stowed away on *Jennifer Jo* beside the lock that day seven or eight years ago. But Danny had started talking again.

"I said that was the last time I saw him, but actually it wasn't," he said. "You see, a few weeks ago, I went round to see mum, like I always do every week, and mum said she wanted to talk to me, so we sat down and had a cup of tea together, while Gran was out shopping. Anyway, she said she'd heard that my Dad was ill, really ill, and he didn't have much longer to live, and that he'd asked to see me, he'd asked if I could go down to see him."

"Well, there was no way I was going to do that, was there? He'd walked out on us, with no warning, and left us to fend for ourselves, hadn't he? And I'd always thought that I'd done something wrong, that had made him not want to live with us any more. And if he'd been there for us when mum was taken ill again, then I'd never have ended up in Grant Hall, would I? So I told her that I wasn't going, that I wasn't interested."

"But then mum said I didn't understand, and she explained to me why he'd had to move out. She told me that when they'd got married and even when I was born, he was in the army, he'd been a regular soldier, you see, and he'd been in the army for quite a few years, since he was a young man, younger than I am now. But I must have been too small to remember him being in the army, because he'd always had a job near home you see, when I was growing up."

"Anyway, while he was in the army, he'd been sent abroad, to somewhere where there was a lot of fighting, she couldn't remember where, and he'd been captured by the enemy and put into some sort of a prison camp. Apparently he was put in a cell with about thirty other people, but it was very small and only had a stone floor and no furniture or anything, with only one very small window very high up in the wall. They were never let out for exercise or anything, and there was no toilet or anything, they all had to pee and mess in a corner and there was hardly any food for them. And there wasn't even enough room for them all to lie down on the floor at the same time and get any sleep."

"She said he was there for about six months altogether, and when he was eventually released he was a changed man. He was discharged from the army after that, because he couldn't fight any more. And ever since then he'd found it difficult to be with other people, even to be with other people in the same room. Even with his own family, just me and mum. It must have been awful for him, it really must. He stuck it with us for a while with me and mum but eventually he found a small cottage out in the open country somewhere and he lived there on his own, he'd got a new job working on a farm, outside all the time in the open, that was what suited him best."

"But she said he never ever forgot his obligations and

responsibilities to us both as a husband and a father. Apparently he always sent money into mum's bank account every month, for me as well as her, and even when I got to be sixteen, the money still came in for me, every month without fail."

"And they kept in touch as well, mum and dad, they used to write to each other, not very often, but two or three times a year. You see, they still loved each other, and mum understood what he'd been though and why he couldn't be with us."

"She said he even came to our wedding, me and Sophie, but he stayed at the back all the time, and when we, that's Sophie and me, when we walked back down the aisle together in the church with Sophie on my arm, he hid behind a pillar, so I didn't see him. I really wish I'd known he was there."

"So because of what mum had just told me about him, and because I knew that she wanted me to, although she said I didn't have to, it was my decision, I agreed to go down to see him. I got the train down to the West country where he lived, one Friday morning it was, I was only going to spend a couple of hours with him at the hospital, and then go back home again the same night."

"I took our photo album with me, you know, with all our wedding photos in it, and pictures of Jenny when she was a baby and since then, growing up. I went into the hospital and up to his ward, and found dad lying there in his bed, he was so pleased to see me, he really was. I sat and talked to him about how things were and everything, and showed him the photos, although I never mentioned anything being in care or about Grant Hall or anything like that. I didn't want him to feel responsible for what had happened to me, it wasn't his fault that being a prisoner changed him so much. And then all of a sudden the nurses were saying that it was time for me to leave, visiting time was over."

"But there was so much more I wanted to talk to him about, so instead of getting the train home, I found myself a bed and breakfast overnight, and went back the next day. They said that it wasn't visiting time till the afternoon, but because dad was so ill they'd let me in to see him. So I ended up spending all day with him. I got him to talk about his life in the army and all the different places he'd been to and that, although he didn't say much about when he was captured, he just said it wasn't much fun being a prisoner."

"I was really sad when they said it was time to go again, so I went back to the B & B for another night, and spent most of the next day, that was the Sunday, with him as well. In the afternoon, I asked the nurse for a sheet of paper and a pencil, and I drew his portrait, just head and shoulders, with no background, and I put a nice smile on his face, although he hadn't got much to smile about, had he?"

But eventually I had to leave the hospital and go home, as I had to be back at work on the Monday, and if I didn't go then I'd have missed the last train home. So I had to say goodbye to him then. He said thanks for coming to see him, and he told me how proud he was of me. I knew then that was the last time I was going to see him, he was really weak. Before I left, I held his hand for a little while and I told him how pleased I was that I'd made the effort to go and see him. And I wished him a good journey. He knew what I meant, I know he did."

"Then I had to leave, so I went out of the hospital and sat down in the bus shelter outside, waiting for the bus to take me back to the train station. I'd just missed one bus, so I had to wait about twenty minutes for the next one, but as I sat there I just started crying, I couldn't help it. The tears just ran down my face, it was awful. The other people waiting for the bus kept looking at me, I know, but I didn't care. You see, there was so much I'd wanted to talk to him about, but we'd never had enough time, and now I was never going to be able to any more."

"And just as the bus came round the corner, this nurse come out of the hospital and asked me to go back inside, they'd seen me still there in the bus shelter from the window in his ward. And they told me that Dad had died a few minutes before. I knew it was going to happen, but I was so upset, I really was. If it wasn't for my dad, I wouldn't be alive, I wouldn't be here now. And there he was gone, and I'll never see him again or talk to him again."

" When I got home, I got the guy in the photo shop to frame the picture of him which I'd drawn, and now it's on the wall at home, with the others I've done of Sophie and Jenny and mum and gran. So at least I've got something to remember him by."

Danny looked up at Alex, staring right into his eyes. "I can't remember the last time I cried," he said. "I think it might have been when I was with you, after Christmas that time, when things got a bit much for me. But I know I never ever cried when I was at Grant Hall, although loads of the other kids did, especially the younger ones. But I didn't. I wasn't going to let Hammond see that he'd got the better of me. But when I realised that I'd lost the chance to ever see and talk to my Dad again, well............."

Danny dropped his gaze to the table as he subsided into silence, deep in his own thoughts. Alex stretched out his hand and put it on Danny's wrist.

"Danny, I feel for you, so much," he said quietly after a moment. "I really do. You've had to learn what is perhaps the most difficult lesson anyone ever has to face. Nothing in life is truly free. Grief is the price we have to pay for love. It is often long delayed, but the more we love someone, then the more severe is the grief, and the more difficult it is to cope with. In your case, because your love for your father was rekindled so late in his life, it's doubly difficult for you."

"But you can be proud that you made the effort to go and see him. And take comfort in the fact that he was so proud of you. And be proud as well that you now understand why he felt unable to live with you when you were younger. Wars do such terrible things to so many people, and yet the human race seems unable to exist without them. All too often, all semblance of civilised behaviour seems to disappear. And the saddest thing of all is that, all too often, people's religious beliefs lie behind it all."

"Every child owes such a huge debt to his or her parents," Alex continued. "They brought you into the world, nurtured and cared for you while you were small and helpless. And the full extent of what your mother and father did for you, you are only now finding out, as you do the same for your own daughter."

"Try to remember your father for all the good things in your life, and in his too. He served his country, and you should honour that. Even though it changed him, because of the terrible experiences he had to go through. It must have been a desperately difficult time for him." Alex paused for a moment, searching for the right words. "Remember, time is a great healer. This hurt you are feeling now will fade over time, I can assure you. I know, Danny, that you will never forget your father. And you never ever should."

"Do you really think so?" Danny asked, looking up.

"Yes, I do, Danny," Alex replied quietly. "Believe me, please."

Danny paused for a moment. "I've really wanted to talk to someone about it, about how I felt," he said. "But there was no one. It's made me really sad. Not being able to talk to anyone about it."

"Do you feel better now?" Alex asked, "now that you have?"

Danny nodded. "Yes, Mister, I do. Thank you for listening, and for what you said. I'm sorry to have shared my troubles with you. Thanks ever so much."

"Counselling can help a great deal in situations like this," Alex responded. "Many people don't rate it very much, but it does have its place. I used to do a little bit at my school, when one of the boys had bad news. I find that it does help to talk things through, usually."

Danny nodded once again. "So you said you went to have a look at Grant Hall?" he asked, changing the subject. "Tell me about that, please."

"Yes, that's right, I did," Alex replied. "it's about to undergo some refurbishment, to convert it into an old people's home, but I found it much as you described it to me once. There's a couple of big signboards been erected outside the main gate in the village, advertising the contractors for the refurbishment, and there's some guys erecting site huts and such near the big wall round the Hall itself. And there's a small hut by the gate in the wall, with a guy inside who checks everyone into and out of the Hall."

"So how are we going to get in there, then?" asked Danny.

"That's simple," said Alex. "We're going to bluff our way in. Here, have a look at these." He handed Danny a small pile of business cards. "Daniel H. Marshall, Trainee Surveyor," Danny read out. "And who's this Ewington David firm, when they're around? I don't work for them, do I?"

"Well, actually, yes, tomorrow you do," Alex told him. "Although they don't know about it. Here's mine." And he showed him his own cards. "I made them up yesterday evening, using some photographs I took yesterday, when I was at the Hall, and some other information which I found on their website."

"While I was there, I spoke with a guy from this firm who was putting up their board at the main gate, and he said that their staff won't be starting on site until Monday. So, we're going in on Friday afternoon, that's tomorrow, and we're going to pretend to everyone we meet that we're quantity surveyors who work for Ewington David. We'll have a good hunt round and see if we can find your tobacco tin. But we'll have to play it by ear. Do you remember those hard hats I bought, years ago, when you helped me do the blacking on the boat? I've labelled them up as well, with the firm's logo, and I've bought a couple of hi-vis jackets, and a pair of clipboards. Most workers on building sites finish for the weekend at Friday lunchtime, so they can go home for the weekend, so we'll go in at around one o'clock, and with luck the site should be pretty quiet by then."

Danny looked a bit dubious. "I suppose it's worth a try," he admitted. "But what if we get caught?"

"We'll worry about that when it happens," Alex told him. "We'll have to play it by ear. Don't worry, it'll be alright. Now, there's nothing much on the television tonight. How about a game of chess?"

Danny nodded. "Alright, Mister," he said, cheering up a bit. "I'll give you a game," as he went to the usual cupboard and took the box out. "I can still remember how to play. It's like riding a bicycle, it's something you never forget. And perhaps you might win tonight. You never have so far!" he added, with his usual grin.

Neither had Alex forgotten how Danny had always beaten him off the board whenever they'd played together, while Danny was living with him on *Jennifer Jo*. And, true to form, Alex lost the game, leaving Danny victorious once again.

CHAPTER 17

Alex had a restless night's sleep, thinking about Danny and how he'd had to cope with the loss of his father, someone with whom he'd had no contact since he was a child, and who had suddenly come into his life once again for just a few short days before he died. Alex knew that Danny would eventually overcome his grief, and he hoped that the counselling he'd been able to give Danny would prove to be of help to him. He knew that Danny was a resilient young man, and that he would eventually come to terms with his belated reconciliation with his father, and with his father's death so soon afterwards. But after a leisurely breakfast and another chat with Danny, who now seemed much happier, they had an early lunch, then started to get ready to go to Grant Hall.

"You've got the business cards I gave you?" Alex asked, as they walked up to the car together. Danny nodded, patting his inside breast pocket as he did so. "That's a smart suit you've got there," Alex laughed.

"Yes, Mister," Danny grinned. "It's the only one I've got. It's the suit I got married in, actually. I don't have much call for a suit, usually."

"No, I suppose not," replied Alex. "But it's nice to dress up occasionally, isn't it? It make you feel good about yourself."

"That's right," Danny nodded, as they got into the car and Alex drove the short distance to Grant Hall. As they drove in through the main gates in the village, and proceeded along the long straight road towards the Hall itself, Alex noticed that Danny had become rather subdued, thinking no doubt about everything that had happened to him while he'd been living there.

"Oh good," Alex exclaimed as he parked the car in the parking area and looked around. "It's definitely the right time for us to be here. There's only seven or eight vehicles still here. That suggests that most of the workers have already left and gone home for the weekend. With any luck we won't be interrupted or challenged about what we're doing here." They put on their hard hats and hi-vis jackets, and then walked up to the ornate wrought-iron gates in the high wall surrounding the Hall, and spoke to the man in the small cabin by the gate.

"Hello," Alex said. "We're from Ewington David, Quantity Surveyors. We're not due to start officially until Monday, but we need to do some preliminaries this afternoon. Here's our business cards." He handed over one of the fake business cards he'd made a couple of days earlier, and motioned for Danny to do the same with his.

The gate-keeper in the cabin looked at the cards, placed them on the counter in front of him, and then turned to pick up a clipboard from the desk behind him, checking the list that was pinned to it. "You're not booked in," he said. "I'm sorry, but I'm not supposed to let anyone in unless they've been booked in first."

"Oh dear," said Alex. "I told my secretary to make the arrangements early this morning. You've got our Mr. David, that's George David, our senior partner, booked in for Monday?"

"Yes," the gate-keeper replied, checking his paperwork. "He's down here on the list for Monday. But there's no-one from your firm booked in today. I'm sorry."

Just then, sensing that they might not gain admittance after all, Danny piped up. "I said you should have got Mr. David's secretary to book us in," he said, turning to Alex. "That new secretary of yours is useless, she's just not up to the job." Turning back to the gatekeeper in the cabin, he added "she's got a lot on her mind at the moment, you see. A bit of a problem. She's pregnant. And she doesn't know whose it is." Then, winking, he added, "but I know it's not mine."

The gate-keeper chuckled. "Silly girl," he said. "They never learn, do they? Well, I suppose it's alright. Sign in here please, on this tally sheet. And be sure to come back here and sign out again when you leave. That way, we always know who's on site by just looking at the tally sheet. Health and safety, you know. You've got protective footwear on?"

Alex nodded, as did Danny. "Yes, of course," Danny replied. "We always wear them when we're on site. Company rules, you see. They provide them for us, a new pair every year."

"That's fine," the gate-keeper replied. "And remember, the site closes at four o'clock tonight, being as it's Friday today. You need to be out by then, or you'll be locked in for the weekend. No-one works over the weekends at the moment, although we might allow it later on, if the schedule is slipping." He turned to put down his clipboard back in his desk and as he did so, Alex swiftly moved to scoop up their fake business cards from the counter, and slipped them back into his pocket, hoping that the gate-keeper wouldn't miss them.

"Thank you," Alex nodded. "Come on, Danny, let's get started." They passed through the gate and walked the two hundred yards to the Hall. "Well done, Danny," Alex said. "You used your initiative really well. That was great. It got the guy on our side, didn't it?" Danny didn't reply, thinking no doubt about going into Grant Hall again after all those years away, and of the hardship Hammond had inflicted upon him and the other boys who'd been there.

Pushing open the main door of the Hall, Danny and Alex stepped inside into the entrance hall, a large open area with a tiled floor, and an ornate marble staircase rising up to the first floor landing above. Danny stood there for a long time, looking around. "It's really strange to be back here," he told Alex. "I almost expect Hammond to come round the corner with his cane and Brutus beside him on the leash at any minute."

Alex laughed. "No, Danny, he's far away now, " he replied. "Nothing to worry about now. Nothing at all. But I can appreciate how this brings it all back to you."

Danny nodded. "Come on, I'll show you where's what," he said. "Let's have a quick look round." He walked forward a few paces, then threw open a door to the right of the entrance hall. It was a large room, with rows of long wooden tables, with equally long wooden benches lined up on either side of each table. At the end of the room a low wooden railing surrounded a slightly-raised platform, where there stood another long table, but this table had upholstered chairs spaced along behind it.

"This is the dining hall," Danny explained "Over there, on that platform, that's where the wardens had their grub. They didn't have the same food as we did. We always used to have stew. They had much nicer stuff. And they got to sit on those nice chairs, we had to sit on the benches, they were pretty hard to sit on, really uncomfortable after a while. Not that we were allowed to sit there for very long after the meal, anyway. And that door over there," Danny raised his hand and pointed, "that's where the kitchens are. We don't need to go in there." Suddenly swinging round, Danny turned and pushed the door to behind them. There, in the corner behind the door, was another chair. "Hey, Mister, this is Hammonds chair, where he used to cane us," he said. "We all had to bend over the back of the chair and take whatever was coming. It wasn't very nice. It really hurt, a lot of the time. But come on, let's have a look at the school room."

Danny led the way back across the entrance hall from the dining hall and opened the opposite door. Here again were rows of long tables, but this time with the wooden benches along only one side of each table, all facing another raised platform at the end of the room, where there was a large blackboard behind it, stretching the length of the far wall. "This is where we had all our lessons," Danny told Alex. "We were divided into three groups, young, middle and older. There was usually only one teacher, who looked after all of us. He'd set one group working on something, and then move on to the next group, and so on. It worked, I suppose, because I learnt quite a bit here, we had a really good teacher some of the time.

Anyway, come on, let's go upstairs to the dormitories."

Danny led the way up the ornate marble staircase, pausing on the landing at the top of the stairs. "This is where we had to do the ball game for the wardens," he said. "That marble stuff, when you fell over, as you always did eventually, it really hurt when you fell on it, it was really solid. It wasn't like falling onto a wooden floor, or even the ground. But I got quite good at it in the end, I didn't fall over half so much as some of the other kids." He turned round again, pointing to two long corridors leading away from the landing. "There's dormitories along there," he said, pointing to the left, "that was called the West Wing, and along there, opposite, there's more dormitories in the East Wing. Mine was in the West Wing. Come along, let go and find it."

He walked a few steps through an archway into the corridor, lit only by the light from small windows located above each of the doors which lined the corridor along each side. "My dorm was the second on the left," Danny explained, "let's go and see if the tobacco tin is still there."

They walked along to the second door on the left, opened it, and stepped into the room. The room was empty, completely empty. Danny walked over to the window and peered out, as Alex followed him. The window looked out onto the front of the Hall, a large parking area with the big gates in the wall beyond which surrounded the hall on all sides.

"Hey, Mister, this is where we stood and watched the cars arrive at night," he explained, "when the pervs and the pedos arrived. That wasn't much fun, either, waiting to see who'd get called down for them to interfere with." He turned and walked back into the middle of the room, then stood with his back against the right-hand wall, about half way along. "My bed was about here," he said. "And we all had a locker, where we could keep whatever personal stuff we had, which wasn't much. But Hammond said the lockers always had to be on the right-hand side of the bed. So my locker was here," he added, as he waved his right hand about. "Now, Stevie, that's Stevie Anson, his bed was opposite mine, so his locker would have been over there." Danny walked across the room, and stood where he thought the locker would have been. Suddenly, he knelt down and started looking at the floorboards. "We had to paint all the floorboards once, while I was here," he said. "All black, all over. But you can see the paint's been worn away, quite a bit now."

Danny spent some time examining the floorboards, and then got up and walked back across the room to where he said his bed had been, and then back again, while Alex looked on. There was nothing that he could do to help Danny at this stage of their search. It was up to Danny to find the tobacco tin, if it was still hidden away under the floorboards.

"There's something wrong, Mister," he said eventually, looking up anxiously at Alex. "There aren't any loose floorboards over there. And by the look of the nails in the boards, there never has been, there's no extra nails at all over there, which there would have been, if the loose one had been fixed down again. I'm sure I've got it right, but it's not the right place, I don't know why. I'm really sorry, Mister. I've brought you on a wild goose chase, haven't I? It's been a complete waste of time."

Danny looked up at Alex, who could see a tear or two in the corner of his eyes. "No, Danny, it's not a waste of time," Alex comforted him. "Lets' check it out again, very carefully, in case we've missed something. Come on, let's go back and start from the landing at the top of the stairs."

They walked back to the landing together, then Alex started talking. "Now, Danny, let's take this one step at a time. Are we on the right landing? Your dormitory might have been downstairs? Or perhaps it was upstairs, on the second floor?"

"No, Mister, downstairs was just the dining room and the kitchens, and the school room. And Hammond's office was down there too, but we weren't allowed to go in there unless Hammond wanted us for something," Danny replied. "It was always kept locked when he wasn't about. And upstairs, on the second floor, that was where the wardens had their quarters. We were never allowed to go up there. All of us kids, we were on the first floor, either in the East Wing, or in the West Wing."

"OK, Danny," said Alex. "That's the first step sorted. Now, are you sure you were in the West Wing? Perhaps it was the East Wing?"

"No, Mister, ours was in the West Wing," replied Danny. "I'm absolutely sure of it. I'd always go up the stairs and turn left at the top to get to my dorm."

"All right, then, let's go into the West Wing," Alex suggested, as they walked through the archway once again. "Now, are you sure that you were in the second dormitory on the left?" he asked. "Not the first or the third? Or maybe on the right?"

"No, Mister, the dorms on the right looked out onto the back of the Hall," Danny replied. "Ours looked out onto the front, that's how we could see the cars arriving at night. And mine was definitely the second dorm, the second on the left," Danny replied. "I'm certain, really certain."

"Alright," said Alex, "let's check all the dormitories out, shall we?" He went to the first door on the left. "Are you sure it wasn't this one? Check if the view from the window is the same as you remember." He swung the door open, and as he and Danny went to go inside they could see that the room was lined with racks of wooden shelving.

"Oh, of course," exclaimed Danny, with a sigh of relief. "This is the linen room. This is where they kept all the clean sheets and duvet covers and pillowslips for the beds. Every month, we had to change all our beds, get clean stuff from here and make our beds up. The dirty stuff, we had to put outside the dorm doors into the corridor, and then whoever was on housekeeping duty had to collect everything up and take them down to the laundry baskets, they were kept round the back in the storerooms behind the kitchens, to get everything ready for when the laundry van came round to collect them. But if Hammond wasn't around, then we'd bring the laundry baskets round into the entrance hall downstairs, they were big wicker baskets on wheels, you see. If you put them in the right place in the hall, well you could just collect up the dirty sheets and stuff, and then, if you aimed them properly, you could sling them over the railings on the landing and get them to drop straight into the baskets. That didn't half save a lot of effort, instead of running up and down the stairs all the time."

Danny turned round and walked across the landing and opened the opposite door, to reveal another room, similarly fitted out with wooden shelving, just like the linen room they'd been in a moment before. "This was the clothing store," he explained. "All the clean clothes were kept here. You know, we never had our own clothes, or anything. With the clothes, everything was done by size. Look, you can still see the sizes written on the shelves." Alex looked at where Danny was pointing. Sure enough, a string of numbers had been pencilled onto the edge of the shelves in various places.

"How it worked was like this," explained Danny. "Like, when I first came here, I always wore a size 32 tee-shirt. So, whenever I needed a clean tee-shirt, I just used to come in here and take one off the top of the 32 pile. Later on, they were starting to get a bit tight, I suppose I'd grown a little bit, so I started taking 34's instead. It was the same for trousers and jeans, shorts and briefs too, and socks and pullovers. The only stuff we really had to call our own were our shoes, and our toothbrushes. Plus our schoolbooks of course, but they were always kept downstairs, in the schoolroom. That was about all we were allowed to have, really."

They walked back across the corridor to the door to the linen room. "So, Danny," Alex asked, "if this is the linen room, and yours was the second dormitory on the left, then it would be the third door on the left, wouldn't it, and not the second door? Let's have a look."

He walked forward and opened the third door, and went in,

closely followed by Danny. Like the previous dormitory they'd been in, this room too was completely empty. "Here, Danny, check this room out, check the floorboards," Alex suggested. "See if you can find any loose floorboards in here."

Danny nodded, and went to the place where he thought his bed was. "Yes, Mister, if this was my place, then Stevie's would have been over there." He walked across the room, and knelt down, examining the floorboards. "Hey, Mister, this board is loose," he exclaimed, looking up briefly at Alex with his usual grin. "Perhaps we're in the right place now."

He pulled at the floorboard, and suddenly it came up, sending Danny sprawling onto his back. "Seems promising," he grinned again, as he lay down on his side on the floor, put the full length of his left arm into the void beneath the boards and felt around. "Nothing there," he said after a moment, "let's try the other side." He rolled over and put his right arm under the boards in the other direction, feeling around the void beneath the boards. "Yes, Mister, here it is," he shouted with glee, "I can't believe it's still here after all this time," he went on, as he withdrew his arm from the floorboards, holding the precious tin in his hand.

Danny handed the tin to Alex, who cracked the lid open. "Yes, Danny, there's some pieces of paper in here, with numbers and letters on them," he said. "But we'll look at them properly, when we get back to *Jennifer Jo*. We should put the floorboard back before we go, though. It's better that no-one knows what we've been up to." He closed the tin and carefully put it in his pocket, away from any curious eyes they might meet before they departed.

"OK, Mister," Danny replied, as he put the floorboard back into place and stamped it firmly down. Then they returned to the corridor, but instead of turning right, back to the main landing above the entrance hall, Danny took hold of Alex's arm and pulled him to the left, towards a door at the end of the corridor. "Come and see the washroom, Mister," he said, throwing open the door. It gave onto a large room, divided down the middle by a row of metal racks with rows of coat hooks on each side, and more wooden benches below, similar to those Alex had seen in the dining hall and the school room a little earlier. The left hand part of the room had a long row of toilet cubicles along one side, and opposite them was a row of washbasins, with a small shelf running along the length of the wall above them, and mirrors screwed onto the wall in front of each basin. The right hand part of the room was fully tiled, with a row of shower heads protruding from the wall.

"I suppose the only good thing you could ever say about this place was that the toilets and showers were always really clean," Danny remarked. "Hammond made sure of that, I'll say that for him. If they ever smelt of anything, they smelt of disinfectant. There was a strict rota for having showers, you know. If you didn't have a shower when you were supposed to, then that was a guaranteed stroke of the cane from Hammond. And do you know something else? The wardens, well, they weren't pervs or anything, none of them ever came in here, while we were all walking around naked, getting showered and the like. They left us to get on with it, although they did usually put one of the older boys in charge of us, sort of like a prefect, but that wasn't really necessary, because, like I just said, we just got on with it. The only time any of the wardens came in here was when they were supervising whoever was on cleaning duty. And if it wasn't all nice and clean, then when Hammond came along to inspect it all afterwards, and if he wasn't satisfied, then everyone on cleaning duty that day got caned."

"Hey, Danny," Alex asked, "if they were so strict about having showers but none of the wardens ever came in here, how did they know that you'd actually had a shower?"

"Oh, come on, Mister," Danny replied with a grin. "You're slipping, aren't you? There was a warden stationed outside the door, with the rota on his clipboard, it was usually Mr. Wilkins who did that, and when you came out, he checked your hair, and if it was still wet, then it was a good clue that you'd had a shower, wasn't it?"

Alex nodded. "Yes, I suppose so," he said, feeling well put into his place. "But come along, let's get on. We've got what we came for."

They returned back down the staircase to the main entrance hall, but suddenly Danny veered off to the right, and opened a door which Alex hadn't noticed, tucked away behind the staircase. "Come down into the cellars, Mister," he suggested. "There's something else for you to see down there."

Alex followed him down the stairs into the cellars, where Danny led the way along a dark, low, corridor, stopping eventually in front of a solid-looking door. On a table set to one side was an old radio set, with several wires leading away from it. "This is the Dark Room, Mister," he explained, adding "have a look inside," as he opened the door. Alex stepped inside the room. It was windowless, with a stone floor and walls, and completely bare, except for a bucket placed in one corner of the room, with a short plank set across it. "That was the toilet," explained Danny, then he called out "I'll just give you a couple of minutes, then I'll let you out," as he swung the door closed behind Alex, leaving him alone in the room.

With the door closed, It was pitch black inside. Turning round, Alex felt his way back to the door in the dark, and found that there was no door handle on the inside. Even though Alex knew that it was a warm summer's day outside, the room immediately felt cold. Suddenly, the room was filled with loud noise, a strange hissing noise pervading the room, impossible to get away from. Alex instantly recognised it for what it was – white noise, radio interference piped into the room from the radio outside, via a hidden loudspeaker somewhere. It was a long two minutes before the door opened, and Alex was able to exit the room.

"How did you like that, Mister?" Danny asked, his grin for once replaced by a more serious expression.

"That wasn't very nice, not nice at all," Alex replied. "And I was only in there for a few minutes. I can't think how awful it must have been for you when you were in there."

"I think I was in there for a couple of days," said Danny. "But you lost all sense of time, when you were in there. That's was what the other kids reckoned, anyway, what they told me after I was let out. And before Hammond and the wardens put you in there, they made you strip naked, completely naked, not because they were pervs or anything, but just to humiliate you all the more. You either had to stand up all the time, or lean against the wall, or just lay down on the floor. It was really cold in there, without any clothes on. And damp as well, you were shivering all the time, even though you were curled up in a corner trying to keep warm. And after a while the toilet bucket started to stink a bit, after you'd used it a couple of times. And when you came out, they made you empty it yourself, of course. They wouldn't dream of doing that themselves."

"This is awful, Danny," Alex said. "Really awful. How anyone could do this to a young boy I just don't know. In a way, I'm glad you've shown it to me, so that I could get some idea of what the Dark Room was like, and what it must have been like to have been shut in there. But I think it's best if we moved on. Come along, it's time for us to leave this place now." They returned to the main entrance hall, and then went out into the bright sunshine and walked back to the gatekeeper, to sign themselves out.

"You're just in time," the gatekeeper commented. "It's nearly four o'clock. A few minutes later and you'd have been in there for the weekend. We'll all be off any minute now."

"Well, have a good one," Alex replied. "We've got done what we needed to do, but we probably won't be back ourselves, as Mr. David is taking over on Monday. Thanks for your help."

As they walked away from the gates, Danny asked "hey, Mister, when you were here before, did you go and see the kitchen garden?"

Alex shook his head, "No I didn't," he replied. "Where is it?"

"It's along here," Danny said. "Come on, I'll show you." He led the way along an overgrown path through the parkland, and after a few minutes they came to a high wall, very similar to the one which surrounded Grant Hall itself. Leading Alex round the corner, Danny stopped at a large wooden door, which stood slightly ajar in the wall. "There's only one door," he said, "in the whole garden. It's the only way in or out, unless of course you do what I did," here he stopped and smiled hugely at Alex, before continuing "and go over the wall."

Alex tried the door, but it didn't budge. "Here, let me have a go," Danny exclaimed, "stand back." He raised his right leg and gave the door a hefty kick, at which it moved a few inches. Danny kicked the door another six or seven times, moving it slightly each time, until at last it was open enough for them both to squeeze through. "That was a bit tight," Danny said, as they went in. "I just imagined it was Hammond standing there. I'd give him a good kicking any day."

What used to be the vegetable garden where Danny and the other boys on gardening duty had toiled under the watchful eyes of the wardens was now once again neglected and well overgrown, as nature had been allowed to reclaim it for its own. In contrast to the parkland outside the wall, where a large flock of free-roaming sheep continually cropped the grass, keeping it short and neat, the garden was a riot of summer weeds and plants, many of them in full flower.

Alex was used to seeing wild plants growing in abundance along the uncut offside margins of the canals, and he had always enjoyed looking at all the wild flowers which in places bloomed in abundance. To him, it was nature at its best and most colourful.

But Danny seemed to be less impressed. "I say, Mister," he exclaimed, "what a mess. It's a bit different to when I was here. We had nearly all this properly cultivated, except for that bit up the back over there, which we were working on when I got away that time. There were potatoes, loads of them, carrots, swedes, onions, parsnips, broccoli, cauliflowers and cabbages, all growing nicely, and we had to keep weeding between the rows all the time, to keep it neat and tidy." Danny pointed to the wall on the right. "And those apple trees were being properly trained up against that wall over there. They're in need of a good pruning now."

Danny turned round to look at the remains of the greenhouse, located beside the entrance door. "That's looking a bit sorry for itself now, isn't it?" he remarked. The once-smart white paint on the woodwork was faded and peeling away, and nearly all the windows were broken. Beside the greenhouse was a small grass-covered mound. "That's where the rubbish heap was," he told Alex. "And over there, just behind it, that's where the pile of boxes was, where I hid that day until they'd all gone back to the Hall. And over there," he shouted, as he ran across the garden through the waist- high weeds, "here's where I built up the boxes to make a stairway to get over the wall. Look, there's a couple of boxes still here!" He bent down and pushed the weeds aside, then picked up a stout wooden crate. "These are what we used to take the produce back to the Hall in," he explained.

They spent a couple more minutes looking round the garden, then made their way back to the car. But as they approached the parking area, Danny veered off to the left and sat down on the trunk of a fallen tree, where he just sat there, staring quietly at the grass in front of him, saying nothing. Alex walked over to him and sat down beside him, waiting. He'd got to know Danny quite well from the year when he'd lived on *Jennifer Jo* with Alex as a boy, and although Danny was now older and in early adulthood, Alex knew from past experience that Danny's thoughts were racing through his mind, and that he would speak again when he was good and ready.

At last, Danny turned his head to Alex. "I didn't really want to come here today, Mister," he said quietly.

"Why not, Danny?" Alex asked. "Were you afraid that it would rekindle old memories, of the bad things that happened here?"

Yes," Danny nodded. "It was horrid here, it really was. All because of Hammond. He was the worst, and I think some of the other wardens got caught up in the atmosphere of violence and cruelty towards us boys and took part in it as well. You know, just like in Germany years ago, when the Nazis came to power and started all the violence towards the Jews, and ordinary civilised people went along with it and became swept up in it, and were encouraged by it to support Hitler and commit such horrid crimes themselves. It didn't need to be like that here. All us kids, you know, we behaved ourselves most of the time. A bit of detention now and again for someone who'd stepped out of line would have been quite sufficient to keep us in order. Nothing more. That's how it was at Harding Court when I was there. They didn't need to cane us, or anything, like Hammond did."

"But some of the wardens here, well, especially the ones who only came in during the daytime, they lived in the village back where the main gates are, not on the top floor like Hammond and the others, I don't think they realised how things were. People like Mr. Wilkins, he was really nice. He was always very kind to us all, considerate as well. Maybe he didn't know. Or maybe he did, but was scared to say anything. Hammond might have threatened him with the sack if he did. He was getting on a bit, he might have struggled to get another job anywhere at his age."

"At least, all of us kids, we stuck together, looked out for each other. United against a common enemy, I suppose you'd call it. I often wonder what happened to them all. I hope they've got over it alright, or as much as I have, anyway. Or better, even, although I'm really happy now, what with being married to Sophie, and with Jenny now as well, of course." Danny turned and looked at Alex. "You do know why she's called Jenny, don't you?" he continued.

Alex nodded. "Yes, Danny, I think I do," he said. "Her full name's Jennifer Jo, isn't it?"

"Yes," Danny replied. "That's right. It's the name of your boat, isn't it? And you said once that you'd named it after your wife, didn't you? You see, there's never been any way I could properly repay you for what you did for me after I got away from Grant Hall, and how you helped me to get myself sorted out afterwards. I realise now how much of a risk you were taking when you took me in. If the cops had found me on the boat with you, well then, they'd have slung you inside for child abduction, and probably much worse as well. But what you did for me, well, it changed my life, it really did. And once I'd got settled in with you, I really enjoyed being on *Jay-Jay*. And you gave me school lessons as well. You somehow managed to make them really interesting, much more than any other teacher I've had, although some of those I have now at the technical college where I go for my apprenticeship, they're pretty good as well. So I thought that it would be a nice tribute to you for everything you've done for me. It's been my way of saying thank you, for how you helped me. I'm really pleased that we met up again, so that you could find out about it."

"Thank you, Danny," Alex said quietly. "That was a very nice thing for you to do. I'm really touched. And, I'm so pleased that I was able to help you when you needed it. But there's something that you should never forget. Remember that by going to the police and laying complaints against Hammond, and giving evidence against him in court, you, in your turn, have changed the life of many other boys whom you've never even met, who were living here at the time, not to mention those who would have been sent here in the years afterwards. Without you, Grant Hall would still be in operation. It's something which you can be really proud of. But, Danny, there's something else. Could I ask you something, please?"

"Yes, of course," said Danny. "Go ahead."

"Well, the last time we met," Alex continued, "Sophie told me that she didn't know why you choose those names for your daughter. I think it would be nice for her if she did know. And does she know about your having to be being here, at Grant Hall when you were younger? She really should be told, in my view."

"Yes, you're right," replied Danny. "I realised that after we met up again, you know, at the pub that day. So I told her all about it a few weeks later. She was asking how we knew each other. She was quite upset about it all when I told her, but she's alright now. If anything, it's drawn us closer together, if that was ever possible. We're so very fond of each other, it's wonderful."

"I hope you don't mind my asking this, Danny, but have you and Sophie ever thought about having any more children?" Alex asked.

"Yes, we've talked about it lots of times," Danny explained, "but we decided against it. You see, when Sophie was expecting Jenny, well she had a really bad time. Right from the start, she had this awful morning sickness, she couldn't keep anything down, nothing at all. And it wasn't just in the morning, it lasted all day, and through the night as well. They'd take her into hospital and put her on a drip, and get her right, then she'd come home and in a few days it would start all over again. It lasted the full nine months, and then, when Jenny was born, well Sophie was in labour for twenty four hours, it was a really difficult birth. I was with her the whole time, and when the baby arrived and they said I could cut the cord to bring my daughter into the world as an independent person, well that was wonderful."

"We've talked about another one several times, but I wouldn't want to put her though all that again, it's not fair on her. We're so happy to have Jenny, she's lovely."

Danny paused for a long while, looking around the parkland with its sheep grazing quietly on the grass, before gazing back at the Hall and continuing. "You know, Mister, I wouldn't have come back here today, except for the chance to find the tobacco tin. I'm really pleased that we found it. I hope that they'll find the people who used to come here and make us do things with them. And put them in jail, where they belong. I knew ages ago, well before the trial, that this place had been closed, but there's no substitute for seeing it for yourself, is there?" He turned and look at Alex, who saw tears forming in the corner of his eyes. "I hope the old people who come to live here will be better treated than we were," he went on. "Much better."

"I'm sure they will, Danny," Alex replied. "But if you're ready to make a move, it's time for us to go. Let's get back to the boat and get some supper together."

Back on *Jennifer Jo*, Alex started preparing their evening meal, while Danny took out his mobile phone. "I'll just go out the back and give Sophie a ring," he said. "I won't be long." But that turned out to be an understatement, as he was on the phone to Sophie for more than a quarter of an hour, finishing his call and coming back into the saloon just as Alex was dishing up their evening meal. "I told Sophie that I'd be coming home tomorrow, Mister," he said. "I hope that's alright? I'm not needed here any more, am I?"

"No, Danny, that's fine," Alex told him. "I'll run you back to the train station in good time to catch your train, and then I can drop the car off to the hire depot."

After they'd finished eating, Danny offered to clear away their dinner things. "I'll clear up, Mister," he said, "while you make a start on the tobacco tin." Alex nodded. "Thank you, Danny," he said, as he opened the tin. "I think the first thing we must do is to make a copy of everything that's written down in here, then we've got a backup if it's ever needed." He took out his laptop and printer/scanner and booted up the computer. "I'll scan them into the computer," he added, "then I'll print off a couple of copies, one for each of us to keep." But as he took out the pieces of paper from the tin and set them out onto the scanner, he realised that there was something wrong. "Hey, Danny," he called out, "all the writing on here, it's just a jumble of letter and numbers. They don't make any sense at all."

"No, don't worry, Mister," said Danny in response. "They're in code. We did that so that if Hammond found them, then he might not realise what they were. Copy them off, like you said, then I'll explain how to decode them. It's quite easy, really."

Danny had just finished clearing away by the time Alex had completed the scanning. "Right, Mister," Danny said, taking some sheets of paper out of the stationery drawer, and sitting down at the dinette opposite Alex. "It's very simple."

He wrote down all the letters of the alphabet from A to Z in a line on the paper, then underneath he wrote the alphabet again, but this time reversed, from Z to A. Then he did the same with the numbers from 0 to 9, followed by a reversed row of numbers beneath from 9 to 0. "Now look, this is what you get," he added, as he passed the paper across the dinette table to Alex.

A B C D E F G H I J K L M N O P Q R S T U V W X Y Z 0 1 2 3 4 5 6 7 8 9
Z Y X W V U T S R Q P O N M L K J I H G F E D C B A 9 8 7 6 5 4 3 2 1 0

"Right, Mister," he went on. "Let's have a look at the first one. What you do, you look at the letter you've got in the code, in the first row, then write down the corresponding letter in the row underneath. The same with the numbers. So this is what you end up with ......"

W Z M M B 9 1 7 9 H K E 6 0 0
D A N N Y 0 8 2 0 S P V 3 9 9

"There you see? That was me, on the 20th August, you see we put the month first, to confuse anyone a little bit more, and the car number was SPV399. Easy, isn't it? Let's do the next one."

It took them just under an hour to decipher all of the pieces of paper which they'd found in the tobacco tin. There were a total of 31 incidents recorded, with 17 boys' names and 13 different car numbers.

"Right, Danny," said Alex, "I'll scan this lot into the computer as well, and then I'll print everything off a couple of times, so we've got a set each. Then we need to decide what to do next, how to move it forwards. I suppose the best way is for you to get in touch with your liaison officer, from the PNCU, whom you dealt with when you first went to the police about Grant Hall, and he'll be able to take it forward from there."

"No, Mister," said Danny. "That's not possible. You see, the PNCU was disbanded a couple of years ago. Didn't you see it on the news? They said it wasn't cost effective, for the small number of cases they handled. All the responsibilities for that sort of thing went back to the local police forces. I don't know what Martin, he was my CLO, my child liaison officer, is doing now. I've got no means of getting in touch with him. He may not even be in the police any more. He was talking once about emigrating to Australia."

"Well then," said Alex, "we'll just have to go to the local police, that's all."

"Actually, no, Mister," responded Danny. "I'd rather we didn't do that."

"Why ever not?" asked Alex. "Surely they're the best people to handle it now?"

"No Mister, I don't think so." Danny looked a bit worried. "You see, I told Martin at the time, when the PNCU were investigating Hammond, long before the trial ever took place, about these cars which came at night, and he tried several times to get the local police to investigate it, and ask Hammond and the others about it. But he never got any feedback about it, none at all. I don't think they ever questioned anyone about it. Martin said to me once that he suspected they were trying not to do it, for whatever reason I don't know, but perhaps someone high up in the local police was involved, and wanted to keep it all quiet and brush it under the carpet. I don't think we should go there, or else it might just be filed and forgotten. We've got to do something better than that, find some other way of moving it forward."

"Well, I think, perhaps, that I agree with you," Alex replied. "So, what do you suggest?"

"Well, Mister, I don't really know," said Danny. "I really wish I did."

"Me too," said Alex. "I don't know either. But it's been several years now since the original trial. Perhaps the people who were blocking it are no longer in the police. Would you like to leave it with me while I have a think about how we can proceed? A few more days won't matter much, will they?"

"No, I suppose not," Danny shook his head. "As long as you reckon you can think of something in the end."

"Alright then, Danny, that's how we'll leave it or the moment. Trust me, I'll think of something. Now, I think there's a good comedy on the TV tonight. Fancy seeing that?"

Danny nodded. "Sure, Mister, that would be good. Let's watch that." Alex switched on the television, and found the film was just starting. It pleased Alex to see Danny laughing uproariously at the funny parts of the film. After visiting Grant Hall, it was just what was needed to push Danny's memories of Grant Hall back into the inner, forgotten, parts of his mind.

The next morning, Alex ran Danny back to the train station in the car, prior to returning it to the hire depot. They found that the car park at the train station was just about full, but Alex spotted a vacant space in the far corner. As they drew near, they could see that an abandoned shopping trolley from the nearby supermarket was blocking the space. "Leave it with me, Mister, I'll sort it," exclaimed Danny, as he opened the door and jumped out of the car. Moving the trolley out of the way , he stood to one side, then waved the car forward, calling out as he did so, "you can bring her in now, Mister,' at the same time grinning broadly. For Alex to hear Danny use that phrase, which had been such a standing joke between them both, brought from the back of Alex's mind perhaps the most enduring and endearing memories of that he had of Danny. It conjured up visions of

Danny at the lock-side, clad in shorts and tee shirt on a warm sunny summers day, with his fair hair waving slightly in the breeze, as he stood beside the open lock gate, windlass in one hand, and beckoning him to bring *Jennifer Jo* into the lock with the other.

Looking at Danny now as he stepped out of the car, Alex saw a fine young adult, self confident and self-assured, married with his own young daughter, making his way in the world with confidence, and with much to look forward to, but still all the while retaining his boyish charm. Alex had no doubt, no doubt at all, that of all the good things that he liked to think he'd achieved during his life, the decision to take in and care for the young, frightened, undernourished child who'd stowed away on his boat all those years ago, was one of the finest decisions he had ever made.

Once the car was parked, they walked together to the station, where they stopped near the barrier which gave access to the platforms. Danny stood there awkwardly beside it, unsmiling now, seemingly reluctant to go. Alex shook him by the hand. " Goodbye, Danny," he said, "and thank you for coming down this weekend. We've done really well."

Danny looked up at Alex. "Do you really think so?" he asked, solemnly, a worried look upon his face.

"Yes, Danny, I do," Alex replied. "I'll find a way to move this Grant Hall thing forward. Don't you worry. In the meantime, Danny, there's something I want to say to you before you go and catch your train."

"What's that then, Mister?" Danny asked.

"It's just this, Danny," Alex replied, serious for a moment. "Be proud. You've experienced difficult times, and some periods of great sadness in your young life, and this weekend has brought some memories of them back to you. But now is the time to look forward once again. Believe me when I tell you, you have much to be proud of. Your wife and your young daughter, your progress in your work, your rediscovery of your father even though it was for just a few days. You are doing well in life, and my hope for you is that you to continue to do so in the future. And always remember, you go with my best wishes." As he spoke, Alex stepped forward and gave Danny a brief embrace.

"Thanks, Mister," Danny responded, now smiling. "And thanks for letting me talk to you about it. It helped, it really did."

"That's fine, Danny," said Alex. "Now, you'd better go and get your train, before it leaves without you."

Danny nodded. "Bye, Mister," he said. "I'll keep in touch, like I always do. And, let me know what you decide to do, won't you?" Alex nodded as Danny strode confidently towards the entrance, head held high.

Alex got back into the car and returned it to the depot, then caught a bus back to the pub by the canal, from where it was just a short walk along the towpath back to *Jennifer Jo*. But as he unlocked the door and stepped inside, he felt a little guilty at having deceived Danny like he just had. He'd said that he'd move things forward, but he had absolutely no idea, none at all, as to how he was going to do that. But he knew that if he sat and thought about it, and kept it in the back of his mind, then in due course an idea would come into his head which might, just might, be worth following up. He could only sit and wait, until inspiration of some sort came to him.

CHAPTER 18

Alex had a light lunch, then started the boat's engine and steered *Jennifer Jo* along the canal for about half a mile to the water point, where he was surprised to see another boat was already in position, taking on a new supply of fresh water. Alex found that It had only just arrived, and he would have to wait for almost an hour before they'd finished and moved off. But that wait gave Alex the opportunity to have a chat with the people on board, who turned out to be holiday makers on their first ever boat trip on the canals, and the time passed quickly. After filling *Jennifer Jo's* fresh water tank to the brim, Alex turned the boat round at a nearby winding hole, and returned to his original location not far from the pub. He knew that he'd be able to stop there a few more days before it would become necessary to move on.

He went inside and made a cup of coffee, and sat thinking about how he could move the Grant Hall situation forward, but nothing came to mind. With no option available with either the police or the PNCU, it seemed that he would have to investigate it himself, and move it forward on his own, until he was able to provide incontrovertible evidence which the police would be unable to ignore. But how?

He sat at the dinette and took the newspaper he'd brought back to the boat after his haircut a few days before, and once again looked at the article about Grant Hall which had first caught his eye. After reading it through a couple of times, looking for inspiration, he noticed the by-line beneath the headline. 'By Robert Jefferies' it read. Alex remembered that name. It was the same reporter whom he'd seen many years ago on the television, when news of the trial and convictions had been widely reported. And suddenly, an idea came into Alex's head.

He was aware that journalists and reporters often had unconventional means of acquiring information which might not be available to ordinary people, so he reasoned that perhaps there might just be a chance that this man Jefferies might be able to point him in the right direction, or even find out something which he, Alex could not. Intrigued by this possibility, he scanned the paper for contact details, and, finding the news-desk phone number, he took out his mobile phone, keyed in the number, and sat patiently as the ring tone sounded. He didn't really expect a response, as it was a Saturday, but to his surprise, the ringtone suddenly stopped, and a voice said, "hello. Robert Jefferies."

"Oh, hello, Mr. Jefferies," Alex replied. "You don't know me, but I wondered if we could have a word together sometime?"

"Yes, of course," Jefferies replied. He always liked to follow-up strange approaches such as these. He knew that they could often lead to an interesting story for his newspaper. "Come into the office, I'm usually around there somewhere, if not they'll ask you to wait, and get in touch with me."

"Well, that's a bit awkward, as I don't have much in the way of transport," Alex said. "Is it possible you could come to me?"

"Well, where are you?" asked Jefferies.

"I'm near the Navigation pub, by the canal," Alex responded.

"Oh, I know it," Jefferies said. "As it happens, I'm coming by that way later on. I'm taking my two boys, I've got twins, 9 year-olds, to stay with their grandparents for the weekend. I could call in on the way back, if that suits you. It would be about 6.30 pm. Is that alright?"

"Yes, that's great," Alex replied. "I'll meet you there, in the pub car park, at half past six. Thank you ever so much."

At the appointed time, Alex walked the short distance along the towpath to the pub, but was surprised to see that the car park was almost full. But he hadn't been there more than a couple of minutes when a car drew up, and parked in one of the last available spaces. Alex walked over to the driver as he got out of the car. "Mr. Jefferies?" he asked.

"Yes, that's right," said Jefferies. "But call me Bob. Most people do."

"Thank you, Bob. I'm Alex," and Alex went on to introduce himself. Then, indicating the pub with a flick of his head, he added "it's a bit busy in there for a quiet chat. Do you mind if we go to my place?"

"No, not at all," replied Bob. They walked out of the car park onto the towpath, and Alex led the way back to *Jennifer Jo*. "Is this boat yours, then?" Bob asked, as Alex stepped onto the rear deck and unlocked the door.

"Yes, that's right," replied Alex. I bought this when I finished work. I used to be a schoolteacher, but when I retired about 10 years ago, my wife and I decided to have this built to spend our retirement on. Unfortunately, my wife died before it was finished, so I live on her on my own now. Live-aboards like me are often called water gypsies, as we're moving around most of the time."

Bob nodded. "I'm sorry about your wife," he said. "But now I see what you mean about not having much transport." He paused a moment before adding "I don't really know much about the canal, I'm afraid. I only just about know we've got one here."

"Well, not many people do, actually," replied Alex. "The pub here is called 'The Navigation', because of the workmen who dug out the canals by hand 200 years ago, using just pick and shovel, with horse-drawn carts to take away the spoil. They were called 'Navigators', which is where our current term 'navvies' comes from. Actually, 'The Navigation' is by far the most popular name for a canal-side pub, by a long way. The canals creep through the towns and cities, behind the backs of the factories and warehouses which they were built to serve, and very few people really know the canal is there. And out in the country, the canals mainly go through open countryside, behind tall hedges, skirting round even the smallest villages."

"So can you go far, then?" Bob asked, obviously intrigued.

"Oh, yes," Alex responded. "There's over 2000 miles of canals and inland waterways in this country. North, South, East, West, you name it, the canals are everywhere if you know where to look for them. The canal system goes all over the place. And canals which were abandoned many years ago are now being restored and re-opened, opening up new possibilities all the time. It's an interesting period for the canals now, a bit of a renaissance really. But come on inside."

Alex stepped down into the boat, and beckoned Bob to follow him through to the saloon. "Here, take a seat at the dinette," Alex suggested, and as Bob sat down, Alex moved to the fridge. "We're not in the pub, but that doesn't stop us having a drink. Would you like a beer?"

"I'd love one," Bob replied. "But I'm driving. I can't afford to lose my licence. A coffee would be nice, though."

Alex put the kettle on the stove to boil, and then sat down at the dinette opposite Bob, who asked, "now, what's this all about, then?"

Alex paused for a moment. Given the delicacy of what he was about to ask, he knew that he needed to choose his words carefully. He didn't want to spoil this opportunity to move things forward. But eventually he spoke. "I just wondered if you could help me with something," he asked eventually.

"So, what do you need help with?" Bob asked curiously.

Alex took a piece of paper which he'd printed out from his computer earlier that afternoon, which bore the list of 13 car numbers which he and Danny had decoded from the papers in the tobacco tin the day before. "I need to find out who these cars belong to," he said quietly.

To his surprise, Bob sat back and started laughing. "You can't be serious," he said, as he pushed the paper aside, without giving it even a cursory glance. "Do you know what you're asking for? The only people who can access the DVLA computers in Swansea to find out this sort of thing are police officers, plus a few selected top level senior council officials. Even if I was to ask any of them to find out this sort of thing for me, which I'm not prepared to do, they'd almost certainly lose their jobs because of it. You see, every time a police officer logs on or uses his computer at the police station to check anything, it's all logged. Every enquiry they make, everything. And when the logs are checked, if they can't justify that what they're looking for is in connection with a current enquiry, then they'll be for the high jump. It's just not possible. No way."

After pausing for a moment, he added, "what's this all about, anyway? What exactly are you up to?" looking up at Alex as he spoke.

Alex didn't reply. Instead, he took the newspaper which he'd taken from the hairdresser's van a few days before, opened it at the page which carried the article about Grant Hall, and without speaking, laid it on the table in front of Jefferies.

"Yes, that's my article," Jefferies said. "I wrote that. So what?"

Once again, Alex didn't speak, but quietly tapped the photograph of Grant Hall in the paper. "Yes, I know," Bob said. "It's going to be a care home for old people, or senior citizens, as they say these days. That's old news now. It's been empty for some years now, ever since the children's home that used to be there was closed down. The guy who ran it, Hambles his name was – no, no, Hammond, that's right, well, he got put away, he wasn't being very nice to the kids who lived there. In fact, if you believe all the accounts of life there, which came out at the trial, he made things quite unpleasant for the kids. I seem to remember he got six years, but he's out now."

"It all came out when some kid who was there, well, he ran off, and they never found him. There was a huge hunt for him, but despite that, he completely disappeared. Until, that is, about a year later, he walks into a police station up in the North somewhere, bold as brass, and makes these accusations against Hammond and the other people who helped him run Grant Hall. Apparently the kid was living up there with his mother, but he'd only been there for just a few weeks, before he went to the cops. It seems that the kid had run off from Grant Hall before, but they got him back after a couple of days, then a few weeks later, he's off again, but this time he gets clean away, they don't find him."

"They still don't know how that boy got away, how he did it. All round here, stretching for miles, there's these CCTV cameras, everywhere is under surveillance, being watched all the time. Not just towns either, villages, landscapes, everywhere. And they've got all these ANPR cameras as well, you know, Automatic Number Plate Recognition cameras, they're everywhere now, on all the main roads, and all the lanes and country roads too. They're disguised as lamp-posts, so most people don't even know they're there, or where they are."

"The police tell everyone that they're just to get the car numbers, and to catch those which aren't licensed or haven't got insurance, but what they don't tell you is that they also look at the driver's face, and the front passenger too, and check them against their computer databases. Depending on the angle the camera looks at the car, they quite often get the rear seat passengers as well. If that boy had left by car, or on foot, walking along the road, or even across the fields, they'd have got him. But he got clean away. They've still got no idea how he managed to get away and evade capture."

"The authorities up North asked around, asked all the neighbours who lived near his mother, and they all said the same thing, that the boy had suddenly appeared there a few weeks before. And they asked at the kid's school too, he'd started there the week after he appeared at his mother's place. But the teachers said that they'd had no concerns about him at all, he'd obviously been well looked after and well cared for, he'd been well fed and wasn't skinny or anything. It would still have shown if he'd been living rough or anything, but it was obvious he hadn't been. And how did he get from here to his mother's, that's more than two hundred miles, as I remember? Although the cops kept asking both the kid and his mother as well, whom they were sure knew all about it, they wouldn't tell. Neither of them would."

Just then, the kettle on the stove began to whistle, and Alex got up to make the coffee. While he did so, Bob stood up and had a good look round the saloon. "Nice and cosy in here," he said, as he looked out of the windows, examined the books on the shelf by the television, and studied the pictures hanging on the wall.

But then, as Alex set the coffee mugs on the dinette table and Bob Jefferies sat down again, opposite Alex, Bob leant forward and spoke again, very quietly. "It was you, wasn't it?" he asked.

"What do you mean?" Alex replied, suddenly a little nervous.

"It was you who helped that boy, wasn't it?" Bob repeated. "Helped him get away, take him up North? To his mother's place?"

"What on earth made you think that?" Alex asked, shaking his head.

"You practically told me yourself," Bob replied. "Like I said, if he'd made it away by car, or a van, or even across the fields, they'd have spotted him, and nabbed him. But as you just said yourself, the canal goes round the backs of the warehouses and factories, no-one knows they're there, you said. It has to be an ideal way to spirit a young kid away, who doesn't want to be found by the authorities, from right under their noses."

Bob paused for a short while before continuing. "And there's other clues too, if you look a little bit harder. For some reason you're interested in Grant Hall, where the kid ran off from. Why, I ask myself? Then there's the school books on your bookshelf. You say you retired from teaching ten years ago. Then why are there school textbooks on your shelf? 'Elementary Science'? 'Mathematics for Years 7 and 8'? 'GCSE Geography'? And a few others as well. Not many, but just right for teaching a kid of the age he would have been when he ran off. They're the same books my two boys use at school now, they bring them home when they've got homework to do." He raised his hand and pointed at the wall near the galley. "And to cap it all, there's a picture on the wall, over there, with you and the kid sitting on the balance beam of a lock. And over there, above the television, there's another, the two of you are working the boat through a lock, by the look of it."

He turned and pointed at the picture above the television, the picture Danny had given him as a Christmas present, the Christmas that he's spent on *Jennifer Jo* with Alex. And the first picture Bob had spotted was the one which Alex had found hidden under Danny's mattress after he'd left *Jennifer Jo* to live with his mother. Alex had proudly had them both on the wall of the boat ever since Danny had given them to him. Although he was well familiar with the scenes they portrayed, he looked at them again as Bob continued. "I sat through all the two weeks of the trial, and that kid gave evidence in court, face to face with Hammond, staring at him most of the time. He was in the witness box for a whole day, he was, maybe more. And a really good witness he was too, the defence counsel tried to trip him up several times, but he stuck to his guns, I'll say that for him. I'd recognise him again anywhere. They're really good pictures, though. Did you do them?"

"No, he did," Alex blurted out, before instantly realised that by what he'd just said, he'd well and truly given the game away. But Bob just sat back and laughed.

"It always works," he said, still smiling. "Sneak in the simplest, most innocent question when they're least expecting it, and you usually get the answer they didn't really want to give."

Alex nodded. He would have to admit to his part in Danny's escapade. "Yes, it was me," he said eventually, after a long pause.

"You're really lucky, then," Bob replied.

"How do you mean?" Alex asked curiously.

"Well, as I remember it, the police up North, they gave the case on to the PCNU. It was them that handled it. The local cops, they had to do what they were told. If the police up North had just passed it on directly to the local force here, without the PCNU getting involved, well they'd have come after you, make no mistake about that. They'd have leant on the kid till he told them all about you. They'd have put you away for sure, you know, for abducting a child, that sort of thing. And they'd probably have bullied the boy into saying that you interfered with him as well. And that would have added years to your sentence, they don't like that sort of thing. Like I said, Hammond was let out years ago. But you'd probably still be serving time now."

Jefferies paused for a moment, drinking his coffee. "So, now, these car numbers. I presume they've got something to do with Grant Hall?"

Alex hesitated. "I don't know if I can tell you," he replied. "I don't want it all over the front page tomorrow."

Bob shook his head. "No, that's not how we work here," he said. "Not on my watch, anyway. We're only a small local paper. We don't print anything until it's been confirmed, checked and then double-checked again. If we got it wrong and someone took us to court, that would be curtains for us. Even if we won, the legal costs would be crippling. So, we don't publish anything until we're absolutely sure about every single thing in whatever article we print."

Bob paused again, draining his cup before continuing. "I'd been onto the case at Grant Hall for a long while," he said. "Many years before it was closed and Hammond was in court, in fact. I'd always had my suspicions that there was something else going on there, apart from what came out at the trial. Am I right in thinking this might be something to do with that?"

Alex nodded. "I'll tell you all about it," he said. "But please, please, don't publish it."

Bob shook his head. "Tell you what," he offered. "I'll only publish it if this comes to something. After all, what you did, looking after that kid, well, it's old news now. If something new comes of it, then I'll come and see you, do an interview with you, or something like that. Is that alright?"

"I'm not sure," Alex said, his mind full of doubt.

"You've got to trust me on this," Bob replied. "Otherwise we're not going to get anywhere."

"Alright, then," Alex agreed, after a long pause. "This is what happened." They sat together for almost an hour, as Alex recounted how he'd come to take in Danny after finding out from the boy about life and abuse at Grant Hall, and how Danny had lived with him for a year, travelling the canal network on *Jennifer Jo,* before going to live with his mother, and how they'd met up again a few months previously. He finished by describing how he and Danny had gone to Grant Hall, bluffed their way in, and retrieved the tobacco tin with the car numbers encoded onto the pieces of paper hidden in the tin. When he'd finished, he sat there silently, waiting for Bob's response.

"Thanks for telling me all this," he said eventually. "It was a very brave thing to do. I admire you for what you've done. As I said earlier, I've got two boys of my own, they're really happy little kids, but perhaps they're not quite so little now as they used to be. I'd hate to think they'd have had to live at Grant Hall while all that was going on. Just think of those poor boys who were there, having to live in a closed environment like that, in a climate of fear, intimidation, and continual violence towards them, with no-one to turn to, no-one to speak out for them and protect them. It must have been a perfect place for the perverts to go to, to interfere with the kids, carry out that sort of abuse, all sorts of things. They must have loved it. But I bet the kids didn't."

"I can understand the choice you made," he went on. "I'd like to think that I'd have done the same."

As he spoke, he reached out his hand and picked up the paper with the car numbers on it, the paper he'd brushed aside without a glance a little earlier. Alex watched his face intently as he read through the numbers on the list. He was sure that Bob recognised at least a couple of the numbers, as his eyes narrowed slightly several times as he scanned down the page.

"But, tell me, why haven't you gone to the police with this?" Bob asked, as he put the paper down on the table once again.

"Well, our first thought was to go to the PNCU again," Alex told him. "But I understand that they've been disbanded now."

Bob nodded. "Yes that's right," he replied. "They didn't get enough cases to justify the cost of maintaining a separate nation-wide outfit like that. Loads of skilled detectives and so on, sitting about all the time, with not a lot to do. Perhaps there aren't as many pervs about as they thought there were."

"So, we discussed it, Danny and I," Alex continued, "about going to the local police. But Danny felt a bit dubious about that. He'd gained the impression, during the original investigation, which was overseen by the PNCU, that the local police here, who did a lot of the ground work for the PNCU, he suspected that they weren't particularly keen to follow it up. He had this suspicion that they were trying to shelve it, hoping that it would go away. Which it did of course, after Hammond's trial and conviction. Danny's liaison officer from the PNCU told him that without something else for them to go on, there wouldn't be sufficient evidence to make it worthwhile."

"No," Bob responded. "The local police here, they've got a bit of a reputation for being, how shall I say, a little bit less than diligent, when they're asked to investigate things they don't really want to."

"But now we have this additional evidence to move it forward," Alex continued. "But how exactly, we just don't know. That's why I called you. I thought you might be able to point us in the right direction, to help us find out how to find the drivers of these cars." Alex picked up the paper and handed it back to Jefferies.

"Leave it with me," Jefferies added after a pause, as he carefully folded the paper and slipped it into his jacket pocket. "I'll see what I can do. I'll be by again in a fortnight, my boys go to their Grandparents for a sleepover every couple of weeks. Saturday fortnight, then. Same time, same place?"

"Well, yes and no," Alex replied. "But let me explain. Every boat on the canal has to have a licence, and because I'm on the move all the time, without a permanent mooring, the licence I have is called a 'Continuous Cruising Licence.' Under the terms of the licence, I cannot stay in the same place for more than 14 days, and in some places much less than that, sometimes only 48 hours. I've been here several days already, so I need to move on before you come back. But what I'll do, I'll cruise up the canal for a few days, there's a boatyard about three or four days away, where I can get some more gas for the stove, and some diesel, and a few other things I need. Then I'll come back and moor up along this stretch somewhere, not far from the pub. So I'll certainly be here when you return, but not necessarily in exactly the same place. Is that alright? But I can meet you in the pub car park like we did this time. Would that be alright for you? I'll give you my mobile number so you can get in touch earlier if you need to."

"Yes, that's fine," Bob replied. "Have a nice few days, the weather forecast is set to be good all this coming week anyway. And thanks for the coffee. Bye." And with that, he got up and made his way to the back of the boat, and before Alex had a chance to say goodbye, he'd stepped off the boat and was walking back along the towpath back to his car. Alex watched him go, with a certain amount of misgiving. Could he trust this reporter Jefferies not to splash it all on the front page? Would he able to find out any information about the car numbers? Alex felt mildly anxious, but he quickly realised that the cat was now well and truly out of the bag. There was nothing that he could do now, except sit and wait, and see what transpired.

It was a full 13 days later that Alex returned to a mooring not far from the Navigation pub. He'd carried out all the tasks he'd set himself, and whilst at the boatyard, he'd met a couple of live-aboards whom he'd met a number of times over the past few years. He'd last seen them on the canal system on the Kennet & Avon Canal three or four years before. They'd spent several congenial evenings together reminiscing about the places they'd visited, about interesting people whom they'd all met at one time or another, and talking about all things canals and boats. But it was with a certain amount of trepidation when, the next day, Alex walked along the towpath to meet Bob Jefferies once again. Would he have kept his part of the bargain? Would he even turn up at all? As Alex waited anxiously, he was relieved to see Bob Jefferies' car turn into the car park, and wave him a greeting as he parked his car.

"Hi, Alex," he called out a greeting as he stepped out of his car. "Just dropped the boys off. It's their Gran's birthday tomorrow, so they're a bit excited. They always are for birthdays, I don't know why. You get too many of them, if you ask me. I'd rather stay 42 all the time, if you ask me."

Alex smiled, as they walked back to *Jennifer Jo* along the towpath. Once inside the boat, Bob sat down at the dinette, while Alex made the coffee. Setting the mugs down on the table, Alex sat down opposite Bob and enquired quietly, "Well? Did you manage to find out anything?"

Bob smiled, and paused for a long, long moment, before replying. "Alex," he said at last, "If this is what you say it is, and I'll make it clear right now that I, for one, do believe what you've told me, then this is dynamite. No wonder it was suppressed."

"So you've managed to find out who these drivers were, then?" Alex asked.

Bob nodded. "Yes, he said. "I called in a few favours. Well, quite a few actually. And one or two people stuck their necks out for me, quite a long way in fact, once I'd found out the first two or three, and chivvied the others up a bit."

"So you've found out who they were, then?" Alex asked, quite pleased that he was at last getting somewhere.

Bob nodded once again. "Yes," he said, taking the paper out of his pocket and placing in on the table in front of them. "On here you've got a solicitor. A bank manager. A company director. A police officer, and not a lowly constable either. A magistrate. And a few others too. Like a councillor, and a doctor. Plus a few more top people. Out of the 13 numbers you gave me, I got 12 names. The 13th was blocked."

"So how did you manage to get this information, then?" Alex asked, curiously. "When we first met, you told me that it wouldn't be possible. 'No way', I think you said. So how come you've been able to get it after all?"

"Well, of course I'd say that at first," Bob replied, smiling broadly. "You don't think I'd just tell a complete stranger, as you were to me a couple of weeks ago, that I could perhaps access confidential information do you? That's bending the law, and it's not the sort of thing anyone would easily admit to. It's only because this is about Grant Hall, and about people messing about with the young kids who were there, that I felt it worthwhile following up. But there are ways and means, if you know how."

"So, exactly how, then?" Alex persisted.

"Well, Bob replied, still grinning broadly. "You've heard of the three-card trick?"

Alex nodded as Bob continued. "Well, it's not that exactly. We used the wild-card trick, or at least the people who cracked this for me did. You see, when anyone logs onto the police computers and makes an enquiry about a car number, then it's logged, who, when, where, etc. That's how the people in charge can find out who's been accessing that information. But sometimes, you see, whoever's making the enquiry hasn't got a complete number. Perhaps the number-plate was dirty, or maybe a victim only got a fleeting glance before the car which hit them drove off. Then it's an incomplete number. What they do then, they put in the parts of the number which they do know, and then put an asterisk in for the characters they don't know. The asterisk is what they call a wild card. The computer then displays all the numbers which contain the known characters in their right order, plus the wild card. So, for example, take this first one on the list, SPV399. Let's say the last 9 is actually the unknown character. So they type in SPV39*, and the system spits out all the numbers in the range SPV390 to SPV399. But the search is only shown as SPV39*. It doesn't show up as a search on the individual record for the actual number, which in this case is SPV399 of course."

"I'm starting to see how you did it, then," smiled Alex."

There's more," Bob replied, still smiling. "Most of these cars are local to this area. But none of the enquiries into the computer were made in this area. I've got my contacts in other areas too, as well as this one. I gave each of them just one number, only one, that's so they only had to make just the one enquiry. They all took a risk on my behalf, but the risk for them is reduced by their only going after one number, instead of a whole bunch of them."

"That's very good," Alex thanked him. "So," he continued, as he took out a piece of paper and a pen from his stationery drawer, "who exactly are these people then?"

Bob grinned again. "No, Alex, it doesn't work like that. I can't tell you. This information is confidential, and the means by which it was obtained is, shall we say, rather unorthodox, a little questionable. You've got to understand that if it gets out, and they start trying to find out how and where this information came from, then I'm finished, and so are a lot of my contacts too. I'm sorry."

Alex was dumbfounded. "So, where do we go from here?" he asked quietly. "Is this the end of the road?"

Bob didn't answer. Instead, he stood up and went to the window, looking out at a fisherman sitting on the opposite back with his young son, their rods and gossamer-thin lines dangling out over the water. "There's always people out fishing along the canal, isn't there?" he asked.

"Yes," Alex agreed, "especially in the summer, on a nice evening like this."

"Do you fish much?" Bob asked. "Got a rod and line, all that sort of stuff? After all, you're right close and handy, being on the boat all the time, aren't you?"

"Well, yes," replied Alex, wondering where Jefferies was going with this line of conversation. "It's tucked away in one of the lockers, underneath my bed. But to be honest, I don't fish very much. It seems such a waste of time, just sitting about all day, waiting for something to happen, and with nothing much to show for it in the end. Fishing's often been called the best ever excuse for sitting around doing nothing. The trouble is, on the canals, the kingfishers and other predators take most of the fish. They're never left swimming around long enough to grow to a decent size. Very few people catch anything more than a few tiddlers. But I suppose it can be fun if you're a young lad, like that boy over there with his father."

"You ought to take it up again," observed Bob. "Especially on Monday."

"Why Monday in particular?" asked Alex. "What's special about

Monday?"

"Well," Bob replied. "If you were to go fishing on Monday, just past that bridge just after the garden centre, you might find someone else sitting there fishing as well, someone who would like you to talk to him."

"So who is this person, then?" Alex asked, curious to find out what Bob had planned.

"His name is Rudolph Ampersandi," Bob replied. "But don't be fooled by his name. He's just about as British as you and me. His name comes from his great-great grandfather Antonio, who came to England in the 1920's, just after the first world war. Antonio set up a small factory making ice cream, with a shop next door to go with it. He did very well, ending up with several shops and cafes and several mobile vans selling ice cream as well. After he'd been here for a few years, he applied for British citizenship, and when it was granted, the day he got the letter in the post from the authorities, he was so pleased, he gave all the kids who went into his shops, and all those who bought ice-creams off his vans, well, they all had free ice cream, just for that day. That year, It coincided with the last day of term before the schools' summer holidays. The firm's still going strong today, it's Rudolph's elder brother George who runs the ice cream business now. But, ever since then, every year, without fail, on the last day of summer term, all the kids get given free ice creams. And they all love him for it."

"So, how is this Rudolph Ampersandi going to help with this, then?" asked Alex.

"Well, I'm coming to that," Bob smiled. "Rudolph, well actually most people call him Ralph, he went to university after leaving school, took two degrees at once, in aeronautics and electronics, I think they were. Then he joined the Royal Air Force, where he was for about 8 years, during which time he took another degree, in sociology. He's a clever kiddo, there's no doubt about that. Then, after the RAF he joined the police force. He used to be an inspector here, in this division. He's alright, we had a nice arrangement going between us."

Alex's eyes narrowed. "I don't want to get involved with anyone who's bent the law," he said anxiously. "But forgetting what you've already done about the car numbers, that is."

"No, it was nothing like that," Bob went on. "You see, years ago, I got wind of a story. But I needed some sort of confirmation, before my editor would clear it for publication, so I contacted the press office, and was passed on to Ampersandi. He was the inspector on the case. He confirmed what I already knew, which would have been enough for me to proceed, but then he asked if I could delay publishing the story for a few days, because the suspects he was investigating would have scarpered, had they got wind that someone knew about what was going on, they'd have sussed that the cops were after them."

"So I agreed, and a couple of days later, Ralph gives me a call, and suggests that I be in a certain place at a certain time, with a photographer in tow. So there I was, and we witnessed the whole chase and arrest. It made a great story, especially having pictures to go with it as well. And we helped each other out like that several times since then. Certainly nothing more than that."

"Anyway, he's on gardening leave right now, and he likes fishing. He's been a Chief Superintendent on our neighbouring force to the East for several years, but he's just been appointed to be the new Chief Constable for our patch. He's taking over at the start of next month. His previous post as Chief Superintendent was terminated early, before his new position was free, to let their new guy take over."

"So, will this guy Ampersandi be OK?" Alex asked. "I don't want it to be hidden under the carpet again."

"No," Bob shook his head. "He's a straight, by-the-book guy. He's got a bit of a reputation as a zero tolerance man. I'll give you an example, back from when he was an inspector here. There's a number of council estates on the patch he used to run. Most of the people who lived there were decent, law-abiding people. But there was a lot of petty crime. You know, taking cars, joyriding, thieving, break-ins, muggings, the occasional sexual assault. Plus loads of graffiti, vandalism, a bit of dealing, that sort of thing. Well, Ralph, he put just eight officers into the patch, just two on each shift, 24/7. They spent all their time on the estate, starting by concentrating on vehicles, cars and vans, motorbikes as well. They'd go round, checking every single car, the licence, insurance, MOT, tyres, ineffective silencers, you name it, if they found it they'd book the guy and give him a ticket, no messing. Everyone got a ticket. No exceptions."

"These tactics at first got up the noses of a lot of people, who felt they were being unfairly victimised. For example, there's a primary school in the middle of the estate, and the road outside is quite narrow, so the council had put double yellow lines down both sides of the road for about 100 yards each side of the school. However, all the parents dropping off their kids in the morning, and collecting them in the afternoon, they just ignored the double yellows, parking wherever they fancied, and because the road was so narrow they pulled all their cars onto the footpaths, so the cars obstructed the paths, and those kids who walked to school had to walk along in the middle of the road. It was chaos. All this despite there being a free public car park less than 5 minutes walk away."

"So he put a couple of coppers out there every morning and afternoon, and got them to give a ticket to every single vehicle parked on the double yellows. Some parents got 10 tickets in the course of the first week, and so they kicked up a stink and complained. They asked for a meeting with Ampersandi, and bitched to him about it. Ampersandi's answer to them was that the double yellows were there for a reason, and by parking their vehicles there they were breaking the law, and asked them why they thought the law didn't apply to them. He told them that just because they'd been getting away with it for so long, it didn't mean that they could carry on ignoring their responsibilities to obey the law."

"Eventually the penny dropped, and it became much better round there, and much safer for the kids as well. I dare say the kids benefitted too, from walking to and from the car park, they never seem to get enough exercise these days. The cops went for everything they could find on that estate. People riding their bikes on the pavement, parking their cars on the wrong side of the road at night, riding a bike at night without lights, you name it, he did them for it. Wherever possible he had them in court, to embarrass them, not just letting them get away with a ticket or a fine through the post."

"But that wasn't all. Everyone who got given a ticket, the cops went round to their house, and asked to come in and talk to them about it, that was so they could have a look round without the people realising it. If they were let in, then usually they'd find nothing and be on their way after a few minutes. But if they were refused entry, then the cops would go and see the magistrate, who was very accommodating, and get a search warrant, on the grounds that they guy must have something to hide. Within a few months, the crime in that area dropped to about one-tenth of what it used to be. And all with just two coppers on the patch at any one time."

"So then he pulled all but two off that patch, and put them on the next one. The 2 coppers who were left there managed to keep the crime levels down to what they'd dropped to, and then the same tactics were put into place in the next patch. Within a couple of years the whole place was one of the safest in the country. This guy is the right one for you, don't worry. Most people round here acknowledge that in the years since then after Ampersandi moved on, things have got a bit slack, and Ampersandi has been parachuted in, to tighten things up. And he will."

"On Monday, talk to him, tell him everything you've told me, and he'll do the business, don't worry about that. And he'll need a statement as well, of course. But that's something you can sort out with him."

"Thanks, Bob," Alex said, "for fixing that up. But there's one thing that I still want to ask you. You said you couldn't trace one of the cars. Something about the number being blocked. What do you mean by that?"

"Well," replied Bob. "The guy who checked that particular number, what he does, he keys in the number with the wild card, like how I told you, but when he gets up the screen with the range of applicable numbers, well, there's no information displayed for the one we're interested in. There's just a message giving a phone number to contact at the Home Office, because special authorisation is required to access that information. Needless to say, our guy logged off at that point, he wasn't going to go any further, and I don't blame him, that was without doubt the right thing to do."

"So why would that number be blocked? " Alex asked. "I don't understand."

"Yes, that's the question," replied Bob. "But I suspect that particular number is a government car. Used by a government minister. I told you there were some top people on the list. You don't get much more top than that. But I just don't know."

Bob paused for a moment, before continuing. "Anyway, I must go. I'll be in touch, to see how you got on with Ampersandi." Bob rose from his seat and walked to the back of the boat, then, turning to Alex as he stepped out onto the towpath, he added, "Ampersandi's all right. You can trust him. He'll follow this up, don't you worry." And with that last remark, he turned and walked off down the towpath, back to the pub where he'd parked his car.

Alex stood and watched Jefferies as he went. It seemed that he'd been right to trust Bob with his story about Grant Hall, but it remained to be seen how things would turn out. He went back inside *Jennifer Jo* and washed up the coffee cups, then took out his laptop and wrote an email to Danny, giving him a brief update about what had happened. Having clicked on the 'send button' he opened his web browser and did a search for Rudolph Ampersandi. To his surprise he found quite a number of links.

First he looked at Ampersandi's biography. It confirmed everything that Bob Jefferies had told him, and much more besides. It also showed a photograph of Ampersandi, taken only a few weeks before, on the news of his appointment to be the new Chief Constable of the local force. Alex studied it closely, so that he would be sure to recognise Ampersandi on the Monday, when he hopefully would find him sitting beside the canal, fishing rod in hand. On the web, there were also links to two books Ampersandi had published, about policing in the 21st century. More disturbing was a link to a civil liberties website, which complained that the zero tolerance tactics which Ampersandi advocated were a heavy-handed abuse of his powers. But Alex also found other comments as well, mostly favourable, from the residents of the areas where Ampersandi's policies had been implemented, saying that he'd transformed their areas from a place where ordinary people were afraid to go out at night, into a pleasant neighbourhood in which to live.

He was just putting his laptop away when his mobile phone rang. It was Danny. "I just got your email, Mister. Well done," he congratulated Alex. "It was a good idea, to get this guy Jefferies involved. It's great, what you've managed to do. Let's hope this guy Ampersandi comes up with the goods."

"Yes, Danny, I really hope so," Alex told him. "But I've just had a look on the net, he seems to be alright. You have a look as well. But we'll just have to wait and see. Anyway, how's the family?"

"They're all fine," Danny replied proudly. "And Jenny's growing every day, she's lovely."

Alex chatted with Danny for another ten minutes or so before they said goodbye to each other. "I'll let you know how I get on, on Monday, Danny," Alex said in farewell. "Wish me luck."

"Of course, Mister, Danny replied. "And enjoy your fishing, won't you?" Alex smiled as he switched off his mobile and put it away. Danny was on the ball, as usual.

The next morning, Sunday, Alex sat over his breakfast and thought about what he had to do the next day. Suddenly he realised that Ampersandsi would need something more than just what Alex was going to tell him whilst they sat fishing together, something altogether a bit more tangible. Almost certainly, he wouldn't take any action on just Alex's word of mouth. He would need a written statement, Alex realised, and without that, Ampersandi would be reluctant to proceed further, however serious were the allegations that were made.

He took out his trusty laptop, and spent most of the day writing up his statement, confirming all that he proposed to say to Ampersandi the following day, recounting all that had happened since that very first day he'd come across Danny stowed away in the cratch aboard *Jennifer Jo*. After printing it out, Alex pinned the sheets together, then printed off a copy of all the scans he'd made of the scraps of paper he and Danny had found in the tobacco tin during their clandestine visit to Grant Hall. Then he delved into the locker under his bed, took out his fishing gear, checked it out, and made it ready for the next morning. He had no bait, but hopefully Ampersandi would bring some, and let him use some of his.

After an early supper, Alex went up onto the rear deck with a cup of coffee, to relax and enjoy the cool of the early evening. It had been a warm day, and the sun was now starting to dip below the line of weeping willow trees which lined the offside bank. As he sat on the rear rail and enjoyed the view, he spotted a couple of young lads, aged about thirteen or fourteen, walking back along the towpath towards the pub car park, carrying their fishing gear with them. Alex recalled seeing them being dropped off from a car which had pulled into the pub's car park earlier that morning.

"Caught anything much?" he enquired of them as they drew level with him.

"Nah," the older of the two boys replied. "A few tiddlers, that's all. But Andy here, he got a nice tench. About a pound and a half, we guessed. But we threw it back, of course. But it's been a nice day to sit out. Better than being at home, my mum and dad row all the time these days."

"Yes, it's been quite pleasant today," hasn't it?" Alex replied. "I'm going to try my hand tomorrow, to see what I can catch. But, may I ask you please, I need some bait, maggots preferably. Do you know where I can get any?"

"Yes, there's a fishing shop in town which sells them," Andy, the younger of the two lads, replied. "But it's quite a way from here. But we won't be fishing tomorrow, as we're back to school on Monday. You can have the rest of ours, if you like. Hey, Billy, that's alright, isn't it?" As he spoke he dug into his bag and handed Alex a tin, lifting the lid as he did so. "Here you are," he said, "there should be enough to last you most of the day, If you're careful with them."

"That's very good of you," Alex replied. "May I pay you for them please?"

"No, don't bother," Billy, the older lad, replied. "We'll only throw them into the water anyway. You may as well have them. And anyway, we're always told not to accept money from strange men, if you know what I mean."

"Yes, I'm afraid I do," Alex replied, as the two boys turned to each other and started laughing and giggling together. Obviously they'd been well briefed about 'stranger danger'.

"But, what about a licence? I'll need one for tomorrow," Alex asked. He well knew the rules about fishing. Fishing from the back of

'Jennifer Jo' was allowed by the terms of his boat's licence to cruise the waterways, but anyone fishing from the bank needed a licence, as local angling clubs paid large fees to the waterway authorities to reserve the fishing for their own members. But most clubs were happy to sell day licences as well.

"We're members of the local Angling Society," Andy replied. "They do special rates for junior members. So we've got a licence for all the year round, both of us have, for the open season anyway. But I'm sure they sell day licences at the pub, over there," he added, pointing towards the pub. "And there's a Garden Centre, a bit further along, they do them as well."

Just them they heard the sound of a car horn in the distant car park. "Hey, Andy, your dad's here," Billy interjected, turning back to Alex. "We've got to go, sorry. You're welcome to the maggots. Bye." And they walked off, back to where their lift was waiting for them.

The next morning after breakfast, Alex made a couple of sandwiches for his lunch, then locked up *Jennifer Jo* and walked along the towpath to the Garden Centre, where he purchased his day licence for his fishing. And then, returning to the towpath, sure enough, just beyond the bridge past the Garden Centre, Alex found a middle-aged gentleman, sitting on a stool with his fishing rod stretched out over the water. After hesitating for a moment, Alex went up to him, and asked "Do you mind if I join you? It seems like you've chosen a good spot."

The fisherman turned and looked at Alex, who instantly recognised him as Ampersandi from the photographs he'd seen on the internet. "Yes of course," he replied. "Once the sun moves round a bit and there's some shade under those trees on the opposite bank, that's where the fish will congregate. Sit here," he added, indicating a nice patch of grass to his right hand side.

Alex sat down and assembled his fishing gear, then cast his float out over the water. They sat there together in silence for about ten minutes, broken only by the passing on the water of a couple of brightly-painted narrowboats, before Ampersandi said quietly, "I'm Rudolph Ampersandi, by the way. But most people call me Ralph." He paused for a moment before continuing. "I understand that you have something you want to tell me. I must say I've got no idea, no idea at all, what this is all about, but our mutual friend told me that it would be well worth listening to you. So, please go ahead when you're ready. I'm all yours."

Alex paused for a moment. He'd thought that Bob Jefferies would have told him the main gist of his story about Grant Hall. But, on quick reflection, he realised that Bob had been wise not to say anything. If he knew how far Bob's enquiries had gone, Amersandsi might suspect that Jefferies had acquired information, confidential information, by questionable means. It was much better that Bob kept his information to himself. Ampersandi, Alex figured, would be able to find out the same information about the drivers of the cars, and by the proper official means to boot.

"Well," Alex started, "it all started about 8 or 9 years ago, when I found a stowaway on my boat. You see, I live on a narrowboat, I'm what's called a liveaboard. And one afternoon, not that far from here, actually, I was working my boat through a lock when ...."

Alex spent most of the morning telling how he'd first met Danny, a frightened young boy on the run from the abuse he'd been subjected to at Grant Hall, and how he'd taken the lad into his care on *Jennifer Jo* for the better part of a year, before had Danny left the boat to live with his mother. He went on to describe how during that time he'd gradually gained Danny's confidence, and how he'd given the boy a thorough schooling in the meantime. He told of the huge coincidence when he'd met Danny again, and finished with an account of their recent visit to Grant Hall to recover the tobacco tin with its contents still inside. All the while, as Alex recounted his story, Ampersandi listened carefully, only interrupting now and then to clarify a point.

As Alex finished, Ampersandi sat quietly for a minute or two before speaking. "Thank you so much for telling me all this," he said to Alex. I'm sure you know who I am, and what my new job is, which I start next month. I can assure you that this will be followed up, as a matter of urgency. But be warned, whilst we will busy on this behind the scenes, you will probably not hear anything more about it for some time. This sort of enquiry takes a long while to pursue properly, and it has to be done properly to ensure that, if and when it comes to court, the case doesn't fail on a technicality. But I can assure you, we will be in touch eventually." He paused again. "I will need a signed statement from you, of course, confirming what you've told me today. And the evidence, the tobacco tin and the papers you found inside."

Alex nodded. "I've already done the statement," he replied. "But it's not signed yet. I'll sign it for you now, if you like. I thought you might like to see me sign it in front of you."

"That's a good Idea," Ampersandi said. "But leave it for the moment, shall we, and let's carry on fishing for a bit? I can collect the other stuff when we've packed up for the day."

"Sure," Alex acknowledged. "It would be a shame to spoil an afternoon's fishing."

It was late afternoon before they packed up their fishing tackle and strolled back along the towpath to where *Jennifer Jo* was moored. "Would you like to come inside for a moment?" Alex asked, as he unlocked the rear doors. "Follow me."

Ampersandi followed Alex down into the saloon of the boat. "Take a seat at the dinette," Alex invited him, "while I find the tobacco tin." He delved into the back of the locker where it had lain hidden since the day he and Danny had found it in Grant Hall.

"Here you are," Alex said, handing it to Ampersandi. "Please forgive me for asking this, but can I have a receipt for it please?"

"Of course you can," Ampersandi smiled. "Let me have a piece of paper, and I'll write it out for you now. If you have a camera, you can photograph me with the tin and the papers, as well, if you like." Alex nodded, and did as Ampersandi had suggested, although he realised that it almost certainly wouldn't be necessary to dispute the fact that Ampersandi had been given the pieces of evidence. He took his statement which he'd prepared the previous day, signed it, then handed it to Ampersandi, who countersigned it as a witness, and then placed the tobacco tin and its contents into a plastic bag and tucked it into his pocket.

"That's fine," Ampersandi thanked him, as he stood up and made his way to the back of the boat, and out onto the towpath. "Thank you for what you've told me today, and for this too," he added, as he patted the pocket containing Alex's statement. "I can assure you that this will be followed up, but as I said earlier, it will take some time. So, please be patient. Goodbye. It's been nice to meet with you."

Alex shook his hand, then stood on the back of *Jennifer Jo* and watched as Ampersandi made his way along the towpath and disappeared round the bend of the canal. Had he done the right thing, he wondered? But he realised that the die was now cast, and there was now nothing further that he could do except wait, and see what transpired. He went back inside *Jennifer Jo* and started to get his tea together, and while it was cooking he sent an email to Danny, telling him what had happened that day. A short while, later, he received a short reply from Danny. "Well done!" he'd sent.

While Alex sat and ate his tea, he thought about his next move. There was nothing else that he could do here, and it was time to move on. He looked at the canal guide a for a bit, then decided he'd go along to Oxford, thence onto the River Thames, then join the Kennet and Avon Canal towards Bristol. It was several years since he'd travelled that route, and there would be many new things to see, and hopefully some old friends to meet up with once again.

CHAPTER 19

Alex was sitting on the back rail of Jennifer Jo, having a cup of tea after his evening meal, when his mobile phone rang. He picked it up and saw that it was Danny calling. "Any news, Mister?" Danny asked.

Alex knew exactly what Danny was enquiring about. It was more than four months since he'd passed over his statement to Rudolph Ampersandi, together with the tobacco tin and the papers inside it. But since then, neither he nor Danny had heard anything further about it. He was well aware that Ampersandi had told him that things would take some time to progress, but as time went on with still no news, Alex had been getting more and more anxious.

"Well, no, none at all, Danny," Alex replied. "What about you?"

"Yes," Danny exclaimed excitedly. "A couple of plain clothes policemen came round to our house this morning, asking for me. Sophie told them that I was at work, and they asked her where that was, so she told them, and they left. Then she phoned me at work to tell me they'd called. She was worried about it, she thought they were after me because I'd done something wrong."

"But you'd told her all about Grant Hall, hadn't you?" Alex asked. "She knew all about your going to the Hall with me, and getting the evidence I gave to Ampersandi?"

"Yes, of course, she knows all about that now, I told her some time ago," said Danny. "I told her not to worry about the police officers, but I knew she would. Anyway, a little while later I got called over to reception, I was working on the lathe in the workshop, turning some balusters for an oak staircase we're making, and there were these two blokes asking to see me, they said they were policemen and needed to talk to me. The lady on reception was ever so nice, she let them have the use of an empty meeting room that wasn't needed that day."

"Once we'd all got sat down she brought us in some coffees, then they started asking me all about Grant Hall, and so on. But as soon as I found out what they wanted, I excused myself for a couple of minutes while I went out and rang Sophie back, and told her what it was all about, so she didn't worry any more. And then we sat there all day, except for a quick break for lunch. They asked me loads of questions, and I told them all about the cars and the men who came to Grant Hall at night, and us kids getting called down to be with them so they could interfere with us. And then they wanted to know all about when I went back to Grant Hall with you, and got inside there and found the tobacco tin under the floorboards, with all the papers inside, with our notes on them. They were all in code, if you remember."

"Yes, Danny, that's right. Quite clever really. Only a simple code but it helped to hide what you were up to."

"Yes, Mister, but no one ever found them. Anyway, these two coppers, they were asking questions all day and typing it all up on their laptops which they'd brought with them. Then, in the end, it was just about 5 o'clock, they took it to the receptionist and she printed it off for them, and I signed it, it was my statement, and then they signed it as well as witnesses, and then they left."

"So they're moving forward, then, Danny," Alex replied. "I'm so pleased. Ampersandi did say to me that it would take some time. Did they give you any indication as to how long it would be before anything else happened?"

"No, not at all," came Danny's voice over the phone. "But they did say that they'd been trying to trace the other kids who were at Grant Hall the same time as me, you know, the ones whose names were on those pieces of paper in the tobacco tin. They asked me If I was in touch with any of them, but I had to say no. I haven't had any sort of contact with anyone from Grant Hall since I climbed over the wall in the kitchen garden that night and ran off. That's quite a few years ago, now, isn't it? I wonder where they all are now, and if they're doing OK, like I am."

"Yes, well, the police have lots of means at their disposal," said Alex. "You know, driving licences, National Insurance numbers, that sort of thing. They can all be used to trace them. And there will be the records from Grant Hall in the Council Archives. They'll get there in the end, I'm sure."

"I hope so, Mister," Danny replied. "Anyway, I've got to go now. It's time to give Jenny her bath, and Sophie's gone to see her mum and her Gran tonight, so I'm in charge. Jenny really likes her bath, splashing about. It's great fun."

"Well, enjoy, Danny," said Alex. "We'll keep in touch and see how things progress. Bye."

"Bye mister," came Danny's response, as Alex put the phone down. Whilst he sipped his tea, almost cold now after his conversation with Danny, he sat back and thought about what Danny had told him. So Ampersandi had taken his evidence seriously, and moved things forward, as he'd said he would. Alex wondered how long it would take for this business to be brought to a conclusion, if indeed it ever would. There was a strong possibility that the team which Ampersandi must have assigned to the case would not find sufficient supporting evidence to bring a case to court, and seek justice for those boys who'd been sexually abused whilst they were at Grant Hall.

It was a good four months later before Alex heard anything more about Grant Hall. He'd been outside on the towpath one evening, talking to a fellow live-aboard boater who'd moored close by, and whom he'd met several times before, the last time being some nine months previously. They'd spent a good couple of hours chatting, well into the evening. That was one of the things that Alex liked most about being on the waterways – being part of a community who were always pleased to help each other, and happy to spend some time in conversation, discussing their boats, where they had been on the canal network in them, and about some of the interesting people they had met.

After saying goodbye, Alex went back inside *Jennifer Jo*, and turned on the television to catch the 10 o'clock news, whilst he tidied up the galley and made himself a cup of tea. The second item on the running list caught his attention, and as the newsreader read through the story, Alex watched and listened with keen interest.

'A total of 12 men appeared in court today charged with historic offences of sexual abuse against young boys.'

......the story began. The newsreader paused, before continuing...

'The offences are alleged to have taken place over a period of several months some 8 years ago at Grant Hall, which was then run by an ex-army officer called Augustus Hammond as a care home for boys with behavioural difficulties.'

Here the screen picture cut away from the newsreader in the studio, and showed film footage of Grant Hall. It was just as Alex remembered it from his visit there with Danny, with the high wall around the house, the ornate gates in the wall which gave access to the house wide open, giving a view of the gardens within, now neatly-tended compared with the riot of weeds and undergrowth which he and Danny had seen when they were there. But the newsreader was speaking again:

'Grant Hall was closed 7 years ago after Hammond and a number of other men who were employed there as wardens were found guilty and

imprisoned for their part in the physical abuse of the boys in their care there. It is understood that none of those charged today worked at or were employed at Grant Hall at any time. After being empty and unused for some years, Grant Hall has recently been re-opened as a residential care home for elderly people after a considerable amount of refurbishment.'

The newsreader then proceeded to name those accused, and gave brief details of each of them. Alex was horrified by what he heard. A solicitor, a company director, a local councillor, the owner of a local golf club, no less than three police officers, two still serving and one retired, and several other local businessmen, presumably all of them well-respected pillars of their communities, were amongst those charged. The newsreader went on:

'At today's hearing, the accused said nothing except to confirm their names and addresses, and all entered 'not guilty' pleas. They were all released on bail, and the case was referred to the Crown Court for a full trial at a later date, the date to be decided once further evidence has been obtained.'

'Outside the court, a police spokesman declined to say why this case had taken so long to be brought to court, and why these charges had not been brought at the same time as Hammond and the others accused of physical abuse against the boys had faced trial and been jailed. She did confirm, however, that there had been suggestions of sexual abuse at the time, but they had not been fully followed up due to a lack of evidence. It does appear now that new evidence has come to light in recent times, which has enabled the police to re-open the case.'

The presenter moved on to the next story, a continuing tale about MP's once again fiddling their expenses. Alex switched off the television and sat back, sipping his tea, as he considered what he'd heard. So Ampersandi had been as good as his word. He'd obviously followed up Danny's evidence, and presumably sought out and made contact with some of the other boys who'd been at Grant Hall at the same time as Danny had been there.

Just then, his mobile phone gave a beep, and, picking it up, Alex found he'd just received a text. It was from Danny, and simply read 'YIPPEE'. Alex smiled to himself. That single word said a great deal. Of all the people who would be pleased at today's news, Danny was perhaps entitled to be the most pleased of all.

Whilst he washed up his tea cup and cleaned the small sink in the galley, Alex thought a bit more about what he'd just heard.*'....suggestions of sexual abuse......not fully followed up due to a lack of evidence....* ' the presenter had said. With a number of influential people apparently involved, including no less than three serving or retired police officers, Alex was not surprised that Danny's original allegations of abuse had been brushed under the carpet. Subtle pressure would have been applied, arms gently twisted, and quiet words gently whispered in the right ears, the ears of the people in charge of the investigation.

It saddened him a great deal that the proper process of justice could be maligned in this way, but he was a man of the world, and was well aware of the rampant dishonesty that seemed to be on the increase in all areas of the public services. It started at the top, as exemplified by MP's found to having been fiddling their expenses, and appeared to be percolating down to all levels of society. And perhaps worst of all, those caught and exposed seemed to express no shame once their wrong-doings had become revealed for all to see. Public confidence in the integrity of those appointed to serve them was at its lowest ever level. And it was people like Danny, honest to the core, just starting out on his journey through adult life, who were being taken advantage of. It was indeed a sick society he was living in, Alex surmised, as he walked through to the bathroom and prepared to turn in for the night.

A further 5 months passed by before the subject of Grant Hall came up again. Alex had been pretty relaxed about it, knowing that Ampersandi's staff would have been working on the case, and preparing it to go to court. So he was only mildly surprised when one afternoon, just as he was mooring up *Jennifer Jo* following a short cruise along the canal to charge his batteries, his mobile phone rang. After checking his identity, the voice on the other end of the phone asked "I believe you live on a canal cruiser and have no permanent address, is that right?"

Alex grimaced. He disliked it when people didn't use the right terminology for his way of life. "Well," he replied, "you're partly right, in that I don't have a permanent address. I live on a boat, it's more properly called a narrowboat, and I am indeed moving around all the time. But, how can I help you?"

"My name is James Walton," the caller on the other end of the phone replied. "I work with the Crown Prosecution Service. I have to serve some legal documents on you. Normally, we'd send them via registered post to your home, but in your case that doesn't seem to be possible, since you don't have a permanent address. Can you suggest any other way we can get them to you? They'll have to be signed for on receipt, of course."

"Yes, of course," Alex replied. "Would you like to give me your number, please? I'll just have a think about it, check out a few details and get back to you." He took down the number he was given and thought for a moment, then locked up *Jennifer Jo* and took a short walk back along the towpath to the lock which he'd negotiated just fifteen minutes before, where he'd noticed there was a small lockside shop and cafe. Going into the shop, he purchased a loaf of bread and a pack of freshly baked homemade cherry scones, and whilst paying for his purchases, he introduced himself to the shopkeeper and explained his predicament. He liked to give his custom to the small shops that were to be found by the cut, especially since he was about to ask a favour. It got the conversation off to a good start, and he'd found that people were more likely to be of assistance if the person asking the favour had just bought something from them.

"That's not a problem, no problem at all," the lady behind the counter confirmed with a welcoming smile. after he'd told her what he wanted. "We often help people out with post and that sort of thing. You say this package you're expecting has to be signed for?"

Alex nodded. "That's right," he agreed. "I was wondering if I could give your address and postcode here, and when the postman comes, could you send him along the towpath to my boat, it's called *Jennifer Jo*, it's only a couple of hundred yards away above the lock. Would that be alright?"

"Yes, that would be fine," she replied. "If you can just write your name down on this piece of paper here, and your boat's name as well, I'll put it by the till, so then if my daughter is looking after the shop while I'm busy in the kitchen, she'll know as well. I'll tell her as soon as she gets back from town, the bus is due any minute now. Would that be alright for you?"

"That's very kind of you. Thank you very much," Alex replied, as he placed his shopping into the carrier bag he'd brought with him. "Goodbye, and thank you once again." He walked slowly back to *Jennifer Jo*, and phoned back to the number he'd been given, asked for James Walton, and told him what he'd arranged.

"Thank you," Walton confirmed. "The package will be with you tomorrow sometime. I thought we might have had a bit of a problem, but what you've arranged seems fine. Thank you for sorting this out for me. Goodbye."

"Goodbye," Alex replied, as he put the phone down and started to put his shopping away and prepare his evening meal.

Late the following afternoon, Alex was busy polishing the brass ventilation mushrooms on *Jennifer Jo's* roof when he saw a postman walking along the towpath towards him. He quickly signed for the fat official-looking envelope the postman gave him, then put down his polishing cloths and went inside the boat to make a quick cup of coffee. Mug in hand, he returned to sit on the back deck and enjoy what was left of the afternoon sunshine whilst he examined the contents of the envelope.

He found it was a court summons to appear as a witness for the crown in a court case scheduled to take place in 7 weeks time. As he looked at the list of defendants and the charges they would be facing, Alex realised that this was the end result of the visit he'd made to Grant Hall with Danny. A total of 12 names were listed, all of whom were facing charges of gross indecency with a child under the age of 13, during a short period some eight years ago. In every case, the location where the offences were alleged to have been committed was given as Grant Hall. Alex allowed himself a wry smile. So Ampersandi had been as good as his word. The abused boys would have their chance to see justice done in the end.

He was just starting to prepare his evening meal when Alex's mobile phone rang. Before picking it up, Alex guessed it would be Danny, and he was proved to be right when he heard Danny's voice on the other end. "Hey Mister, guess what I've had come in the post today?" Danny exclaimed.

"Well, Danny, I reckon it's a summons to appear as a witness in a court case. About what went on at Grant Hall. Am I right?"

"Well, yes, Mister, that's right. How did you know that?" Danny sounded a bit disappointed that Alex had outsmarted him.

"Danny, I've had one as well, it came this afternoon," Alex explained. "I'll take *Jennifer Jo* down there, of course. If I don't hang around too much I can get there in good time. Would you like to stay on the boat with me while the trial is taking place?"

"Yes please, Mister, that would be great," replied Danny. "Just like old times again. Thanks very much. I'll have to clear it with the people at Smart Brothers, because I don't have any holiday left. Do you think they'll let me be away for however long it's going to take? And they'll probably stop my wages as well, they won't want to pay me for not being there, will they? I can't really afford for them to do that."

"I'm sure they'll let you be away, Danny," Alex reassured him. "You see, you don't have any choice in the matter. It's not optional, you're obliged to be there, at that trial. If you read the small print in the papers you've received, you'll see that. And if Smart's won't pay you for the time you're away, then you can claim an allowance from the court, so you shouldn't lose out financially. Why not have a chat with the personnel people in the office? Show them the court papers you've received, and hopefully it will all work out alright."

"That's a good idea, Mister," Danny responded. "I'll do that, and see what they say. Anyway, I've got to go, tea's ready now. The trial starts on the Monday, so I'll come done on the train to meet you the Saturday before, if that's alright. But we can sort out the detail later. Bye."

"Bye, Danny," Alex replied, but Danny had already put down his phone and rung off. After having his tea, Alex sat down with the Nicholsons and worked out which was the best way to go back down south again. As long as there were no stoppages on the canal system which might impede his progress, he worked out that he'd be able to get to where he needed to be with a few days to spare.

CHAPTER 20

It turned out that Alex had been right. He'd gradually made his way down south once again through the canal system on *Jennifer Jo*, and arrived at his usual mooring position with just a couple of days to spare. It was the same location he'd used before, a pleasant spot where he'd met the newspaper reporter Robert Jefferies over a year ago now, and where a few days later Rudolph Ampersandi had come aboard and collected the tobacco tin with its incriminating slips of paper inside.

The following day Danny had arrived, and they'd spent the Saturday evening and all of Sunday catching up on what had been happening to each of them since they'd last met. And on the Sunday evening, rather than sit and watch television, the chess board came out, with Danny once again wiping Alex off the board, eventually gaining the upper hand after a tight game which at one point Alex was pretty sure of winning. "Do you know, Danny," Alex remarked as they put the board away, "we've played chess together quite a few times, you and I, but I don't think I've ever beaten you, not even the once."

"You've got to be really good to beat me, Mister," Danny replied, smiling broadly. "I told you that years, ago, if you remember, when I was living on *Jay-Jay* with you. You've got to have a good strategy. Obviously something I've got and you haven't," he added with a cheeky grin, the grin which Alex would always remember was usually never far away when Danny was around.

Bemused, Alex could only shake his head and smile ruefully. "Next time, perhaps," he added.

But of course Danny had an answer. "Fat chance, Mister," he grinned. "Like I said, it's me you're playing against. It's about time you got used to losing against me. You're really lucky we don't play for money, aren't you?"

"It's just as well we don't, then," Alex replied. But anyway, it's time to turn in, we don't want to be late in the morning, do we?"

The next morning, they caught the bus from the bus stop near the pub, just a short walk down the towpath from where *Jennifer Jo* was moored, and arrived at the court house in good time. They'd been told to be available from 10.00 am onwards, but it was barely twenty-past nine when they walked up the steps and were met by a uniformed official as they entered the building.

Are you witnesses?" he asked. "I'm Peter Bracer, the witness support officer. Can I have your names please?" Alex and Danny identified themselves, and Bracer checked off their names on a list secured to a clipboard he was carrying. "Would you like to make your way to the witness waiting room, please?" he asked. "It's up the stairs, turn right at the top, and along the corridor to the end. You'll find there's a notice on the door. Please make yourself comfortable. The judge doesn't sit until 10 o'clock, and there's all the jurors to be sworn in first, before any witnesses are called. So it might be some time yet, several days even, before you're needed. I'm sorry, but I don't know when you'll be called, or how long the case will go on for, I'm afraid."

Alex thanked him, then he and Danny made their way upstairs to the witness waiting room. It was a pleasant, spacious, room, furnished with a range of easy chairs, coffee tables, and a couple of writing tables. Large windows looked out onto a colourful garden with a neatly-trimmed lawn which lay to the rear of the building. A table in one corner of the room bore a tea urn and a large flask of coffee, with a tray of cups and saucers beside them, and beside the table was a vending machine offering fresh sandwiches and soft drinks. A bookcase with a range of paperback and hardback books stood against one wall, and beside it was a rack holding the day's newspapers, together with an assortment of magazines.

"This is nice, Danny," Alex remarked as they made their way to a small group of chairs arranged round one of the coffee tables, and sat down. "I suppose, sometimes witnesses must have to wait for ages before being called to give their evidence, so they powers-that-be in the Justice Department have made a good effort in helping to make their time pass as pleasantly as possible." Looking round the otherwise empty room, he added "since there's no-one else here at the moment, we must be the first to arrive."

Danny nodded. "Yes, Mister, you're right. But I'd rather be early than be late. It's not a bad place to relax before the ordeal of being in court, though."

"Are you nervous, then, Danny?" Alex asked. Danny didn't reply, but nodded silently. Alex suddenly realised that Danny must be feeling a bit unsure of himself. "I'm not looking forward to it, not at all," he admitted after a pause. "But I want to see those perverts put in jail for what they did to us all those years ago. After all, that's what I'm here for."

"Yes, Danny, that's right," Alex consoled him. "This is the end result of our going back to Grant Hall last year, and finding the tobacco tin. Now we have to hope that justice will be done."

Just then the door opened and a man in a smart suit, covered by a legal gown, swept in and came across the room to greet them. "Hello," he said, "My name is George Crumber. Peter Bracer told me you were here. I presume you're Daniel Marshall?" he asked, turning to Danny and proffering his hand.

"Yes, that's right," replied Danny, shaking his hand, and then Alex introduced himself. "It's nice to meet you both," Crumber greeted them. "I'm a junior counsel for the prosecution. My senior, William Willoughby-Woodward QC, is leading for the prosecution in this case. He's one of the top barristers in cases of this nature, I've worked with him on several similar cases in the last couple of years. By engaging him for this case, it shows that the CPS, that's the Crown Prosecution Service, is really keen to secure the convictions of all the defendants."

Suddenly, Danny burst out laughing. "I'm sorry," he said between chuckles, "but what a name to have! William Willoughby-Woodward, did you say? Fancy having to go through life with a name like that!"

"Yes it's a bit of a mouthful, isn't it?" Crumber smiled. "But wait till you hear who's leading for the defence. Are you ready for this?"

Danny nodded again. "The leading defence counsel is Sir Cecil Sissingston-Smithson QC," said Crumber. "He's appearing for all of the defendants in this case." He paused for a moment before continuing. "It's him whom I've come to warn you about," he added, but he stopped speaking as Danny sat down in his chair, leaned back and started giggling uncontrollably. Alex allowed himself a chuckle as well, as Crumber smiled and waited patiently for Danny to find his self-control once again. "I'm ever so sorry, Mr. Crumber," Danny managed to say eventually. "You must think it awfully rude of me to laugh like that. I just couldn't help it. It's just so funny, the posh names these people have."

"That's alright," Crumber smiled at Danny. "You're not the first to find it amusing, by a long way. The Judge in this case, Mr. Justice Henderson, just calls them Mr. Smithson and Mr. Woodward whenever they appear before him. It's much simpler, and they don't seem to mind, not that they have any choice in the matter anyway. Anyway, back to Smithson."

"Yes?" asked Alex. "What is it that you wanted to warn us about?"

Well," Crumber paused for a moment. "Smithson has a bit of a reputation. He really knows the law, and he's a very good barrister, make no mistake about that, but his favourite tactic when he's acting for the defence is to destabilise the prosecution witnesses. He adopts a rather hostile stance towards them, trying to discomfort them and trip them up, undermining their evidence at every opportunity, casting them in a bad light, and generally destroying their credibility in every way he can. He's already had two warnings from the Bar Council for his aggressive attitude, but it doesn't seem to have made much difference. If he's not careful he's going to get a formal reprimand soon. But if he tries it on here, as he almost surely will, then at least you will have been warned."

"Thank you," Alex responded. "At least we'll know, and hopefully be prepared."

"That's fine," Crumber replied. "Anyway I must go now. Mr. Marshall, I'm sorry but it may be several days before you're called. There are four other witnesses scheduled to give evidence before you're going to be needed." Turning to Alex, he added, "but you're first on the list. See you in court. And by the way, please remember, both of you, that you should not talk about this case to each other, or to any of the other witnesses, you may see someone here whom you know from years ago." And then he turned and went out of the room, which had been gradually filling up whilst they'd been talking.

As Alex and Danny watched him go out of the door, they saw a tall, smartly dressed dark-skinned man with tightly-curled hair enter the room, wearing a light-grey suit with a light blue shirt and dark blue tie. After quickly glancing around, he took a newspaper from the rack and went and sat in front of one of the windows. Making himself comfortable, he opened the paper and held it up in front of him to catch the light from the window while he started reading the front page.

"Do you fancy a coffee, Mister?" Danny asked. "I think I need one myself anyway." Seeing Alex nod, he added "I'll go fetch them, you wait here." He walked over towards the refreshment area, but suddenly veered across the room to the new arrival, who was still sitting reading his paper. Putting his hand on the top of the paper and pushing it down, Danny said in a loud voice "you're crazy!"

Alex looked on in amazement. In all the time that he'd known Danny, he'd never ever seen him speaking in such a rude manner to a complete stranger. He'd always had him down as an extremely polite person. What had happened to upset him, what had that man done for Danny to speak like that?

But to his astonishment, Alex heard the man reply quietly, "yes. And who are you?"

"I'm Danny. Danny Marshall," Danny exclaimed. "We were at Grant Hall together, weren't we?"

The black man stood up and stared at Danny for a moment. Then his face broke into a smile. "Of course," he said, as he and Danny embraced warmly. "It's great to see you again."

"Why don't you come and join us?" Danny asked, indicating Alex sitting nearby. "And, I'm just getting some coffees, would you like one as well?"

"Yes please, that would be very nice," the man replied, as he walked over and sat with Alex, who shook his hand and introduced himself.

"My name is Kwodmo, Akrasi Kwodmo," the man responded. "And I was indeed at Grant Hall when Danny was there. All the other kids there, they used to call me Krazy, it was short for Akrasi. I didn't mind, I didn't mind at all, all us boys were good pals there, united against a common tyranny, as it were."

Alex nodded. He vaguely remembered that when he and Danny were decoding the scraps of paper from the tobacco tin, one of the boys named in those papers was indeed Krazy. Danny had told him at the time that it was just a nickname. "So how did you end up at Grant Hall?" he asked Akrasi.

"Well," Akrasi answered. "I was born in Ghana, in West Africa. When I was aged about seven or eight, a lot of fighting broke out in one of the northern provinces, where we were living at the time. To get me away from the fighting, my parents sent me to England to live with my grandmother, she'd married a British colonial official who was in the country when it was being prepared for independence. You may remember, the country was called the Gold Coast in those days. After independence they both returned to England together, but my parents stayed behind, they'd just married and didn't have any right of entry to England anyway. But because of the fighting and because I was a child, I was allowed in to live with my grandmother. She was living on her own, my grandfather had died two or three years previously."

"After about a year living with my grandmother, she died and the Social Services people put me into care. I was sent to live at Willen Place. It wasn't very nice there, some of the kids were really quite horrid to me. I was the only coloured kid there you see, and they used to call me nasty names and that sort of thing, just because I had black skin. The people in charge, they knew about what was happening, but they never did anything about it, and sometimes they joined in as well. It wasn't very nice at all, really unpleasant. I had to stick up for myself, and the only way I could get them to stop calling me nasty names was to hit them, and it always seemed to end in me being involved in a fight. That's how I seemed to get a reputation for always fighting, and that's why I got sent to Grant Hall."

"It was different there, in more ways than one. I'd only been there a couple of days when Hammond, he was the man who was in charge of everything, he heard one of the older boys calling me names about my skin colour. He took that kid straight to his office and caned him, I think he got six strokes. And at supper that night, he told everyone that if anyone ever called me names again about my colour, then they'd get six strokes of the cane every night for a week. That really did put a stop to it, no one ever called me names again, and after a little while I was just accepted for who I was."

"That's one of the strange things about Hammond," he went on. "He never allowed any racism at all, he was very strict about that, and he always made certain that the place was spotlessly clean, not just when there was going to be an inspection or something, but all of the time. If it hadn't been for the beatings and the canings and the poor food and the ball game, I had to do that as well, especially after Danny went, it would have been a tolerable place to live."

By that time Danny had returned with the coffees, placing them on the table in front of them. " So what are you doing now, Krazy?" he asked.

I'm back in Ghana now," he replied. "After I left Grant Hall, I was there all the time until it was closed, I trained as a teacher. Then I returned back to Ghana a couple of years ago. I'm teaching English as a foreign language. A lot of the schools there don't have English teachers, and mostly the children only speak their native tongue, which varies from district to district, generally in line with the old tribal areas. English is seen by the authorities there as a common language, because if everyone speaks the same language then it helps to unify the country and all the different ethnic groupings in it. And of course, English is the international language of science, commerce, industry and business, the world over."

"I'm surprised the British Department of Justice here managed to trace me back to Ghana, but they did, they sent a detective out to Ghana to interview me and take my statement. And now, they've paid for my air fare so I could come back and testify, and they're putting me up in a nice comfortable hotel, it's only about ten minutes walk away. It's nice to be back in England for a while, but my heart really belongs to where I was born, back in Ghana. I can contribute much more, teaching there, than I ever could do if I'd stayed in England. All the children there are keen, very keen to learn. It's a joy to teach them, it really is." He paused for a moment, before continuing. "But that's enough about me. What's happened to you, Danny, since you went over the wall?"

Danny briefly told Akrasi how, after he'd absconded from Grant Hall, he'd found shelter with Alex on his narrowboat, and then gone to live with his mother in the north of England, how he was now a trained carpenter and joiner after serving an apprenticeship with a large building firm, and was now proudly married with a young daughter.

"That's great, Danny," Akrasi responded. "I'm really pleased for you." He paused for a moment, then continued. "You know, Danny, you became the stuff of legend at Grant Hall after you went over the wall, especially since they never managed to catch you. I mean, you were the only kid who ever got out, and to cap it all you got out twice."

"I'll never forget the day you disappeared from the kitchen garden, I was on gardening duty that day as well. When the wardens there discovered you were missing, they phoned Hammond, he was away that day, then we all got marched back to the Hall. We were having supper when Hammond got back, it was a bit strange because there was this empty space where you normally sat. He called out the wardens who'd been on duty at the kitchen garden that day, they had to go into his office, and he was so cross, and shouting at them, we could all hear what was going on even though the doors were closed. He was beside himself with rage, we thought he might even take the cane to them but he didn't."

"I was on gardening duty again the next day, and it was Hammond who took us down there. He'd got Brutus, the Rottie, with him of course, like he always had. He unlocked the gate into the garden, and we all filed in and lined up in front of the greenhouse, as per usual, waiting to be given our tasks for the day. That's when we saw the pile of wooden boxes stacked up against the wall. You see, until then no-one had any idea how you'd been able to get away, because everyone knew that the wall was far too high for anyone to climb over, and the young fruit trees trained against the wall were no way strong enough to take your weight. We twigged then that you must have hidden in the garden somewhere and got out over the wall later, when it was dark, even though Jamie Blanchard had told the wardens he'd seen you climb up the trees and got over the wall that way, and I think Jonny Raeburn told them the same as well. All of us kids knew that those fruit trees would never have taken your weight, but the wardens didn't realise that."

"Anyway, once we were all inside the garden, Hammond locked the gate behind us, like he always did, then he came in and when he came round the greenhouse and saw the stack of boxes piled up against the wall, his face went purple with anger. He stalked over to the wall and got hold of some of the boxes and started throwing them to the ground. It was then that one of the kids started laughing, I don't recall now who it was. Then someone else started laughing as well, and before you knew it we were all standing there laughing at him and pointing at the boxes. We laughed and laughed, and the more we laughed the more mad Hammond became, he was beside himself with rage. You know, it was great, absolutely great."

"I can guess how Hammond reacted to that," remarked Danny.

"Yes, you're right," Akrasi replied. "Several times he shouted at us to be quiet, but of course no-one took any notice of him, we were all having too much fun laughing, there really wasn't much to laugh about usually, if you were living at Grant Hall. Anyway, he called Brutus over and took the lead off the Rottie, and then he called us up one by one, we had to bend over with our hands on our knees and we all got two strokes of the lead on our backsides for being impertinent to him. It was worth it, though. No-one had ever got away before. Nor since, either."

The room was starting to fill up now, with witnesses arriving and waiting to be called into court, and Crumber popping in and out checking names and trying to make people feel at ease. Danny and Akrasi kept wandering round the room, greeting and chatting with other people whom they recognised from their time together at Grant Hall, leaving Alex to sit on his own reading the newspapers. He found it interesting to see how different newspapers managed to put a different slant on the same story, in support of their own particular political policy.

It was well past mid-day before Alex and Danny bought themselves some sandwiches from the vending machine and sat and had their lunch together, and in the early afternoon, a court usher entered the room and called Alex's name. Standing up, Alex replied, "'yes, here."

"Thank you," the usher replied, "can you follow me, please."

Alex followed him out of the room and along a corridor, up a flight of stairs, then along another corridor before the usher opened a door into the courtroom and led him to the witness box. As Alex took the oath and confirmed his name, he felt slightly intimidated by his surroundings. The room was relatively dark, with subdued lighting, the wall lined with wooden panels which had obviously darkened with age. A small amount of daylight filtered into the room from long, narrow, windows set high up along the top of one wall. The judge, clad in his formal scarlet robes, was seated to Alex's right behind a high desk, with a couple of clerks seated in front of and below the judge's desk.

Opposite Alex sat the twelve members of the jury, and to his left was the dock, where behind a low glass screen sat the twelve accused men, most of whom were smartly dressed with collar and tie. In the body of the courtroom were the legal teams for both the prosecution and the defence, resplendent in their legal gowns and wigs. The public gallery ran across the back of the room at a high level, where Alex saw the newspaper reporter Robert Jefferies seated in the front row.

He thought suddenly of 13-year-old Danny, who eight years before at the trial of Augustus Hammond had chosen to give his evidence in open court so that he could face his abusers in person. A courageous decision by a brave young boy to face such an ordeal, Alex thought to himself.

After the initial formalities, the prosecution counsel started his questioning. Woodward's charm and friendly easy-going manner soon set Alex at ease as he carefully encouraged Alex to recount how he'd first met Danny and decided to give him shelter in his narrowboat, and how the boy had stayed on *Jennifer Jo* with him for the following twelve months. Then Alex was asked to describe how, years later, he'd gained access to Grant Hall with Danny whilst it was being renovated, and how they'd found the tobacco tin with its papers inside.

At that point Woodard asked "Can the witness please be shown exhibit 12c?" The court usher hurried forward with a sheet of paper enclosed in a plastic bag. "Is this the tally sheet you signed when you gained access to Grant Hall that day?" he asked Alex.

Alex looked closely at the sheet. Ampersandi's team certainly had been thorough, to have made sure that evidence was produced to confirm that he and Danny had actually been at Grant Hall. "Yes it is," he confirmed.

"Thank you," was Woodward's response, as he consulted his notes. "And now please show the witness exhibit 17a." As the usher brought him another plastic bag, Alex recognised the tobacco tin which he and Danny had found under the floorboards. "And is this the tobacco tin you say you found under the floorboards that day?" Woodward asked.

Alex looked at it carefully. The tin had a small dent in the lid, near the top left-hand corner, a dent he recognised from months earlier. "Yes, that's the one," he told the court. He was not surprised when the next items he was asked to identify were the slips of paper they'd found inside the tobacco tin.

By the time Woodward told the judge "no further questions, your Honour," and sat down, it was past four o'clock, and the judge closed the proceedings until 10 o'clock the next morning. Alex left the court and made his way back went to the witness room to collect Danny, where he found him still in deep, good-natured conversation with his fellow witnesses.

On their way back to *Jennifer Jo*, Danny asked "how did it go, then, Mister?"

"All right, I think, Danny," Alex replied. "But I don't think I should say anything else at the moment, not until you've been in the witness box yourself."

"No, I suppose not," Danny replied. "I shouldn't have asked really, should I?"

"Well, it's natural to be curious," Alex remarked as they reached *Jennifer Jo*, and he unlocked the door and they went inside.

The next morning, back at court, Alex returned to the witness box as the defence counsel, Sissingston-Smithson, started to put his questions. In contrast to Willoughby-Woodward, the prosecution counsel, Alex took an immediate dislike to Smithson, a tall, skinny individual with thinning slicked-back black hair, who spoke in a sneering manner and who never seemed to open his mouth wider than a very narrow slit whilst he was speaking.

Smithson's very first question raised alarm bells inside Alex's head. "What work do you do?" he asked. Alex became a little anxious. How could that be relevant to this case? "I don't work any longer, I'm retired," he replied cautiously.

"And what work did you do, before you retired?" was the next question.

"I was a schoolteacher," he responded.

"And what sort of school did you teach at?" Smithson sneered.

"It was a boy's boarding school. I was a housemaster there, for twenty-five years almost, in charge of one of the boarding houses," Alex explained.

"Describe this boarding house to the court," Smithson asked. "The layout of the building, and that sort of thing. And the age group of the boys who lived there."

At that, Woodward rose to his feet. "Your Honour, is this really relevant?" he exclaimed. "How can this have anything to do with the nature of this trial? None of the accused have ever been anywhere near this witness's place of work."

"Mr. Smithson?" the judge asked.

"If your Honour would bear with me," Smithson responded, rising to his feet, "the connection will become clear later in this trial," he responded.

"I very much hope so, Mr. Smithson," the judge remarked. "You may continue." Woodward sat down and Smithson rose to his feet once more.

"Well," Alex began, wondering where all this was leading to.

"There were ten boarding houses altogether. The teaching blocks were separate from the boarding houses, and there was a central dining and catering facility. The boarding houses provided living accommodation for about eighty boys each. On the ground floor were the common room, a games room, a television room, and a couple of quiet rooms as well with a small library of books to read, also a changing room for use when the boys were undertaking sports activities, and where their outdoor clothes were kept. On the first floor were the boys' dormitories, with bathrooms, toilets, and showering facilities."

Alex paused for a moment, but immediately Smithson pressed him to continue. "And how were these dormitories arranged?"

"Well, the ages ranged from nine to fifteen," Alex went on. "The younger boys were in dormitories eight beds to a room. As they got older they moved to rooms with six beds each, and the fourteen and fifteen year olds were in dormitories which had four beds to a room. All the rooms were the same size, so as the boys grew older they had more space to call their own. There was a separate accommodation block for sixth form students, but that wasn't part of my remit."

"I see, Smithson sneered yet again. "And your own accommodation, where was that?"

"In the same building," Alex replied, getting more and more worried by the minute. What on earth had this to do with Grant Hall? "Downstairs were our living room, dining room and kitchen, we did our own catering, we didn't eat with the boys at all. Upstairs were our bedrooms and bathroom."

"And was there any access between your quarters and the boy's areas?" pressed Smithson.

"Yes, there was a connecting door between them, on both the ground floor and first floor," answered Alex.

And were these doors locked at all?" the questions continued.

Alex paused for a moment, fearful now of the direction in which the questions were moving. But he was well aware that any reticence on his part could be construed as an admission of something that other people might think he wished to hide. Taking a deep breath, he replied "no."

"Not even from the boys' side?" came the next question.

"No," confirmed Alex. "We needed to get to the dormitories quickly and easily should there have been a problem with one of the boys during the night, you know, if a lad was ill for example, or if there was a pillow fight or something that might have got out of hand. My wife, you see, was the....."

"It not your wife we're talking about," Smithson interrupted immediately, giving Alex an icy look. "It's you we're interested in. If we need to ask your wife anything, then we'll ask her to come to court and tell us. I'm sure she'll tell us all about you," he sneered.

"So you could wander at will into the boys' part of the accommodation?" he went on. "Whenever you wanted? Into the changing rooms? Even into the dormitory and bathroom areas, when they were getting dressed or undressed, or getting ready for bed, wearing just their pyjamas, or even naked in the showers, or anything like that?" Smithson asked, peering over the top of his glasses as he did so.

"Yes," Alex replied after a pause, feeling sick at the unspoken insinuations which Smithson appeared to be implying.

But Smithson wasn't finished with his insinuations. "So your work brought you into close proximity to young boys then. You were with them for most of the waking day, and they were not far off at night either. Is that correct?"

"Yes," Alex answered glumly.

"That must have been nice for you. Very nice," Smithson sneered. Alex didn't answer, shaking his head slowly from side to side.

Smithson spoke again, apparently now on a different tack. "Did you enjoy your work?" he asked.

"Well, yes, I did," Alex replied, as he heaved a sigh of relief. Perhaps the difficult questioning was at an end. "Teaching can be a most rewarding profession," he added.

"So let us see where we are now, then, shall we?" Smithson looked at the jury with a hint of a wry smile on his face. "You enjoyed your work, surrounded as you were by young boys practically all the time, and the nature of schooling is that there is always a fresh supply of boys coming into your boarding house to live very close to you."

He paused for a moment to give extra emphasis to his next statement to the jury. "As you've just told this court, you enjoyed being with young boys. I *bet* you did."

There was another pause. before Smithson continued. "And when you found young Daniel Marshall, a scared twelve-year-old boy hiding on your boat, you took him in, not handing him over to the authorities when you should have done, and you kept him with you on your boat for a whole year. I wonder why you should choose to do that?" Alex stood quietly in the witness box, not deigning to reply.

"They're not very big, these boats are they?" Smithson went on. "You and this young lad must have been very close together for all of that time. I wonder what that vulnerable youngster had to do for you in return, for you to allow him to stay with you on your boat? When that boy hid away on your boat, you must have thought your lucky day had arrived! Because, as you've just told the court, you like being with young boys, and having them around you all the time, day and night."

Alex glumly shook his head, but said nothing. He realised that Smithson had very cleverly twisted the facts and painted him into an unpleasant corner, and he'd unwillingly been obliged to assist him, having had no option but to answer his questions.

"No further questions," Smithson muttered to the judge, as he sat down with the hint of a smirk on his face. The Judge nodded. "Thank you, Mr Smithson." Turning to Alex, he said "You may step down now. And I think it's time to adjourn for the afternoon," he announced. Court will reconvene at 10 o'clock tomorrow morning."

"All rise," the usher instructed, as the judge swept out of the court. Alex made his way out of the court and found George Crumber waiting for him in the corridor outside.

"I'm so sorry," Crumber remarked anxiously. "I did warn you about Smithson, did I not? He really went out of his way to discredit you, I'm afraid, but that's his way. He was very unkind to you. I'm not exactly sure what he's up to, but I fear that when Mr. Marshall takes the stand it will become clear. Anyway, goodbye until tomorrow."

Alex made his way to the witness room, where he collected Danny, and as they made their way down the steps at the front of the court building, Robert Jefferies came up to Alex, who introduced him to Danny. "Nice to meet you, Danny," Jefferies remarked. "You're the boy who lived on the narrowboat with Alex for a year, aren't you? And did that nice picture of the boat?"

"Yes, that's right," Danny replied.

"Is it still on your wall, Alex?" Jefferies added, turning to Alex.

"Yes, it is, actually," Alex confirmed.

"But, Alex," Jefferies asked, "you got a right going over this afternoon, didn't you?"

"Yes, I did," replied Alex, with a shrug. "But we'll have to see how things go in the next few days. I don't like a slur being cast against my name, especially when it's completely untrue."

"Yes, reputations can sometimes be completely trashed for no apparent reason," Jefferies agreed. "But, that's the nature of court sometimes. You don't always get justice, you get the law. They can be two very different things sometimes. But don't worry, I'll make sure that nothing which Simpson implied is in the report for my newspaper."

"Thanks, that's much appreciated," Alex responded. "Thank you very much. Anyway, Danny, let's go and catch our bus, I can see it at the end of the road now." They made their way back to *Jennifer Jo,* with Alex tight-lipped, not saying much to Danny, who was of course completely unaware of the day's proceedings in court.

The next day, on arrival at the court buildings, they separated, with Danny returning to the witness room, whilst Alex took a seat in the public gallery. During the morning, three witnesses were called in quick succession. The first to be questioned was a collector of tobbacciana, namely all things to do with tobacco. On being shown exhibit 17a, the tobacco tin, he confirmed that the design on the lid was first introduced some 8 years ago, and was only in production for about 9 months before it was withdrawn and a new design introduced. So it seemed pretty conclusive that the tin did indeed date from the period when Danny and the other boys at Grant Hall were being abused and taking down the numbers of the cars which turned up at the Hall late at night.

The second witness was a forensic scientist, who described the tests he'd carried out on the slips of paper which Alex and Danny had found inside the tobacco tin. He confirmed that the paper had aged by about 8 years, and appeared to have been stored in a dry location away from daylight.

The final witness of that morning's proceedings was a cryptographer, who explained to the court the simple code which had been used to conceal the true nature of the notes on the scraps of paper. As the court adjourned for lunch, Alex could only admire the thoroughness with which the prosecution's case had been put together. It seemed that Ampersandi and the CPS were leaving no stone unturned to secure the convictions they were hoping for.

After lunch, with Alex in the public gallery once again, it was Danny's turn to be called and give his evidence. Alex watched as Danny confidently made his way through the courtroom and into the witness box. All afternoon, under questioning from the prosecution counsel, Danny recounted how he and the other boys at Grant Hall had seen the cars arriving and being called down to be with them. At one point, Mr. Woodward asked him to describe in detail the exact nature of the abuse he personally had suffered.

Danny turned to the Judge. "Must I, Sir?" he asked. "It's really rude, you know. I'd rather not talk about it, if you don't mind."

"I know how distressing this must be for you, Mr. Marshall," the

Judge replied. "But for the court and the jury to be aware of just how serious these incidents are, then you have to tell everyone exactly what happened. Please answer the questions."

Danny nodded. "Yes, sir, if I must," he responded. And for the rest of the afternoon, he very reluctantly described what had taken place during those late nights at Grant Hall with those strange visitors.

The final question from Mr. Woodward, before the Judge adjourned the proceedings for the afternoon, was quite simple and straightforward. "Mr. Marshall," he asked. "The man, or men, who made you do all these things with them, do you see them here in this court today?"

Yes, " Danny replied, raising his right hand and pointing to the dock. "It's that guy over there, on the left in the front row, in the blue jacket," he said. "He told me once that he always asked for me, whenever he came to Grant Hall, because he really liked me." Danny paused for a moment before shouting out vehemently "THE DIRTY BASTARD!" Alex glanced across at the witness box, where the man whom Danny had identified sat very still, showing no emotion whatsoever, staring resolutely across the room with a vacant expression.

A murmur rang through the court as the usher called for silence. "Let the record show," Woodward said as quiet descended once again, that the witness is pointing to Charles Morritt." Then, turning to the Judge, he added "no further questions."

"Thank you, Mr. Woodward," the Judge replied. "I think that's enough for this afternoon. The court will reconvene at 10.00 am. tomorrow morning." As the usher called out "all rise" the Judge rose and left the court.

The next morning, Danny returned to the witness box to face questioning from the defence counsel, Mr. Smithson. Sitting in the public gallery, and mindful of how he'd been treated by Smithson whilst he'd been in the witness box, Alex had a dark sense of foreboding. 'What nasty tricks is Smithson going to pull out of the bag this morning?' he wondered, as Smithson rose to his feet.

But the session started off quite well for Danny. "These cars which you say arrived late at night, Mr. Marshall," Smithson asked. "If it was late at night, as you claim, surely it was dark when they arrived. How then, if it was dark, could you see the numberplates?"

"That's simple," Danny replied confidently. "There were these security lights out the front, see? They came on automatically whenever anything moved outside. It was just like daylight out there. The rottie used to set them off all the time. It was easy to spot the car numbers, ever so easy, no problem at all."

The Judge leaned forward. "The rottie?" he asked.

"Yes sir," Danny turned to the Judge. "Brutus."

"Brutus?" asked the judge again.

"Yes, Sir. Hammond's dog. Hammond was the chief warden at Grant Hall. Brutus was his dog, a rotweiler. We all used to call it the rottie. He let it run loose in the grounds most nights. The security lights, they were going on and off all the time. We got used to it in the end." Alex allowed himself a wry smile. Smithson seemed to have scored an own goal with that question.

"Thank you," the judge nodded. "Mr. Smithson?"

"Thank you, your honour," Smithson rose to his feet again. "Mr. Marshall," he began, "yesterday, you identified one of the defendants as the man who you say abused you. But these alleged incidents took place more than eight years ago. You were only a young child at the time, and people's recollections of their young childhood are well known to be unreliable as they get older. I put it to you that you are just guessing. You choose that man at random out of those in the dock, and in fact it wasn't him at all. These things never really happened, did they? You're making this all up as you go along, aren't you?"

"No I'm not," Danny snapped back. "When you're only eleven years old and having that sort of thing done to you, things that you know are wrong, then you never forget it, and neither do you forget the face of whoever's doing it to you. It's him, I tell you." He once again pointed at the dock to Charles Morritt, who continued to sit impassively in the dock, slowly shaking his head from side to side. Alex smiled again. 'Round two to Danny,' he thought, as he wondered what tack Smithson would try next.

But Smithson was ready with his next question. "Let the witness be shown exhibit 12c, please?" requested Smithson. As the usher handed the exhibit to Danny, Smithson asked '" Do you recognise this piece of paper?"

"Yes," Danny replied. "It's the tally sheet we signed when we went to Grant Hall, to get the tobacco tin."

"Can you read out the headings at the top of the four columns on the tally sheet, please?" Smithson asked.

Puzzled, Danny peered at the paper through the plastic wallet in which it was contained. "Name," he read out. "Company. Time in. And, time out."

"Thank you Mr. Marshall," Smithson acknowledged. "And now, can you please tell the court what you understand by the word 'company' on the tally sheet?"

"Well, it's where you write in the name of the firm you work for," Danny replied, looking a little anxious now.

"And what firm were you working for, at the time that you visited Grant Hall?" Smithson asked. Danny paused for a moment, beginning to realise the trap which Smithson was leading him towards.

"Well, Mr. Marshall?" Smithson asked.

"Smart Brothers," Danny answered reluctantly. "I still do."

"And could you please read out to the court what you wrote on the tally sheet in the 'company' column?" Smithson pressed him.

"Ewington David." Danny said quietly. "Quantity Surveyors."

"Now isn't that really strange," Smithson continued. "You've just told us that you worked for Smart Brothers at that time. And yet you wrote 'Ewington David' on the tally sheet. Both of those can't be true, can they? Which one did you actually work for?"

"Smart Brothers," came Danny's reply, now clearly starting to lose his confidence, his hands tightly gripping the front rail of the witness box.

"So when you wrote 'Ewington David' on the tally sheet, you knew that it was untrue?" Smithson pressed his point.

"Yes," Danny acknowledged quietly.

"So it was a lie then?" sneered Smithson.

"Yes," replied Danny reluctantly, after a long pause, and now looking visibly upset.

"So you're a liar then?" Smithson sneered. "A LIAR? An L..I..A..R liar?"

"Yes" Danny mumbled, almost inaudibly, as he glanced desperately round the court. Alex felt for him. Smithson was performing true to his reputation, doing his best to discredit a prosecution witness. But worse was to come.

Smithson allowed himself a wry smile as he turned and faced the jury. "So," he stated. "This witness has admitted he is a liar. Let us take a moment to wonder what else he's lying about. I don't doubt that the abuse he's described to this court actually took place."

Turning back to face Danny in the witness box, he continued, "but it was never at Grant Hall where it happened, was it? After having absconded from Grant Hall, you were on the run from the authorities. You were taken in by a complete stranger, a man living on a canal narrowboat, and he let you stay with him for over a year. Why should he choose to do that, we ask ourselves? What ulterior motive did he have? That man has already admitted to this court that he enjoys the company of young boys, he likes having young boys around him at all times of the day and night. What did you have to allow him to do to you, we all wonder, so that he'd let you stay on his boat with him, and not get sent back to Grant Hall?"

Smithson paused for effect. "Well, now we know, don't we?" he continued. "For over a year, the abuse which you allege took place at Grant Hall was actually taking place within the narrow confines of that canal boat, wasn't it? The canal boat where the two of you lived, oh so very close together, for all that while. My client Charles Morritt is totally innocent of all the charges against him, and shouldn't be in the dock at all. Standing there in the dock facing these charges should be the man who kept you on his boat for more than twelve months, and abused you all that while, before you plucked up the courage to run away from him and go and live with your mother. That's the true story of this abuse, isn't it?" Smithson thundered.

"No, it wasn't like that at all," Danny said weakly, struggling to hold back his tears but almost ignored as a loud murmur swept round the court and Smithson, wearing a big smirk on his face, turned to the judge and said "no further questions, your honour."

Sitting in the public gallery, Alex felt furious at the allegations Smithson had just made to the court. Now he knew why Smithson had asked him about his teaching career and his life as a housemaster. He'd been building up a foundation onto which these latest smears could be laid. Alex knew them to be completely untrue and without foundation. But how much would the jury believe?

The judge turned to Danny. "Thank you, Mr. Marshall," he said. "You may now step down." Still visibly upset at what had just transpired, Danny turned and started to make his way out of the witness box, when he suddenly turned round, bounded back up the two steps leading to the box, and with a newfound confidence raised his hand and pointed it once again at Charles Morritt in the dock.

"He's' got a scar!" he shouted. "I've just remembered. Three, in fact." Dropping his right hand to his tummy, he continued, "I've had my appendix out, when I was a little kid, and course I've still got the scar from the operation, it's about here." He waved his hand around his lower abdomen as he continued. "His scars are about midway between there and his.... well, you know," he added. "In fact, they make a sort of triangle shape. And he doesn't have any hair down there on that side either. I always wondered about that, when he was interfering with me, but of course when you're only eleven you don't really know much about that sort of thing, do you?"

As Danny spoke, Alex looked down at Morritt, who, in contrast to his previous impassive stance, was now leaning down with his head in his hands, rocking slowly backwards and forwards. But Danny wasn't finished yet. He turned to the judge and asked, "why don't you get someone to look at him? They'll find out I'm right. There's only one way I could know that, isn't there? It was him that interfered with me. No one else ever did. Have it checked out and see!"

The court erupted in a loud chatter as everyone started commenting to the people sitting nearby. After three calls for silence, quietness was restored and the judge turned to Woodward, asking, "Mr. Woodward, would you like to ask any further questions of this witness?"

Smithson immediately rose to his feet. "Your honour, the prosecution counsel has already had his chance to ask questions," he said. "Not long ago, he told the court 'no more questions.'"

The Judge drew himself up and frowned at Smithson. "Are you telling me how to run my court, Mr. Smithson?" he asked.

"No, your honour," Smithson apologised quietly, as he sat down and the prosecution counsel rose to his feet once again. Under Woodward's questioning, Danny recounted all that he could remember about Morritt's scars, and the lack of hair on that side of his body. As the questioning finished, the judge said "I think that's enough for this morning. Court will reconvene at 1.45pm this afternoon," and as he rose and left the court a hubbub of chatter erupted about Danny's latest revelations.

No longer able to use the witness room as their time as witnesses had come to an end, Alex and Danny had a sandwich and a cup of tea in a cafe just across the road from the courthouse. Whilst they ate, they discussed the events which had taken place in the court that morning. "Danny, it's a good job that you remembered about that guy's scars," Alex remarked. "How is it that you never remembered it before, and didn't think to tell the police about it when they came to interview you a few months ago?"

"I just don't know, Mister," Danny replied. "It just never occurred to me, and if it had then I probably wouldn't have thought it relevant, or worthwhile mentioning. But when that horrid man Smithson accused me of being a liar, and making the whole thing up, I thought that we were going to lose the case before it had really got started. So I thought and thought, and racked my brains to see what else I could remember, and I came up with that in the nick of time. It was when he suggested that it was you that abused me, well, that really did get me thinking, to see what else I could remember about that guy Morritt. You know, I never knew what his name was before today. But anyway, what exactly did Smithson mean when he said you'd admitted you liked having young boys around you? What was that all about?"

"Well, Danny," Alex paused for a moment. "As you found out this morning, Smithson is very clever at twisting what you say to suit his own devious objectives. He asked me about my career, and so I had to tell the court about my time as a schoolteacher and housemaster at a boys' boarding school. And then he asked if I'd enjoyed my work, which of course I did. You see, I did enjoy the satisfaction of giving the boys in my care a good education, and as they grew up, helping to shape them into thoughtful and considerate people of good character. But he almost made me out to be a pervert, he twisted it around so much. It's just the same as the way that he made you out to be an inveterate liar, just because of the slight deception we used to get into Grant Hall. But it should be interesting to see what this afternoon brings."

"That's right, Mister," Danny agreed. "I'm a bit disgusted at how Smithson twisted the facts like he did. But I think we've got a much better chance of our side winning now."

"I hope so, Danny," Alex agreed. "I really do hope so," as they walked back across the road and returned to the courtroom. They were now able to sit together in the public gallery, where there seemed to be a lot more people now than there was earlier. No sooner had the judge sat down when Mr. Woodward, the prosecution counsel, stood up and addressed the judge. "Your honour," he said, "in the light of the previous witness's testimony this morning, I wish to ask for an adjournment whilst I seek a medical examination of the defendant Charles Morritt. I believe a seven day adjournment would be sufficient?"

The judge turned to Smithson, the defence counsel. "Mr. Smithson?" he asked.

"That won't be necessary, your honour," Smithson answered quietly as he rose to his feet. "My client Mr. Charles Morritt has intimated to me that he wishes to change his plea to guilty. As also do my clients Mr. Stanley Gordon and Mr. Anton Gileskivych."

The court erupted in noise at the latest revelations. "YES!" shouted Danny loudly, his face beaming as he turned to Alex. "What do you make of that? The bastard's admitted it!"

Alex could only smile. Danny was entitled to rejoice for a few moments. But once order was restored, the normal process of the trial continued, with Akrasi Kwodmo being called as the next witness. But after about twenty minutes, a court official entered the court from the judge's entrance and whispered something into the judge's ear. The judge nodded, then announced, "the court will adjourn until 10.00 am tomorrow morning," after which he stood up and left the room.

On their way out, Alex and Danny were making their way out of the building when they saw Robert Jefferies, the newspaper reporter, who'd been in the public gallery at every session since the trial started. Alex asked "why the adjournment, Bob?"

"It's nothing to do with this trial," he answered. "There's an urgent application for an injunction which has to be heard today. Apparently some newspaper, and not mine I'll hasten to add, has got hold of some dirt on some celebrity and they're trying to stop it becoming public. That's all I know, I'm afraid. Anyway," he added, turning to Danny, "you certainly turned the tables on Smithson, didn't you? He was up to his usual tricks, smearing you both as is his usual style, but now, thanks to you, he's already got three of his clients pleading guilty. And I suspect that all the others will go the same way when the jury's heard the evidence against the rest of them. The CPS seems to have put a very good case together. Anyway, I must be off and file my report. These three changing their plea to guilty should be front page stuff in tomorrow's paper. Bye."

As Jefferies hurried off, Danny and Alex made their way back to *Jennifer Jo*. On the way, Alex thought about the trial. "Danny," he asked, "now that we've both given our evidence, and the guy who abused you has pleaded guilty, I don't think there's any useful purpose to be served by my being there every day. What's going to come out over the next few days won't be much different than what's already been said. It will just be the different people who used to be at Grant Hall with you giving details of the abuse that was perpetrated against them. To be honest, I think personally, I've heard enough about that. And I've got plenty to do on the boat, we need some more gas and diesel, and the fresh water's going to need replenishing soon. And I need to do some shopping too. What do you think?"

"You're probably right," Danny replied. "Why don't you stay on *Jay-Jay* and see to what needs to be done. I'll still go and watch the trial every day, if you don't mind, because I knew all the people involved. I'm a lot closer to what went on at Grant Hall than you, if you know what I mean."

"Yes I understand that," Alex agreed. "That's settled, then. But I'd like to hear the jury deliver their verdicts, and see what sentences the judge hands down afterwards."

It was a full week before Danny came back to *Jennifer Jo* one afternoon and told Alex that the jury had retired to consider their verdicts. "The judge's summing up went really well," he said. "He covered all the important points, from everyone's evidence. They went out at around 11 o'clock this morning, and I was talking to Bob Jefferies just before I came away. He said the word was that the jury was expected to return tomorrow sometime. Are you going to come along tomorrow then?"

"Yes Danny, of course I will," Alex confirmed. "I want to see the wheels of justice grind to their logical end. I hope our visit to Grant Hall will turn out to have been worthwhile in the end."

It was almost 12 o'clock the next day when Alex and Danny, who'd been in the visitor's lobby at the court building all morning and were about to go across the road to the cafe for a spot of lunch, heard a court usher announce "the jury is about to return to court 12." They filed into the public gallery and took their seats as it quickly filled up to capacity, with several late-comers left standing. It seemed that this case had sparked a great deal of public interest. Some of the last people to enter were Bob Jefferies, closely followed by Rudolph Ampersandi, who took care not to be seated next to each other. With a smile, Alex realised that it was not a good idea for a Chief Constable to be seen chatting to a newspaper reporter.

After the judge had taken his seat, the jury filed in. With three of the defendants having changed their pleas to guilty during the trial, there were just nine verdicts due to be delivered. In turn, the usher asked each defendant to stand whilst he asked the foreman of the jury for their verdict regarding that particular defendant. The first defendant hung his head in shame as the foreman, a young man not much older than Danny, stated simply 'guilty', and then confirmed that it was the verdict of them all. Danny allowed himself a small smile, which quickly became broader and broader as, one by one, each defendant was asked to stand, and one by one the verdicts came back the same. Guilty.

He turned to Alex in delight. "That's about right, Mister," he said excitedly. "They've been found out good and proper now. I hope the judge slings the book at them, I really do. You know, I never thought it would end like this, when we went into Grant Hall to get the tobacco tin, but it's been worthwhile, hasn't it?"

"Yes, Danny, that's right," Alex agreed. "Ampersandi told me, right at the start, that he'd follow it through, and he certainly has. I'm as pleased as you are, I really am." He stopped speaking as the judge began to hand down the sentences on the now-guilty men. Nine of them were given sentences of either six or seven years in prison, with the three who had changed their pleas to guilty during the trial were rewarded with lesser sentences of five years each. As the usher called out "all stand" and the judge left the court, the room once again erupted into a loud chatter. The public gallery gradually emptied into the lobby outside, and everyone started drifting down the stairs to the main exit.

As they exited the building, they saw a television news crew had set up on the grass outside the court building, where a news reporter was interviewing Rudolph Ampersandi. Alex walked over to listen to what was being said, "...... let the outcome of this trial today send a clear message to anyone who abuses children," the Chief Constable was saying to the camera. "Such behaviour will not be tolerated in today's society, and however long ago an incident took place, we will make every effort to find and punish those responsible."

As the interview continued, Akrasi came up to Danny. "Hey, Danny,'" he said, "some of the ex-Grant Hall kids are going to the pub to celebrate. Are you going to join us?"

"Of course I will," Danny replied, with his usual trademark grin. "Just try to keep me away." He turned to Alex. "I'll make my own way back to *Jay-Jay*, if you don't mind, Mister," he said. "I'll see you later."

"That's fine, Danny," Alex nodded. "I'll expect you when I see you."

Together with a number of other people whom Alex recognised as having been in the witness waiting room, Danny and Akrasi walked off down the road to the pub on the corner, just beyond the bus stop. Turning back to Ampersandi's interview, Alex saw that it was just coming to an end, as the camera swung back to the interviewer, who was just signing off with the familiar words "and now back to the studio." Then, to Alex's surprise, Ampersandi came over and greeted him. "Hello, Alex," he said. smiling broadly as they shook hands. "How nice to see you again, since we met whilst fishing that time. I told you I'd follow up what you talked to me about, didn't I?"

"Yes, indeed you did," replied Alex. "Although I did start to get a little anxious when nothing seemed to happen for ages."

Ampersandi nodded. "I'm not surprised, not surprised at all. There are procedures which have to be followed, and they all take time. And don't forget, I was new to the job. There were lots of important things which needed to be done, and they couldn't be all done at once. But I'm pleased to say that we got there in the end."

"That's right," Alex agreed. "You must be very pleased with the outcome today, though. It 's been a good result, hasn't it?"

"Yes it has. My team, and the CPS, have done a good job, I'm pleased to say." Ampersandi paused for a moment. "But I do have one regret, though," he added.

"What's that?" Alex asked, a little puzzled.

"Well, I'm more than a little annoyed," he said, "about the one that got away." Ampersandi frowned. "You see, those papers in the tobacco tin which you gave me, which the boys at Grant Hall had used to note down the car numbers, they mentioned thirteen car numbers in total. We managed to trace twelve of them, found their drivers, and they've all been in court at this trial and found guilty, as you know. But all our enquiries as to the last one, the thirteenth, came up against a brick wall. We just couldn't find the information we needed to follow it through. Whoever it was seems to have got away with it and escaped justice, as every line of investigation seems to have come to a dead end in that respect. We know that he's still out there somewhere, but I don't know if we'll ever find him now."

"Anyway," he added, looking over Alex's shoulder, "it seems my car's just arriving, I'll have to go. But before I do, may I say one thing, please? Don't be too worried about the way Smithson stitched you up in court the other day. He does it to most witnesses who're testifying for whatever side he's up against. No-one who knows him takes his insinuations seriously, but he seems to think that he can sway the jury by using smears and innuendo like that. Perhaps he'll learn one day, but probably not. It's just part of his *modus operandi*, if you know what I mean."

"Anyway, It's so nice to see you again, and thank you for your part in all this. Goodbye." They shook hands and Alex watched as Ampersandi strode over to his car and was driven away, quickly disappearing amidst the busy traffic.

Alex looked at his watch. It was early afternoon, and Danny was in the pub celebrating with his old friends from Grant Hall, where Alex expected him to remain for some time. He went across to the nearby cafe and had a quick snack for lunch, then decided to walk back to *Jennifer Jo* in the bright sunshine. As he walked along he thought about what Ampersandi had said a little earlier, about the one person whom the police hadn't managed to identify. 'Why was it,' he wondered, 'with all the resources which they had at their disposal, that the police hadn't been able to trace the one remaining car and driver?'

But suddenly he remembered something which Bob Jeffferies had said to him some months before. He'd told Bob about the visit he and Danny had made to Grant Hall, and given him the car numbers. And

Jefferies had returned a couple of weeks later and reported back about the discreet enquiries he'd asked his contacts to make. They too had traced twelve of the thirteen, but not the last and final one. It had appeared that the data on that particular number was blocked from access without special authorisation. Jefferies had speculated at the time, Alex remembered, that it was a government car, used by a high-up official. 'Was that official still blocking the police enquiries?' Alex asked himself. As he reached *Jennifer Jo* and stepped aboard, he decided he had to accept that the answer to that particular riddle might never be revealed.

When it was past nine o'clock, darkness had fallen, and Danny still hadn't returned to *Jennifer Jo,* Alex started to become a little worried, although he was well aware that Danny was a responsible young man and, hopefully, well able to look after himself. So it was with a slight sigh of relief that he heard a heavy tapping on the window. Going out onto the back of the boat, he saw, not Danny as he was expecting, but a small, lightly built, middle-aged man with receding hair standing on the towpath beside the boat.

"Is this boat called *Jennifer Jo*?" the man asked.

"Well, yes, that's right," Alex replied. "How can I help you?"

"Well, my name's Wansfield, George Wansfield," the man replied, smiling broadly. "I'm a taxi driver. I've got a passenger who asked me to bring him here, but he's a bit worse for wear, if you know what I mean. I don't think he could manage to walk along the towpath to get here to this boat without falling in, and I wouldn't want that to happen. The thing is, I'm not strong enough to handle him and bring him here on my own. Would you be able to come along and give me a hand?"

"Yes, of course," Alex replied. It was his turn to grin now. This had to be Danny returning back to the boat. He walked back to the pub car park with the taxi driver and hauled Danny out of the cab, then they took an arm each and walked Danny back to the boat between them. Alex carefully helped the young man down the stairway and laid him on his bunk, throwing a blanket over him before returning to the back deck, where he found the taxi driver still there. "Thank you so much, Mr. Wansfield," he said. "That's very thoughtful of you."

"It's all right," the driver replied. "Not the first time I've had to do that sort of thing, if you know what I mean." He winked, then spoke again. "The young man there, he didn't have any money," he added. "He said you'd pay the fare?"

"Yes, of course," said Alex, the grin disappearing from his face now. "How much is that, please?"

"Its £9.85, if you don't mind, please?" the driver asked. Alex slipped inside the boat and returned with a £10 note. "Keep the change, please," he asked. "And thank you once again for bringing him back here. I'll sort him out in the morning."

The taxi driver thanked him and departed back to his taxi in the pub car park. Alex went back inside to find Danny already fast asleep in his bunk, and now snoring loudly.

The next morning, Alex was clearing up his breakfast things when Danny appeared, walking very slowly into the saloon and sitting down very carefully at the dinette. Alex made him a mug of really strong coffee and set it on the table in front of him. "Here you are, Danny," he said, smiling. "Better drink this."

"What's that knocking sound I can hear, Mister?" Danny asked blearily. "Is there someone banging on the side of the boat?"

"No Danny," Alex laughed. "There's no-one there. There's no-one banging on the boat. That's your headache, making you think you're hearing things. I presume from this that you had a good time yesterday afternoon with the Grant Hall boys?"

Danny nodded, as he placed his elbows on the table and rested his head in his hands. "They can really put it away, some of them," he said, speaking very slowly, as if he was difficulty getting his words together. "They drank me under the table, just about." He took a sip from his coffee, then added, with a rueful glance at Alex, "I was going to go home today. But I think I'll leave it until tomorrow now. I'll phone Sophie later, when I'm feeling a bit better, and tell her." He looked up at Alex with an anxious expression. "Please, Mister, don't tell her about this, will you?" he asked, managing a slight smile. "She wouldn't be too pleased."

"No, Danny, I'm sure she wouldn't," Alex replied. It was his turn to smile now. "Sometimes there are things which things are better left unsaid, aren't they?"

Danny managed another slight smile. "I think so, Mister," he said. "Unsaid is the word." And Alex could only nod in agreement.

CHAPTER 21

Alex was just setting about making his evening meal when his mobile phone gave a soft 'ping', signifying that he'd just received a text message. He picked it up and was pleased to see that it was from Danny. Since the trial six months ago, when the men who'd abused the boys at Grant Hall all those years ago had been convicted, he and Danny had continued to keep in touch regularly, every two or three weeks or so, usually by email, but also sometimes by a simple text message, and occasionally by a phone call as well. Alex had always been interested to hear how Danny was getting on, and learn about the progress of his young daughter Jenny.

Opening the text, Alex was surprised to find that it consisted of only 4 words, 'BBC News, 6 o'clock.' Danny liked to do this, drawing Alex's attention to something that had caught his eye, something that he thought Alex might take an interest in. Looking at his watch, he realised that he'd got half-an-hour before the bulletin was due to start, just time to finish cooking. He'd be able to watch it whilst he ate his tea.

Unsurprisingly, the main features of that night's news consisted of follow-up stories from the General Election which had been held the previous Thursday. Since he had no permanent home address whilst living afloat on *Jennifer Jo*, Alex was unable to register for or vote in elections, but that didn't prevent him from taking a keen interest in politics in general, and in how the country was being governed. As in the last few days, the news was full of stories about how the previous Labour Government, which had been in office for the last 9 years, had been soundly and convincingly thrown out of office after nearly a decade of gross economic mismanagement.

It hadn't surprised Alex one little bit that the Labour party had lost the election. Their union paymasters, now the source of some 90% of the party's income, had been flexing their muscles as never before, insisting on the adoption of hard-left policies. Repeals of the Thatcherite reforms to trade union law had led to countless strikes and abysmal labour relations across the country, as the unions flexed their newly-restored industrial muscle at every opportunity. Days lost through strikes had mushroomed, and the resultant strife had forced many firms and employers to close and go out of business.

It had saddened Alex, when cruising along the canals which wound through the once-great industrial heartlands of the big cities, past the factories which the canals were built to serve, to see that so many buildings had had their roofs removed, rendering them unusable, in order to avoid the crippling property taxes that had been imposed on empty industrial buildings. This short-sighted and misguided attempt to generate additional tax revenue just made it much more difficult and expensive to bring jobs and prosperity back to the country.

With its eyes constantly focussed on generating public support for itself at the next general election, the Labour government's foolish answer had been to hugely expand the public sector to create jobs for the newly unemployed workforce, at vast cost to the public purse. Even so, unemployment was over four and a half million, and taxes had skyrocketed to pay for these excesses, with interest rates nudging nine percent. And the Cabinet, comprised mainly of poorly-educated ministers with few academic qualifications, who had risen to the top of the party solely through their trade union background, seemed to have had no idea as to how to fix the economy, and return the nation to an environment of growth and prosperity.

A goodly first half of the news bulletin was devoted to the new government's announcements about newly-appointed ministers, and the fleshing out of policy statements. But eventually the newsreader came to the piece Alex was watching out for, the item which Danny had forewarned him about. He turned to the screen and listened intently, as the newsreader continued.....

"And now for some other news..... Mystery surrounds the identity of a young boy whose body was found last week by workmen installing a new drainage system at Grant Hall. Our reporter Amanda Freeman has the details......"

The picture then cut to a young woman standing outside the gates in the wall surrounding Grant Hall. Alex immediately recognised it from his visit there with Danny a few years before. The camera panned around the site, and then zoomed in through the gates to an area at the side of the Hall where some workers in hi-visibility jackets and hard hats were busy at work behind some temporary security fencing, with a bright yellow digger busy excavating beside a heap of freshly-dug soil. Then the reporter started her voiceover.....

"After standing empty for some years, Grant Hall opened several months ago as a retirement home for elderly people, but it was found that

the sewerage system continually gave problems, and so contractors moved onto site last week to install new sewerage outfall pipes. Whilst excavating a trench for a new pipeline, workmen uncovered the body of a young boy, buried in a shallow grave not far from the Hall. Police were called, and the area immediately cordoned off and work halted whilst they carried out their investigations."

"It appears that the body had been in the ground for a number of years. However, the peat-rich nature of the soil around here has meant that decomposition of the body has been slower than would normally have been expected, and so police forensic experts have been able to make a detailed examination of the body. The body is that of a young boy, aged around 10 or 11 years old at the time of death, but it appears from preliminary reports that in the months before death, the child's development had been mildly restricted, probably due to a lack of nourishment."

"Previous to its current use as an old people's home, Grant Hall had been in use as a children's home, catering for boys who exhibited behavioural difficulties. At first it was thought that the boy whose body was found had been in some way connected with that era, but a detailed examination of Grant Hall's records from that time, which had fortunately been retained in the archives at County Hall, showed that all of the boys who'd been in care at Grant Hall had been properly accounted for."

"That is, with the exception of one boy who absconded from here some years ago, but was soon apprehended a few days later. However, that same boy absconded again a few weeks later, and despite an exhaustive search, he was never found. But he turned up again eighteen months later, when he walked into a police station in the North of England accompanied by his mother, with whom he'd been living for the previous six months and attending a nearby school. The boy filed accusations of physical abuse which he and most of the other boys at Grant Hall there had been subjected to whilst living there, his accusations backed up by inconvertible evidence. The Hall was immediately closed and the boys resident there were transferred to other care homes. Charges were subsequently brought by the police against a number of members of staff, most of whom received hefty jail sentences for their part in the abuse which had been taking place there."

"Investigations into the boys' body are continuing. The cause of death has been established, but the police are not releasing further details at the present time. DNA samples have been taken and analysed, but no match has been found with the missing children's register. Anyone with any information about the possible identity of this young boy is asked to *contact their local police station. And now, back to the studio......"*

As the newsreader continued with the next item on the running list, Alex leant forward and switched off the television, then stood up and took his cup of tea out to the back deck, where he sat on the gas locker, thinking about what he'd just heard, while enjoying the view across the cut to where some sheep were munching contentedly on the grass. This was the part of the day he liked most, the calm and quiet of the evening. But he hadn't been sitting there for more than a couple of minutes when his mobile phone rang. It was Danny.

"Hello, Mister," Danny said excitedly. "Did you see it? What do you make of it?"

"Yes, Danny, I saw it," Alex replied quietly. "I thought everything that had happened at Grant Hall had been sorted and put to bed. But this is really disturbing isn't it?"

"Yes, I know," came Danny's response. "But the thing is, I think I know who it might be."

"So, who do you think it is?" Alex asked.

"I think it's Jamie Roberts," said Danny. "He was at Grant Hall the same time as I was, you see. We were In the same dormitory together. He got called down one night, and he never came back. He simply disappeared, and we were never even allowed to ask about him. I've often wondered about what happened to him, and why he never came back. We all knew that something horrid might have happened, or maybe he'd been taken away, but we just didn't know. We wondered about him for ages. I really hope that it isn't him, because that would mean that he was dead. I'd much rather that he was alive and happily married with a family, like I am. But I'm really afraid that it might be him. Perhaps something bad happened to him after he was called out to go downstairs, and he died, and Hammond and the others, they buried him in the grounds. And they've just found him, now that they're sorting out the drains."

"You know, Mister," he continued, "the drains were always giving problems, even back when I was there."

"What sort of problems were there, Danny?" Alex asked.

"Well, I'd only been there a couple of months, when the drains got blocked," Danny answered. "We were all having showers one morning, when the water stopped draining away, it just stayed on the floor and got deeper and deeper. And then the toilets started overflowing, it was awful, all the mess and water everywhere. Hammond was away that day, and the other wardens, they didn't really know what to do, I think they were always afraid to make any decisions without Hammond being there. So, whenever we wanted to go to the toilet, they let us out of the back door of the Hall, and we had to go in the bushes. Hammond, when he got back in the afternoon, he was furious, we could hear him shouting at them for leaving it like they had, and not doing anything about it. And less than an hour after he'd got back, he must have got on the phone and organised it all, this lorry arrived with a load of portable toilet cubicles, you know like they have on building sites. Smarts, where I work, they've got some, they take them out to the sites where they're working."

"Anyway, before long there was all these cubicles lined up outside the back, and we were alright again, although we got a bit wet nipping out there when it was raining. Then, another load of workmen arrived and they set to clearing the drains, they took up all the manhole covers and were rodding the pipes through, they ended up working most of the night, and by morning they'd managed to get the drains clear. But there was still all this mess in the washroom, I thought I d have to help clear it all up, because I was on cleaning duty that day, but Hammond, once the drains were clear, he got this firm of cleaners in, and it only took them a couple of hours to get everywhere all clean again. The washrooms smelt really strongly of disinfectant after they'd finished. But it never really solved the problem, because every few months the drains would get blocked again, and we went through it all again."

"Anyway, Danny, what makes you think that it's this boy Jamie?" Alex asked.

"Well, do you remember that those big black cars used to pull up outside? And the men would get out and come into the Hall to see Hammond, then after a little while one of us kids would get called out to go downstairs and be with them? It all came out at the trial a few months ago, didn't it? Well, it was Jamie who got called out one night, and he never came back. And the next morning, his bed had been stripped and his locker was empty. Nobody knew what had happened to him. He just sort of disappeared."

"I don't see how that can possibly be him," Alex responded. "They said on the news that all the archive records had been checked, and all the boys who'd ever lived there had been properly accounted for. Except one, of course," he added with a smile, "and we both know who that is, don't we? And where he is now?"

Alex could hear Danny chuckling over the phone. "Yes, Mister, you're right there. But remember what they said on the TV, the exact words they used. All they said was that the records they'd got in the archives didn't show anyone not accounted for. The records could easily have been fiddled, anyone could have done it, before they got to the archives."

"How do you think that could have happened, Danny?" Alex asked.

"Well, when I was there, at Grant Hall, all the records were kept in Hammonds office, they were kept in a row of filing cabinets along the side of one of the walls of his office. I only went in there a few times, when I got called in to see Hammond about something, but I can clearly remember them, they were kept locked nearly all the time. But when he wanted to get your record out, he'd unlock the cabinet where your record was and fish it out, they were all kept in brown manila folders, there was one there for each of us. It would have been really simple to just have dropped a folder into the shredder, he had that in a corner behind his desk, and when the shredder had finished, then whoever's folder it was, well they would have just disappeared from the records, wouldn't they? Simple really, isn't it?"

"Yes, Danny, but the Social Services people, they'd have had records of all the children who they sent to Grant Hall, wouldn't they? Surely the police would have checked the Council's foster carers lists, or something like that?"

"But I don't think Jamie ever had a foster carer," Danny replied. "You see, I think he went straight into Harding Court, where I was before I was sent to Grant Hall, after the accident in which his parents got killed. They had to find somewhere for him straight away, after the accident, and I don't think they had any immediate vacancies with any of the foster carers on their approved list."

"Oh, the poor kid." Alex felt a little upset. "What accident? What exactly happened? Do you know?"

"Yes, Mister, there was a road accident," said Danny. "I can remember Jamie telling me about it, soon after he arrived at Harding Court. It was a Saturday morning, he and his mum and dad and his sister too, she was a couple of years older than he was, they were all in the car together, they took him to football, he was in one of his local boys club's teams, they were playing away that week. They dropped him off at the football pitch, then the rest of them went off to do some shopping while he played in the match, then they were supposed to pick him up again afterwards. But while they were on their way back to collect him, after the shopping, there was this road accident. Apparently a big articulated lorry came out onto a roundabout without stopping and it hit their car. The car was rolled over, and his mum and dad, they were in the front seats, they were both killed straightaway, and his sister, she was in the back, she was badly injured and her head was hit, she got some sort of brain damage."

"Anyway, Jamie, after the football match finished, everyone else went home, but of course his mum and dad, they never turned up to collect him, so he ended up sitting on the grass on his own waiting for them. After a while it started raining, really hard, so he went and sat under a tree, but that wasn't much good because it was raining so hard. He was there all day, in the pouring rain, there wasn't anywhere else for him to go, he just sat there soaked through to the skin in the cold."

"Then just as it was starting to get dark, this woman walking her dog came along and found him and took him home and gave him a bath and some blankets to put round him while she dried his clothes. And then she phoned the police and told them she'd found this young kid sitting on the ground in the rain. So the Social Services people came to collect him and took him straight to Harding Court. They had to tell him that both his parents had been killed and his sister had been very badly hurt as well. That can't have been very nice for them either, having to tell him that."

Danny paused for a moment before continuing. "I can remember him coming to Harding Court, I'd already been there about a couple of months before he arrived, they put him in the same dorm as I was in. He didn't settle down at all, it's not surprising I suppose, after all that, every night he'd cry for ages before he cried himself to sleep. I felt like I wanted to get in his bed and give him a big cuddle like I used to give little Freddie when I was with Mrs Bradley, but of course I couldn't do that with all the other kids in the dorm watching, everyone would have called us gays or something worse. So I swapped beds with someone else so that we could be next to each other, and I used to sit on my bed and talk to him and try to settle him down as best I could, but he was still ever so upset about everything that had happened. It's not surprising really, is it?"

"And he never went to church or joined in any of the religious services they stuffed down your throat there, he just refused point-blank to have anything to do with anything like that. He said he didn't see why, if there was a god, why god had allowed his mum and dad to be killed like they were. And all the people in charge at Harding Court, all they ever told him was that if he went to church and prayed, then he'd find the answer. I don't think he appreciated that at all. They were really cross with him, because he wouldn't go to the church services or do bible study or anything, but they couldn't force him to go without grabbing hold of him and physically dragging him there, and of course they weren't allowed to do that."

"So, when some of the other kids started complaining about him crying all the time and stopping them from getting off to sleep, that was the excuse they were looking for to get rid of him, and that's how he got sent to Grant Hall."

"Actually, Grant Hall seemed to be a bit of a dumping ground for all the kids what the other children's homes didn't want," Danny continued. "All the dregs seemed to end up there. But they weren't bad kids, none of them were, it's just that they'd all had bad luck of some sort or another. I think you'll find that they all turned out alright in the end. I mean, look at me. I reckon I turned out OK, don't you?" Alex could hear him chuckling at the other end of the phone.

"Anyway," Danny continued, "me and Jamie, we were both taken there, to Grant Hall, from Harding Court where we were, on the same day. We both had to sit in the back of some social worker's car, and someone from Harding Court came with us, he had all the paperwork. When we arrived there, we sat together on a bench in the entrance hall while they went into Hammond's office and all the papers got signed. We'd asked on the way there if we could be put in the same dormitory, like we were before, and they must have got Hammond to agree to it, because we were together all the time, from the day we arrived."

Alex felt really sad about what Danny had told him about Jamie's life. "That poor boy," he said, "he didn't have much of a life after the accident, did he? But, going back to the identity of the body they found, if it was this boy Jamie whom you've just been telling me about, surely they must have checked the records from Harding Court, then? And confirmed that it was Jamie?"

"Well no, Mister, they couldn't," Danny's voice came over the phone. " You see, there was a fire. Harding Court got burnt down, not long after I left there. All the records were destroyed. That's why my mum couldn't find me, when she came out of hospital."

"Oh yes, I remember now," Alex recalled, "you told me about that, a long time ago. So, are you going to go to the police, and tell them who you think it is, this boy Jamie?"

"Yes, I think I should, don't you?" Danny asked.

"Yes, I do," Alex agreed. "It could at the very least be a lead in the right direction. And if they're able to trace Jamie's sister, who must be in nursing care somewhere, then they could try for a DNA match, which would prove whether or not it is young Jamie. Will you go to your local police station, or go back to Ampersandi? That might mean you have to travel down South to see him, or one of his officers."

"I'll go to our local cop shop, I think," Danny replied. "The Child Liaison Officer, who was my main contact with the police when I first went to them about Grant Hall, you know, after I left you and *Jennifer Jo* and went to live with my mother, he's still there! Smart Brothers, where I work, we built an extension to our local police station last year. I helped make all the roof trusses in the workshop, and then went out on site and helped to build the roof, and then later I went back and did the second fixings. That's when I met him again, he's an inspector now. I'll phone in and ask to have a meeting with him, he's sure to know what to do next."

"That seems a good idea, Danny," Alex said. "Do please let me know how it goes, won't you?"

"Of course I will," Danny replied cheerfully. "I'll keep you informed. Anyway, I've got to go in a minute, because it's Jenny's bath time soon, but before I do, there's something else I want to ask you."

"What's that, Danny?" Alex asked. "Ask away."

"Well, where are you on the boat, at the minute?" Danny asked.

Alex smiled to himself. He wasn't amiss to mildly teasing Danny from time to time. He knew full well what Danny wanted to know, but he restricted himself to answering just the question which Danny had asked. "I'm at the back of the boat, sitting on the gas locker, looking out at the view," he replied.

"No, that's not what I meant," came Danny's response.

"Well, it's what you asked," Alex rejoined. "I gave you a truthful answer to what you just asked me."

" All right, I'll try again," Danny sighed. "What I meant was, where is *Jay-Jay* at the moment?"

"She's moored up against the towpath," Alex replied, smiling again. "Opposite a meadow with some sheep in it. And I've just seen a fox lurking in the undergrowth not far off. He's probably looking for his supper right now, eyeing up which sheep to take. The farmer won't be very happy, I don't doubt."

"Probably not," replied Danny, "but I give up. Let me ask again. What canal is *Jennifer Jo* on at the moment?"

Alex smiled again. Danny had at last asked the right question.

"I'm on the Shroppie right now," he told Danny. "The Shropshire Union canal."

"At last, Mister," Danny replied. "About time. That's what I wanted to know. But do you think you might be able to go back down South again, to be there in a couple of months time?"

"You know me, Danny," Alex rejoined. "I'm a water gypsy. I go wherever I fancy. But tell me, why should I want to go down South again?"

Well, Mister, I've had this letter from Ampersandi, it came last week," said Danny. "It was a big surprise."

"What did Ampersandi want?" Alex asked. "What was the surprise?"

"Well do your remember, a few months ago, the Home Office announced that they were introducing a new award, for people who've given outstanding help to the police and the justice system, in bringing criminals to justice? It's called the Citizenship Award. The Chief Constable in each police area is only allowed to nominate one person every year, and Ampersandi has nominated me, because of all the help I gave about Grant Hall, not just in this trial that finished a few months ago, but way back the first time as well, after I'd been living on *Jay-Jay* with you, and then went to live with my mum."

"That's wonderful, Danny," Alex congratulated him. "That's a great surprise. I think you really deserve it. Well done."

"Actually, Mister, I didn't really know whether or not to accept it," Danny continued. "I thought that sort of thing was only for posh people, but mum and gran, and Sophie's parents as well, they all said I should. So I need to send the forms back and tell them that I've agreed to accept it. I'll have to attend the awards ceremony down south, to be presented with it, and I'm allowed to take one guest as well. If you don't mind, Mister, I'd like you to come there with me, to be my guest."

"That's very nice of you, Danny," Alex thanked him. "But really, it shouldn't be me who goes with you. It has to be your wife, Sophie."

"But she can't come," Danny explained. "You see, we've got Jenny to think of. Normally, Sophie's mum and dad might have been able to have her, but they're going to be away on holiday that week. They're going to America, California actually, to see Sophie's aunt who lives out there. They haven't seen each other for years, and they're really looking forward to it. We can't ask them to cancel now, they'd lose all the money they've already paid for their tickets and everything."

"Well, I can understand that, but what about your Mum? Or your Gran?" Alex asked. "They should go, surely, not me. They must be really proud of you, to get the award."

"Yes, Mister, they are, but they can't come either," Danny told him. "Gran's hurt her leg, she had a fall, and she needs a bit of looking after at the moment, and mum won't leave her alone while she's like that. So neither of them can come, either. I'd really like you to come along. Please say yes."

"Well, if you're sure, Danny, then yes, I'd love to," said Alex. "Thank you so much for inviting me."

"Oh, good, that's settled then," Danny agreed. "I'll put your name on the form. And while you're down there, I presume I can come and stop on *Jennifer Jo* with you, as I've done before? It would save me the cost of a bed and breakfast somewhere."

"Of course you can," Alex smiled. "It will be great to have you aboard again. You can have your old berth in the back cabin, just like you always have."

"Thanks ever so much," Danny replied. "I'll scan in all the instructions and details about the awards ceremony, and email them down to you, so you know what it's all about."

"That's fine, Danny," said Alex. "By the way, this award, what exactly do you get?"

"There's an illuminated scroll,' Danny replied. "That's actually just a rolled up parchment, that's a posh sort of paper, and it's got some coloured motifs on it. It's not a piece of paper with a light in it, like some people think. And I get a medal as well, and a certificate in a frame to hang on the wall, and a citation saying why I've received it. And, also, I'm entitled to put the letters CM after my name, that's short for 'Citizenship Medal'. But I don't think I'll use that very often."

"No, I suppose not," Alex smiled. "But it will serve to impress whenever you go to see your bank manager, I don't doubt."

Danny chuckled again. "It sure will, Mister," he laughed. "Anyway, I must go, it's Jenny's bath time now. I'll call into the police station tomorrow and arrange to see my liaison officer, and let you know how it goes. Bye."

"Goodbye, Danny," Alex replied, as he switched off the call and sat back to think about what Danny had told him. He had little doubt in his own mind that the body that had been found was that of the boy Jamie Roberts, who'd been living at Grant Hall during Danny's time there. But there was little that he could do. He would have to leave it with Danny to move forward the question of the boy's identity with his liaison officer.

But he was really pleased that Danny had been awarded the

Citizenship Medal. With each Chief Constable being permitted to make just one award each year, the Citizenship Medal would bestow a real measure of exclusivity upon the recipient. Without Danny's evidence, at both of the trials relating to events that had taken place at Grant Hall, there would not have been any convictions, indeed without what Danny had done there would not even have been any trials at all. Danny's actions had been instrumental in bringing justice to bear onto the wrong-doers, and for that Danny's award was really well deserved. As Alex turned, picked up his cup, and went back inside *Jennifer Jo* to wash up and clear away after his meal, he allowed himself a small sense of pride that he'd been able to make a small contribution to what Danny had achieved.

The news item which Alex caught about a month later was short and succinct. It was the penultimate item in the half-hour bulletin he tried to catch every day, placed almost last in the running list behind the earlier, major pieces, featuring as was usually the case, politics, the economy, and the world situation, especially new tensions in the Middle East. 'Some things,' Alex thought to himself as he listened, 'never change, and probably they never will.' But he listened intently as the newsreader continued with the final pieces of the bulletin.

"........Police announced today that they had confirmed the identity of the young boy's body which was found last month buried in a shallow grave by contractors working on a new sewerage outfall system at Grant Hall, which at one time was in use as a children's home for boys with behavioural difficulties. Initially, police thought that the boy might have been resident at Grant Hall at some time in the past, but an in-depth study of Grant Hall's records from that time, now held in the archives at County Hall, had failed to give any clues as to whose body it might be."

"However, following information received from someone who had also been resident there, police were led to believe that the body was that of a boy named Jamie Roberts, who was indeed at one time being cared for at Grant Hall. Whilst it appeared that the body had been in the ground for a number of years, decomposition had been slow due to the nature of the peat soils in that area of the country. Police forensic scientists were able to recover good DNA samples from the body, and profiling against samples provided by a close relative has enabled the boy's identity to be confirmed as Jamie Roberts."

"It is understood that the cause of death has been established, but police are not releasing any further details at this time, save to confirm that a murder investigation has been launched."

Alex switched off the television and sat back, saddened by what he'd just heard. So Danny had been right after all. He sent a quick text message to Danny on his mobile, and shortly after received a reply. 'Yes, I know,' he'd sent. 'I sent you an email to let you know, the police told me yesterday.' Alex wasn't surprised that he'd not yet received Danny's email. Whilst he could usually get a good mobile phone signal, which used the 2G system, emails and internet connectivity, both of which required a good 3G signal, was still somewhat patchy at times. But Danny's text continued: 'I wonder what bastard did that to him. I hope they get him, and send him down for ever. And then the other lags in whatever jail they send him to will cut his bits off, and with any luck finish him off properly as well.' Alex allowed himself a grim smile. It was not like Danny to make comments like that. It showed just how upset Danny was about the whole business.

"Very smart, Danny," Alex opined a couple of months later as Danny stepped up onto the back deck of *Jennifer Jo,* resplendent in his smart suit, it's dark charcoal grey making a nice contrast to his pale blue shirt, which was neatly set off by a dark blue tie, with matching handkerchief just showing above the hem of his breast pocket. It was the day of the awards presentation, and they were just about to set off.

"You don't scrub up badly yourself, Mister," Danny retorted with his trademark grin, as he cast a glance at Alex, also wearing a smart suit and tie.

Alex smiled. "Well, they say clothes mature with age," he responded, "but it seems to have shrunk a touch since I last wore it."

"No, perhaps you've put on a bit of weight!" Danny sniggered.

"Maybe, just a touch," Alex laughed, "although working *Jennifer Jo* through the locks keeps me pretty fit. But I've had this suit for quite a while actually, probably eight or nine years now. There's not much opportunity to wear smart clothes when you're a live-aboard boater, you know," he added, as he locked the boat and they set off, walking along the road together.

Danny nodded. "What number bus do we need?" he asked, as they approached the bus stop. "There's a number 29 now coming."

"No Danny, it's not the bus today," Alex replied. "An occasion like this demands something a little better than that. I've ordered a taxi, it should be here presently, we're a couple of minutes early." It was indeed less than a minute before their taxi arrived, and they climbed aboard, Alex asking the driver to take them to County Hall, where the awards ceremony and reception was due to take place.

Their taxi dropped them directly outside the steps of County Hall, where a small crowd had already gathered. But, going briskly inside, they presented their tickets to one of the ushers, and were guided to their seats, only three or four rows from the front. Alex noted that whoever had set out the seating plan had done their job properly, with Danny being located on an aisle seat, thereby making it easy for him to approach the platform to receive his award without having to push past other people seated in the same row.

The hall quickly filled up, and it wasn't long before the dignitaries made their way onto the platform and the ceremony got under way. The event was being hosted by the Lord Mayor, resplendent with his mayoral chain of office draped over his shoulders, with the awards all being presented by the County's Lord Lieutenant, dressed in his smart black outfit with red trimmings, a ceremonial sword swinging at his side. Alex recognised none of the other people on the platform, with the exception of Rudolph Ampersandi, the Chief Constable, sitting quietly at the end of the front row, happy to let others take the limelight. Alex was aware that Ampersandi much preferred to keep a low profile on occasions such as this, and be judged by what he had achieved.

It was the first function of its type that Alex had ever attended, and he followed the proceedings with interest. Most of the awards were for staff from the services which drew their funding from the County Council, such as the fire service, children's and educational support services, and social services. There were long service awards, retirement awards, awards for meritorious service over many years, and several awards for exceptional work by volunteers in the recipient's chosen field.

The final category of awards were for members of the police, and as these were presented, one particular recipient caught Alex's attention. In contrast to the others who stepped up to collect their awards, this award, for outstanding initiative, was presented to a young police constable named Frederick Stephens, by far the youngest recipient in the whole of the morning's presentations. Alex was pleased to see that even newcomers to the police were recognised for their contribution to society, and were not overlooked at events such as these.

Eventually, as the proceedings arrived at the last award of the day, the Citizenship Award, Rudolph Ampersandi stood up and addressed the assembled crowd. "I'm immensely pleased to be able to present this award to a very worthwhile recipient," he stated. "On no less than two separate occasions, this person came forward with compelling evidence of wrongdoing on a serious scale, the first time when he was just a young lad of 13 years of age. The evidence he provided enabled the offenders to be brought to trial, and they were subsequently found guilty by the courts and sentenced to long periods in prison. And in the past few weeks, he's been assisting us with our enquiries into another incident which we've been investigating for some time. I would like it to be known that public spirited actions such as those displayed by this person are and always will be appreciated and acted upon with diligence. It gives me great pleasure to be able to present this very well-deserved first Citizenship Award to . . . . . . Mr Daniel Marshall."

To a round of polite applause, Danny stood up and moved forward to the platform where Ampersandi shook his hand, and together they turned to the nearby to pose to the photographer, who'd snapped all the awards, for the handover of Danny's medal. Then, blushing slightly, Danny returned to his seat as the Lord Mayor brought the proceedings to a close, and everyone moved through to the adjacent room for the informal reception and buffet that followed.

Alex and Danny slowly circulated round the room, visiting the buffet to partake of a light lunch, whilst several people, whom neither of them knew, came up to congratulate Danny on his award. But after a while, the crowd began to thin out as some of those present started to make their way home. But just as Alex was thinking that he and Danny should be on their way themselves, the young policeman who'd so impressed Alex by receiving an award for outstanding initiative came up to Danny. "Hello, Mr. Marshall," he said to Danny. "I hope you don't mind, but I think I know you. Do you remember me?"

Danny shook his head. "No, I'm sorry, I don't think so," he said, "but congratulations on your award."

"Thank you, Mr. Marshall," the young policeman replied. "And congratulations on your award too," he added. "It's much more important than mine. But I do think I know you, from years ago. Your first name's Daniel, isn't it? But did you used to be called Danny, when you were a kid?"

"Well, yes, actually, I did," Danny responded. "Most people still call me that now."

The policeman nodded. "And, when you were younger, were you in care?" he asked eagerly.

"That's right, I was," said Danny. "For quite a while, in fact. But they let me go in the end."

Alex smiled to himself at the understatement of the year, as the policeman went on. "Were you in foster care once? With a Mrs.

Bradley?"

"Yes, I was," replied Danny, curious now. "She was ever so nice."

"Yes, she was," said the policeman. "She was nice to me too. You see, I think you were there, with Mrs Bradley, at the same time as me. My name is Frederick Stephens, but back then, before I was formally adopted, my name was Frederick Norton. But everyone used to call me Freddie. They still do. It's only Frederick for formal occasions like this."

"You're Freddie? asked Danny, incredulously. "Little Freddie? We shared the same bedroom at Mrs. Bradley's?"

"Yes, that right, we did," Freddie replied excitedly. "Do you remember me now?"

"Yes I do," Danny exclaimed. "I'm really sorry that I didn't recognise you earlier. But you've changed a lot since then, though."

"I suppose so," Freddie laughed. "But so have you, as well. You know," he went on, "I thought such a lot of you, back then. I really did. I can still remember how unhappy I was at first, when I first went into care and went to Mrs. Bradley's. But when you arrived, and started to look after me, well, that helped me so much to put the unhappy times behind me. I'll never forget what you did for me, how much you helped me. I don't suppose I ever thanked you then, so can I please say a big thank you now?"

Freddie took Danny's hand and shook it vigorously as Danny responded. "It's very nice of you to say that," he replied. "You were such a cute little kid, you know. I can remember how miserable you were at first. I'm really pleased that I was able to help you. You've obviously put it all behind you now."

"Yes," Freddie replied, "I had some wonderful adoptive parents, they looked after me as if I was one of their own children. They'd already had two kids of their own, and they felt they still wanted to help other kids after their own two left home. That's my mum here now, over there." He pointed across the room where a small group of people were chatting to the Lord Mayor. "If you can excuse me, I suppose I'd better go and be sociable. Once again, thank you so much for what you did. I'm really pleased that I've met you again. Bye." They shook hands together, and with that, Freddie made his way across the room to rejoin his mother.

Danny turned to Alex, a wide smile upon his face. "Fancy that, Mister," he exclaimed. "Did I ever tell you about Freddie?"

"Yes, I recall that you did," Alex replied. "But that was a long while ago now, just after you came to be aboard *Jennifer Jo*. It's really nice that you've met up again. By the way, you've collected your medal now, but what about the other things they said you were going to get? The illuminated parchment and the framed certificate, and stuff like that?"

"Oh, that will come in the post," Danny explained. "Next week sometime, I think. They only presented just the medal this morning. It's really nice, isn't it?"

He opened the case and showed Alex the medal, securely fastened onto a purple felt backcloth, with its purple and blue ribbon above. "I'm really proud to have been awarded it. Mum and Gran and Sophie, they'll all be pleased as punch when I show it to them."

"I'm sure they will," replied Alex. "But anyway, there's nothing much to keep us here now, and we don't know anybody, so if you've had your fill from the buffet, shall we make our way back?"

"I think so, Mister," said Danny. "I've had enough to eat at the moment, but I'll try to put some supper away when we get back to *Jay-Jay*. Let's go," he added, grinning once again.

"Right-oh'", Alex nodded. "Let's go, then."

They walked back to the entrance foyer, then, as they started to make their way down the majestic steps in front of the County Hall, Rudolph Ampersandi came out behind them. "Hello, Alex," he called. "Sorry I couldn't get to chat earlier. Nice to see you here. And you, too, Mr. Marshall. It's good to meet you at last, the police up North spoke very highly of you. Your input on all these cases you've been involved in really has been most valuable. You were by far the most suitable person to receive the Citizenship Award, believe me. Well done."

"Thank you, Sir," Danny replied, blushing slightly. "I only did what anyone would have done."

"Well, I'm not so sure everybody would have done what you did," Ampersandi replied. "But you've been certainly instrumental in bringing two serious cases to a good conclusion."

"Speaking of which," Alex asked, "did you ever get any further on that last suspect? You know, after the trial a few months ago, about the historic sex abuse of the boys at Grant Hall, twelve of those thirteen people who paid night-time visits to molest the boys were sent down. You'd been able to trace them from the car numbers we gave you from the tobacco tin. But you told me then that you'd not been able to trace the last one, the last of the thirteen. 'The one that got away', you called him. Have you been able to make any progress on that since we last met?"

"It's funny you should ask that," Ampersandi said, with a wry smile. "In just the last few days we have actually managed to identify the one that got away. But we'll not be taking it any further. Anyway, are you still on your boat? In the same place where I met you that time?"

"Yes, I'm still boating," Alex nodded. "And yes, I'm moored in the same place as usual, it's quite a nice place to stop for a few days. Danny's staying on board with me at the moment as well, I'm providing B & B for him while he's down here to collect his award."

Ampersandi smiled. "Almost like old times, then," he said. "You're right, It is a nice spot. I like to fish there whenever I get the time, which unfortunately is not very often these days." He glanced down at his watch before adding, "perhaps if you go straight back now, you might just be back in time to catch the six o'clock news. Anyway, I must go, my car's just arrived. Goodbye." He shook hands with both Alex and Danny, then set off down the steps to his waiting car.

Danny gave him a quick wave as his car sped away, then they walked together down the steps to the pavement. "Where's the taxi, then, Mister?" Danny asked, grinning once again. "I could get used to going around like that. It's much better than being thrown about on the bus every time it goes round a corner."

"Don't push your luck, young man," Alex smiled. "It's the bus for us now. Or you can walk if you like, but I'll warn you in advance, it's quite a long way."

"The bus it is, then," said Danny, with an imitation groan. But then, as they stood waiting at the bus stop for their ride back to *Jennifer Jo*, Danny turned to Alex with a question.

"I say, Mister, there's something I don't understand. About what Ampersandi said just now."

"What's that, Danny?" Alex asked.

"Well, If they've found the last man from the car numbers, the one that got away, who they've been looking for, then why aren't they taking it any further? It doesn't make any sense to drop it, and not take him to court. And, why should Ampersandi say we could get back just in time for the six o'clock news? It doesn't make much sense to me, no sense at all."

Alex smiled. He well knew that Danny was a bright young man, but he'd obviously missed the subtleties of what Ampersandi had said. "I think you'll find, Danny," he replied, "that when you find the answer to your second question, then that will answer your first question as well."

"What exactly do you mean?" asked Danny. "I still don't understand. You're talking in riddles now, as well."

"Well, Ampersandi has to be very careful as to what he says," Alex told him. "But that doesn't stop him dropping a few gentle hints when he can. Let's get back and see the news, and perhaps that will make things much clearer. In fact, I'm sure it will. And, don't forget, it's your turn to make the tea tonight. Anyway, here comes our bus. Let's go."

Alex and Danny had just sat down to enjoy their meal when the news started. They listened intently as the regular news presenter David Bathurst presented the first item......

"The Shadow Home Secretary, Darren Armitage, has died. He was found dead at his home this morning. Our reporter Jane Walmsley has the details..........."

The picture then cut to a view of a large country house, with Jane Walmsley standing outside the entrance gate. Through the gate could be seen several police cars, and a tent erected in front of the double-garage at the side of the house. A number of policemen were moving around, with a uniformed constable on duty by the gate, which had a couple of the familiar blue and white 'no entry - police line' ribbons stretched across it. Some forensic specialists wearing white overalls and face masks were talking amongst themselves in the background. Then Jane started her piece to camera....

"Yes, thank you, David. The police are releasing few details at this stage of their enquiries, but they have confirmed that a dead body was found here at Darren Armitage's home this morning, and it is that of Darren Armitage, the Shadow Home Secretary."

" We understand that Mr. Armitage was due to present himself at a local police station this morning for an interview, but when he did not turn up, a couple of police officers were sent here to his country house, where they found no-one at home. However, whilst scouting around the house, they noticed the sound of a car engine running inside the garage, which was securely locked from the inside. Upon forcing entry to the garage, they found Mr. Armitage slumped in the driver's seat with the car windows open. Paramedics were called immediately, but it was soon determined that Mr. Armitage had been dead for some little while before the police officers first arrived, presumably from the inhalation of exhaust fumes, but this will need to be confirmed at a post-mortem."

"Police are not releasing any further details at this stage, and have refused to comment on why Mr. Armitage had been asked to attend

for interview. The coroner has been informed and an inquest will be held at a later date. Mr. Armitage leaves a wife and three grown-up children, who are all said to be very upset at his untimely death. And now, back to David in the studio."

Bathurst immediately introduced the news team's chief political correspondent, who went on to present a summary of Armitage's political career. Appointed Shadow Home Secretary when the Labour Party moved into opposition after the recent general election, Armitage had been Home Secretary in the previous Labour government, having previously held a number of junior positions over many years in both government and opposition, all of them in the Home Office. Alex and Danny listened in silence, then as the new bulletin moved on to the next item, Alex leaned over and switched off the television.

"So, Danny, what do you make of that?" Alex asked.

Danny was quiet for a short while before he spoke. "Well, Mister," he said at last, "I think that Armitage has to have been the one that got away. That must have been what Ampersandi was hinting at when we left the reception."

"Yes, Danny, I think you're right," Alex confirmed. "I can think of no other explanation. Probably the interview he was supposed to attend at the police station was something to do with Grant Hall? I just don't know. And perhaps now we never will."

"Why do you say that?" asked Danny, curiously.

"Well," Alex went on. "Armitage is, or rather was, an important figure in politics. And if this is to do with Grant Hall, then it will be hugely embarrassing to the Labour Party. The dirty deeds that such high-profile people in senior positions in politics do whilst they're alive are usually hushed up after they're dead. There'll be a lot of pressure applied to the police to keep a lid on it, you mark my words."

"That's not right, is it?" Danny asked. "Everyone should be called to account for their actions. Especially if they've been interfering with young kids like we think he has. I don't follow politics that much, but from what I've heard, he's not a very nice person anyway."

"You're right there," Alex agreed. He was well aware that Armitage, who'd left school at the age of 16 with no academic qualifications whatsoever, had always been a very aggressive character, right from his very early days as a trade union official and convenor. He'd had a 'no compromise' approach to industrial relations, often referring to employers as 'the enemy', and he'd orchestrated any number of bitter strikes, the end result of which, on quite a few occasions, had been that the companies involved had moved production overseas, or simply gone out of business altogether, ironically putting many of his trade union members out of work. In fact, by comparison with Armitage, Arthur Scargill had been a fairy godmother. Entering parliament sponsored by his trade union, Armitage's prominent hard-line left-wing views had made headlines many times. And in government he'd been a continual thorn in the side of the Prime Minister, whose trade union paymasters had insisted that Armitage be given one of the key offices of state.

"He's a bit of a bruiser, certainly," Alex added. "And that's putting it mildly. He's not going to be a great loss to society, in my view."

Danny nodded in agreement. "And if he is the one that caused Jamie to die, then he's a right coward, isn't he? Avoiding a court case like that?"

Alex had to agree. "Right again, Danny. You put it very well. Anyway, since you cooked the supper, I'll do the clearing away. OK?"

"Sure thing, Mister," Danny smiled. "But I'll wipe up for you."

They'd just finished washing up their supper things when there was a loud knock on the side of the boat. Looking out of the window, Alex saw the newspaper reporter Robert Jefferies standing outside. He and Danny went out onto the rear deck to greet him, and found he had with him two young lads, about nine or ten years of age.

"I thought I might find you here, Alex," Jefferies said. "Nice to meet you again. And you too, Danny. Congratulations on your award, by the way. It's well deserved. I saw you both at the ceremony this morning, but didn't get a chance to speak with either of you. I was only allowed to be at the back during the presentations, and I wasn't allowed into the reception afterwards at all. By the way, these are my two sons. The one on the left is Ricky, and him on the right, that's Reuben. As you can see, they're twins," he smiled. "I'm taking them to their grandparents, they go there every other weekend, but we're a bit early, and so I thought I might drop in for a chat."

Saying hello to the two boys, Alex caught his breath with astonishment. He'd seen a number of pairs of twins before, as over the years quite a number of twins had passed through the school where he'd been a teacher and housemaster, but never before had he seen two boys so alike. Usually there were slight distinguishing features which he could easily notice and remember, but these two boys really were like peas in a pod. But Jefferies was speaking again. "They've never seen a canal narrowboat," he said. "Do you mind if they can have a look inside?"

"No, of course not, that will be fine," Alex replied. "Danny here, he'll show them around." Danny nodded. "Come along with me," he said to the boys, "and mind these steps on the way down, they're quite steep until you get used to them."

As the two boys disappeared inside *Jennifer Jo* with Danny, Alex turned to Jefferies again. "How do you tell which of your two boys is which?" Alex asked. "They look so much more alike than any other twins I've seen."

"Funny you should say that," replied Jefferies. "I often get asked. But I just do. I can't really explain how, but I can tell them easily. You know, most twins have DNA which is about 98% or 98.5% identical, but these two, well, theirs come in at around 99.99994% the same. The doctors and geneticists were amazed when they did some tests, soon after they were born. They think that the fertilised egg split into two separate embryos much later than it usually does when there's twins. The specialists wanted them to have loads more tests, but my wife and I, we said no, we didn't want them to become laboratory animals."

"It was really difficult for us at first," he went on. "What we did, when we first brought them home from the hospital, we tied large labels with each name on, onto their ankles, and never took them off. And every time we attended to them, you know, like feeding or nappy changing or bathing or whatever, anything like that, we'd take that one out of earshot from the other, and talk to him all the time, making sure that in every single sentence we'd say his name, saying it over and over again, in every sentence, trying to imprint his name onto his brain as much as we could."

"And eventually, we could go to them when they were together and just say a name, and one of them would respond, like moving his eyes or his head to look at you, or something like that. That helped a great deal, but we kept the labels on for a good three years or more, I can't remember exactly how long now, until we were both fully confident about which was which. My wife was always more confident than I was, I suppose it comes from being their mother who carried them, I don't really know."

"One thing we noticed quite early on," he continued, "once they got to be able to walk around, was that they always sat together the same way."

"What do you mean?" asked Alex.

"Well, when they sit together, side by side, it's always Reuben sits on Ricky's right, and Ricky is always on Reuben's left. That's another hint as to which of them is which. We think it's because that's the position they were in, when they were in the womb together before they were born. And, from very early days, they've always hated being apart. We've got a three-bedroom house, so they could have had their own rooms ages ago, but they've always insisted on sharing the same room together. And at the dining table, when we're having a meal, we started them off with me and Pauline sitting at opposite ends of the table, with the boys on opposite sides facing each other. But they kicked up such a fuss, we had to have a change round, with the two boys along one side, and me and Pauline together on the other side. And of course Reuben always had to be on Ricky's right."

Jefferies paused a moment before continuing. "We had trouble when they started school, too. The head teacher, she thought she knew best, she insisted they were put into separate classes, although we had warned her that they'd much prefer to be in the same class together."

"Well, they didn't do very well, not taking part much at all in what was going on, and at times being a little disruptive, I'm afraid, it has to be said. But then Ricky's teacher fell ill, and they had to put the two classes together in the same room for a few weeks until she recovered. As soon as the boys found themselves in the same class, their work improved tremendously, and they were much better behaved. And the boys arranged it with one of the other kids to swap seats so they could sit together at the same table. The penny dropped with the head teacher after that, and they were allowed to be together from then on."

"It's not just being together, either," he went on. "They always need to be as close together as they can. For example, as I said just now, they're in the same bedroom. We originally put their beds parallel to each other, on opposite walls, to give some space in the middle of the room for them to play, but it wasn't long before they'd moved their beds into the middle of the room, side by side and close together, touching in fact, so that they could be as near to each other as they could."

"That's really interesting," Alex commented. "You must find it really strange."

"Yes we do," Bob continued. "They seem to have a real empathy with each other, too. Like at football."

"What happens there?" asked Alex, growing more and more curious every minute.

Well," said Bob. "They play football in our local boys sports club, they're both been members for some time now. If they're playing in different teams, well, they take part in what's going on, but not really that much, it's more like they're just going through the motions. if they're in opposite teams, playing against each other, it's even worse, they both just stand around and take very little part at all in the match."

"It's when they're playing together, on the same team, that they really start to shine. For example, if Ricky has the ball and needs to pass, nine times out of ten he'll choose to pass it to Reuben. But the thing is, looking at what's going on from the sidelines, I quite often go to watch them play, Reuben is usually in the right place to receive the pass, he's the obvious player to pass the ball to. The team manager has realised now how well they play when they're together, and he nearly always arranges his team list like that now. Their team is second in their league at the moment, they got promotion from the league below at the end of last season, they're doing really well."

"That's fascinating," Alex remarked.

"There's more," Jefferies went on. "When they were about five, I was with them at home, Pauline was out. I was cooking the tea in the kitchen, but the boys, Reuben was in the living room playing on the floor with some toys, and Ricky was at the dining room table with a colouring book. They couldn't see each other, but from where I was in the kitchen I could see both of them. Suddenly Reuben caught his elbow against a cupboard, it must have hurt him a little bit, because he stopped what he was doing to rub his elbow. And immediately, Ricky in the dining room put down his crayon and rubbed his elbow as well, the same elbow of course. There's loads of little things like that happen all the time."

"But I think their bond is becoming stronger, and stranger too, as the years go on," said Bob after a pause for reflection. "There's something even more remarkable happened about a year ago. Reuben was in the dining room, building a model out of Lego. And Ricky was upstairs playing with his model railway, he always has liked his trains, much more so than Reuben, who prefers Lego. They do have different interests at times, you see, they're each their own person, if you know what I mean. Anyway, Reuben, he couldn't find the particular piece of Lego he was looking for, he was hunting through this big tub of Lego parts and getting more and more frustrated because he couldn't find the piece he wanted. And then suddenly, without a word being spoken between them, Ricky comes downstairs with a piece of Lego in his hand and passes it to Reuben, he says 'here it is,' then goes off upstairs again. And of course it was the piece that Reuben was looking for. Pauline and me, we just looked at each other, we couldn't believe our eyes."

"Then last year, Reuben had to go into hospital, he'd got appendicitis. Ricky was really miserable while he was away, and the day

Reuben had his operation, Ricky goes up to the bedroom and starts groaning. Pauline was with Reuben in the hospital, so I went upstairs to see what was wrong, and there's Ricky holding his side and crying, saying it hurt. But after about three quarters of an hour, he stopped groaning and came down stairs, saying I'm alright now. I checked with Pauline when she got home, and the time when Ricky was groaning was the same time that Reuben was having his operation. It's absolutely unbelievable, but I tell you, it really happened."

"Well, at least there's an easy way now to tell them apart," laughed Alex. "Reuben is the one with the scar on his tummy!"

"That's right," agreed Bob. "All you've got to do now is persuade him to show it to you! Anyway, while I'm here, did you see the news tonight?"

"About Darren Armitage, you mean?" asked Alex. "I presume it's to do with Grant Hall?"

"What makes you think that, then?" asked Jefferies, smiling broadly.

"Well," Alex replied. "I had a brief chat with Rudolph Ampersandi after the reception this afternoon, and he dropped a subtle hint, and Danny and I, we've put two and two together and come up with a lot more than four."

"You're right, of course," Bob Jefferies confirmed, still smiling. "I don't know how much of this I'll ever be able to publish, but what I've been able to put together, from various sources, is this."

"Really, we need to start with the body of that young boy they found buried there, Jamie Robson, his name was, no, Jamie Roberts, that's right. It's not generally known yet, as the police haven't released this information, but the cause of death had been established quite early on in their investigations, he died from a perforated bowel. Given what those night-time visitors to Grant Hall went there for, you can imagine how that happened."

"Anyway, the forensic scientists, they did a thorough job examining the boy's body, and they found someone else's DNA up where the sun don't shine, if you know what I mean. Of course, they ran it through against the national DNA database, but there wasn't a match. So that line of enquiry seemed to have come to a dead end."

"So, now we go back to the car numbers which Danny and his mates noted down when the night-time visitors came. Do you recall, when we met here that time, after you'd told me all about the tobacco tin and the car numbers, I got some of my contacts to have a look into the

Police National Computer and check out the car numbers? They'd never be able to do that now, by the way, they've tightened things up a great deal since then. Anyway, the guy who was looking into one particular number didn't get very far, there was just a screen giving a phone number and saying permission had to be obtained to access the information. Do you remember that?"

Alex nodded. "Yes, I do," he said. "I thought it a bit strange at the time."

"That's right," Jefferies continued. "I said then that I thought it was the number of a government car, if you remember. Apparently Ampersandi tried quite a number of times to get the info he wanted, to find out whose car it was, but the people on the other end of that phone, whoever they were, they always blocked it, so he never got very far with it. He even approached the Prime Minister when they were at a policing conference together, but the PM simply said it was a matter for the Home Office and he couldn't, or wouldn't, interfere. Talk about the toffs sticking together. That Labour crowd seem to be the worst of the lot. It was high time they got slung out of office at the election the other month."

"But Ampersandi never did get that information, did he?" Alex asked. "He can't have done, because otherwise he'd have found whoever's car it was, and had him into court ages ago, with those others who were sent down."

"You're right, he had to let it rest," Bob Jefferies confirmed. "He wasn't happy about it, but in the end he just went after the ones he could identify. And that's why the one that got away, as Ampersandi called him, never made it into court."

"So how did they find him now?" asked Alex. "After all this time? They didn't let it rest after all?"

"Well they did really," said Bob. "They had to, they were obliged to close the files. You see, after the case against all those other men was sent for trial, Ampersandi pulled all his men off the case. There's been a big increase of drugs into this area recently, there's a team moved in who are flooding the place with cheap supplies, and targeting school kids as well. The street price has never been as low as it is now, and they're making a fortune. And now another team has moved in and is trying to take over the trade, there's a bit of a turf war, so Ampersandi is trying to sort that out. He left just one young copper on the case, to tidy up the files and make sure everything could be put away and archived properly. But this young copper, he had a breakthrough. He did really well, that's why he got a special award this morning."

"Do you mean Freddie? Frederick Stephens?" asked Alex. "That's really strange, that is!"

"Why's that?" asked Jefferies.

"Well, Danny's a few years older than Freddie, but he knew him a long while ago," explained Alex. "They were young lads together, when they were both in care, being fostered by a Mrs. Bradley. They met again at the reception this morning. It was quite emotional, really. But what exactly did Freddie do, to break the case open again?"

"Well," Jefferies went on, "Stephens was convinced that there had to be some way of finding out who's car it was, so he thought about it for a while, then he had a bit of a brainwave. He reckoned that, since there was a different government in power now after the general election, it might be worth while trying again to get the information about that car from the Home Office."

"So he put it forward to Ampersandi, and he agreed, and so the request was put in again, for the umpteenth time, but this time, to everyone's surprise, a few days later back came the information they'd been after for ages. They expected it to be someone important, but they hadn't reckoned on what actually came back. You see, it was Darren Armitages' car, the car he'd had the use of when he'd been a junior minister at the Home Office. They'd never expected to catch such a big fish as that. Now they could understand why all their requests for information had been refused in the past. I mean, Armitage wasn't going to own up to being at Grant Hall, was he, after all that had been going on? No wonder he quashed all the requests for information."

Alex nodded in agreement as Bob went on. "But that didn't really get them very far, because on its own, it didn't link him with the abuse that was going on, all it proved was that Armitage had been to Grant Hall. It was insufficient for them to re-open the case, especially since he was such a high-profile figure, and they'd already had a trial and put a few important people away, although none as important as Armitage was."

"And there was no way that Ampersandi could give his guys a photo of Armitage and go round the people who testified about the abuse at the trial, asking them if this guy had abused them as well. Just imagine if one of the tabloids had got hold of it, they'd be headlines on the front page two feet high, screaming that the Shadow Home Secretary was suspected of abusing young kids. Don't forget the type of person Armitage was, there'd have been writs flying around all over the place in thirty seconds flat, and Ampersandi would have been slung out of his job in no time. So once again, although things had moved forward a little with

Armitage's car being identified, that wasn't nearly enough to warrant any action being taken. So it seemed that they'd come up against another dead end."

"But that young copper Freddie Stephens, he'd got the bit between his teeth now. He was convinced that Armitage had something to do with Jamie Roberts death, and so he decided to look a little deeper into Armitage's background, and see if he could dig anything else up. So he started trawling through Armitage's career history, and that sort of thing. He'd been in the limelight for quite a while, firstly as an MP, then after that either as a government minister or a shadow minister, always at the Home Office, and before that he'd been a really tough guy in the trade union movement. So there was plenty of material for young Stephens to go through."

"Well, eventually Stephens finds something interesting. You see, years ago, when it was first realised that this DNA testing procedure was going to be such a useful tool for the police, the government had to get the law changed to permit the police to take samples from suspects and have those samples analysed. So there'd been a bill presented to parliament, and the guy who'd been made responsible for piloting the bill through parliament was none other than our friend Armitage. He was a junior minister at the Home Office at the time. And once royal assent had been granted, there'd been a press photo-call to publicise it, and at the photo-call Armitage was pictured having a sample taken, a swab from inside his mouth, I think it was."

"So Stephens started to wonder what had happened to that sample. Had it ever actually been sent for analysis? He makes some enquiries, and finds that at the start of the DNA testing programme there were only three laboratories approved to carry out the tests, so he gets on to them all and asks them if they'd received Armitage's sample for analysis. One of the labs came back and said yes, they'd had it and analysed it, and sent the results back to the Home Office. So he asks them if they've still got a copy of their results in their archive, and they confirmed that they had. Next, he asks for the results, but they wouldn't release them, because of patient confidentiality, and because the tests had been commissioned by the Home Office and not by the police."

"So Ampersandi has to go back to the Home Office and get them to give permission for the results to be released, which they did, and eventually the results they'd been waiting for, for all that time, they finally came through. The final piece of the puzzle was to compare that against the analysis of the sample found in Jamie's body, and bingo, they've got him. You can imagine how Ampersandi felt about that."

"Yes, I'm sure he was pretty pleased," Alex remarked.

"Indeed," Bob replied. "Armitage was due to present himself at his local police station this morning for questioning, and I think they would have proceeded to bring a murder charge against him. Ampersandi had tipped us off, so we had a photographer and a reporter waiting there to catch him, we've helped him quite a bit on the drugs investigation, so it was a bit of a payback time for us, but of course he didn't show up. There will be a lot of pressure now to hush up why he was wanted for interview, but I suppose it will leak out in the end. It's a shame that I can't publish it in my paper, because a lot of what I've just told you I shouldn't really know."

Just then, Danny reappeared from inside *Jennifer Jo* with Bob's two boys, who went and stood next to their father. Alex seized the opportunity to surprise them, and hopefully Danny as well. "Now, let me see if I've got this right," he remarked casually, pointing to the boy on his right, "You're Ricky, aren't you? And you," he added, pointing to the boy on his left, "you must be Reuben."

The two boys looked at each other in astonishment. "Gosh, you're really good," Reuben exclaimed. "How on earth can you tell, after only just meeting us? Most of our teachers at school can't tell us apart, and we've been at that school for a couple of years now."

Alex smiled as he cast a sly wink at their father, un-noticed by the boys, and by Danny too. "Just being observant," he said. "It's called experience, being able to notice the little things." He wasn't going to let on that Bob had told him only a few minutes before that Reuben always stood on Ricky's right, to the left as he stood looking at them. "Anyway, boys," he added, "what do you think of my boat, then?"

"It's really surprising inside," said Reuben. "It's amazing how much you can get into quite a small space if you try. It must be nice living on a boat like this. Dad, can we hire a barge next year, and have a holiday on the canal? Please?"

"Hang on a moment," Alex said, grimacing slightly as he did so. It annoyed him to hear the wrong terminology being used. "It's not a barge, it's a narrowboat. A narrowboat is no more than 6 feet 10 inches wide, whilst a barge is 10ft or more in width. But don't worry, everyone makes that mistake at first."

"What about it, Dad," Ricky piped up. "Can we please? It would be good fun!"

"I'll have a word with your mother, and we'll think about it," Bob replied, smiling. "But I'm not promising anything. You'll have to work the locks though, don't expect me or your mother to do them."

"We will, Dad," they chorused in unison, smiling at each other.

"Anyway, Alex, we've got to be on our way," Bob added. "It's been nice to meet up with you again. Just remember please, what I've just told you isn't generally known yet. So be careful who you talk to, please. And goodbye to you too, Danny. Come on, boys, let's go."

Alex and Danny went back inside Jennifer Jo, where they sat in the saloon while Alex told Danny all that he'd just heard from Bob. Unsurprisingly, Danny was a little upset to hear about how Jamie Roberts had died, but when Alex had finished, he said quietly "I'm glad that bastard Armitage is dead. I hope he rots in hell for what he's done."

Just then Alex's mobile phone rang. He answered it, making notes as he did so, then putting the phone down he turned to Danny. "Danny, that was Ampersandi's secretary," he told him. "Now that Armitage is dead and there won't be a court case, the police have released Jamie's body for burial. The funeral is tomorrow, at the village church near Grant Hall. I said I'd go. Would you be able to come along as well?"

"Yes, of course I will," Danny responded. "I have to say a last goodbye to Jamie. As you know, I was supposed to go home tomorrow, but I'll phone Sophie and tell her I'll be back a day later. It's Saturday tomorrow, anyway, and I'm not due back at work till Monday, so that will be fine."

"That's good," Alex responded. "I'll hire a car for the day, that will be easier for us."

The next morning was bright and sunny. As their car approached the church, situated just outside the large iron gates which gave access to the long drive into the grounds of Grant Hall, Alex was saddened to see the flag at the top of the church tower flying at half-mast. He and Danny were surprised to see so many cars in the car park, in fact they were lucky to get one of the last spaces. Going inside the small but elegant country church, they found it was packed, almost full. They sat down on a pew near the back, and a minute or two later Bob Jefferies came in and sat down beside them.

"Who are all these people?" Alex asked him. "I didn't expect there to be many here at all."

"Ah, you can thank Ampersandi for that," Bob replied. "The lady in the wheelchair at the front, I think that's Jamie's sister, there's a couple of carers with her. There's several from Social Services too, and the rest, they're mostly either police officers or civilian police support staff. You see, when he became Chief Constable, Ampersandi made a point of encouraging all his people to attend the funerals of murder victims whose cases they've worked on. It's a policy which has become very popular amongst all his staff, to give a good farewell to the deceased." But then, the group of bearers entered with the small coffin on their shoulders, placed it on the stands at the front of the church, and the service got under way.

The funeral service lasted about half an hour, then everyone slowly trooped outside to the churchyard to the place where the interment was to take place. The priest said a few more words, then silence fell, as Jamie's coffin was slowly lowered into the ground. Suddenly, Alex heard a choking sound coming from Danny. Turning to him, he saw a stream of tears running down Danny's face. Alex reached out took hold of Danny's hand, grasping it tightly. Danny looked round to Alex, and nodded an acknowledgement through his tears. 'That,' thought Alex to himself, 'says it all'.

As the crowd round the grave gradually dispersed, Danny walked with Alex back to their car. As Alex drove off, Danny reached into the glove box and took out a road atlas. "Can we go somewhere please, Mister?" he asked. "Before we go back to *Jay-Jay*? It's not very far, I'll give you directions."

"Yes of course, Danny," said Alex. "Wherever you like."

Alex followed Danny's instructions until he was asked to pull up on a grass verge, out in open country. "We can walk from here," Danny said, and the two set off along the road, walking along in silence. After about 300 yards they turned a sharp corner and Alex found himself on a humpback bridge, and looking over the parapet, he saw the canal beneath. He didn't immediately recognise exactly where he was, as his usual view of canals was not from atop a bridge, but from the back of *Jennifer Jo*. It was a quite different perspective from which to view the waterway.

"Follow me," Danny said, as he disappeared through a gap in the hedge and down a grassy slope onto the towpath, sitting down on a bench beside the nearby lock, to Alex just one of the many locks that he'd encountered during his years on *Jennifer Jo*. Alex sat down beside Danny, knowing it was best to stay quiet, leaving him alone with his thoughts. They sat there in silence for a good five minutes before Danny, still staring at the water, spoke at last.

"Jamie didn't deserve to die like that," he exclaimed bitterly. "The poor little kid. He didn't deserve to die at all."

"Yes, Danny, I know," Alex consoled him. "Life can be very cruel at times. Cruel to those who die before their time, especially when it's because of the selfish actions of others. And cruel too, to those left behind. But be happy now that Jamie is at rest where he should be, and be satisfied as well that those who were responsible for what happened to him have at last been called to account, and paid a price for what they did."

Danny nodded glumly. "I suppose so, Mister," he agreed, "but it doesn't make it any easier, does it?"

"No, Danny, it doesn't," Alex responded. "But time is a great healer. Everything that happened at Grant Hall can at last be allowed to fade into history, now that the final piece of the puzzle has been put into place. Now is the time for us to leave all this behind us, and look forward to better things. You have a great deal to look forward to, with your wife and daughter."

"Remember, Danny, your life is not a rehearsal, it's the real thing, and you only get one chance at it. So seize the opportunities that present themselves to you, make the most of your life, and enjoy it as much as you can. That's the best advice I can possibly give you."

Danny didn't reply, just nodding in agreement, then falling silent again for a couple of minutes. "You know, Mister," he said eventually. "This is where it all started. You and me."

Alex suddenly recognised the place where Danny had brought him to. This was the lock where he'd moored up that afternoon many long years ago, and spent the afternoon helping other boaters take their boats through the lock. This was the place where a young boy, scared, frightened, and on the run from the abusive environment at Grant Hall, had lifted Jennifer Jo's cratch cover and crept aboard, while Alex was busy at the lock. And later that evening, a little further along the cut, whilst looking in the cratch for coal to feed his fire, Alex had found him, shivering in the cold, and thus starting a relationship that had now spanned many years.

"Yes, Danny," I recognise it now," he replied. "I was moored up under those trees over there. They've grown a bit since then, though."

"I suppose so," Danny replied. He stretched out his hand, pointing. "I was hiding up that tree, the tall one on the right. I saw Hammond come down the road and talk to you. He'd got that awful dog Brutus with him, if I remember right. That dog, it was pure evil. I've never like dogs, ever since Brutus got too close to me, several times."

He was quiet for a short while, than began speaking again. "What happened here changed my life, you know, Mister," he said quietly.

"Deciding to hide in your boat was one of the best things I've ever done. You took me in, hid me from the authorities, looked after me, you even waited at bridge 45 after I got took back to Grant Hall until you'd run out of supplies, you were out of almost everything. You taught me school lessons. And you helped me find my mum again. Not many people would have done all that for a young boy who they didn't know, who they'd never even met before."

"You know, I did wonder about you a bit at first, why you took me in, the very first day," he went on. "Especially when you took those photos of my injuries, even my backside if you remember. Do you remember, when you said that first night, that I needn't sleep on the floor by the stove, and you went and made up a bed for me in the back cabin? I think that's what decided me to see how things turned out with you. And you were all right, right from the start."

"And without those photos, without that crucial evidence, Hammond and those other wardens at Grant Hall might never have been put away, and there might still be young kids going through god-knows-what there today."

"I did what was right, Danny," Alex replied quietly. "Anyone would have done the same."

"No Mister, they wouldn't," Danny responded. "Anyone else would have handed me in, just washed their hands of me. You didn't. You did so much for me. I wish I could find some way to thank you properly, to repay you for what you've done."

"There's no need, Danny," said Alex. "The fact that you appreciate what I was able to do for you is thanks enough."

They were quiet again for a while as they sat and watched a crew work their boat through the lock, not wanting to share with anyone else what had become a very private conversation. Then Alex turned to Danny and started speaking again. "Danny, there something I need to tell you," he said. "It may come as a surprise to you, but I've decided to sell *Jennifer Jo*."

"You what?" exclaimed Danny in astonishment. "What will you do? Where will you live? You love being on the canal, I know you do. And it doesn't seem right that someone else will be living on *Jennifer Jo* instead of you."

"Hey, Danny, one at a time, please," Alex smiled. "You're right, I do love being on the water. It's been wonderful to move around, there're over 2000 miles of canal to explore, and I've travelled just about all of them. No matter how many times I go along the same stretch of water, there's always something different to see. And it's a great way of life, I've really enjoyed being part of the boating community, where everybody is so friendly and always willing to help each other. And also, over the years, I've provided a quite bit of entertainment to the hordes of gongoozlers along the bank, who like to come out on a sunny afternoon and watch the boats work through the locks."

"But I only have a 'continuous cruising' licence for *Jennifer Jo*, and the terms of my licence mean that I have to keep on the move most of the time. In some places, I'm allowed to stay for fourteen days, in others it's only forty-eight hours, and in a few of the most popular locations just twenty-four hours is permitted. Being on the move means locks, and believe me, there's a lot of locks on the canals. You must remember that from when you were on *Jennifer Jo* with me. And locks mean hard work."

Danny nodded. "Yes, Mister. It was fun doing the locks," he laughed.

"So it might be, when you're the age you were when you were with me," Alex smiled. "But I'm a lot older than you now. Until recently, like you, I thought nothing of tackling fifteen, maybe twenty locks in a day. But lately, I find I'm getting tired after just half-a-dozen. I did think about getting a permanent mooring for *Jennifer Jo* somewhere, either on-line or in a marina, and continue living aboard. But after a lot of thought, I've decided to go back to the bank and live on dry ground again, and have a bit more space to myself."

"So where will you go, then?" Danny asked anxiously.

"Well, I'm not leaving the cut altogether, Danny," Alex responded. "I've bought a lock-keepers cottage, up North, at lock 14 on the Moreland Canal, so I'll still be pretty close to the water. It's not that far from your neck of the woods, actually. I'm pretty sure we passed through it once, when you were with me. I saw it advertised in one of the waterways magazines a few weeks ago, so I hired a car for the day and went up to have a look at it. It's about 200 years old, but the structure is really sound, they built pretty well in those days, and the roof doesn't leak or anything like that. It does need a bit of work, though, since it's been unoccupied for about a year. I'll put in new carpets and redecorate throughout, and probably a new kitchen as well. The garden is well overgrown too, but none of that worries me, I can take my time and sort it out gradually. Directly after I'd had a good look round, I put in an offer to the agent, and it was accepted. And then I placed *Jennifer Jo* with a broker, who's found me a buyer. Everything should go through in about a couple of months, maybe a bit more. I'm quite looking forward to it, now."

"But it doesn't seem right that someone else will be living in *Jennifer Jo*," Danny complained. "It's your boat. Your home."

"Well, yes, Danny, but remember, your home is where you make it," Alex replied. "I'm going to be very happy in my lock-keepers cottage, I'm pretty sure, and of course I'll be able to help a few boats through the lock when I feel like it, although it's not one of the busiest canals in the country. There's probably only about a dozen boats go through it every day, and of course less than that in the winter months."

"Anyway, the new owners who're buying my boat are planning to be liveaboards as well, but in a sense they won't be living in *Jennifer Jo,*" Alex explained. "You see, I insisted that, as part of the sale agreement, the boat's name was to be changed. Jennifer and Jo were my wife's names, and I couldn't let anyone be as close to her as I have been."

"Do you remember," he continued, "when you were with me on *Jennifer Jo,* you helped me to black the bottom? It was just after Christmas that year?" Danny nodded. "Well, as soon as they assume ownership, the new people are going to have her taken out of the water to have her bottom blacked once again, and while it's out of the water, they're going to change the name. I think they said they were going to call it '*Will O' The Wisp*'. You see, it's considered to be bad luck to change the name of a boat while it's still in the water."

"Well, Mister, it won't seem the same, you not being on your boat," said Danny. "And I do hope you'll like it being on dry land, but I bet you'll find it strange at first. Anyway, I'm starting to feel a little hungry. Shall we go and find a pub somewhere? I'll buy you a meal, to say thank you for having me on *Jay-Jay* this week?"

"That would be very nice, Danny," Alex thanked him. "It's been good to have you aboard once again." They made their way up over the bridge and set off back to where their car was parked. As they walked along, Danny turned to Alex, "Hey Mister," he said. "There's something I've been meaning to ask you. Those two boys yesterday, Bob Jefferies' twins. How on earth could you tell which of them was which, when we came up out onto the back after I'd shown them round *Jennifer Jo*? I couldn't tell them apart at all."

Alex smiled to himself. This was a chance to tease Danny once again, and he wasn't going to part with his little secret that easily. "You just had to look closely, Danny," he told him. "All you needed to do is to just keep your eyes open, and look closely. There were loads of differences between them."

"You should try to be a bit more observant in future," he chuckled, as they reached the car and drove off down the country lane to the pub in the nearby village.

CHAPTER 22

Alex looked up from his map, and turned to Ben, the driver who'd picked him up that morning, and driven him north in the white van he'd hired for the day. 'Funny,' Alex had thought when the van first arrived at the boatyard that morning, 'how all delivery drivers seemed to have white vans. Really strange.' It was as if the manufacturers only had one colour paint nowadays, similar to, but a direct opposite of, Henry Fords' famous maxim - you can have any colour you want, as long as it's black. And now here they were, just about to arrive at their first destination.

"It's along here, on the left hand side," he said to Ben. "If you just pull in and let me out, this will be fine. As I remember it, there's a car park just along a bit further, a couple of hundred yards or so, on the right, just before a small park. If you park up there, I'll come and find you when I've finished in the estate agents." As he got out of the van, Alex reached into his pocket and took a £20 note from his wallet, and handed it to Ben. "Here, this will cover the cost of the car park, and then get yourself some lunch, there's a sandwich bar we just passed, a little way back. I'll be about 30 minutes, I suppose. And can you get me a sandwich, please, it doesn't matter what filling it's got, and a carton of orange juice as well, please?"

"Yes, Alex, of course," Ben replied, as he took the money Alex held out, and then drove off. Alex walked the few steps back to the estate agents, went in, and asked the receptionist if he could to see the manager, Mr. Holdgate, the agent who'd first shown him the lock cottage three months ago, and taken his deposit after checking with his client that Alex's offer to buy the cottage was acceptable. And now, with all the formalities completed, he was about to take possession of the keys to his new home.

As he sat and waited for Mr. Holdgate to appear, Alex thought about the events of that day. He'd spent most of the last two days, Wednesday and Thursday, in *Jennifer Jo*, packing up his belongings and putting everything carefully away into cardboard boxes, throwing out items he'd kept in case they might prove useful - but never had - and tidying up and cleaning as much as he could. And then, today, early on Friday morning, he'd motored his boat, his home for the last twelve years, the short distance along the cut to the boatyard where he'd arranged to hand over *Jennifer Jo* to her new owners. He'd moored up his boat securely for it to await their arrival, and then walked to the office and passed over the boat's keys to the broker who had arranged the sale. It had been an emotional time for Alex. As he'd sat on the bench on the grass beside the canal, waiting for the van to arrive, Alex had had an opportunity for a short period of quiet reflection. He'd finally reached the end of his time on the water, having decided some three months before to sell the boat which had been his home. He'd had a good time on *Jennifer Jo* over the years, and had never once regretted his decision to become a water gypsy, a live-aboard boater on a canal boat. He'd made many new friends along the cut, and quite often provided entertainment for myriads of gongoozlers who sometimes came to the canal in their droves to watch the brightly-painted boats pass by and work through the locks. He'd enjoyed being part of the boating community, always exchanging a friendly wave to every other boater he'd passed on the waterway, and always ready for a chat.

Alex knew that he would miss the way of life he'd become accustomed to over the years, but he also knew that he'd made the right decision. At 58ft long, *Jennifer Jo* was a heavy boat, and single-handedly working her through all the locks on the canals had, in the past year or so, become somewhat arduous at times, as his strength started to wane, no doubt aggravated by his advancing years.

He'd met a fair number of single-handed live-aboard boaters, usually men well into their 70's and now suffering from various degrees of ill-health, who'd refused to accept their situation. They refused to sell their boats and move ashore, and were still living afloat and struggling to cope, without the fitness needed to manoeuvre a boat on the waterways, lacking the strength to pull on the ropes and keep their boats under control. That's how they would end their days, unable to move far because of their inability to work the locks, until one day they would pass away, and lie dead inside their boat for weeks, until someone knocked and asked why they hadn't moved on in accordance with the terms of their licence. Alex hadn't wanted to end up like that. It was, he was sure, the right time to move on.

And then Ben had arrived in his white van, helped Alex to load up all his boxes and other items, and they'd set off. They'd had a good chat along the way, with Ben being very interested in Alex's stories of life on the cut. And Ben, a young man of around 25 or so, had told Alex of his plans to go travelling round the world, backpacking, once he'd earned enough money to fund what he described as the trip of a lifetime. Their conversations had made the time pass much quicker than Alex had expected, and helped to make the long journey north seem much shorter than it actually was.

His thoughts were disturbed as Mr. Holdgate came out and escorted Alex into his office. "As I told you on the phone yesterday," he said, "everything's in order, and been sorted out satisfactorily. My client's solicitor notified me yesterday afternoon that he's received your funds from your solicitor, and I can release the keys. Just sign here for their receipt, can you please?"

Alex signed where Holdgate had indicated, and passed the forms back over the desk. "Thank you," Holdgate replied as he gave Alex a copy of the receipt, together with a large bunch of keys. "As requested, we've arranged the insurance for you," he continued. "The cost of the first premium was included in the money your solicitor sent over. Here's the documentation for you to keep." He produced another sheaf of papers and handed them to Alex, then, standing up, he extended his hand to Alex and they shook hands. "Congratulations on acquiring your new home," he added. "I hope you enjoy living there. And you'll have a little surprise when you see it. Good day to you."

"What do you mean, surprise?" Alex asked, but all Holdgate did was smile. "You'll see," he said. "Goodbye. It's been nice to do business with you." And he showed Alex the way to the door.

Alex walked along the street a short way, and entered Whistlers, the largest department store in town, and made his way to the customer services desk, where he confirmed that the furniture and kitchen appliances he'd ordered some time ago would be delivered to the cottage that afternoon, as he'd requested on the telephone a few days before. Then he walked back to the car park and located Ben's white van, but found it locked and no Ben in sight. But, looking round, he spotted Ben sitting on a bench in the adjacent park, and walked over to him.

"Everything sorted, Alex?" asked Ben, as he handed Alex his lunch and the change from his £20 note.

"Yes, fine, thanks," he replied. "I'll just tuck into this and then we can be on our way. We're in good time."

It was only a short while before they were walking back to the van and setting off again. As they drove along, Alex took out his map and gave Ben directions out of the town and down a maze of small country lanes. "We're nearly there," he said after about ten minutes. "Turn left here, then a little way along you'll go over a hump-backed bridge, then directly after the bridge, as the road turns to the right, there's a pull-in off the road, can we stop there, please?" Ben nodded, and a moment later brought the van to rest on a hard-standing area beside the lane.

"Are you sure this is the right place?" asked Ben. "There's nothing here."

"Yes, I'm sure," laughed Alex. "That little bridge we just came over, that's the bridge over the canal. My place is about 200 yards away, along the towpath. There's no road access to it, this is the nearest we can get to it in the van."

"So do we have to carry everything along the towpath, then?" Ben asked, curious as to how they were going to get Alex's possessions to their final destination. "It's a long way to carry heavy stuff, especially along an uneven path like that."

"No," Alex laughed again. "I've ordered a flat for the afternoon, that should be here shortly, at two o'clock. We'll use that to take everything the rest of the way."

"A flat?" Ben asked, intrigued. "What's that? You don't mean a flat in the cottage, do you?"

Yes, a flat," Alex replied, smiling as he did so. "But not the type of flat you're thinking of. In this context, a flat is nothing more than a canal work boat with a solid flat top," he explained. "We can put everything on the boat I've hired, and then the boat will take it along the cut to the cottage. Easy! Just a floating equivalent to your van, really, I suppose."

"Yes, of course," Ben replied, laughing as he did so.

"Anyway," Alex added, "would you like to wait here for the flat to arrive, please, while I go ahead and unlock? And there should be another van turn up here soon, from Whistlers, with my new furniture and some other bits and pieces. Can you please make sure they know they're in the right place, and give them a hand unloading it all onto the flat when it arrives? And when all the stuff in the van is loaded on as well, once that's done, then you can be on your way home, it's quite a long way. Thank you for all your help today."

Ben shook his head. "No," he said. "We deliver door to door, that's what we say, and just because the final stretch is by boat, that doesn't change anything. I'll come along on the boat, after its been loaded up, and take it all indoors for you. No problem. It's all part of the service we offer."

"That's very kind of you," Alex replied. "Thank you very much. I'll see you in a little while." He set off down the towpath towards the cottage, tucked away from the road a couple of hundred yards away round a bend in the canal. Whilst he was aware that it needed some attention, having been unoccupied for about a year, he was looking forward to seeing his new home again, not having been there since first viewing it with the estate agent three months before. But as he rounded the bend in the canal and the cottage came into view, Alex suddenly realised that the cottage was not as he'd last seen it. It was now completely different.

Back then, the cottage had had a dilapidated air to it. The picket fence round the outside of the plot, once white, had been a dirty grey, and In bad need of repainting, with some of the slats broken, and blank spaces in a few places where other missing slats needed to be replaced. The garden had been waist high in weeds. On the cottage, the barge boards and fascias, the doors, the windows and the window frames, all had been in need of a good clean down and repainting. And the inside of the cottage had been just as bad. All of this Alex had known and accepted. The state of the property had been reflected in its low asking price, after having remained unsold for 12 months. And he had not been put off by the amount of hard work that would be needed to bring everything back to good condition. After all, he'd thought, he'd have plenty of time on his hands to do all the work, he could take his time.

But now, the cottage and its surroundings were completely different. The picket fence round the garden had been repaired, with the broken and missing slats replaced, and the whole fence had been treated to a fresh coat of white paint, gleaming in the bright early afternoon sunshine. Alex walked up to the gate, opened it, and made his way into the back garden. Where there had previously been a glorious riot of weeds, there now lay in front of him a neatly-cut lawn, with the edges neatly trimmed. In the flowerbeds around the lawn, against the inside of the picket fence, was a variety of neatly trimmed shrubs and bushes, surrounded by a wide assortment of flowers, mostly just coming into bloom, with many new buds about to burst into life. And down the far end of the garden, a wooden cage had been erected, with a black plastic net securely fastened around it, to keep the birds off the fruit bushes and young brassica plants recently planted inside. And at the side of the cage were a couple of young rhubarb crowns, too.

'So this is what Holdgate had meant by a surprise," thought Alex, as he turned round and took a closer look at the cottage. All the external woodwork had been cleaned down and repainted, the brilliant white of the doorframes and window sills gleaming in the early afternoon sunshine, while the doors themselves and the window frames had been repainted in a coat of shiny black paint. Alex immediately recognised the traditional black-and-white colour scheme used on the canals for over a hundred years, ever since the first canal companies started painting their buildings and canal equipment. It neatly complemented the black-and–white of the lock gates and paddle gear of the lock beside the front of the cottage.

Alex sat on the garden bench and thought for a moment about what he'd just discovered. Who on earth had done all this work? He'd realised, when he decided to buy the cottage, that a great deal of work would lie ahead of him if he was to bring it up to scratch, and here it was, already done for him. Apart from his solicitor, the estate agents, and the vendor's solicitor, and of course the previous owners themselves, no one knew of his plans to buy the cottage. And he hadn't given any instructions to anyone to carry out all this work. It was a real mystery.

He walked round to the front door of the cottage, by the lock-side, unlocked the door and stepped inside. Here, another surprise awaited him. The small hallway had been re-decorated, with a new carpet neatly laid, and also stretching up the stairs in front of him as well. Alex slowly walked up the stairs to the upstairs landing, which he found also brightly repainted, with the same carpet extending to the doors of the two bedrooms. Each of them he entered in turn, and in both, he found the same – walls newly re-decorated with fresh emulsion paint, new carpet laid, and skirting boards and windows all freshly painted. And in each room, a pair of brightly-coloured curtains hung in front of the windows. 'How has this all happened?' he asked himself, as he walked down the stairs back to the hall.

He made his way to the kitchen, and found that too had been completely refurbished. The old tatty kitchen units, with their doors hanging off, had gone, replaced by smart new units and cupboards, and a granite worktop over them, with space left for a refrigerator and washing machine. A shiny stainless steel sink and drainer sat recessed into the worktop beneath the kitchen window. The old lino on the floor had gone, too, replaced by a new vinyl floor covering.

Alex went through the small rear lobby into the bathroom. It had been a later addition to the 200-year-old cottage, having been added only about 60 years ago, but the previous owner had refurbished it only 18 months before the cottage had been put up or sale, so Alex was not surprised to see the original sanitary ware still in place. But the whole bathroom had been thoroughly cleaned, the floor tiles cleaned and polished, and the faint smell of disinfectant lingered in the air. There was even a fresh roll of toilet paper, its end neatly folded, in the holder.

Alex turned and went back through the kitchen to the hallway, and through into the only room he hadn't yet inspected, the living room. It was a nice airy room with windows at the front and back of the house, looking out onto the lock at the front by the small front garden, and the now-tidy back garden at the rear. As he had come to expect after looking at the rest of the cottage, he found this room to be in the same condition as the others, newly decorated, with new carpets and new curtains in place.

He walked over to the window and watched as a boat worked through the lock, a hire boat with a load of holiday-makers aboard. But as he stood there watching, one big question remained in his mind – how could all this have happened? He turned to go out of the room and await the arrival of the flat with his belongings aboard, when he noticed something he'd missed a moment earlier. Above the fireplace hung a large picture. It was drawn throughout in pencil, and neatly coloured in with coloured pencil crayons. He didn't need to look at the name neatly written in the bottom right-hand corner of the picture to know who'd drawn it. He recognised instantly whose style it was. But he looked anyway, just to confirm what he already knew. And the name he saw read 'Danny Marshall'. Alex realised it was a clue to what had been going on here.

Alex had discussed his prospective purchase with both of his two children. Apart from them, who both lived and worked abroad, the only people who knew that he was buying the cottage were the estate agent, the vendor, and their respective solicitors. Just four people. No more. But Alex suddenly remembered that when Danny was last with him on *Jennifer Jo*, he'd told him about his plans, and how he was set to leave his life on the water, and how, a few days previously, he'd paid the deposit on a lock cottage located about half-an-hour's drive from where Danny lived with his wife and young daughter. Somehow, Danny must have been involved in some sort of way in all this renovation work. A small part of the puzzle had fallen into place. And Mr. Holdgate, the estate agent, obviously, had known what had been going on. That must have been what he'd meant when he'd said 'You'll have a little surprise when you see it.'

Alex sat down on the carpet opposite the fireplace with his back to the wall, and studied the picture carefully. It was a picture of the lock, with the cottage behind, drawn from a vantage point just across the canal, on the other side of the lock from the cottage. The water in the lock was full, and by the bottom gate of the lock stood a young boy with his mouth slightly open, clad in a blue shirt, shorts, and neat white ankle socks above his trainers. Alex immediately recognised it to be Danny, depicted as the 12-year-old boy who'd lived with him for a year on *Jennifer Jo* all those years ago, wearing the blue polo shirt with the *Jennifer Jo* logo he'd bought him for Christmas that year. He remembered that Danny had lived almost all the time in polo shirt or tee-shirt and shorts throughout most of that spring and summer he'd been on the boat with Alex. The boy was holding a lock windlass in his left hand, and his right hand was raised, beckoning to a boat which was just entering the lock through the open top gate. The boat, with its smart blue livery, was *Jennifer Jo*, its name neatly inscribed along the curve of the bow. And standing on the back of the boat, hand on tiller as he carefully steered the boat into the lock, was Alex, also wearing a matching blue polo shirt.

Standing up, Alex stepped nearer to the picture to have a closer look. The pictures Danny had drawn whilst he was living with Alex aboard *Jennifer Jo* had been good, but Alex hadn't seen any of Danny's work since then, quite a few years ago now. It was obvious that Danny's technique and style had developed considerably over the years. His pencil lines were now extremely thin, and in places much closer together, enabling him to give a much better texture and depth to the scene. And his colouring, too, had a wider range of shades to it. All in all, Alex thought, it was a superb piece of work. If all the portraits that Danny was doing were as good as this, then it was no wonder that his talents were in such high demand.

Suddenly Alex noticed a caption written along the bottom of the picture. Moving closer, he found it read: 'YOU CAN BRING HER IN NOW', obviously the words that Danny was calling out to Alex in the picture. Alex realised that the picture was intended to be a reminder of Danny's time on the canals with him. Certainly, in the months after that Christmas which they'd spent together, Danny had seemed to have put behind him the horrors of Grant Hall, and started to really enjoy his time afloat. And the picture encapsulated so well the standing joke that had developed between them every time they'd worked their way through a lock. Tears welled up in Alex's eyes as he realised the unspoken tribute to Alex which it portrayed, and how perfectly the scene reflected their time together on *Jennifer Jo*.

Looking at the picture again, he realised that it must have been drawn very recently, in the past few days in fact, as the flowers in the cottage garden were shown with some heads in bloom, and many others in bud and about to burst out into full colour, just as they presently were outside in the garden. So Danny had been here very recently, maybe drawing the picture here, or perhaps taking photographs from which he could recreate the scene at home.

Just then, Alex heard the sound of a diesel engine in the distance, gradually getting louder, and as he walked round to the front of the cottage, he saw the flat coming towards him round the bend in the canal, propelled by a motorised work boat, tightly roped to the back of the flat. The work boat seemed to be quite new, resplendent in the traditional waterways livery of blue and yellow, a sharp contrast to the unpainted rusty brown steel of the flat, which was loaded with his goods and belongings, together with the new furniture he'd ordered. Ben was standing in the work boat, together with a couple of men in smart Whistler's work coats. He ran down to the lock landing on the other side of the canal, caught the rope the steerer threw to him, and helped make the boats fast, assisted by Ben handling the flat's front and rear ropes.

The older of the two Whistler's men walked up to the lock and studied the scene. "This is going to be really difficult, you know," he said, "getting all this stuff off the boat, then carrying it up that steep slope by the lock, and then struggling over those two lock gates with it. It's too dangerous, when you've got your hands full carrying all this stuff, some of it's quite heavy, you know. I don't think we can do it. I'm really sorry."

"No, don't worry, it's not a problem," Alex laughed. "It's easy really. We'll open this bottom lock gate, and put the boat into the lock. Then we'll close the gate, fill the lock, and as the water level rises, the boat will come up. When the lock is almost full, we'll close the paddles, and the flat will be on the same level as the ground in front of the cottage. Then it will be simple to just take everything off the flat and walk it through the gate and take it inside. Easy!"

"Right, we'll try that then," the Whistler's man replied. "Let's get going, then. We haven't got all day, you know."

It turned out to be a good solution, but It still took most of the afternoon before Alex's belongings and new purchases had been moved into the cottage, and his new refrigerator, washing machine, and cooker all installed and checked out. Alex said goodbye to Ben and the Whistler's staff, and as they set off to walk back along the towpath to the road, he went and helped the work boat reverse out of the lock and moor up the flat. Then the work boat was uncoupled from the flat, turned round, and roped up to the other end of the flat, and after saying farewell to the steerer, it moved off, taking the newly-coupled pair along the canal back the way they had come a few hours earlier. Alex went inside the cottage, closed the door, and sat down to relax in his new home. It had been a long day. He would rest for a while before making some tea.

The next day, Saturday, Alex spent most of the morning assembling a couple of new flat-pack bookcases which had been delivered along with the rest of his goods the previous afternoon, and made a start unpacking one of the cardboard boxes he'd brought with him from *Jennifer Jo*. Then he made himself some lunch, and took it outside to the bench in the front garden beside the lock, where he sat and ate it in the warm afternoon sunshine. As he ate, he watched a couple of boats as they worked through the lock, one in each direction, and chatted to the lock crews as they stood waiting for the lock to fill or empty. The last boat hadn't been gone more than a few minutes when he saw some people walking round the bend of the towpath towards the cottage, from the direction of the road.

As they drew closer, Alex recognised who they were. In front was Sophie, Danny's wife, carrying a large bouquet of flowers. Following on behind her, with his young daughter Jenny sitting on his shoulders, was Danny. Alex got up to greet them as they arrived, giving Sophie a quick embrace and shaking hands warmly with Danny.

"Hello, Mister" said Danny, smiling broadly. "This is Jenny. I bet she's grown a bit since you last saw her."

"My word, yes she has, Danny," Alex replied, as he looked at Danny's young daughter. She was a pretty girl, with fair hair tied back in a small pony-tail, and with freckles on her cheeks. But what struck Alex most of all was the expression her face. She'd inherited Danny's cheeky grin, and seemed to be smiling all the time. Obviously a very happy child.

But Danny was speaking again. "I thought you'd be moved in by now, Mister. I reckoned it would be about now."

"Yes, Danny," Alex replied. "Yesterday, in fact. I'm still in the throes of unpacking loads of boxes and things from *Jennifer Jo*, though. But come through into the back garden, then Jenny can run around in safety away from the lock and explore the garden, while we sit and have a chat."

They walked through to the back garden, and Alex and Danny sat on the garden bench while Jenny wandered round the garden exploring. "Shall I take these indoors and find a vase for you?" asked Sophie, indicating the flowers still in her hand.

"Yes, please, Sophie," replied Alex. "I unpacked one this morning. You'll find it in the cupboard next to the kitchen door."

"Right-ho, thanks," said Sophie. "I'll put the kettle on while I'm there, and make us some tea. Is that alright, Alex?"

"Thank you, Sophie, that would be nice," he replied. "You'll find everything you need in the kitchen, just have a look in the cupboards."

"I won't be long," Sophie responded. "Danny, keep an eye of Jenny, will you please?"

Danny nodded. Turning to Alex, he asked "so, you're settled in alright, then, Mister?"

"Yes, thanks, Danny," said Alex. "It all went quite smoothly yesterday, I'm pleased to say. But still lots of unpacking to do, though." He told Danny about his journey north in the white van with Ben, and how it had been a wrench to leave *Jennifer Jo* and hand over the keys after all his years afloat. "But I'm amazed at one thing though."

"What's that, then?" asked Danny, keeping an eye on Jenny as she disappeared behind the bushes at the back of the garden.

"Well, the cottage. It's been completely renovated. And the garden. It wasn't at all like this when I was here last, when I decided to buy it. I expected to have to do it all after I moved in. And I haven't been here since. It's all been done for me, but I've got no idea who did it. Did you have anything to do with that?"

"Me, Mister? No way, Mister. How could I have done?" Danny replied, his gaze still firmly fixed on Jenny, who was now investigating the water-butt. "I live 20 miles away. And I've got a job to go to. I couldn't possibly have spared the time to do anything at all to this place, let alone renovate it like you say it has been. I've got enough to do looking after my own place. And Mum's house as well, there's always something to be done there. I've got no idea. No idea at all."

Alex sat and wondered about what Danny had said. If it wasn't Danny then who could it possibly have been? Was Danny telling the truth? He was about to ask Danny about the picture hanging in the living room, surely he couldn't deny any knowledge of that, but just then Sophie returned bearing a tray of tea, and a glass of squash for Jenny. Alex decided to leave it until later, until he was alone with Danny again.

They sat down together and sipped their tea, while Danny updated him about how things had been for him since they last met.

"Mum and Gran are alright," he told Alex. "But Gran's slowing down a bit now. She still goes out a fair bit, though. Once upon a time, a few years ago, she'd walk almost everywhere. But she tends to use the bus a lot more now, although she's still pretty sprightly for her age. I slip round to see them every week or two, just to make sure everything's alright, and see to any jobs that need doing."

"What about your work, Danny," Alex asked. "How are things going there?"

"It's great, Mister," he replied. "They're giving me more of the difficult work to do now, I can cope with most of it. I really enjoy it. And I've been asked to run a course at the local training college this autumn, too."

"What about," asked Alex, curious. "Woodwork and joinery?"

Just then, little Jenny got up and tugged at her mother's dress. "Mummy, shall we play hide-and-seek?" she asked. Without waiting for an answer she went on, "I'll go and hide. You count to twenty, alright?" And with that she ran off and hid behind the water butt, giggling as she went.

"No, Mister," Danny laughed as he answered Alex's question. "They've got some really good lecturers there in that department, they taught me when I went there on day-release while I was doing my apprenticeship. This is for the Art Department. They want me to teach drawing, two evening classes a week, a couple of hours each night. This lecturer at the college, he saw one of my pictures in the window of the art shop where they take the orders for them, and he went in and asked who the artist was. That's how he found me. He got in touch with me and suggested that I run a course for them on drawing. I said I'd give it a go and see how it went, so he's gone back to the college principal and asked to have it put in the prospectus for next year."

"That's really good, Danny," Alex replied. This was an ideal opportunity to ask Danny about the picture hanging in the living room inside the cottage, but he didn't want to broach the subject while Sophie was with them. Fortunately, at that moment Sophie stood up, calling out "I'm coming, ready or not," and she wandered off round the garden, pretending to be oblivious to Jenny standing behind the water-butt in full view, giggling all the time as she did so.

Alex paused for thought for a moment. Danny wouldn't be able to deny drawing the picture, but he wanted to find out more from Danny about who'd done all this work at this new home. Then suddenly he remembered the way Robert Jefferies, the newspaper reporter, had tricked Alex into admitting that he'd sheltered Danny when he was on the run from Grant Hall, by asking a seemingly innocent question. Alex decided to try the same approach now with Danny.

"Danny, there must have been a lot of people busy here, to get all this renovation work done in just a few weeks," he remarked casually, wondering what Danny's response would be.

"No, Mister, I did it all myse........." he blurted out, before he stopping short, then added belatedly "myself," as his face turned bright red, blushing furiously.

Alex smiled. Danny had fallen into the little trap which he'd set, just as he himself had fallen into Bob Jefferies' trap years before.

"You did it all? Alex asked. "Everything?"

After a long pause, Danny slowly nodded. "Yes," he added reluctantly. "You weren't supposed to know I did it, though. It's my present to you. Back then, when I was a kid on the run from Grant Hall, and afterwards, you did such a lot for me. I've never been able to repay you properly for what you did for me then, so when you told me you were buying this place, I thought I could give something back to you for a change. I've been wanting to repay you, to do something for you, for ages. And this was my chance. I hope you don't mind."

"Of course I don't mind, Danny," Alex responded quickly. "I really appreciate it. It would have taken me ages to do all this, and you've done it all for me. It's great, really great. I can't thank you enough. But it must have been a lot of work for you. Thank you so much, it's very kind of you. But I don't think I did that much for you, really."

Danny was very thoughtful in his reply. "Yes you did, Mister. You did a great deal for me." He waved at Jenny running round the lawn, closely followed by her mother, the two of them giggling as they did so. "Without what you did, I wouldn't have my Mum and Gran again. I'd never have seen my father that last time. I wouldn't have the great job I've got now, which I'm really enjoying. And I wouldn't have Sophie and Jenny. It's all down to you, because of how you helped me when I needed it. I'm really glad I've been able to repay you, even if it's only just a little bit."

"Well, Danny," Alex replied. "It's very nice of you to say so, but it hasn't been all down to me. You know, we all make our own pathway through life. It's you who has made your own route, through the choices and decisions you've made."

"What do you mean, Mister?" asked Danny, puzzled.

"Well, Danny. Think about it for a moment. You chose to run away from Grant Hall. The only boy who ever did, in fact. No-one else did that, and more than that, you managed to do it twice. You chose to stow away on *Jennifer Jo*. You could have made off at any time, but you chose instead to stay with me. You chose to go and live with your mother, once you found her by a remarkable coincidence. You chose to walk home with Sophie when she was being teased by those other girls. You chose to marry her. And together you chose to have a child. No-one else made those choices for you, Danny. All of those choices were yours, not mine or any else's. It's good that all of your choices turned out to be good ones. Not everyone has that good fortune. Many make choices for the best of reasons which, in the fullness of time, turn out to be bad choices. But that can't be known at the time they made their choice."

Alex paused for a moment, before continuing. "But to me, Danny, one of the best choices you made was to go to the police, after you left *Jennifer Jo* to go and live with your mother, and tell them about the abuse you and the other boys had suffered at Grant Hall, and show them the evidence you had. I think that was very brave of you. Not everyone would have done that. You could easily have forgotten all about Grant Hall, put it behind you, and moved on. But you didn't. And thanks to you, Grant Hall was closed, and the abusers punished. All of the boys who were there at that time owe you a great deal."

"You know, Mister," Danny said quietly, "at first, when I told Mum all about it, and showed her the photos you took, and the account you got me to write about what happened there, well, she was upset and cross about what I'd been through, but she didn't want me to go to the police or anything like that. She said to forget all about it, just like you said some people might. But I knew that I had to do it. I couldn't just leave it. Mum tried to talk me out of it, but I insisted, and in the end she agreed, and came to the police station with me, and supported me. I'm really glad I did."

"Being in court and giving evidence against Hammond, while I could see him sitting there in the dock right in front of me when I was being questioned, that was really frightening. But he got put away in the end. I'm glad. It serves him right." Danny turned to Alex with a pained expression on his face. "I hope he got a load of stick from the other prisoners while he was inside," he added. "He deserved it, for what he did to us kids."

Alex nodded. "I can understand how you feel," he said. "I really can. But really, looking back at your time on *Jennifer Jo* with me, all I've done is to have been there when you were in need of help, and to have given you a helping hand. And for my part, I'm glad that I was in the right place to help you, at the right time, when you were most in need of it."

"I suppose you're right, Mister," Danny replied, after a long pause. "But I realise now what a terrible risk you were taking when you took me in. If they'd have found me with you on *Jay-Jay*, they'd have done you for kidnap and child abduction, or worse, and put you away for years. And I'm glad, really glad, that I've now been able to give you something back. What you did for me, Mister, will never be forgotten. I suppose you realised why we named our daughter Jenny?"

"Yes, Danny, I did," Alex assured him. "It wasn't difficult to figure that one out. I must say, I was really pleased about that."

"I was a little unfair to Sophie with that, I'm afraid," Danny admitted. "We agreed when we got married that it would always be 'us', not 'me' or 'her', we decided that we'd always make all our decisions together. But when we found that our baby was a little girl, I insisted that we called her Jennifer, Jennifer Jo. And I don't think I told Sophie why, not at the time anyway, because I wanted to shield her from what happened to me at Grant Hall. But of course she does know why now."

Danny sat quietly for a moment, before continuing once again. "You know, Mister, I've never talked to you about this before, but you really did save my life back then."

"How do you mean, Danny?" asked Alex, a little surprised by what Danny had said. "Isn't that a bit strong?"

Danny shook his head in disagreement. "Well, when I was on the run from Grant Hall, it was early summer, wasn't it? Living rough wasn't easy, but it wasn't particularly difficult either. It was never really cold, and there was a bit of food to be found if you looked around a bit, without pinching, because I'd never do that. And as summer moved through to autumn, there would have been loads of food about, berries in the hedges and that sort of thing. But then, suddenly one night, the cold weather would have arrived with a vengeance, and remember I was only wearing a thin summer tee shirt and an old pair of jeans. I'd have sneaked into a farmer's barn out somewhere beside an isolated field, and snuggled down in a corner under a couple of sacks to try to keep warm, and only been found days or even weeks later by some farm hand, stiff as a board, all the life frozen out of me. I'm certain that's how it would have ended if it hadn't been for you, because I'd never have handed myself in. Never!" he added vehemently. "I wasn't ever going to go back to Grant Hall voluntarily. Hammond would have caned me to pieces. After all, I was the only kid who ever got to get away from there. And as you said just now, I did it not once, but twice. Hammond would never have forgiven me for that. He'd have taken it as a personal insult to him."

Danny and Alex sat on the garden bench for several minutes, not talking, just watching Jenny as she darted around the garden, with her mother in tow. But eventually Alex spoke again. "Well, Danny, actually I feel a little humbled by what you've just said. I must confess I was very dubious about taking you in as I did, but with hindsight it turned to have been the right thing to do. But once again, thank you for doing so much here, at my new home. And you really did it all yourself? Inside and out?"

"Yes, Mister, just about," Danny replied, now smiling once again. "After I got back home from the Citizen's Awards reception, you know, after you told me that you were going to move up here, I came out here to take a look at where you were going to live, and I was shocked to see what sort of condition the place was in. I thought it wasn't going to be very nice to move in to a place like that, even though you knew what sort of state it was in when you bought it. But the agent's board was still up then, so I went back to town and went in and asked if I could have a key, because I wanted to do some work here. But the guy I saw, a Mr. Holdgate it was, he said no, they don't hand out keys to anyone who just walks in through the door. So had to leave it, but I didn't want to give up, so I thought at least I could come out here and do the garden and mend the fence, I wouldn't need a key to get inside to do that."

"So I got on with the garden," Danny continued. "I got that all sorted, the lawn and the flower beds and the bushes, then I dug over the vegetable plot and put up the cage round it, to keep out the birds. Some of the guys I work with, they grow all their own veg from seed, and they swap young plants with each other, and they gave me some spare ones they had, to put in. There's sprouts and cabbages and cauliflower, and some broccoli too as well. I wanted to plant out each sort together, but the plants got a bit mixed up, they all look the same when they're that size, don't they? So by the time I put them in I couldn't tell which was which. But it's easy really, Mister isn't it, when they get a bit bigger? If they've got knobs on the stalks then they're sprouts, if they've got green curly bits on the top then its broccoli, and if they've a white bit at the top then they're cauliflowers." He turned to Alex and grinned. "And anything else, well they must be cabbages, mustn't they?"

Alex smiled. "Bang on, Danny," he said, laughing. "I reckon I'll be able to tell them apart from your very accurate description."

Danny grinned once again. "So I'd just about got everything outside finished," he continued, "then one Sunday, we were round at Sophie's Mum and Dad's house for tea. They like to see Jenny, she's their only grandchild, and I told Sophie's Dad what I'd been doing out here, and how I couldn't get in to do the inside, and he asked me if that Bob Holdgate was still the manager of the estate agents. So I told him yes, it was, he was the bloke I'd seen, and he said to leave it with him, he knew Holdgate because they'd been to the same school, actually they were in the same class together. Then, a few days later, I got a phone call from the receptionist there, she said to call in and I could have a key, because Mr. Holdgate, he'd come out here and seen what I'd done with the garden, and Sophie's Dad had vouched for me, so he'd take a chance on me."

"Danny, I'm impressed. You did very well to get it all done in time," Alex congratulated him. "There was a lot of work that needed doing."

"Yes, Mister, I did it all," Danny said proudly. "I never had to buy anything, nothing at all. I had loads of half-full tins of paint at home, so I was able to use most of those up. But the new curtains, Mum made those for me, she's a dab hand with her sewing machine. She works part time a couple of afternoons a week in the drapery department at Forrester's, that's the big department store in our town. They let her have some remnants they weren't able to sell, she made the curtains up from that."

Danny paused for a moment, as Jenny came racing past once again. "The kitchen units came from Forrester's too," he added. "They've got a big kitchen and bathroom department, and every two or three years, they renew their displays, and Smart Brothers, that's where I work, we have the contract to take out all the discontinued ranges and put in the new ones, we do all their maintenance work and that sort of thing. I got put on that job, me and some other blokes, we did it all in a couple of weeks, the people at Forrester's were really pleased with how quickly we did it. Anyway, the old units, the ones we were taking out, we were told to just put them in the skip, so I asked if I could have some of them, and because we'd done the job so quickly, they said yes, I could have them for nothing. Otherwise, I'd have made all the kitchen stuff myself, but it would have taken me much longer, and I didn't really have enough time anyway. I wanted to make sure I'd got everything done before you turned up."

"Actually, Forrester's did quite well for you, you know, because the carpets came from there too," Danny smiled. "And the vinyl in the bathroom. Sophie's Dad sorted them out. He's the manager of the flooring department at Forrester's. He started there as a carpet fitter years ago, when Sophie was little, then after a few years he got moved onto the sales floor selling carpets and the like, then when the existing manager retired, he was promoted to be the new manager. They've just finished a big contract to provide all the carpets and so on for a big office building which Smart Brothers had been refurbishing, I worked on that job for quite a time as well. Anyway, Forrester's had a load of off-cuts left over. Fortunately, your rooms here aren't that big, so we could get enough pieces to do all the rooms. So Sophie's Dad laid all the carpets, and the new vinyl in the bathroom. Otherwise I've done it all. It's been interesting doing it, I've really enjoyed doing it for you."

"Talking about carpets, Mister," Danny went on, "do you know what Sophie's Dad told me? He said the people who run Forrester's want to be able to provide everything you would want for a home, but carpets and flooring are really difficult to sell properly and make a profit out of it."

"Why's that, Danny?" Alex asked, intrigued now.

"Well, big stores like Forrester's, they buy the carpet in from the manufacturers in these huge rolls, you see. They have to sell at least half of it before they've recovered the money that they paid for it. Then the next 25% is to pay the staff wages and company overheads, like heating and lighting and business rates, and after all that, then the next 15% is your profit. But that last 15% what you're left with is a remnant which you've got to sell off cheap to get rid of it. But Sophie's Dad has got that sorted. You see, they didn't want to be seen to be selling off remnants, it detracts from the image they like to present as high quality retailers. So what he does, he sells the remnants on to a guy who used to work there, who left to start up his own shop selling carpets and the like. He can't afford to buy the big rolls like Forrester's can, so he takes the remnants off their hands at a really good price, and the sort of customers he sells to, they're on low wages or benefits, so they like a bit of cheap carpet. This guy is never going to be serious competition to Forrester's, but the way it is, everyone wins."

"No, Danny, I can imagine the retail trade can be pretty difficult at times," Alex responded. "But please, tell me about the picture."

"Oh, yes, the picture," said Danny. "You do like it, don't you?"

"Yes I do, Danny," Alex thanked him. "I like it very much indeed. I shall treasure it, always. Your technique has developed a lot since you were with me on *Jennifer Jo*. It's improved a great deal. I'm not surprised you've been invited to run a course at your local college."

"I nearly didn't do the picture, you know, Mister," Danny replied, as he blushed slightly once again. "You see, I'd worked really hard last weekend, and by Monday evening I'd just about finished everything, and as I was clearing up and running the vacuum round, I thought that the wall above the fireplace was a bit bare, and a picture would fill it nicely. So I decided to draw a picture of the cottage from across the lock, and I sat out there and made a start, then took some photographs to finish it at home."

"Then I thought that if it was going to be a picture of a canal cottage beside a lock, then really it should have a boat in the lock, with some people as well. And if I was going to draw a picture with a boat in it for you, then the boat just had to be *Jennifer Jo*. And if the boat was going to be *Jay-Jay* then the people just had to be me and you. So that's what I drew."

"I only finished it on Thursday night, then I took it straight round to the photo shop where they sell my drawings, and knocked up the guy who owns it, he's got a flat above the shop. He framed it for me while I waited, he did it in about ten minutes, he's ever so quick. Then I came out here and hung it on the wall, and dropped the keys back through the estate agent's letter box on my way home, Holdgate's secretary had phoned me a couple of days earlier to let me know he had to have the keys back by Thursday night because you were planning to call in and collect them on Friday."

"Well, you did jolly well, Danny," Alex thanked him once again. "I really am most grateful."

"I'm glad you like it," said Danny. "But I thought you would. Did you see the caption at the bottom?"

"Yes, Danny, I did," Alex smiled once again. "I thought it was quite apt."

It was Danny's turn to smile now, his trademark grin spread wide across his face. "I thought you'd like that. I must have said that to you hundreds of times, mustn't I? At just about every lock we worked *Jay-Jay* through, when I was the guy on the bank working the lock for you." And he started giggling at the thought.

They both sat there quietly for a few moments. "You know, Mister," Danny said after a while, "I really got to like my time on *Jay-Jay* with you. Not at first, because it was so strange living on a boat which moved about all the time, and I didn't know you at all. And it took me a long while to get used to it. Also, back then, well, I was always afraid of being found out, and being taken back to Grant Hall. But after a while, I reckon it was around Christmas time, you know when we were in that marina with those other people off their boats, we all had such a good time together. It was like a widespread family all coming together for a couple of weeks and then drifting apart again, with us all going on our separate ways. After that, I seemed to settle down and really got to like the way of life we had. I quiet enjoyed it in the end. Before that Christmas, I always seemed to be looking back, trying to forget about Grant Hall and everything that happened there, but never being quite able to. But afterwards, I was able to look forward to finding my mum, knowing that every day that passed was one day closer to finding her and being with her again."

"You know," he continued, "I was a little reluctant to leave you and the boat when I found my mum, but of course I was so glad that I found her. But I did miss being on the boat with you, for quite a while afterwards."

As Danny fell silent, Alex thought about what Danny had said. He could recall exactly when Danny had turned that particular corner, and become able to put the horrors of Grant Hall behind him. It had been the night after the quiz, the last night they'd spent in the marina before moving off to do the blacking to *Jennifer Jo*'s hull, the night when Danny had suddenly broken down in tears, fallen into his Alex's arms and buried his head on his chest, sobbing. Alex knew that was the moment Danny had let out all his anger about his situation, the anger he'd hidden so deep down inside him for so long, to tumble out. It had taken a long time for it to happen, much longer than Alex had expected, but Alex had known that sometime, happen it would. And Alex also knew that the longer it took for Danny to vent himself of that anger, the deeper it had been concealed within him. That moment had been a very sad time for Danny, but one that had pleased Alex more than a little, for he'd been waiting and expecting for it to happen ever since he'd told Danny that he could stay with him on *Jennifer Jo.*

Just then, Sophie came up to them, out of breath. "Gosh, Jenny's tired me out today, she just loves to run around. But Danny, it's time we were on our way. Don't forget we need to call in to the shops on the way home and get some things for your mother."

"Alright, Sophie, I'm ready," he said, getting up from the bench. But just then, Jenny started tugging at her mother's hem, and whispered something to her. Turning back to Danny, Sophie smiled. "Well, I'll be ready in a just a moment, too," she said, adding in a quiet whisper, "toilet stop first," as she took Jenny's little hand and they walked off together towards the back door of the cottage.

Danny sat down again. "Before I go, Mister," he said, "there's something I want to ask you. I've been meaning to ask you for a long while now, but the time never felt right before."

"What's that, Danny?" Alex asked. "You can always ask me anything you want, you should have known that by now."

Danny nodded. "Well Mister," he said after a slight pause. "I've always called you Mister, all these years I've known you. I don't want to be familiar, but would it be alright if in future I called you Alex?" He turned to look at Alex, with an eager look on his face.

Alex smiled. "That would be very nice, Danny," he said. "I would like that very much indeed."

"Alright, Mister - I mean Alex," Danny grinned. "That's settled then." He paused again, looking round at the nice neat garden, with the cottage nestling at the end of the garden, with the canal lock just visible at the side. "You've got a nice place here. I really envy you. We're trying to save up a deposit to buy our own place, me and Sophie, but we aren't getting very far with it at the moment. Where we live now, it's a nice house, in a nice neighbourhood, but the rent is quite expensive. And we always like Jenny to have nice clothes, not the cheap stuff out of the pound shop, or off the bargain racks at Tesco's. Sophie did say she'd go out to work again, her Mum would be happy to have Jenny some of the time, but I said no. I want her to be there at home for Jenny until she's grown up. We neither of us want her to be a latchkey kid. But we'll buy our own place one day, I'm sure of it. I'd just love to have a place like this."

"Anyway, here they come," he added, standing up as Sophie came round the corner with Jenny. Alex got up from the bench, and walked with his visitors to the garden gate. "Goodbye, Sophie," he said, as he gave her a nice smile. "And you too, Jenny. But especially to you, Danny. Thank you once again for everything you've done for me here. And thank you for coming round this afternoon. It's been great to see you. Please feel free to come again, whenever you like. You're very welcome, all of you, any time you like."

He shook Danny by the hand as he gave him a quick embrace, and then sat on the bench at the front of the cottage by the canal lock and watched as Danny and his young family made their way back along the towpath back to the road bridge over the canal where their car was parked.

As he watched, he realised how proud he was of Danny, how well he'd put Grant Hall behind him, and how he had rebuilt his life after meeting up with his mother again. And Alex was also truly proud of the small part he'd been able to play during Danny's formative years, as he was making his progression from childhood to adulthood. It struck him what a contrast there was between Danny as he was now, a mature young adult with his own family, compared to the scared and frightened little twelve-year-old boy who'd stowed away on *Jennifer Jo* all those years ago.

But long after they'd disappeared from view, Alex sat there still, thinking about what Danny had said just before he'd left. How pleased he'd been to hear Danny say those few words – 'I'd love to live in a place like this'. For there was something that Danny did not know, something he was not aware of, something which Danny would not learn about for some time to come, but which he would eventually discover in the fullness of time.

When Alex had been to see his solicitor to arrange the purchase of the cottage, the solicitor had surprised him by asking a simple question. 'Now that you're due to become a property owner, there's something you need to consider,' he'd asked. 'Do you have a will?' And Alex had been obliged to admit that he did not. He'd never considered it necessary. During all his years as a schoolteacher and later as a Housemaster, his accommodation had been made available as part of his contract, although he'd always had to pay a market rent for it. And when he'd retired and purchased *Jennifer Jo*, although it had not been cheap, it had not been anywhere as valuable as a house on dry land. And so he'd never thought it necessary to have a will.

But during his time on the waterways, his circumstances had changed. He'd enjoyed a good inflation-proofed pension from his teaching days, and later he'd started to receive the state retirement pension as well, which also was index-linked. His living costs, together with the cost of running and maintaining *Jennifer Jo,* had been relatively modest compared with how much it cost to live in a house on dry land. And so, over the years, he'd been able to accumulate a quite considerable sum in savings and investments.

And now, he'd suddenly been obliged to consider how his estate should be distributed on his death, something which he'd not thought about before. He'd discussed it with both of his children during some of the regular weekly video chats he had with them through the internet. His son Robert lived in America with his wife and two young children, working for the Department of Agriculture there. And his daughter Christine was also married, living in New Zealand, with her first child expected shortly. After some discussion, it had been agreed between them all that Alex's savings and investments would be cashed in and distributed equally between the two of them on Alex's death. But neither Robert nor Christine had wanted the cottage, and had left it with their father to decide what should happen to it.

Alex had known that it could be sold and the proceeds passed to his children with the rest of his assets, but he'd had in mind a better solution. He'd decided that in his will he would leave the cottage to Danny, in the hope that Danny would welcome the gift, and move in with his family and make their home there. And now it pleased Alex more than a little that Danny had told him how much he'd like to live there.

Alex's thought next turned to what he should do in the months ahead. He'd expected to have been busy renovating the cottage, but Danny had already done all that work for him. So now, there was the opportunity to move on to his next project. A project that he'd had in the back of his mind for some time now.

The books he'd written a few years before, about the history of his school, had been well received. Although Alex had never expected them to feature in the best-seller lists, they had enjoyed a small but steady number of sales, mainly to alumni of the school, their parents, and other supporters of the school. He'd often been congratulated on his easy-to read style of writing. And he'd thought for some time that he'd like to write another book.

And he knew what it would be about. It would be a book about life on the canals. He knew that many books had been published about the early days of the canals and their builders, names such as James Brindley and Thomas Telford. And there were quite a number, too, telling of the canal-carrying days of the early boatmen, both fiction and non-fiction. But there were very few books about present-day life on the canals. And he had just the storyline in mind.

It would tell the story of a live-aboard boater, a retired

schoolteacher, a water gypsy cruising the canals single-handed, who one evening finds a stowaway, a young boy on the run from a nearby children's home where he'd been subjected to physical and sexual abuse, trying to find his mother with whom he'd lost contact. It would tell how the schoolteacher reluctantly decides to give shelter and support to the boy, how he gradually gains the boy's trust, and how their relationship develops between them. It would tell how the boy eventually finds his mother again, and how, over the years that follow, the boy and the schoolteacher work together to bring the abusers to justice.

It would be presented as a work of fiction, and with the names of people and places changed, only a handful of people would ever know that it was based on fact, on events that had actually happened. And Alex had already decided upon a title for his book. The title would be a play on the boater's live-aboard lifestyle, and also on the boy's journey to find his mother.

The book would be called 'Floating Home'. It would, Alex believed, be an interesting tale to tell.

GLOSSARY OF CANAL TERMS

ANODES Also known as sacrificial anodes. Metal plates, usually made from Zinc or Magnesium, secured to the hull of a narrowboat to prevent corrosion by stray electrical currents. The currents corrode away the anodes in preference to the steel hull. Anodes usually need to be replaced every 4-5 years.

BOTTOM The underside of the narrowboat, but more generally used to refer to that part of the hull which is below the waterline. Usually painted black.

BOW The front (sharp end) of a narrowboat.

CRATCH A wooden framework over the front well-deck of a narrowboat, usually fitted with a rubberised roll-up cover. Also refers generally to the frontal area of the boat ahead of the cabin.

The **CUT** Boaters' term for the canal. Derived from the manner in which the men building the canal 'cut' it through the countryside with pick and shovel.

GALLEY A boat's kitchen.

GREASER A hand-operated device to pack the seal round the propeller shaft with grease where it passes through the hull of the boat.

GONGOOZLER A non-boating member of the public, a sight-seer.

LOCK A brick-built chamber between two pounds on the canal which are at different levels. Has water-tight gates to enable boats to enter from the higher level (the top gates) or the lower level (the bottom gates)

OFFSIDE The side of the canal opposite to the towpath.

NEARSIDE The side of the canal adjacent to the towpath.

PADDLE GEAR Winding mechanism at each end of a lock, used to raise or lower sluices which permit water to fill or empty a lock. A windlass is required to operate the paddle gear.

PILING Metallic galvanised steel edging driven vertically into the side of the canal to prevent erosion. Provides good secure mooring facilities.

PINS Solid metal rods, usually about 18" long with a sharp point at one end, and a loop for a rope at the other. Driven into the towpath bank with a mallet to provide an anchoring point for mooring ropes. Removed and taken onto the boat when casting off and continuing your journey.

POUND A stretch of canal between two locks.

STERN The back end of a boat.

TURNOVER BRIDGE A bridge located where the towpath crosses from one side of the canal to the other. Has special access ramps on both sides to enable the towing horse to easily cross the bridge.

WINDING HOLE (Rhymes with finned, not find)
A short length of canal which is much wider than the rest of the canal. Provides an opportunity to turn a boat around, as narrowboats are much longer than the canal is wide. Derives its name from the days of horse-drawn boats, when the boatman would use the wind to turn the boat around.

WINDLASS A removable hand-held winding handle used to operate the paddle gear at the locks. Carried on the boat from one lock to the next.